JONATHAN JANZ

THE SIREN AND THE SPECTER

This is a **FLAME TREE PRESS** book

Text copyright © 2018 Jonathan Janz

FLAME TREE PRESS
6 Melbray Mews, London, SW6 3NS, UK
flametreepress.com

Distribution and warehouse:
Baker & Taylor Publisher Services (BTPS)
30 Amberwood Parkway, Ashland, OH 44805
btpubservices.com

Thanks to the Flame Tree Press team, including:
Taylor Bentley, Frances Bodiam, Federica Ciaravella, Don D'Auria,
Chris Herbert, Matteo Middlemiss, Josie Mitchell, Mike Spender,
Cat Taylor, Maria Tissot, Nick Wells, Gillian Whitaker.

The cover is created by Flame Tree Studio with
thanks to Nik Keevil and Shutterstock.com.
The font families used are Avenir and Bembo.

Flame Tree Press is an imprint of Flame Tree Publishing Ltd
flametreepublishing.com

A copy of the CIP data for this book is available from the British Library
and the Library of Congress.

HB ISBN: 978-1-78758-007-7
PB ISBN: 978-1-78758-005-3
ebook ISBN: 978-1-78758-008-4
Also available in FLAME TREE AUDIO

Printed in the US at Bookmasters, Ashland, Ohio

JONATHAN JANZ

THE SIREN AND THE SPECTER

FLAME TREE PRESS
London & New York

For Peach, my youngest child.
Thank you for bringing
me joy and laughter every day.

'If I knew something to keep us safe, don't you think I'd be doing it right now? I used to think I knew what would keep us safe, but I don't anymore. One time they gone see a cross and they gone back off, and next time they just gone laugh and make you feel like a fool. That's real meanness in a spirit. And I tell you, they laughing now, they laughing real hard.'
Michael McDowell
The Elementals

'Depending on one another's hearts, ye had still hoped that virtue were not all a dream. Now are ye undeceived. Evil is the nature of mankind.'
Nathaniel Hawthorne
'Young Goodman Brown'

PART ONE
THE LAST HAUNTING

CHAPTER ONE

David Caine motored toward the Alexander House, his Camry jouncing over a lane that was little more than twin wheel ruts. There was gravel here, but only enough to prevent the path from being washed out by a good rain. When he glanced at his phone, he was unsurprised to find the map of the area gone. He'd lost contact with the satellite. David signaled a right turn.

The next lane was even more primitive, with dense woods on both sides. Ahead, David spied hints of a broad river the color of Indian ink.

The Rappahannock.

Nostalgic images clutched at him. He eased back in his seat, willed himself to breathe through the thickness in his throat. His college buddy Chris Gardiner appeared in a few of these images; several more were comprised of nothing more than the water, the trees, the lazy nights rolling past tobacco fields. But one figure, one face, recurred more than any. This was the cause of his burning throat, the source of his throbbing chest and sweaty hairline.

Anna Spalding.

The Camry bounced over a pothole. Jolted from his reverie, he discovered an elderly man peering at him through a screen door, the house around it white aluminum siding with red shutters. The Camry swept past, the trees less frequent now, and although David was afforded better views of the river, the man's craggy face hovered in his memory.

David shifted in his seat, noted how the forest to the right of the lane formed an unbroken jade wall. As if the woods weren't forbidding enough, its lower regions were clogged by chain ferns and thorny shrubs, a haven for poison ivy and other insidious plant life. No, David decided, this forest was not intended for exploring. More like a barrier to keep outsiders away.

To the left the woods thinned rapidly, the Rappahannock visible through the overgrown ryegrass and wildflowers. Then, a couple hundred yards distant, he spotted the white clapboard structure with a russet-colored roof.

Despite his eagerness, David slowed the Camry to a crawl and inspected the home. He'd studied the Alexander House in countless pictures, yet now he realized he'd never really seen the house at all. People said it all the time about famous landmarks: "You have to be there to believe it." And even if the platitude made him roll his eyes, he'd found it to be true. The Eiffel Tower, the Empire State Building. Yellowstone and the Grand Canyon.

In its own way, the Alexander House surpassed all of these.

Not in size, of course. Two stories tall with a peaked attic above, the house was a hair under three thousand square feet. From the pictures online, he remembered the structure having two dormered facades, one facing the lane, the other pointing south, toward the river.

David was pulling into the oak-canopied driveway when Chris Gardiner stepped out onto the porch. For a moment David sat there with his foot on the brake, his hand unable to work the gearshift. There was a look on his old friend's face that made him appear hostile, almost alien. During an interval that could not have lasted more than a few seconds, David was convinced his old friend wished nothing more than for David to die a slow, torturous death.

Then Chris smiled and David was able to move again.

Still, he couldn't help notice how his hand shook as he slid the gearshift into park and twisted off the engine.

David climbed out and gazed at the oldest haunted house in America.

CHAPTER TWO

"Sure you want to make this a rental?" David asked as he approached. "This is like owning your own island."

Chris looked around as if noticing the property for the first time. "It's not ready yet. It's hell getting the caretaker out here. You'd think we weren't paying him twenty bucks an hour."

David ascended the porch steps – eight of them, and steep. He supposed you had to build a house high if it was only a few feet above river level. Chris waited for him, no offer of a handshake yet. No sign of the wife, either.

David made it to the top and smiled. He was just under six four, a few inches taller than Chris, who up close appeared a bit beaten down by life. Chris jolted, as if remembering his manners, and began to extend his hand, but David muttered, "Come on, man," and wrapped him in a hug. Chris's body remained stiff, and when David pulled away and squeezed Chris's shoulders, he noticed a blush creeping up his friend's cheeks.

"Want to come inside?" Chris asked.

David made a show of looking around. "I thought I'd camp out the first night. You know, get to know the native fauna a little better."

Chris stared at him for a moment before his ruddy face broke into a grin. "You're an idiot."

David clapped a hand on Chris's shoulder, moved him toward the screen door. "I want to meet this wife of yours. I still can't believe I didn't get to stand up with you at your wedding."

Chris opened the door, a look of panic flitting across his face. "It was a small ceremony, David. I had family members who didn't get invited."

Chris led him through a long hallway that bisected the house. The clapboard continued down the corridor, the wood painted a faded aquamarine. The walls were festooned with fishing poles, crab buckets, tackle boxes, plastic bags containing colorful lures, orange lifejackets, and sheet-metal maritime-themed signs. One read 'EDUCATION

IS IMPORTANT BUT FISHING IS IMPORTANTER.' Another: 'WHAT HAPPENS ON THE RIVER STAYS ON THE RIVER.'

Chris followed his gaze. "I know they're tacky, but the agent says they help add local flavor…ambience…whatever."

"Your wife pick them out?" David asked.

"I did," Chris said. "If Katherine had her way, this place would be done up like Halloween."

David shot him a look. "Don't tell me she's one of those ghost fanatics."

Chris went a shade redder, his face reminding David of an oversized rhubarb.

"Right through here," Chris muttered, leading David toward the screened-in porch and a breathtaking view of the river. They stepped onto coarse green outdoor carpet, and David saw Chris's wife.

She was facing the backyard, gazing out over the water beyond. The house had no doubt been constructed with this view in mind. To the right, where the river bent, the water was only a football-field wide. But straight ahead, where Katherine was looking, the farther shore was only vaguely discernible. There were houses over there, but they were merely white splotches, errant brushstrokes on a rustic nature scene.

"David Caine," Chris said, "this is my wife, Katherine Mayr."

David nodded. Half the married female professors at Purdue retained their maiden names, although most of those chose hyphenates. That Katherine hadn't taken Chris's name meant nothing. Less than nothing. Still, for reasons he couldn't explain, it surprised him.

Her grip was warm enough to conjure thoughts of fever. She beamed at him, showing white, sharklike teeth. Her chestnut hair was arranged in a series of cloudlike whorls that framed her attractive face, reminding him very much of the nighttime soap opera stars of the eighties, women like Linda Evans and Joan Collins and that blond lady from *Falcon Crest*. Susan Something. He couldn't remember, perhaps because he'd hated the show, only pretended to like it because his mother let him stay up past his bedtime to watch it with her. Anything to avoid going to bed. Anything to avoid being alone with the night.

She eyed him up and down. "You never told me your friend was so tall, honey." Her expression changed, grew hungry. She didn't let go of his hand. "You feel something, don't you?"

David's smile became strained. "I'm not sure—"

"The energy," she said, pale blue eyes boring into him. Jesus, he thought. She could find work as a mesmerist with those eyes. She nodded as if they'd just agreed on something. "I felt it the first time I stepped inside. Chris experienced tremors even before we reached the property. Didn't you, honey?"

Chris opened his mouth but said nothing, and David was forcibly reminded of the younger man Chris had been back at William & Mary. Never good at thinking on his feet, every remark directed his way a curveball he couldn't hit.

David contrived to break Katherine's grip, but she clung to him a moment longer, scoured his face in a way that reminded him of a scientist examining specimens. "You *will* do it, won't you?"

David raised his eyebrows, glanced at Chris, who was studying the floor.

Katherine shut her eyes, her brow beetling. "Oh, *please* tell me you let Mr. Caine know our wishes when you spoke to him."

"I…." Chris began.

"Your husband asked me to stay here a month," David said. "I'll prove the place is free of ghosts, so the property can begin making you money."

Katherine's smile was gone, in its place an expression not of scorn, but of pity. She interlaced her fingers before the woven gold belt cinched around her black dress. Her pale blue eyes burned into him.

"Mr. Caine," she said, stepping nearer until they were close enough to smell each other's breath. "You know the story of John Weir."

He struggled to quell the surge of annoyance her tone elicited. She'd spoken the name like Weir had been a carnival sideshow freak rather than the most respected debunker of the twentieth century.

"You know I'm aware of him, Mrs. Mayr. You've read my books, after all."

She smiled delightedly. He could see her tongue. "Some of them, yes. You're quite skillful, Mr. Caine."

He glanced at Chris, but his friend was occupying himself by dusting a white metal table with an oxblood-colored rag.

"Since you've read my work, Mrs. Mayr—"

"Katherine, please."

"You know I agree with Mr. Weir's philosophies."

"I'm aware of your pessimistic worldview."

David scratched the back of his neck. "Well, you know, Mrs.—Katherine…some would argue it's more pessimistic to believe there are ghouls and demons around every corner yearning to prey on us. I'd say Weir's view is the rosier one."

"Then why did he die here?"

David stared at her. He wanted to believe his irritation was a product of the interminable drive, but deep down he knew it was hearing John Weir so contemptuously disparaged.

Chris surprised him by speaking up. "There's no evidence Weir died in the house, darling."

Katherine's answering laughter was light and easy, but because of that it jangled David's nerves all the more. "You're right, dear! No evidence at all. Only his every cherished possession found in the house, his last known whereabouts verified by half the neighboring town."

David longed to wipe the gloating smile from her face, but he held back. Remember Chris, he told himself. He's the one who has to go home with this woman. He crossed his arms. "Maybe you should spell out your expectations."

Katherine leaned toward him, eyes wide. "'Spell out my expectations'? You really don't like me, do you, Mr. Caine?"

"Hey, I never said—"

"Doesn't anyone challenge you at that college of yours?"

"Purdue is a respected university, darling," Chris said.

Katherine spread her hands. "I'm not indicting your *credentials*, David. May I call you David? I'm merely questioning your imagination."

"Well, hell," David said, with as much of a smile as he could muster, "why didn't you just say so? And here I thought I was being insulted."

Katherine made a tutting sound. "There I go again, too loose with my tongue." She sighed, gathered herself. "You're the most respected writer in your field."

"There aren't that many writers in my field, Mrs. Mayr."

She made a pained face. "Please, *Katherine*." She bit a thumbnail, looked at him in a way that trimmed ten years off her age. "*Can* I call you David?"

"It's your house."

She exhaled. "Good. We're back to being friends."

David glanced at Chris, but his friend was staring at the floor.

"What my husband told you over the phone was true," Katherine went on.

"I think we interpret that word differently."

"And I know you're shrewd enough to surmise the real reason why we invited you."

"You want me to write a book about this place."

Her smile flared.

"Evidently," David continued, "you also want me to drum up a lucrative ghost-hunting trade as well."

"Oh, I'm sorry I gave you that impression. I don't presume to know the truth about the Alexander House. The fact of the matter is that *no one* knows the truth."

"Certain conclusions can be drawn," David said.

Her eyes gleamed. "But proving them is another matter entirely."

David glanced at Chris. No help there.

Katherine moved over to Chris, massaged his shoulder. "My husband and I view it as a kind of a wager."

"You view everything that way," Chris muttered.

Her pale blue eyes riveted on David. "I'm not asking you to label this site haunted. All I'm hoping for is a disinterested observer."

"Who'll write a book about it."

She spread her arms. "Who *wouldn't* want that? You're known the world over as the authority on all things supernatural."

"I can't promise a book, Katherine. I wouldn't get my hopes up."

She raised a forefinger. "Remember, David. No pessimism."

He glanced at Chris, saw the hint of a smile on his friend's face. Unexpectedly, they both chuckled at the same time. Bemused, Katherine looked from one man to the other.

"I'll do my best to be imaginative," David said.

"That's all I ask," she answered. She eyed him for several seconds, nodded. "You might find it easier than you think."

CHAPTER THREE

Chris and Katherine having departed, David reentered the house, exhaled, and waited for the magic of the Alexander House to wash over him. Standing in the sunless foyer, David scented the slow-moving water, the vegetation around the property, the still-potent aroma of the hand-hewn oak beams overhead, and the walls themselves, from which radiated a whiff of mildew. So much history here, so much to study.

Why did folks have need of the supernatural?

Because, he reminded himself, they had trouble facing what was in front of them. He turned, thinking, It's all about escape, hence the overreliance on technology. Distraction is an oasis. The real world is a thicket of other people, of conflicts, of emotions.

The kitchen was just big enough for an eat-in table. The light filtering in from the single window was shaded by the giant trees, so that the room, at this dusky hour, lay steeped in bluish shadow. David considered switching on a light but decided it wasn't necessary, not yet. Though the notion of a house having a personality was antithetical to his beliefs, he did like to think of a house as possessing *character*. A home's character, he'd decided long ago, was best discernible in natural light, not a harsh electrical glow.

The kitchen was dingy, outdated. He moved on to the dining room.

David couldn't suppress a grin.

Though the kitchen had been updated several times, the dining room reminded him just how old the Alexander House was. The knotty pine table, although assuredly not original to the house, was in keeping with the broad brick fireplace, the exposed rafters the color of milk chocolate. There were hand-carved ducks on every surface. Mallards, buffleheads. A couple that looked like breeding experiments between Canada geese and pelicans. David drifted over, plucked one of these larger carvings off the mantel, and caught sight of himself in a speckled rectangle of mirror. Though he was only forty-four, he looked a decade older in the jaundiced light. There were hints of crow's feet bracketing his eyes, deeper furrows in his forehead.

Disquieted, he turned away from the mirror, made his way through the rear of the dining room and back to the foyer. He paused at the base of the stairs, toyed momentarily with exploring the rooms up there.

No, he decided. First floor first.

David opened a six-panel mahogany door onto a room that was darker than a grizzly bear's asshole. Good God. The wood grain was so sooty it was impossible to discern the type, but whatever it was, it encased the entire…what? Sitting room? Den? There was a chair-and-a-half in here and a couch. Both of them rich leather. There were windows on the northern and eastern walls, but the thick plantation shutters obstructed all but the feeblest suggestions of light. In the corner he found a door. He went in and discovered a bathroom. He'd begun to worry there wouldn't be a bath on the first floor. But here were a toilet, a sink, and a shower stall as narrow as a coffin standing on end. David moved back to the den and through a doorway.

And could finally breathe again.

The master bedroom was light and airy, with tallow-colored walls, muslin curtains, the king-sized bed overlaid with a blue-and-ivory quilt. The room was maybe sixteen by twenty-two, large enough for a sitting area, but the excess space was left empty, making the room seem larger than it was.

David moved through the master suite, noting French doors to the east. He crossed to the southern door and was pleased to note it opened onto the screened-in porch.

David reached out, grasped the old brass knob.

Why are you avoiding the upstairs?

David froze. Now where in the holy hell had that come from? He wasn't avoiding *anything*. Funny how being alone could twist one's thoughts, send them careening down shadowy tunnels.

He checked his iPhone: 7:42 and he was ravenous. Skipping supper had been foolhardy. When he got like this – what had Anna used to call it? Hangry? – his judgment got addled. Everyone, he supposed, needed food, but David more than the average man. Fed, he was as patient as anyone he knew. Hungry, he exhibited all the sweetness of a rabid wolverine.

Maybe, he thought as he returned to the foyer, Chris and Katherine had stocked the fridge with a few items. They knew he was traveling a long way.

He opened the old Frigidaire.

A half-empty ketchup bottle and a butter container brimming with baking soda.

Well, shit. He supposed he'd have to go into town.

Why are you avoiding the upstairs?

He flung shut the refrigerator door. Goddammit, he wasn't avoiding anything. He was merely trying to avoid his body digesting itself.

Dimly, he heard Anna's teasing voice: *You're hangry, David. Get some food.*

It brought a smile. He imagined her with her baseball cap on backward, her flappy flannel shirt open enough at the chest he could see hints of her bra when she moved. Hard to tell what color her shorts were; the flannel shirt drooped so low she looked naked from the waist down. Her neon-pink flip-flops.

She doggedly defended her outfits, declared herself a fashionista, but what David always knew was that anyone else would have looked ridiculous in Anna's getups. Yet on her, somehow, they worked.

Anna, he decided, would have loved this place. An ardent fan of horror novels and creepy movies, she'd believed in all the things he did not. Where he was contemptuous, she was hopeful. Where he was skeptical, she was trusting. God, what a wondrous person she'd been.

There was a tightness in his chest.

"What happened to you?" he asked aloud.

To escape the answering silence, he strode into the foyer. To the right lay the long climb to the upstairs. To the left, the front door and the Camry and, if he didn't die of malnutrition on the winding road to town, food. It didn't matter where. He'd eat McDonald's. Gas station burritos. When a man was this hungry, it was about survival. Hell, he'd strip some bark off a tree and suck the juices if he had to.

He was halfway to the Camry when the question tickled again, an unmistakable note of mockery in it now: *Why are you avoiding the upstairs?*

David turned and faced the house.

Seven dormers jutted forth, three each on the first two stories, one from the attic. With the shadows settling around him and night creeping inexorably nearer, here, in this place of antiquity, it wasn't at all difficult to imagine a writer like Hawthorne being inspired, penning a novel like *House of the Seven Gables*, or a story like 'Young Goodman Brown,' which David had taught this spring semester.

What would Hawthorne, David wondered, make of the Alexander House and its body of Baroque legendry? Would he credit any of it? Or was he really, as David suspected, an atheist who veiled his disbelief in allegory and—

"Meet any ghosts?" a voice called.

David gasped, spun. A man nearly David's height ambled down the lane, a longish silver instrument in one hand. The man appeared to be somewhere between sixty and seventy, athletic-looking, a white growth of beard framing a mouth that grinned with mischief. He wore an ill-fitting white apron with a bloody smear across the belly.

Taking in David's scrutiny, the man said, "Guess bachelors get sloppy, huh?" He extended a hand. "Name's Ralph Hooper."

David shook. "A name like that, you ought to be a baseball player."

"I was," Ralph said. "Played a decent right field."

David studied the breadth of the man's shoulders. "Bet you could hit a little too."

"I could at that," Ralph allowed. "Always had too much swing-and-miss in my game, but when I got ahold of one...."

"Bet it sailed," David said, his eyes returning to the Alexander House.

"Capricious girl, ain't she?" Ralph asked.

David glanced at him. "Why would you say that?"

Ralph shrugged. "Homes have personalities, don't they? Some are sullen, some are cheerful. This one—" he nodded, "—is less predictable. There'll be days when you feel like she's your best friend, like she's smiling at you and wishing she could give you the world. But then she'll turn brooding. Enigmatic."

"Sounds like you've got a fetish for old homes."

Ralph let out a gust of laughter. "Hell, I probably sound like a nut, don't I? Too much time alone, I suppose. And looking at the house every day, I guess I *have* begun to project onto it."

David grinned. "You're the guy I saw staring through the screen door."

"We're neighbors," Ralph said. "I mean, if you're planning to stay." His bushy eyebrows rose infinitesimally.

"A month," David allowed.

Ralph gave a noncommittal nod. "Don't suppose they stocked you up, did they?"

"Uh-uh."

"You wanna eat?"

David took in the blood-smeared frock.

Ralph chuckled. "I promise the burgers aren't raw. Got 'em from the farmers' market in town. Grass-fed."

David's mouth watered. "I should probably get groceries."

"You probably should," Ralph said. "Then again, maybe you shouldn't rest on ceremony and pass up burgers and free beer."

"You've got beer?"

"Yup."

"What brand?"

"The cheap ones. Budweiser. MGD. Coors."

"Perfect."

"Yeah?" Ralph said. "I figured you for a snob."

"That's okay," David said, falling in beside him. "With that bloody apron, I figured you for a serial killer."

Ralph laughed, and they set off in companionable silence down the dusty lane. It wasn't until night had fallen and a ghostly rind of moon had materialized over the Rappahannock that David remembered he hadn't yet ventured to the second story of the Alexander House.

CHAPTER FOUR

David devoured three thick burgers, not worrying that his lips were glistening with juice and beer, not noticing anything at all save the satisfying fullness in his belly. He and Ralph reclined in cedar rocking chairs, the screened-in porch much smaller than the one in the Alexander House and with a much less panoramic view. With the woods encroaching on both sides and a strip of dock scrolling out before them, David felt nestled in, pleasantly anonymous. Ralph had drunk half a six-pack already, David two cans.

"The Bud's nearly gone," Ralph said, cracking open another. "Let's start on the Coors."

"I better not. Too many and I'll be foggy all morning."

"Work to do, huh?"

David studied the man's profile. Largish nose. Slightly protuberant forehead. But instead of dumbing Ralph down, the rough features conveyed a sage virility.

"I'm settling a bet for an old friend," David said and found himself explaining the entire situation.

When he'd finished, Ralph said, "So the wife wants you to write a book, make the house even more famous."

"That's about the size of it."

"But your buddy doesn't?"

"Chris has never been the imaginative sort."

"Neither are you, from the sound of it."

David stared at Ralph, whose expression remained as amiable as before. "I guess that depends on your definition of imaginative."

"You always come out on the same side."

David sat up in his rocking chair. "You've read my books?"

"A couple."

"Let me guess – you hated them."

"Not at all." Ralph sipped his Bud. "You're a mighty fine writer."

"Thank you," David answered, unaccountably touched. Into the silence, he said, "But...."

Ralph scowled. "Hell, I don't know. Who am I to judge?"

"You're as qualified as anybody else. Now tell me what bothers you."

"It's like you watch a movie from the beginning, and it's damned good. Engrossing plot, sharply drawn characters. Really sinks its teeth into you. You can't help but go along for the ride."

"And then...." David said, knowing what was coming.

"It was all a dream," Ralph said. "Or the police swoop in and save the day. Either way, the audience gets cheated. It's an anti-climax."

"I can't ignore the truth, Ralph. I'd be the laughing stock of the academic community."

"Ah, the academic community," Ralph said, mock-primly. "They about as tight-assed as they sound?"

"More so," David said. "You've never seen people take themselves so seriously."

"You ever spent time with a bunch of town selectmen?"

"Never had the pleasure."

"Be thankful. They've got the temperament of bull sharks."

"Huh." David gazed out on the river. "So you believe in the supernatural."

Peripherally, he saw Ralph shift in his rocking chair, the first time he'd sensed any discord in his host. Good, he thought. Let the mask slip so we can see what's underneath.

"I need another beer," Ralph said. "You?"

David shook his head.

When Ralph returned with a six-pack of Coors, David said, "You were telling me about your belief in ghosts."

Ralph threw back his head and laughed. "You're a ballbuster, you know that? No wonder you're still single."

"I wouldn't wish me on anyone."

Ralph cracked the tab on a new can. "I never said I believed in things that go bump in the night."

"You're disappointed when I debunk a haunting."

"That's too strong a word." He shook his head. "Okay, maybe 'disappointed' fits, but not in the way you mean."

"Meaning?"

"The disappointment of a *reader*, not a believer. You wanna know the ride's been worthwhile. You want there to be a payoff."

"So I should make one up?" He was aware of the edge in his voice but made no effort to soften it. Ralph's criticism was too familiar. Why did people crave dishonesty?

Ralph was staring into his beer can. At length, he said, "I don't know what I believe."

David kept quiet, waiting.

"I keep an open mind," Ralph said.

Which means mine is closed, David thought. Hell. It was like his critics were sitting here drinking beer with him.

"You've never seen anything that makes you wonder?" Ralph asked.

David settled in his chair. The cedar armrests felt good under his forearms. "I've spent time in nine – now ten – supposedly haunted places. Written books about all of them. At no time did I feel the presence of anything unnatural."

"You didn't answer my question."

When David could only frown, Ralph went on. "I didn't ask if you ever felt something unnatural. I asked if you ever wondered."

David glanced out at the pine trees. "I've got a receptive nature. Always have. I feel all sorts of things. Emotions, sensory details, memories. If anything, I've got an overactive imagination."

"What I wonder," Ralph said, "is why you rely on all that silly ghost-hunting bullshit. Thermal cameras, voice recorders...."

David was smiling and nodding. "...infrared lights, grid scopes. I know, it's all a bunch of stage tricks. I blame *Ghostbusters*."

"Bill Murray's funny as shit, though."

"That he is."

Ralph's eyes narrowed. "But he's a Cubs fan."

"Thank God," David said. "You like the Yankees, I suppose."

"Hell's bells, man, what kind of a person you think I am? I hate the Evil Empire."

"Red Sox fan?"

"Through and through."

"I don't suppose we get cable out here?"

Ralph shook his head ruefully. "On a clear night you might get one snowy network without audio."

"Damn. And here the Cubs are in first place."

Ralph reached out, patted an old radio David hadn't noticed on the porch ledge. "I listen to the Sox on this thing. If you get bored."

"I don't get bored," David said, "but I'll come anyway."

A few minutes later they toted their empty cans and soggy paper plates inside. As David was making his way through the murk of the front yard, Ralph called to him.

"Yeah?" David asked.

Standing in the half-open doorway, Ralph seemed to debate with himself. "Promise me one thing."

David shrugged. "If I can."

"If something happens, don't ignore it."

David stared at him, but Ralph's face was indistinguishable in the gloom. When it became apparent that Ralph was awaiting some sort of answer, David said, "I'll grill the burgers tomorrow night."

"Hellfire, boy. You think I trust you to cook for me?"

Smiling, David turned away. Ralph said something else, but whatever he muttered, David couldn't make it out.

It wasn't until he was halfway home that the words began to crystallize.

He was pretty sure Ralph had been praying for him.

CHAPTER FIVE

At just past 11:00 that night, he showered, brushed his teeth, downed two tall glasses of water with a couple Tylenol to combat the ghost of a hangover. He wanted to be sharp in the morning. He'd write until noon, then spend the rest of the day poring through his least favorite book, *The Last Haunting: The Curious Disappearance of John Weir*. Sensationalized, puerile, and so crammed with fabrications it made David's head throb, the novel – for that's what it was; David refused to think of it any other way – had been published in 1932 and had become an instant bestseller. Unfortunately, the book's audience had only grown since then and it was still shelved in the non-fiction section.

Yet it was all horseshit. The author, Dr. Isaiah Hartenstein – perhaps the most dubious use of 'doctor' David had ever encountered – had been scratching out a paltry living as a lecturer on the subject of the paranormal when *The Last Haunting* hit. And though Hartenstein's subsequent works never rivaled the success of his first book, he remained a celebrity until his death decades later.

Naked, David ambled into the master bedroom and stared at the stack of books he'd lugged in and arranged on the birch dresser. A couple of them were about this house. He liked to learn about a place on the fly, gleaning the site's history while he resided within its walls.

With a ripple of disgust, he selected *The Last Haunting* and studied the cover. On it, unforgivably, was a photograph of John Weir. David gripped the book harder, the stark truth resounding in his brain: Hartenstein, a bona fide charlatan, made his career by destroying the reputation of a legitimately brilliant man.

David slapped the book onto the dresser, hastily buried it under a trio of superior books. The truth was, David had only read the first forty pages of Hartenstein's hatchet job, and that had been a decade ago. He supposed he was obligated to read the rest of it now.

The beads of shower water had all but dried, leaving David a shade too warm. It wasn't muggy enough to run the air conditioning, but maybe a touch of night breeze would do the trick. He crossed to the southern window and muscled it up a few inches.

There. A pleasing current whispered over his stomach, provided just the right counterpoint to the musty heat. He went to his travel bag, fished out a pair of loose boxer shorts, slid them on, then selected one of his favorite collections from the dresser: M.R. James's *Ghost Stories of an Antiquary*. Book in hand, he cozied into bed and began a re-read of one of his favorites, "Canon Alberic's Scrap-Book."

Why are you avoiding the upstairs?

"Son of a bitch," he growled.

He flung the book aside. Pushing the covers off, he strode around the bed, moved through the impossible blackness of the den, and into the main hallway.

It was cooler in here. Centrally located as it was, the main hall should have been warmer than the windowed rooms, particularly with the doors locked tight. Yet it was perceptibly chillier here than it had been in the bedroom, with the crisp night air circulating.

Go upstairs.

Yes, he thought, grasping the banister. He needed to go upstairs.

He'd climbed to the third step when another thought sounded in his head: *Why do you need to go upstairs? Because you need to prove something to yourself?*

He scowled in the darkness. I don't need to prove a damned—

Then why go up? It's pushing midnight, you have a book to begin in the morning. You need sleep. The only motivation to search the upstairs is to prove to yourself you're not frightened of it. Aren't you a little beyond such absurd displays? At your age?

David hesitated, half turned.

A creaking sound from above.

Feathery fingertips brushed his spine.

That cranky, pragmatic voice spoke up, louder this time. *Sure, David. Be terrified. Because it's totally abnormal for an old house to creak. Jesus, it would be a marvel if you spent ten minutes in here* without *hearing a creak. But go upstairs, by all means. Investigate the eerie noise and prove to yourself there are no ghouls on the second floor. And while you're at it, why not fling some salt over your shoulder and chant a few incantations. You fucking child.*

He rolled his eyes at his skittishness. He *was* receptive – he'd told Ralph the truth about that. What he'd failed to mention – perhaps because he didn't like to admit it – was that he was also, on rare occasions, a bit jumpy. He descended the risers, passed through the den, and reentered the master bedroom. He was retrieving M.R. James when he heard a sound through the open window.

David stared out the sliver of screen and realized what it was he was hearing.

A woman's voice. Singing.

You've lost your damned mind.

But he hadn't. It was faint, it waxed and waned as it drifted on the night breeze. But it was, unmistakably, a woman singing.

A radio on the screened-in porch? Had Chris or his wife left it on?

There's no radio out there and you know it.

The voice swelled, diminished. He could nearly make out the words. Its tone was sorrowful, elegiac. He realized his skin had broken into gooseflesh.

Locking in on the voice, David crossed to the window, grasped the wooden frame, and with an effort, forced it a few inches higher. Damn thing needed oil.

Like whatever's creaking upstairs?

"Stop it," David muttered.

He bent at the waist and peered into the night. For a moment he lost the voice, the chill breeze kicking up. When it died, however, he detected the nocturne again. There was something fragile about it, something lost. He screwed up his eyes to see beyond the screened-in porch, beyond the sparse but gigantic hickory and elm trees in the backyard, where the Rappahannock sprawled like a depthless tarn. Far away on the opposite shore he made out glowing pinpricks, the private security lights like earthbound stars. It struck him again just how vast the river was, how cut off he was from those on the opposite bank.

The voice came to him, insistent now. There was something vaguely Celtic about the song, something lilting and pagan. He imagined pre-Roman hills, a seething pyre. Tear-streaked faces. Flames and a sacrifice.

Or, he thought wryly, someone was blasting a stereo from a distant dock. He knew sound carried over water with uncanny power.

The wind barreled in, the great hickory shivering. A bench swing he hadn't noticed before teetered in the wind as though occupied by an invisible child.

David swallowed, his shoulders tingling. The voice…it was in the yard. He grasped the window frame, strained to slide it higher, but it was jammed fast, the years of grime and disuse stubbornly refusing to loose their hold. He moved to the corner of the master suite, manipulated the lock and deadbolt on the door, and stepped out onto the fake turf of the porch.

Here he felt unaccountably exposed. Despite the lack of neighbors – Ralph was two hundred yards away and screened by a dense grove of trees – David sensed eyes upon him, and yes, the voice was still audible, and not at all distant. Heart ticking along like a frantic metronome, he slipped outside, the dewy grass frigid on his toes. The voice resonated more strongly out here among the burled trees and the undulating shadows. He made out a few consonants, but the language was no more discernible than the singer.

There is no singer. Someone is cranking a stereo across the river, likely a bachelor lothario attempting to penetrate some woman's defenses.

But this wasn't seduction music. This wasn't Marvin Gaye or sweaty jazz. It was a mournful dirge beyond time, a threnody of myth and loss and cruel fate.

Conscious of his racing pulse, rankled by his witless physiological reaction despite the fact that there was nothing whatever to be scared of, David trudged through the wet grass, stopped when he'd ventured to within twenty feet of the rocky shore.

His heart beat harder. The clarity of the voice was striking. It couldn't be projecting from across the river. The aching loss, the unforced sultriness…it was coming from….

He swiveled his head to the southwest, toward the tip of the peninsula. His stomach gave a lurch. Had he glimpsed a hint of flesh? A forearm receding into the darkness? Pallid fingertips beckoning him closer?

His feet refused to obey his commands, his knees locked stupidly. Mouth dry, he stared into the darkness of the river and told himself he didn't see a glimmer of hip, a milky swash of throat as it caught the moonlight.

Drawn by some mysterious gravity, David followed the receding object that couldn't possibly be real, a wraith that dwindled and skimmed over the surface of the water.

When he reached the river's edge, he craned forward to see what had been hovering on the shoreline.

He didn't see anything. Of course he didn't. But he did make out the melancholy strain as it danced on the night breeze. To his right lay the river bend, the dense forest packed on the nearer shore. To his left, the Rappahannock opened to oceanic breadth, the far shore a barely recalled memory. But straight ahead, he now discerned a wild, hoary bank, choked with deadfalls and bizarre humps that could only be uprooted trees. Farther in, cupped by the deep-set bay, he made out an island. It was toward the island that the figure—

There was no figure!

—had drifted. It was there that the woman lived.

Listen, David. If you really believe a woman just floated over the water from that island and back, you might want to head into urgent care for a toxicology test. Maybe Ralph laced your burgers with hallucinogenic mushrooms.

David stared at the distant island. What about the song? he wondered.

You already solved that mystery. It was a stereo. Someone's idea of a soothing late-night mix.

David grunted. Soothing? If the song were so goddamned soothing, why did he feel like he'd just escaped death?

Bed, the practical voice ordered. *Now.*

He backpedaled a few steps, his eyes never leaving the island. The trees there were even larger and older than the ones in his yard. He turned and headed for the screened-in porch. He didn't hear the voice again. But he did walk a little faster until the door clacked shut behind him.

CHAPTER SIX

From the Introduction of *The Last Haunting: The Curious Disappearance of John Weir:*

> *...and it seems that Weir's own haughtiness proved his downfall. The dismissiveness that had made his reputation among like-minded academics (and, incidentally, had ruined the lives of those whose authentic experiences with the supernatural were labeled hoaxes by the contemptuous Mr. Weir) is the quality that doomed him in his final case. The Alexander House, like many of the supposed 'hoaxes' Weir debunked, attracted Weir like a blowfly to carrion. Half a dozen serious-minded researchers had already established the presence of paranormal entities in the isolated peninsular residence; more than two centuries-worth of inhabitants had fled the house in mortal terror.*
>
> *This brings to mind one of Weir's most egregious sins: his recklessness. Weir fancied himself enlightened, a voice of reason in a wilderness of superstition and fear. However, it is precisely this quality – Weir's willful ignorance of hard evidence – that motivated him to accept the invitation of Geoffrey Mansfield, the Alexander House's owner from 1916 to 1940, with the intention of pronouncing the house free of psychic manifestation. Had Weir succeeded, how many future residents would have been, at best, emotionally scarred by their experiences in the Alexander House? Or worse, how many future lives would have been claimed because of Weir's temerity, the way that Weir himself was ultimately claimed by the house?*

With a muttered curse, David shut the book with a thump on the table of the screened-in porch. He poked at the Caesar salad he'd picked up at the grocery store, but though there was nothing demonstrably wrong with the food, he found his appetite was weak.

The morning's writing hadn't gone well. The beer and the late night and – though he was loath to admit it – the incident with the mysterious voice had conspired to fog his brain. He'd only managed eight hundred words before abandoning the project and heading into town. While Lancaster had proved larger than he'd assumed, it was still a twenty-minute drive from the house, and the journey ate into his day.

Now it was past one and sweltering. What he needed was exercise.

He went in, changed into red athletic shorts and his well-worn running shoes. He retrieved his adjustable dumbbells from the Camry's trunk and bore them into the yard. Four sets of military presses, four sets of curls. He jogged inside, a fine sheen of sweat making his forearms gleam in the gloomy kitchen, and poured himself a tall glass of water. He guzzled it, drew himself another, and carried it outside. Eschewing the dumbbells, he selected a low-hanging elm bough that would support his weight and performed three sets of pull-ups.

There. He no longer felt like a cadaver. He stretched lightly and started off at a leisurely trot. Moving away from the Alexander House, he discovered a spindly dock protruding into a miniature inlet. The wood was gray and weathered, but it looked trustworthy enough to support him. More excitingly, there were multiple metal buckets tethered to the dock posts.

He grinned. He hadn't been crabbing since his early twenties, and he resolved to reacquaint himself with the hobby this afternoon. Hell, if he got lucky and caught something he could invite Ralph for a crab bake. That, he decided as he chugged past the dock, would go beautifully with the case of Budweiser he'd purchased.

As he moved, his muscles loosening, he discovered another surprise: a pair of yellow kayaks half hidden in the tall grass. Even better.

He pelted along the shoreline, the dirt path giving way to grass. Still, the terrain was level enough for him to jog without fear of a twisted ankle. To his left the Rappahannock's brown waters rolled along companionably.

Unbidden, a voice whispered, *Anna loved the river.*

David's smile evaporated.

The park you used to visit is nearby, the voice continued. *You know you're in the general area.*

Maybe so, David agreed, chugging faster. But that's ancient history.

Like Anna's death?

"Aw, hell," David said. He put his hands on top of his sweaty hair, got control of his breathing.

You can't pretend it didn't happen, the voice persisted.

He got moving again. Maybe, he thought dourly, he could outrun his conscience. But he'd only jogged a few steps when he detected a stirring in the forest ahead, just a few feet from the riverbank.

It's the Siren.

"Shut up," he growled.

A small shape stepped onto the strip of grass. "Why'd you tell me to shut up?"

The boy was maybe seven, with shaggy black hair and dark, resentful eyes.

David halted. "I wasn't talking to you."

"We're the only ones here," the boy countered.

David opened his mouth to answer but decided against it. The boy had a point.

"You from town?" the boy asked.

David nodded toward the woods. "I'm staying at the house over there."

The boy's eyes narrowed. "Bullshit."

David blinked at him, suppressed shocked laughter. The boy wore a light blue Captain America tank top, green shorts with a faded *Teenage Mutant Ninja Turtles* insignia on one leg.

"Why were you in the woods?" David asked.

"Mom and Dad are fighting again."

That's because people aren't meant to be married.

David stared beyond the boy's shaggy head but couldn't see a house. "Won't they be worried about you?"

"Worried, hell," the boy said.

David glanced at him, adjusted the boy's age up a year. He was too world-weary for seven. Eight, maybe, but small for his age. Malnourished. David felt a tremor of disquiet.

"Come on," David said. "I'll walk you home."

The boy's face spread in a lewd grin. "Mom is sure gonna like you."

CHAPTER SEVEN

The Shelby property was like a vinyl record played at the wrong speed. The flats were too flat, the sharps downright earsplitting. There was nothing overtly wrong with the place, not that David could spot from fifty yards distant, but the closer he and the boy ventured, the more powerfully the wrongness resonated. The boy – Mike Shelby Jr., the kid told him – kept watching David for his reaction. As though the boy understood there was something wrong with this place but needed someone older to articulate it for him.

David had just about decided to say his goodbye when the kid asked, in that same petulant drawl, "Aren't you comin' in?"

David took in the big river house, which was somehow obscene looming here among the native plants and the water. Two stories, brick, probably worth half a million. It was like a contractor had plopped the house here to strike back at a conservationist with whom he'd been feuding. The lawn was tufted and weed-strewn, making it difficult to tell where the countryside ended and the property began.

The boy said, "Come on. Mom'll wanna check you out."

David eyed the house warily. "You said they were fighting."

The kid stared up at David in challenge. "I thought that's why you wanted to walk me home. You turning chickenshit?"

David stared down at the kid.

"I wanna show you my cars," Mike Jr. said.

"What kind of cars?"

The kid put his hands on his hips. "You a retard or something?"

"That's a lousy word."

"Mom uses it."

"She shouldn't."

Mike Jr. shrugged. "Tell her yourself."

David sighed. He'd be here a month. Even in a place this remote, he was bound to run into Mr. and Mrs. Shelby eventually. Why not get it out of the way?

They crossed the yard, where numerous faded toys lay like the corpses of soldiers from some long-ago battle, and onto the porch, which was crisscrossed with fluorescent sidewalk chalk. Bright pink suns were scarcely discernible beneath green and blue monsters with guns. Chalk victims with Xs for eyes sprawled at the feet of gun-wielding werewolves. David was reminded of the *Itchy & Scratchy* cartoons, wondered what the hell kind of parenting the Shelbys were doing.

David expected to hear raised voices when Mike Jr. opened the door, but instead he heard loud music, not from a stereo – too tinny – but from a television. Beneath that….

You've gotta be kidding me, David thought.

He followed Mike Jr. through a white tiled foyer littered with mismatched shoes and sandals, and when they came around a corner, the sounds clarified.

The sounds of people having rough sex.

The acid of his stomach boiling, David followed Mike Jr. past a staircase. At the rear of the house he made out a wall of windows, the Rappahannock beyond. To the right was an expansive kitchen full of granite and stainless steel. To David's left spread the family room. It was from here that the music and moaning emanated.

David found it difficult to process what he was seeing.

On a giant projection TV, the kind that was in vogue during the younger Bush presidency, an over-tanned guy with a blue mohawk was butt-fucking a blond woman with pendulous breasts.

Mike Jr. nodded at a leather sectional couch, where a woman in her late thirties sat staring at the porno. She clutched a glass of some dark liquid. Across the room from her, seemingly oblivious of the sex show, a girl no older than four lay coloring in a *My Little Pony* book.

"Who's our visitor?" a voice called.

David turned and discovered a nondescript man of perhaps forty. The guy had wire-rimmed spectacles, a balding hairline, and a gnomish belly. His clothes were conservative, his expensive shoes in need of a good polish.

Above the mohawked man's grunts, Mike Jr. explained, "This here's our neighbor."

"Ah," the man said. "It'll be diverting to have someone next door."

On the enormous television, the woman rolled onto her back, told her mohawked lover to fuck her harder.

David fought off a wave of nausea. The man and the boy continued to study him. The woman on the couch continued to study the porno.

The man raised a glass. "Drink?"

"I've...." David began, realized he'd have to be louder to be heard above the grunting. "I've got to be going."

The man slapped himself in the forehead. "Where are my manners? I'm Michael Shelby. I see you've met my boy."

"You've got nice arms," the woman on the couch said.

David turned, regarded her, and with an inward start remembered he was as shirtless as the guy with the mohawk.

"Hard abs too," she said, eyes crawling down David's torso. Her ivory dress hung loosely on her chest – no bra that David could see – and was hiked up nearly to her crotch, revealing thighs that were strong and opalescent.

David turned away, said to the husband, "I was on my run. I better...."

Michael Shelby smiled. "We have different ideas here, Mister...."

"Caine," David supplied.

"Mr. Caine. We're...ah...more open. Honey feels that's best."

"Honey?"

"My lovely wife," Shelby said, gesturing toward the couch with his drink. A gout of clear liquid sloshed onto David's sneakers. David realized how slurred Shelby's speech was.

It's early afternoon, he thought.

"You married, Mr. Caine?" Shelby drawled.

"Never," David murmured. He glanced at the little girl with her coloring book. She looked peaked. Her dark bangs were trimmed unevenly on her forehead. She had reddish Kool-Aid stains on the corners of her mouth. He wondered if she'd eaten lunch yet. Or breakfast, for that matter.

"How about that drink?" Shelby asked, a hand on David's triceps.

"Like I said..." David began, then faltered when he noticed the trickle of blood wending its way down Shelby's chin.

Following David's gaze, Shelby wiped the blood off with the back of his hand, glanced at it, and grinned at David a trifle sheepishly. "Honey likes to get physical."

David glanced at the little boy, who was watching the men raptly. "Mike Jr. said you and your wife were fighting."

Shelby smiled. There was blood on his teeth. "Did he now? Well, we're an *expressive* family, Mr. Caine. What you see as fighting, we see as healthy communication."

On the television, the blond woman was taking the mohawked man's oversized member into her mouth.

Jesus Christ, David thought.

"Can we turn that off?" he asked.

Shelby nodded an apology, said, "Please pause it, dear."

"We're getting to the good part," Honey responded.

David made the mistake of glancing at the television and discovered that a petite young woman had sauntered into the bedroom, was slithering between the blond woman's legs.

"You can finish it later," Shelby answered. He shot a nervous glance at David. "Honey does enjoy her pay-per-view."

Grumbling, Honey turned off the television.

Shelby took David by the arm, made to lead him into the kitchen, but David shook free, said, "I really need to finish my run."

"You can use our lane," Honey said, standing and swaying a little. Though barefooted, she was tall. Well-built too. The dress drooped, revealing a great deal of cleavage.

David turned back to Shelby. "Your lane connects with—"

"Governor's Road," Shelby said, nodding.

"How long you on the island?" Mike Jr. asked.

"Peninsula," Shelby corrected automatically. He smiled at David. "My son likes to think of this as an island."

"Might as well be," Honey said, "for all the entertaining we do."

"I imagine," Shelby went on as though his wife hadn't spoken, "Mike Jr. envisions being in the middle of the Pacific Ocean. That's the sort of game I used to play when I was his age. Did you, Mr. Caine?"

"I fight terrorists," Mike Jr. said. "I blow their heads off with my M-16."

"Well," David said, "I really better get moving."

"You timid around pretty ladies?" Honey asked. Although she stood several feet away, David scented a puff of warm whiskey.

He turned and moved away.

"Mama hits Daddy," Mike Jr. called.

David stopped and studied the boy. The declaration had been made with the same casualness he'd used when talking about killing terrorists. He looked at Honey.

"Does that bother you, Mr. Caine?" Honey asked with a lazy grin.

Shelby blushed and adjusted his glasses. "I hardly think that's any of Mr. Caine's business, Michael."

"Name's Mike," the boy said.

"Michael *Junior*," Shelby corrected.

The boy looked like he'd eaten something rotten. "If you say so."

For the first time Shelby's affable demeanor slipped. "Get in your room right goddamned now."

Moving with no real urgency, Mike Jr. passed David, then climbed the stairs.

"See you, Mr. Caine," the boy mumbled.

Shelby forced a smile. "Children are a trial, Mr. Caine. You're blessed you never had any."

David considered telling him his fatherhood or lack thereof was none of his business but decided there was no point.

He'd started toward the foyer when Honey said, "You know why they call it Governor's Road?"

"Now *why*," Shelby snapped, "of all the topics you might broach with our new neighbor—"

"He wasn't really a governor," Honey said.

"Darn it, Honey...." Shelby said.

David glanced behind him, saw Honey approaching with Shelby in tow. She said, "They gave him this territory to limit what he could do."

"Who?" David said, interested despite himself.

"Let's get your movie back on," Shelby said, a hand on his wife's shoulder.

Honey flung his hand off, rounded on him. "It's the only interesting thing about this island—"

"Peninsula."

"*Peninsula*," Honey mocked. "Jesus, you sound like a little girl."

Shelby poked a finger at Honey's chin. "Don't you dare—"

David took a step forward but froze, stunned, as Honey smacked her husband on the cheek, the sound a sickening pop in the two-story foyer.

Shelby put a hand to his face, but rather than being enraged, his features conveyed a wicked species of lust.

David's gaze was drawn to something down the hallway.

The little girl. She was gazing up at her parents with huge eyes.

"Go color," Shelby said.

The girl did as she was told.

"Worried about her, Mr. Caine?" Honey asked. "Maybe you should come back tonight and give me a good, hard parenting lesson."

"Sure," Shelby said, that wicked gleam on David now. "We'd love some instruction."

David left the Shelbys staring after him. He was shaking, queasy. It wasn't until he'd escaped the yard that the midday heat penetrated his icy sweat.

He dashed toward the woods and didn't stop sprinting until the Shelbys' house was a half mile behind him. He slowed, thinking of the little girl with the coloring book.

She hadn't spoken a word.

CHAPTER EIGHT

His run brought him back to Alexander Lane – not its real name, as far as he knew, but that was how he thought of it – twenty minutes later. He'd explored a couple paths off Governor's Road, but both had led to wheat fields with no apparent means of exiting.

He considered stopping by Ralph's but decided against it. He needed a shower in the worst way, the sweat and the dust and – there was no denying it – the Shelbys conspiring to instill a deeply unclean feeling in him. He disrobed in the foyer, which was uncannily cool, and moved into the gloomy den.

David showered, the sensation of hot water on his flesh the perfect balm for his discomfiture. Just what the hell was wrong with the Shelbys?

Rinsing out the shampoo and soap, David considered his options.

He'd witnessed physical abuse of the husband, and he strongly suspected Mr. Shelby sometimes reciprocated. But both of them seemed to *like* it. So where did that leave David?

And the kids? My Lord, it was the kids to whom David's mind kept returning. Mike Jr. growing up with such shitty role models. The little girl, whatever her name was, coloring her ponies while semen geysered over a woman's face on the television a few feet away.

Could Child Protective Services intervene? And if so, what would their legal basis be for removing the Shelby children? That their mother enjoyed watching pornography? That their parents engaged in consensual physical abuse?

Was there such a thing as consensual abuse?

David toweled off, went to the bedroom, and changed into a clean pair of cargo shorts and a light gray *Stranger Things* T-shirt that read 'Hawkins AV Club.'

He had to go upstairs.

Silly, really, that he hadn't explored the second story yet. He'd been here nineteen hours, and he hadn't yet seen half the house.

The most important half.

Absurd, he thought, smiling a little. Barefoot, he started up the stairs. Unsurprisingly, they creaked loudly. On the landing he paused, noticed how cool it was on the second floor.

"Better grab the thermal scope," he murmured. But he wouldn't, of course. He always waited until the end of a stay to break out the accouterments of the paranormal-obsessed.

He was studying the second-story hallway when Honey's words echoed in his brain: *They gave him this territory to limit what he could do.*

Now what the hell had that meant?

David crossed to a walnut trestle table, found a collection of hoary leather books pinned between scrimshaw rowboats. He lifted a pale hunk of scrimshaw and jumped when a leather book toppled with a ridiculously loud boom. David glanced behind him at one of several closed doors, shook his head at his skittishness.

He replaced the rowboat and set the book upright again.

And wondered, to whom did they give this territory and why did he need to be limited?

His toes were freezing. Like they'd been dipped in liquid nitrogen. Going shoeless had been a mistake.

David glanced down the hallway and spotted what just about had to be the house's second bathroom.

You're stalling.

Am not, he argued. I'm taking my time.

The bedrooms, David. They're the whole ballgame.

There *is* no ballgame. Just an old house with a scandalous reputation.

He took a steadying breath, strode over, and grasped a dull brass knob. It was freezing.

Doesn't hot air rise?

He pushed away the thought, opened the door.

A bedroom. Just a bedroom.

There was an old-fashioned walnut bedstead nestled under a crimson-and-ivory quilt. Though there were windows on the southern and eastern walls, the room received very little sunlight. David considered twisting on a lamp, but what was the point? There was nothing interesting about the room, save an aura of moroseness. He imagined a bedridden nonagenarian spending the last dispiriting years of her life under that quilt, opined how monotonous it would have been with only a nurse to spoon-feed her meager bowls of soup and to empty the bedpan. He fancied he could scent the undercurrents now, watery broth and sour black feces. Within this suffocating miasma the woman with the saggy crone's neck and the papery yellow skin would turn, her tiny sable eyes like painted ball bearings rolling toward him, slowly focusing, her taloned hand unearthed from its tomb of blankets, the trembling fingers groping for him, beseeching, a gargling rattle sounding in her throat, a plea floundering in a cauldron of phlegm, and then—

David gasped, backpedaled from the bed, his left shoulder blade ramming the doorframe. He stepped backward into the hall, stared at the bed that was just a bed, but somehow wasn't. He swallowed, hesitated, then lunged forward, seized the knob, and yanked it shut.

He stood panting, his arms and fingers numb, his feet useless hunks of ice. Perspiration trickled down his back; he wondered if it'd freeze before it reached the belt of his cargo shorts.

There's nothing to be afraid of, a voice soothed. But this irritated instead of calming him. He didn't need coping mechanisms. This was merely a house. Old, yes, but a house like any of the others he'd debunked. And while a handful had given him a momentary case of the willies, none had engendered in him a reaction like the one he'd just experienced.

But it was bound to happen sometime, wasn't it? An occupational hazard?

He attempted a smile, but it wouldn't take.

You're building it up too much, David. You know what an important project this is, and you're increasing the pressure on yourself to deliver.

His pulse slackened a notch, his breathing easier. In his other jobs it had been the legend versus his logic, and that was a battle for which he was equipped.

This, on the other hand, was complicated by the need to clear the man on whose shoulders David's career was built.

Sensation returned to his appendages. Yes, he thought, striding down the hallway to the next closed door. He was psyching himself out because of his desire for justice. What did you do to him, Mansfield? How did you murder him, Dr. Hartenstein?

Yes, David thought. In his marrow he knew that Mansfield and Hartenstein – the owner of the Alexander House and the charlatan who penned the fictionalized account of John Weir's death – had brought Weir to this place on false pretenses: *We need you to disprove the legends, Mr. Weir.*

Weir, being the game academic that he was, would have relished the opportunity. Few places possessed the reputation of the Alexander House.

But the invitation was a ruse. Mansfield and Hartenstein had conspired to break down Weir's defenses, to cause a man of advancing years to doubt his own perceptions. There was no doubt Weir saw and heard peculiar things in the Alexander House, but the details chronicled in Weir's journal – exploited and reprinted to hideous effect in *The Last Haunting* – were so fantastical as to defy explanation.

Which, David supposed, was the point. Make Weir believe there were ghosts cavorting through the Alexander House, or at the very least, convince him he was losing his mind. Weir had been seventy-one by the time he journeyed here. Not old by today's standards, but back then firmly in his twilight years. Once he'd begun to deteriorate from the strain, it wouldn't have been difficult for them to consummate their sinister plot.

To murder him.

Yes, David realized. That's what he believed. In the end, Mansfield and Hartenstein, having procured the needed histrionics from Weir's journal, simply murdered the defenseless old man and then…what? Sank him in the Rappahannock? Perhaps, David thought, though there was a problem with that. For one, the river wasn't deep, which made disposal of a corpse risky. Even riskier when one considered the current. On most days the Rappahannock rolled sedately along, as dark and innocuous as an ancient black bear slumbering in its cave. But during a tempest the river could roil and kick, the whitecaps like wraiths capering across the water. How thoroughly would one have to weight a body to make sure it would never surface?

Burial seemed the likelier option.

Musing about where Weir might have been entombed, David opened the door to the second upstairs bedroom.

If the first bedroom had been dimly lit, this room was positively sepulchral. That made sense, David decided. It was directly above the den, which was equally dark. Like the den, this room was furnished in murky colors. Though he couldn't be certain without turning on the lights, the walls appeared to be chocolate brown. The duvet was similarly brown with occasional light brown stripes. The floor and trim had been stained to such a degree that any grain was undetectable.

He reached out, flipped on the light.

The room remained as dark as pitch.

Dammit.

The nearest lamp was a mere six feet away, yet David found himself holding his breath as he advanced into the gloom and twisted it on.

Though the light it produced was paltry, at least he could see now. There was a door in the far right corner, a small closet, no doubt. There was no door opposite, which meant the occupant of the room would have to enter the adjacent bathroom through the hallway. Inconvenient. But then, convenience hadn't been a hallmark of homes constructed in 1664.

Thinking of the house's age, David whistled softly. Granted, this level of antiquity was commonplace in Europe, but for a nation as young as America, a structure so old seemed too fantastical to be real.

He extinguished the lamp and went out. Turned right and entered the bathroom. Experienced a surge of happiness. So there *was* a bathtub. David rarely took baths, but when he did he always wondered why he didn't more often. The tub was nothing special. On the short side, and not particularly deep. But he could take a bath if he wanted.

He gave the rest of the room a cursory scan: toilet, sink, freestanding towel rack in the corner. The only notable characteristic was the northern dormer, which was curiously empty.

David flipped the bathroom switch and advanced down the hall. Coming to the stairwell, he paused, compressed his lips. He chided himself for it, but he'd been about to descend the steps despite the obvious fact that there was another room to explore.

The final bedroom, he decided, must be the biggest by far, for it appeared to occupy the entire western side of the house. Knowing he might lose his nerve if he delayed too long, David pushed open the door and stepped inside.

And immediately realized something was wrong. It wasn't just the dimness – why was every room save the master suite so light-deprived? – it was the *frigidity*. Christ, like a meat locker in here.

The furnishings were antique but unremarkable. Four single beds facing west, aligned like a hospital ward. A brick fireplace. Maritime bric-a-brac lining every surface. David turned to the southern wall and studied the mahogany table that occupied the dormer. There he spied a ship in a bottle. A pair of carved mallards. Another hunk of scrimshaw.

He plucked this last from the table with unsteady fingers and examined it. It was shaped like a canoe, but inside the pale object, where there should have been an empty bench, or perhaps a Native American with an oar, there were tiny severed heads lined up from end to end. Six of them, their eyes agape, their mouths open, as if they couldn't believe it had come to this, set adrift on the Rappahannock without bodies or limbs to guide them. The carvings were executed with exquisite detail. David stared at them, nauseated.

There was someone in the room with him.

He whirled. Beyond the row of single beds, thirty-five feet away, he made out the window, and in that somber spill of light, a rocking chair. As David stared at it, limbs turned to stone, it leaned forward, tilted back, leaned forward, tilted back, the creak of its runners audible.

David darted for the door, which was somehow closed. He scrabbled for the knob, realized there was something in his hand, glanced down stupidly, discovered the accursed canoe, and flung it away with a gasp. It hit the floor with a teeth-jarring *clack*. He was certain the door would be locked and he'd be imprisoned in this icy tomb, but then the knob turned and David burst through, nearly tumbled headlong down the stairs. He took them two at a time, slipping repeatedly, his heels thudding painfully on the risers, his groin damn near ripping from his graceless blundering. Somehow, he made it to the foyer, where he tore open the heavy front door, shouldered open the screen door, and dashed down the steps into the driveway.

Hands on knees, David tried to corral his ragged breathing. In movies this was the moment when a neighbor wandered by, declared how spooked the protagonist looked. But a quick glance around the yard showed him he was alone.

This should have reassured him, but it didn't. Though he hated to admit it, he craved company now, Ralph in particular. He could head down the lane, see what the older man was up to. Maybe take in an inning or two of the Red Sox, if they were on.

Or you can do the job you came to do, you pussy.

He cringed. The voice had sounded eerily like his father's.

David scowled at the seven dormers of the Alexander House. He hated his father's voice. It represented everything that could go wrong when notions of masculinity were bound up with stoicism, with callousness, with proving one's strength to the detriment of others. But maybe, for once, he needed to heed his father's advice.

The book wouldn't get written if he cowered out here.

He told himself it had all been in his head. The legends, *The Last Haunting*, and his overactive imagination conspiring to conjure spirits when there was nothing here but an old house.

The sweat drying on his skin, David moved reluctantly toward the porch.

He kept his eyes down, studiously shunning the window of the long bedroom.

CHAPTER NINE

"It is the evening of June the second, and I'm staring out at the Rappahannock from the screened-in porch of the Alexander House," David said into the voice memo recorder of his phone. "The facts of the case are these...."

He shook his head, pushed stop, and erased the recording. This wasn't a 'case'; it was an *assignment*, a job. Calling it a case gave it a more mysterious aura, and though there *was* a mystery to be solved – how Mansfield and Hartenstein murdered John Weir – the present circumstances were far more straightforward: Katherine Mayr wanted David to turn this property into a tourist attraction by admitting the existence of the supernatural. David would not. David would, however, help Chris by proclaiming the house as normal as any other.

At the thought of Chris, he experienced a pang of guilt.

You abandoned him. Him and Anna both.

David blew out an aggravated breath, pushed *record*. "The...situation is this: the Alexander House has a notorious reputation. The home's age, the deaths of a handful of its occupants, and the unfortunate popularity of a lurid work of sensationalism have imbued this venerable property with that dreaded appellation: haunted house."

He pushed *stop*. Not bad, but he'd have to curtail his contemptuous tone when he committed these words to paper. As his agent was fond of reminding him, the majority of his audience bought his books because they *wanted* to believe in ghosts.

Okay, he thought. Then humor them. Just a little.

"Having completed my first twenty-four hours in the Alexander House, I must confide how impressed I am. It was only by screwing up my courage that I was able to explore the second story today, and when I was skulking through the rooms, I did feel, if only for a moment, that something unnatural might dwell here."

David smiled. His agent would love that, as would his editor. David knew very well what both of them wanted, so he reveled in withholding it. And when he did give them a passage of fright, they responded orgasmically and clamored for more.

Well, they'd been loyal to him. David supposed he could string them along.

"I teach a story in my American Gothic Tradition course called 'Moonlight Sonata,' by Alexander Woollcott. The tale was made famous by its inclusion in the sublime *Great Tales of Terror and the Supernatural*, one of the class's required texts. In that story, the main character discovers a figure in a rocking chair, sitting in a spill of moonlight, plucking the hairs, one by one, of a severed head. Despite the fact that the discovery renders 'Moonlight Sonata' a simple tale of murder, the image is an indelible one, and I confess to experiencing a shiver of delight when my students gasp aloud at Woollcott's gruesome revelation.

"I also confess to a recollection of Woollcott's macabre tale this afternoon. Despite it being June in Virginia with temperatures regularly in the nineties, the long bedroom proved to be uncommonly frigid. Aside from that...." David hesitated, experienced a moment's reluctance at mentioning the scrimshaw canoe, finally decided he'd throw that in as well.

By the time he finished recounting his experience in the bedroom, he'd begun to sweat, and not from the humidity of the evening. He wished Ralph had joined him for dinner, but when six o'clock had come and gone with no sign of the older man, and David had ventured down to Ralph's house, he'd found a note taped to the front door declaring that Ralph wasn't feeling well and had gone to bed.

David drummed his fingers on the table. The burgers he'd made were overcooked and sat uneasily in his belly. Even the beer David was nursing tasted foul, the Budweiser too metallic, the heat making the can sweat in his grip.

He sat forward, eyeing his phone. He considered deleting the voice memo. How ironic would it be, he mused, if David were to go missing and the only record of his stay here was a breathless recording of his weird experience upstairs? He would become an even truer successor to John Weir: another skeptic claimed by the spirits he was attempting to debunk.

As far-fetched as this was, it made him restless. He stood and pocketed the phone, resolving if anything did happen to him, he'd make sure his last words on earth didn't sound like a recanting of everything he believed.

What to do now?

David craned his head toward the dock, his mouth opening in a smile.

The kayaks!

Oh man, he thought, setting off in that direction, how lovely it would be to scythe through the water in the deepening dusk. In another twenty minutes it would be full dark, just him and the moon and the Rappahannock. And he knew where he'd go, too.

The island. He knew his experience of the night before had been imagination – the notion of a woman floating backward over the water while serenading him was the stuff of overripe Gothic romance – yet it had wrought one positive outcome: it had made him aware of the island.

The prospect captivated him. He remembered an island just like it in college. He and Chris and Anna whickering through the night on a rope swing, somersaulting into the river, lazily backstroking out to the island, where they'd lazed in the shallows, the sand gritty but somehow pleasing to the touch. Funny, he thought as he reached the tall grass half concealing the kayaks. The island from here looked a good deal like the one they'd frequented back then. This was, after all, the same area of the Rappahannock they'd once explored back in their days at William & Mary.

David shook off the thought. Coincidences happened, but that would be too much. For how long did the Rappahannock meander through the countryside? A hundred and fifty miles? The odds that this was the very same island they'd once loved were too scant to consider.

He waded through the grass, the dew dampening his leg hair, and grasped the edge of a kayak. He overturned it and sucked in breath as a long black snake slithered toward him. David danced away, nearly fell, and was about to take off at a sprint when the snake changed course and headed toward the shore.

"Jesus," he muttered. Six feet long at least. He didn't know what species it was, but it looked like something that could kill a man.

Moving with more caution, David returned to the kayak, selected a plastic oar, and dragged the boat toward the bank. He placed the oar inside, nosed the kayak into the water a few feet from the dock. When he thought he'd reached a point where he could safely enter the boat but still push off with the oar, he climbed inside. He was out of practice and nearly capsized, but after a minute of fuss, he found himself floating toward the main Rappahannock.

Lord, but the night was beautiful. He had a momentary worry of some angler's bass-fishing boat appearing out of nowhere and nailing him broadside, but as the kayak sliced through the water, the river opening up around him, he realized he was entirely alone out here, the only signs of human existence the twinkling lights on the distant shore, and those so intermittent they might as well not have existed.

He was twenty yards into the main river before he noticed the large brick house to his right. His good spirits vanished. The Shelby home was lit up like a gambling riverboat, the picture windows plating the waterside glowing tangerine and yellow and, in the family room, the antifreeze blue of the giant projection television. David wondered what kind of porn Honey was watching tonight and whether the little girl was still in the corner with her coloring books.

Had the kid eaten anything but Kool-Aid today? Had the boy spent the afternoon machine-gunning terrorists and evading the fisticuffs between his mom and dad?

David's stomach performed a slow, sickening roll. He switched his oar to the right, dug into the water to move away from the Shelby house. As the kayak knifed through the water, moving steadily toward the place where the Rappahannock opened up, he again considered reporting the Shelbys to Child Protective Services. He couldn't imagine CPS making his name known to the Shelbys, and even if they did, who the hell cared? He wanted them to know his contempt for them, wanted them to know that someone was aware of their negligence and...

...and abuse. Hell yes, he thought, paddling steadily. It sure as hell *was* abuse. David had experienced firsthand what it was like to be ignored, to be treated like dirt, to be hit.

The tide of remembrance slugged him in the throat, made it difficult to breathe. God, he hadn't thought of his childhood forever, and the way those dark times had been dredged up made him hate the Shelbys even more.

Be quiet, Davey. Daddy's home.

Shhh, sweetie. We can play when Daddy goes.

Then his father: *What the hell have you been doing all day, Shelly? Don't fucking work, the house looks like a landfill. You and David probably spent the afternoon watching TV, didn't you?*

In fact, David and his mother *did* used to spend all afternoon watching TV. It was calming, she used to inform David. Easier on her nerves. He hadn't realized then she was popping pills. How could he? He was a fucking kid.

Quit crying, goddammit. I mean it, Shelly. You're the reason our son's such a sissy.

A slap for Shelly.

A spanking for David. On one occasion his dad swatted him so hard that David had shat blood.

When his dad had finally tired of abusing his wife and son and left for good when David was eight, David had believed life would be grand.

It turned out, the pills' hold on his mother had tightened to the point that she was incapable of mothering. With no money, no car, and no real family – her parents had died in a car accident, and David's paternal grandparents were as nasty as his father – David and his mom had subsisted on food stamps and the charity of neighbors. By the time David was eleven, it was apparent that Shelly was unfit for motherhood. She handed David over to the county, and he never saw her again.

The tears streaming over his cheeks caught him unawares. David placed the oar in his lap and wiped them roughly away.

He was nearly to the bend in the river, where he shifted the oar to the left and made for the shoreline. The approach to the bay would be calmer there, the current less swift.

The gigantic deadfalls along the shore reminded him of fantasy novels, post-apocalyptic epics in which the planet had been obliterated by nuclear war or an alien attack. The moon broadcast its ghostly luminescence over the uprooted trees and the piled, glistening boughs. Though it carried him into a stronger current, David steered well clear of the shore. He had no desire to ram a barely hidden stump or capsize on a snarl of lurking branches.

With a glance ahead he saw the island. It was larger than he'd judged last night. The sandy shore ringed this side of the island in a luminous white penumbra; the trees stood sentry several yards in, their mossy trunks uniformly spaced, the underbrush thick and obeisant.

David twitched, a psychic whisper passing through him. *Yes, there are many islands in this river, but how many are there like this one?*

Impossible, he thought.

It's the same island. The one you shared with Anna.

The current had towed him toward the broader part of the river. Not wanting to spend all night fighting his way back, David went to work, his powerful upper body more than equal to the task. By the time he made it past the deadfalls, he was perspiring freely, but dammit, it felt good. Since his humiliating experience in the long bedroom, he'd been feeling reduced and weak. Now, with the moon spangling the black water and his muscles pumping, he was back in control, strong again.

But when he discovered the public beach that had been hidden by the outcropping deadfalls, his arms went slack, the oar clunking on the kayak floor between his feet.

It couldn't be, but it was. There could be no mistaking the swings, the slide, the shelter.

The sign reading 'Oxrun Park.'

The sight of this place, the realization he'd come to it accidentally but unerringly, suffused him with a nameless dread.

Oxrun Park.

The last place he'd been with Anna.

A month before she committed suicide.

CHAPTER TEN

David rowed toward shore, but he couldn't arrange his thoughts, which tumbled over him like boulders in a rockslide:

This was where he and Anna had spent their last evening together.

The last time she'd asked David to make love.

The only time he'd refused her.

The most cruelly he'd ever treated her. Ever treated anyone.

Chris had told him he'd forgiven him for Anna's death, but what if he hadn't? Had Chris bought the Alexander House because of its proximity to the park, the island? And if so, what bizarre aim could Chris possibly have in doing so? He must have known David would discover the truth eventually.

Unexpectedly, the nose of the kayak met sand, and David was catapulted into the hard plastic coaming. Rubbing his chest, he climbed out and dragged the kayak onto the beach.

Oxrun Park was the same in most details. One exception: an old-fashioned teeter-totter had been replaced with a pair of seahorses on giant steel springs that allowed you to rock back and forth.

Here was the slide. He remembered Anna whooshing down its satiny silver length, not quite nailing the landing.

Gracefully clumsy. Endearingly goofy. God, he'd loved her.

He could almost see her, her Red Sox cap worn backward – Ralph would have approved – as she raced toward the swings. She'd worn gray shorts that night that showed her tanned legs to delirious effect. A red tank top. Bare feet, her flip-flops abandoned in Chris's car. Chris was always the driver so David and Anna could drink.

David could almost smell the beer as he roved over the sandy beach. He remembered tasting the beer on Anna's mouth, their hot tongues clashing. A wave of desire scudded through him, and he allowed himself to imagine her body. She wasn't tall, wasn't built like a supermodel, but she'd aroused him like no woman had then or since. Yet she'd only been twenty-one, a year younger than David and Chris. An intelligent but emotionally raw girl who told him she loved him after the third date, who scared him with the power of her affection.

Perhaps, he reflected as he reached a copse of trees, it had been his love for her that had doomed them.

She wasn't clingy. Had she been possessive, like so many women David had known, breaking up with her wouldn't have been so painful. But she hadn't been needy at all, had merely told him how she felt and made it clear she wanted a future with him.

And God help him, he'd wanted it too. Or part of him had. And not just the libidinous part of him, the creature of the night he indulged too often, who was maybe no better than Honey with her porn flicks.

No, it had been the emotional, receptive compartment within his… he dared not call it his heart…within his *being* that longed to remain with Anna. When they'd been together – only a year, but in many ways the best year of his life – he'd found himself entertaining the possibility of marriage, of raising children with her.

Yes, he thought, weaving between the trees. Breaking up with Anna had been the levelheaded decision. He couldn't have known what it would do to her, couldn't hold himself responsible for her suicide.

David emerged from the trees and froze, mouth opening.

The nearest swing pendulumed back and forth.

The wind, he thought hollowly.

But there was no wind, no breeze at all. And the other swings, three of them, didn't stir.

Laughter, light and insouciant, echoed behind him.

David whirled, heart thundering, and peered through the trees. He leaned forward, straining to see through the shadows to the beach beyond. He heard a scraping noise.

David plunged through the trees, his shoulder gored by branches. He angled toward the beach, but that carried him off the path. He stumbled over a bent sapling, half twisted his ankle on a root. Teeth bared, he charged on, and through the remaining trees he caught the sound of splashing, of a disturbance along the shore.

David burst through a tangle of bushes and scampered toward the beach.

The kayak was gone.

No, he realized, not gone, but adrift. Someone had dragged it into the water and given it a shove. It was already fifteen yards out. Soon it would catch the current and be swallowed up by the Rappahannock. Without pause, David bolted toward the water, leaped, realized he might be hurtling straight at the shallow river bottom. He entered at too steep an angle and raked his chin along the river floor. The pebbles harrowed his chest. He scarcely registered this because he glimpsed something trawling through the water in the other direction. For a moment he almost followed. But if he didn't reach the kayak soon he'd be stranded out here, and then what? It would be, at minimum, a forty minutes' swim across the Rappahannock. He thought he could do it, and he was relatively certain he could touch the river bottom most of the way there. But what if it dropped off? Even at a seven-foot depth he could drown. Then his worst nightmare would be realized: FAMED MYTHBUSTER DISAPPEARS ON FINAL CASE!

He was closing on the kayak, but the current was taking hold. It propelled him in the right direction, but it was urging the kayak along too, and David was growing winded. His back muscles bundles of flame, he put his head down, stroked and kicked with maniacal intensity. He pushed himself as far and as long as he could and then looked up, praying he'd closed the distance.

He had. The kayak was only six feet away. Despite the complaint of his aching limbs, he gave a final burst of effort, and then his fingers brushed hard plastic. The damned thing goosed away from him, and it took another thirty seconds of painful toil to draw even again. This time he stroked abreast of the kayak and slung a forearm over the side. The boat wrangled, he glided along with it for a few seconds before realizing he could touch the bottom. Not comfortably, but if he strained, he could brace his toes on the river bottom and keep the kayak relatively stable. He'd try to climb into the boat in a minute or two. For now, it was enough to have caught it.

The Rappahannock lapped against his armpits, the mingled aromas of dead fish and damp foliage somehow pleasing now that he was safe.

He became aware of movement in his periphery. He screwed up his eyes, but it was impossible to discern the object in the water. Breath coming in labored sips, he tried to climb over the rim of the kayak, but as expected, it was a hell of a lot harder to accomplish in deep water than it had been in the shallows. David compressed his lips, took a chance and dropped down in an underwater crouch, then exploded to the surface and shot both arms over the kayak's center. He only succeeded in overturning it.

Damn it!

He attempted a different tack. After situating the oar inside the kayak, he drew himself up gradually, attempted to use his upper body to keep the boat from overturning. It wobbled a bit, but eventually he was able to flop inside. Though his muscles were overtaxed, he began paddling toward the object moving away from him, which was dark and circular, almost like…

…the top of someone's head. But it was almost to a dock that sprouted from the bank about fifty yards from the park. He closed the distance, but it was evident he wasn't going to intercept whoever it was. David watched, mesmerized, as the figure reached the dock, climbed onto it, and rushed down its length toward the densely wooded shore.

It was a woman, David saw. She wore a white two-piece. She had a beautiful body, but this scarcely registered. He couldn't help thinking that this was the woman he'd seen last night floating over the water.

There was no woman!

The woman whose sad, melodic nocturne had summoned him from the house. Why had she set his kayak adrift? Why had she fled?

For a time, he simply gazed into the woods after her and willed her to appear again. When his trance fractured, he realized the current had been hauling him away, toward the main Rappahannock.

David rowed himself around, started back toward the peninsula.

He thought of Anna, of how he'd broken her heart, left Virginia, left everything he'd known to begin a new life.

And in doing so, ended hers.

Far off, so softly he couldn't be certain it existed at all, David heard the melody of the night before. Sorrowful. Yearning. The song cleaved his soul.

The voice sounded like Anna's.

PART TWO
THE LONG BEDROOM

CHAPTER ELEVEN

"Dammit, Ralph, I know you're in there."

David peered through the screen door, imagined he saw movement in the cramped kitchen. The morning was overcast, but he could make out the small table, a vacant chair that hadn't been pushed in.

He rapped on the metal frame again, harder this time. "The Red Sox suck balls!" he called. "Carl Yastrzemski is a communist!"

A throaty chuckle from within.

David visored his eyes and stared through the screen. A figure ambled toward him.

Ralph pushed open the screen door, his expression sheepish. "You're probably miffed at me, huh?"

"At least when a woman stands me up, she's civil enough to send a text."

"You get stood up a lot?"

"I need some water. I forgot how sultry Virginia was in June."

Ralph eyed him. "'Sultry'? You sure you don't write romance novels?"

David armed sweat off his brow, but his forearm was sweaty too. He blinked against the stinging in his eyes. "Damn."

"Get in here," Ralph said, holding the door for him. "You're a goddamned mess."

He followed Ralph into the kitchen, where the older man handed him an ancient dishrag.

"The mosquitoes are out too," David said through the towel, which smelled faintly of shoe polish. He drew it away from his face. "This thing clean?"

"How can a big strong guy like you be so delicate?"

David chuckled, tossed the towel on the kitchen table. There were four brands of cereal boxes lined up there, most of which David associated with little kids. He identified the half-eaten bowl as Fruity Pebbles.

"Didn't have an appetite this morning," Ralph remarked, moving toward the screened-in porch.

"That why you stood me up?"

Ralph grunted in the negative. David trailed the older man onto the porch, but Ralph went out, down a pair of rickety wooden steps, along a flagstone path, the stones having sunk so far that they were scarcely visible in their nests of grass.

"Dock's wide enough for both of us," Ralph said.

Although the view off the end of Ralph's dock wasn't panoramic due to the heavily wooded yard, to the south you could see a long ways. If you gazed straight ahead, the Rappahannock went on forever.

"Bet you paid a lot for this view," David said.

When Ralph didn't answer, David looked at him and noticed how tight his face had become.

"Ralph?"

With the air of a man working himself up to something, Ralph glanced down at the water, said, "Guy loses his wife at fifty and decides he's gonna go live on the river. Fish, drink beer, smoke all he wants."

"I didn't know you smoked."

"He looks around, but all he finds are rundown shacks priced like French chateaux, places that claim to be on the river but actually have 'river access.'" Ralph looked at him. "You ever hear that phrase, run screaming the other way. 'River access,' 'lake access,' those are just real estate parlance for shitty property nowhere near the water. I don't know how many places the lady showed me before she got it through her head I didn't want to strap on hiking boots and pack a week's provisions just to make it to a fishing hole."

"I dated a real estate agent," David said. "She told me she always tried to sell her own properties before she'd show any others."

"Didn't want to split the commission," Ralph said. "This house wasn't even listed. I only found out about it by happenstance."

"Driving around?"

Ralph shrugged. "In a manner of speaking. I was scouting for properties when I stopped at The Crawdad. You see it before you turned off the highway?"

"Uh-uh."

"Not surprised. Looks like a derelict garage. But it's still in business. Good thing, too. Otherwise you'd have to drive fifteen miles just to gas up.

"Anyhow, I'd just finished buying groceries at The Crawdad when I happened to glance at this old bulletin board littered with notes." Ralph meandered over and tested a fishing rod sheathed in an iron holder. The line moved easily, nothing on the other end. "'One bedroom, one bath, two acres, Rappahannock,' was all the ad said. Wasn't even a price listed. I asked the old fart who used to run the gas station – he's been dead more than a decade – where the property was. He had wrinkles on his wrinkles, but I could see he was uncomfortable talking about it. I didn't know why then. Didn't know why until after I'd bought the place and moved my stuff in."

"He the one selling it?"

Ralph glanced at him. "If he was selling it, why would he be hesitant to talk about it?"

"Good point."

Ralph nodded over his shoulder. "You can have some cereal, get the blood flowing to your brain."

"Piss off," David said, grinning.

Ralph smiled too. "I finally got out of the man that the house was on Governor's Road, and he gave me directions. Wouldn't give me a number for the owner, not yet, but he told me how to get here.

"When I arrived, I felt despondent."

David looked at him questioningly.

Ralph shook his head. "Oh, I loved the house. That was the problem. No way, I figured, was this gonna be in my price range. It's not like the place was in great shape, but the view off the dock, the screened-in porch…." He shrugged. "I came back to The Crawdad and told him I was interested. Didn't even bother wearing a poker face. I wanted this house. After my wife…." He glanced at the river, his expression pensive. David let it go.

Ralph hawked, spat. The loogie smacked the water, where it floated and spread. "Turns out the house had been part of an estate, and a lawyer from Virginia Beach was in charge of it. He sold it to me – not cheap, but not as salty as I'd figured – and I moved in a few weeks later."

Ralph fell silent. The day had grown gloomy, a breeze kicking up around them. Rather than cooling the day, however, the sensation of being stuck inside a vast cauldron only increased, the febrile wind swirling about them like some devil's stew. Just when David was about to prompt him, Ralph went on.

"I didn't notice the Alexander House until after I'd moved in." He turned to David. "You find that strange?"

David thought about it. "Your property is pretty overgrown – no offense."

"I prefer to think of it as rustic."

"You can't see the Alexander House from inside the house. Too wooded."

Ralph said nothing, but David could tell by the way the older man had cocked his head that he was hanging on David's every word.

A bit uneasily, David went on, "You can't see it from the screened-in porch either. Again, too wooded. The backyard is jammed with trees and brambles. And from here…." David paused, glanced to his right, where the Alexander House, two hundred yards away, stood silent and watchful.

"And from here?" Ralph prompted.

"Well," David said, gave a little shrug, "you can see it from here, but it would be easy enough to miss if you weren't looking."

"Would it," Ralph said. Not a question.

David tore his gaze off the house. "I admit it's arresting, but I can understand the oversight."

"Maybe you can help me understand it."

He realized Ralph was staring at him now, his eyes imploring.

"Ralph, what do you—"

"*That fucking place*," Ralph said, his voice a harsh croak. His eyes were starey, his teeth bared. "It's like it was…hiding from me. I looked this house over, even walked the property in all directions…." He leaned toward David. "*And I never saw the Alexander House.* Can you explain that?"

David peered down the shoreline. "There are several possibilities."

"I'm listening."

David shifted from foot to foot, aware he had been thrust into his accustomed role of skeptic. "For one, the weather could have been bad. There's a lot of mist in the mornings—"

"I visited this property eight times before I moved in." A trace of a smile. "You know how exciting it is to move into a new house. Especially if it's your dream home."

David couldn't argue with that. The place he lived in now he'd scouted two dozen times before making an offer, and after closing on it, he'd hung around like a gnat until the previous occupants moved out.

He chewed his lip, inspected the long run of vacant land between the properties. "There might have been more trees then."

"There weren't."

"Oh."

"Nor," Ralph continued, "was there an ancient mountain range that sank due to the shifting of tectonic plates."

"Smartass."

"Just taking away that argument."

"Is it possible you're just unobservant?"

"You have a scar under your hair," Ralph said. He tapped behind his right ear. "Back here. You can only see it when you're facing a certain angle and the light is just right."

David fingered the scar behind his ear self-consciously, which was shaped like the onyx stone in the ring his father used to wear. He shoved his hands in his pockets. "I don't know, Ralph. Maybe you were just excited about your new home and didn't pay attention to the neighbors."

"That place," Ralph said, his lips writhing into what David was certain was an unconscious snarl. "That place is diseased."

"I'll admit it looks foreboding."

"You don't feel anything?"

"What the hell do you want me to say?"

"No need to get testy."

"I'm not testy," David snapped.

"I won't judge you."

"Judge me all you want," David half shouted. "I deserve it. I...." He stopped, massaged his brow. "Maybe I'm just putting too much pressure on myself."

Ralph reached into his pocket and came out with a well-worn pouch of Red Man chewing tobacco.

Watching Ralph pinch out some black leaves, David said, "You're just full of vices, aren't you?"

"It's unhealthy," Ralph agreed. "But it's better for my lungs than stogies." He stuffed the wad into his cheek.

"Was someone living in the Alexander House back then?"

The color drained from Ralph's face.

When the older man didn't speak, David asked, "What happened there?"

"They were beheaded."

David could only stare. He realized with alarm that Ralph was on the verge of tears.

Ralph said, "They were a nice, normal family. He was a trifle strange. A writer, like you."

When David opened his mouth, Ralph waved him off. "You wouldn't have heard of him. His wife had a good job, so he was free to pursue his dream of writing full time."

The contempt in Ralph's tone was evident, but David made no comment.

Ralph spat brown juice into the water. "I had them over once, nice little boys, one no older than five, the other a toddler. Wife read x-rays... oh, I forget the—"

"Radiologist."

"Radiologist," Ralph repeated, with a frustrated shake of his head. "Old age."

Another silence.

David glanced at the Alexander House. "Who...you know...."

"Cut off their heads?"

David cringed. "*Man.*"

"No idea."

"You didn't find them, did you?"

Ralph spat into the water, armed juice off his lips. "As a matter of fact, I didn't."

"Who—"

"Should've known you wouldn't let this go," Ralph muttered. He scratched the back of his neck, sighed. "The woman – Clara Raftery

– used to drive to work every morning, except on weekends and holidays, and sometimes even on those." He shook his head. "Hard worker. Good woman. It got so I'd sit on the front porch and smoke just so I could wave to her." A fond smile. "If she'd been twenty years older...." The smile faded. "One morning she didn't go to work. Then the next.

"I was worried she'd taken ill. Their cars were in the driveway, so I knew they hadn't gone on vacation. Besides, it was early November, not exactly prime traveling time."

Ralph looked up at the dingy sky. "The fourth day I finally went down there. You know, to make sure things were okay. I'm a shitty cook, but I could've whipped up some chicken noodle soup or something. She was always bringing me leftovers...." The smile again, but there was pain in it. "I knocked, but nobody answered. I walked around the house and called out, but...nothing. They didn't respond to phone calls... didn't...."

Ralph spat straight off the end of the dock, the stream an impressive splurt that must have traveled at least twelve feet. "It was the smell that told me."

"You called the police?"

Ralph smiled a ghastly smile, tobacco-streaked and half-mad. "I was a good citizen, all right. Did my duty and dialed the authorities."

David frowned. "I don't—"

"Don't you *see*?" Ralph barked. "It made me a coward, that place. Even now I can barely look at it."

David found himself thinking back a couple days ago, the evening he'd arrived. Yes, Ralph had greeted him, but he'd been restive. And he'd balked at entering the Alexander House.

It's making you a coward too, a voice whispered.

"They'd been strapped to the dining room table," Ralph said, his voice gruff. "Strapped down and vivisected."

David's stomach muscles contracted. "All four of them?"

"Their heads were lined up on the mantle. Like those wooden ducks."

David couldn't keep himself from imagining the woman and the man and the two little boys staring sightlessly from atop the mantle. "You saw this?"

Ralph spat. "Can you understand English? No, I didn't *see* it, I was told about it. I'd no sooner set foot in that house than I'd use my testicles as catfish bait."

"*Damn*, Ralph."

"The part that keeps me up nights…the part I've never gotten over… it's that what happened to that family…those poor kids…it happened on my watch."

David arched an eyebrow. "Your 'watch'? Don't you think that's going a bit far? You bought a house on the river. You didn't sign on to be some kind of sentry."

"No, I didn't," Ralph agreed. "But after what happened, I did discourage folks from buying it."

Ralph glanced toward the lane. David followed Ralph's gaze and saw Chris Gardiner's black Mercedes rolling toward the Alexander House.

"Those idiots wouldn't listen," Ralph remarked, watching after the Mercedes. "The others, they'd turn white when I'd tell them the story. But not those two. They were hell-bent on buying it. And when they brought you here…. I woke up last night in a cold sweat. I'd dreamed that your head was staring at me from the mantle."

"On that note," David said, "I'll be on my way."

The fishing line jerked. Ralph gaped witlessly at it for a moment. Then his trance broke and he removed the reel from the iron sheath. "Feels like a big one."

"Bet it'll taste like tobacco spit," David muttered as he walked away.

CHAPTER TWELVE

When he jogged nearer, Katherine Mayr made no pretense of averting her eyes. Instead, she stared at his chest, his stomach, his crotch.

"I knew it," she said. "I pegged you for a fitness junkie."

"Where's Chris?" he asked.

She nodded toward the house. "Stomach complaint. Chris gets diarrhea more than anyone I've ever met."

And I'm sure he'd be delighted to know you were making that information public, David thought.

"Have you experienced anything unnatural yet?"

He hesitated, then regretted it when she smirked at him.

"Look, Katherine...."

"You can admit it, David. *Everyone* feels it."

"Then I'm in the minority," he said with more heat than he'd intended. "Because I haven't felt a goddamned thing."

She favored him with a speculative look. "You *will* report any occurrences, won't you?"

David crossed his arms. "Calling me a liar won't help your cause."

"Don't be so grumpy! I only meant that men can let pride get in the way." She gave him a comprehensive glance. "Would you like to shower before we talk?"

David glanced at the house. "Isn't your husband using the facilities?"

"Go upstairs." She smiled. "Unless it makes you nervous."

Unable to formulate a comeback, he broke eye contact.

He spotted the adjustable dumbbells on the gravelly edge of the driveway. Good thing it hadn't rained. He made a mental note to store them in the house when he was done lifting. He dialed the weight up to sixty on the dumbbells, pointedly faced the dock so he'd have his back to Katherine, and began to squeeze out a set of twelve shrugs.

The knowledge of Katherine behind him proved distracting. Come on, Chris, he thought. Finish your gastrointestinal explosion and save me from your rapacious wife.

But Chris didn't appear. Between sets David glanced back at Katherine, and sure enough, she was eyeballing him. Scowling, he completed his shrugs and dialed the weight down. He positioned his left hand on his right hip, hoisted the thirty-pound dumbbell above his head, and began cranking out triceps presses. After ten reps, he switched hands and repeated the exercise.

He'd performed three sets when the front door opened with a creak, and Chris appeared on the porch. He was sweating and red-faced.

David strode toward his friend and said, "Hey, buddy. Let's you and I talk in private."

Chris shot Katherine a nervous look, but she said, "Fine. I'll walk the grounds." She glanced at David. "That is, if you don't mind."

David shrugged. "Your house."

With a sphinxlike smile, she headed toward the dock.

Chris joined David in the yard, both men watching after Katherine.

Chris's grin was shy. "She's something, isn't she?"

David studied his old friend's face. "You were in there awhile."

Chris touched his belly gingerly. "I get gurgly when things get tense."

"Everything kosher with you and Katherine?"

"It's this house. She's obsessed with it. Talks of nothing else. She would've been here last night if I hadn't persuaded her to give you some space."

David grunted. "She started firing questions at me the moment I was within earshot."

"What did you tell her?"

"There's nothing to tell."

Chris looked crestfallen.

"I thought you didn't want there to be ghosts," David said.

Chris ran a hand through his thinning hair and moved toward the water. "I gotta tell you…it'd make my life easier if Katherine got her way. She's adamant."

"I'm not sacrificing my career to placate her."

Chris peered toward the dock, where Katherine stood gazing toward the opposite shoreline. The deadfalls.

David nodded that way. "Why didn't you tell me what was over there?"

Chris grew very still.

"On the other side of those trees," David continued. "Where that big bay begins. That's Oxrun Park, the place Anna—"

"*Don't say her name,*" Chris snarled.

David drew back. Chris's round face was livid. His hands had balled into knots, and for a crazy moment David was sure his friend would strike him.

In a measured voice, David said, "I know you were fond of her...."

"*Fond,*" Chris repeated, his face twisting.

"I cared about her too."

"Would you drop the bullshit niceties?"

David half smiled. "It was almost a quarter of a century ago."

"So it didn't happen?"

"I didn't—"

"Or it doesn't *matter?*"

"I never said that."

"Did you even cry, Davey? Did it even bother you when you heard Anna killed herself?"

And staring at his old friend, David was forcibly reminded of the time his pet dog, Lady, had developed a festering wound on her forepaw. David was ten or so, his mom on the verge of checking out for good, so a vet was out of the question. Way too expensive, and David had no way of getting the suffering animal – a good-sized black lab – all the way across town. So he'd raided the medicine cabinet and found an old tube of congealed Neosporin and attempted to spread the ointment over the wound. Afterward, he'd try to remember if there were warning signs, but of course there hadn't been. One moment Lady was lying on her belly, her forepaws spraddled on the olive-green living room carpet; the next she was sinking her jaws into his hand and shaking it like a rabbit. David had been home by himself, and it had taken a good ten seconds to free his hand from the viselike grip of Lady's incisors. When he'd escaped, the sight of his savaged flesh made him woozy. He'd somehow made it outside, where, eventually, a woman who lived one block over found him stumbling down the sidewalk, a steady patter of blood trailing after him.

At the hospital, they'd sewn him up, pricked him with needles, fed him more than he usually got at home. When his mother had shown up, the doctors and nurses had been frosty with her, and maybe, he decided when he was old enough to view his childhood with more objectivity, that was when the state's mechanism for removing him from his home and placing him in foster care had been activated. Whatever the case, his mom had treated him with nothing but resentment for causing so much fuss, and the next day had informed him, "Lady got put down because of you." He remembered not only her wording, but her manner. It was as though he'd applied poison rather than medicine to the dog. His mom hadn't even *liked* Lady. He'd been feeding Lady portions of his own food for months since his mom seldom purchased dog food. But now his mom behaved as though David had murdered her dearest friend.

The part that stayed with him was being bitten by Lady, the radical change in her. He read the same vicious intensity in Chris's eyes now.

David sighed. "Look, buddy—"

"Don't 'buddy' me," Chris said. He took a step forward, prodded David in the chest. "Don't act like you care. We both know you don't. We both know you were born without that trait, the one that gives a shit about people."

"You act like I'm the Zodiac Killer."

Chris stepped closer. "Anna was worth a thousand of you. She would have done anything. All you had to do was let her down easy, and then maybe we could have...."

Chris trailed off, and with a mental thud, the idea slammed home. My God, how had David not seen it before? Did Chris really believe he and Anna would have ended up together, had she lived? As ludicrous as the notion was, he could see that, yes, this was precisely what Chris believed.

In the silence that followed, Chris hiked his belt up, but his ample belly pushed it back down. He took a few aimless steps away, moving in the direction of the house, and as he did David discovered something. The weeds on this side were in dire need of pruning, but beyond them, down in a shadowy swale, there was a door at basement level, its white paint peeling in leprous curls.

"What's down there?" David asked.

When Chris didn't answer, David took a step in that direction.

Chris finally said, "The cellar."

"What do you guys store in there?"

"Stay out," Chris said flatly. "Katherine?" he called. "We're going."

Without a backward look, Chris stalked to the Mercedes. Katherine glanced inquisitively at David but didn't ask what had happened. She climbed inside, and the Mercedes reversed, made a half turn, and rumbled off down the lane.

David glanced down at the cellar door. What's inside? he wondered.

CHAPTER THIRTEEN

Disturbed by the conversations with Chris and Ralph, and knowing he couldn't write any more that evening, he figured exploring the cellar would be diverting enough to take his mind off the house's past.

More importantly, off *his* past.

It was 7:35, the gloomy dusk making it seem much later. He waded through the knee-high weeds and tried the doorknob on the off-chance it was unlocked.

It was.

A surge of adrenaline coursed through him at the discovery. He drew open the door, but it scraped the ground stubbornly, and after moving a few inches it stuck fast. A formidable odor, wet earth and dank cinder blocks, assailed him. David glanced down, saw the rotted base of the door lodged in the dirt. He'd have to locate an implement to scrape the earth away so the door could swing wide enough to accommodate him.

Problem was, he hadn't seen a spade or any other gardening equipment anywhere. There was no garage. He could head down to Ralph's, borrow a hand tool, but at the moment David preferred being alone.

Come on, he told himself. Think.

He set off toward the Rappahannock. Without making a conscious decision, he moved toward the tip of the peninsula, the spur of rock and crabgrass that pointed toward the island. His tennis shoes squelching in the sodden grass, he found what he was looking for: a slender rock with a keen edge.

He moved back through the yard, the evening blowing damp breath over his skin. Storm approaching, he thought. Fine. Maybe it would wash away some of the brooding atmosphere that had, like some unseen but toxic gas, pervaded the property.

He stepped down the decline and knelt among the weeds. He elbowed the door shut and began scraping the dirt and grass with the flat edge of the river rock. Though the weeds rasped over his bare arms, the work was satisfying in an elemental way.

After a few minutes' toil, he tried the door, and though he'd only bought himself about six more inches, the passage was now broad enough for him to slip through.

Inside, the smell was appalling, like someone had distilled all the clammy basements in the Southeast and piped the formula down here. Images of rats and cobwebs and cisterns flickered through his mind. It occurred to him he hadn't bothered with a flashlight.

He was halfway out the door when he remembered his iPhone. He retrieved it, activated it, saw the battery was down to seven percent.

Damn. It would almost certainly work long enough for this brief expedition, but in the past few weeks it had been behaving erratically, shutting off without warning, claiming it had plenty of battery when it was actually nearing a temporary death. For one alarming stretch it had actually made calls to the wrong people, like the time David pressed a colleague's contact info and instead phoned up the garage that did occasional tune-ups on his Camry.

He swiped the screen, selected the flashlight button, and the basement lit up.

It was a disaster. Like someone had made a bet about how much junk could be piled inside the thirty-by-thirty space. Lawn chairs of several different species were stacked to the seven-foot ceiling, the chair legs in a couple spots wedged between ceiling joists. There were half-deflated rafts and inner tubes draped like molted skin over jagged junk piles. Dented crab buckets and damaged cages were strewn at weird angles, their rusty faces tinseled with cobwebs. Splintery oars protruded from the shadows.

David ventured toward the nearest heap of rubbish, the phone light unsteady in his grip. He lowered the phone to better illuminate the heap, but despite the light's brilliance, its reach was curiously limited, as if, in touching the nearest surface, it lost its nerve and refused to penetrate the deeper shadows. David made out a fishing net with a rusty frame, a beach ball skewered by a tent spike. On the grimy cement floor he spotted the faded red handle of an oversized whiffle ball bat. David loved those bats as a kid. The sensation of squaring up a tennis ball and knocking it to kingdom come…God, how exhilarating.

Smiling, David reached for the handle and a rat the size of a Chihuahua clambered over his fingers. Hissing, David jerked his hand away. The rat was dark gray, mangy-looking, its tail dragging like a rubber cord as it disappeared inside a spill of cardboard boxes. As he watched after the rat's tail, a shivering fit gripped him. He straightened his arms to get the willies out of his system, and the iPhone winked out.

The darkness was shocking. Either he'd been in here longer than he'd suspected or the clouds outside had grown denser. Whatever the case, the cellar resembled a crypt now. He thumbed on the phone, but it was unresponsive – seven-percent battery, my ass – and the only thing to do now was to get the hell out of the basement and come back with an honest-to-goodness flashlight instead of a treacherous iPhone.

David turned and discovered a small child barring the door.

CHAPTER FOURTEEN

His scream wasn't exactly soundless – he was aware of noise emanating from the depths of his throat. But it was a breathy, impotent sound.

The outline of the child clarified: dark hair, slumped shoulders, bony limbs. His mind leaped to the story of the Rafterys, of Clara the radiologist and her poor, vivisected children.

When the child spoke, David gasped, staggered back, half sprawled on a pile of plastic chairs and fishing nets.

"What did you say?" David demanded.

"Mom and Dad are raging," the boy said.

David squinted at the boy. "Mike Jr.?"

"Don't call me that," the boy said. "Don't care what you call me, but don't call me that."

David stepped closer, noting as he did how Mike Jr. took a step backward. He felt a moment's fury. They'd better not be hitting the kids, he thought. So help me God, Honey and Michael, if you're hitting these kids....

"Smells like shit in here," Mike Jr. said.

"Watch your mouth," David muttered and cried out as thunder shook the house.

Mike Jr. stared fearfully up at the ceiling joists. "Fuck."

"C'mon," David said, taking the boy by the shoulder and guiding him toward the door.

"We supposed to get a storm?" Mike Jr. asked.

"I look like a meteorologist?"

"What's a—"

"Weatherman," David said, shooing Mike Jr. through the door. "Move it."

David was halfway through the door when a squiggle of lightning lit up the western sky. He mentally counted to three before the thunder rolled over them.

"Storm's close," he said in an undertone. He put a hand on the boy's shoulder. "We gotta get you home."

Mike Jr. swatted his hand away. "Ain't goin' home. I told you Mom and Dad was raging."

Rain began to patter the yard, wetting David's cheeks and mingling with the sweat in his hair. "What do you mean 'raging'?"

"Mom starts talking about fuckin' some other guy, and Dad gets pissy 'cause he didn't get to watch."

David made a face. "Could you not…I'd rather not hear the details."

"You asked."

"What I meant was…did it get physical?"

"You mean the fucking?"

"*Jesus.* No, I didn't mean the— I'm asking you if they hit each other."

Mike Jr.'s snort was horribly world-weary. "Hit each other all the time. They like it."

It was out of his mouth before he knew it. "You don't belong in that house."

Mike Jr. gave him a wry look. "Hell, I know that. Why you think I'm over here?"

"I meant…ah, come on."

He led the boy toward the front porch. In his periphery lightning flashed again, and though he didn't count, the attendant thunder sounded nearer than it had previously.

David stopped. "Wait a second. Where's your sister?"

"Half sister. She's got a different daddy."

"Whatever." David glanced toward the woods, the shoreline path that led to the Shelby home. "Is she…you know…."

"No idea," Mike Jr. said. "Ivy don't go out of the house much."

"So she's still in there. Terrific." David imagined the girl sitting in the corner with her coloring books and her Kool-Aid stains. Goddammit….

"We've got to get her," David said. "If it's not safe for you in there, it's not safe for her."

He'd taken a few steps when a girl's voice sounded behind him: "Where you goin'?"

David whirled, a hand on his chest, and found Ivy sitting on the porch, clutching a light green stuffed animal. A lion, he saw upon further inspection.

She caressed the lion's fur. "Minty's scared. He doesn't like storms."

David approached. "I don't blame him."

Now what? he wondered. He couldn't very well keep them for the night, nor could he cast them back into that freak show.

Child Protective Services?

The rain was falling harder now, thick, punishing drops that matted his hair and changed Mike Jr.'s Captain America shirt from light blue to navy. Thunder rumbled over the river.

"We gonna stand in the rain all night?" Mike Jr. asked.

"I'm thinking," David muttered.

"Kinda slow at that, ain't you?"

David arched an eyebrow at the kid, but Mike Jr. stared impassively back.

"Mr. Caine?" Ivy said.

"David."

"Mr. David?"

He sighed. "Yes?"

"Minty's hungry."

David looked at the little girl, took in her knobby shoulders. "Well, we better get Minty something to eat then."

CHAPTER FIFTEEN

Freshets of rain drilled the kitchen window. The lights kept flickering on and off. It was only a hair after eight but it was darker than soot outside. David hoped they didn't lose power.

"Got any pork rinds?" the boy asked.

"If I did," David said, slathering peanut butter on bread, "I wouldn't give them to you."

"Just like my dad," Mike Jr. said. "Gets barbeque chips, Doritos… think he shares them with me?"

"You sneak them," Ivy said from the kitchen table.

"Fuck off," Mike Jr. said.

David dropped the butter knife with a clatter. "First off, you're not going to cuss—" Thunder shook the earth, made the dishes and appliances rattle. "—in my house."

"Ain't your house," Mike Jr. said, chin upraised. "This here belongs to Governor Judson Alexander."

One mystery solved, he thought. David flipped the peanut butter-covered bread on top of the jelly slices, began the job of cutting the sandwiches diagonally. "As it currently stands," David answered, "Judson Alexander is worm food."

Something solemn permeated Mike Jr.'s voice. "Shouldn't joke about that."

He glanced at Mike Jr., assuming the boy was afraid of death, but what he read on the malnourished features was something deeper than normal fear.

David placed the sandwiches before the children and asked, "What are you talking about?"

"He chopped people up," Mike Jr. said in a small voice.

David glanced at Ivy, saw she was hunched over her sandwich. She was nibbling, but her shoulders were drawn in, her face even paler than usual.

David went over to the fridge. "Maybe we shouldn't talk about it now."

"That's why you're here, isn't it?" Mike Jr. asked. "Dad says you're going to desploit what happened here."

"Exploit," David corrected. He came out with a gallon of milk and crossed to the counter. "I'm not going to exploit anything. In fact," he said, removing a pair of glasses from the cabinet, "I'm here for the opposite reason." He poured the milk and brought the glasses over. "You see, when a house is as old as this one, there are bound to be legends about it."

"Like choppin' people up?" Mike Jr. asked.

Ivy's eyes were huge over the slice of sandwich.

"Let's forget it, okay?"

Through a mouthful of peanut butter, Mike Jr. said, "You gonna call the cops on my folks?"

David stared at the boy. "Has anyone done that before?"

That snorting laugh again. "Course. We been with Granddad twice. Once we lived with…I forget what they're—"

"Foster parents?"

"They was assholes."

David glanced at Ivy. Lightning cracked very near, the thunder rumbling a couple seconds later.

David sat across from Ivy. "Maybe we should call your grandfather."

Ivy twitched and stared down at her plate.

"Uh-uh," Mike Jr. said.

"But you said—"

"He's like Mommy and Daddy," the boy said. "Everybody thinks he's this great guy…."

Ivy sipped her milk.

David glanced from face to face. "He hit you?"

Mike Jr.'s eyes were downcast. "He ain't the hittin' kind."

Rain splashed over the window in gouts, as if a film crew were standing outside heaving buckets at the panes.

"You don't feel safe there?" David asked.

"Granddad's always wanting one of us to stay in the bedroom with him."

It was only with an effort that David kept from vomiting or screaming.

He glanced at the rain-besieged window. "Maybe we can…."

"What?" Mike Jr. asked.

David scowled. "Hell, I don't know. There's got to be something."

Ivy's voice was scarcely audible. "Can we stay here?"

How did I get into this? he wondered.

"Ain't stayin' at Granddad's," Mike Jr. said.

"No, I don't suppose that would be prudent."

Mike Jr. tilted his head. "You sound like my teachers sometimes."

"I am a teacher."

"Thought you was a writer."

"I'm a writer too."

"Dad says all teachers is socialists."

"Can we stay the night, Mr. Caine?" Ivy asked.

David looked at her, rifled through the possibilities again. Came up with nothing.

"Maybe your parents have cooled off by now."

"You don't know them," Mike Jr. said.

"Please don't make us go back," Ivy said. David noted how tightly she was clutching the sandwich, her tiny fingertips disappearing inside a snowdrift of bread.

David sighed. "I need to tell them where you are."

"They won't answer the phone," Mike Jr. said. "Too shitfaced."

"Then we'll have to go over there."

Thunder boomed, making all three of them jump.

Mike Jr. stared with dread out the window, where lightning strobed in three quick flashes. "You're gonna make us go out in that? We'll get fried."

"Fine," David said, rising. "I'll go."

"Can you grab my iPad?" Mike Jr. asked.

"No." David started toward the doorway.

"Mr. Caine?" Ivy said.

"What?" he answered too brusquely. When Ivy only watched him with wide eyes, he said, more softly, "What is it?"

"Don't get fried," she said.

He nodded and went to leave. Paused to pluck his iPhone off the charger.

"You got anything other than white milk?" Mike Jr. asked.

"Water."

"Got any Dr. Pepper?"

David didn't answer.

"Bet you got you some beer for yourself," Mike Jr. called.

David moved toward the door. "Drink your milk."

"Milk sucks ass."

"Watch your damned mouth."

Mike Jr.'s reply was lost in the sound of the screen door closing. David hustled down the steps, the rain already slanting down at him in stinging drops. He'd dragged on a black T-shirt, but it was already soggy. His shorts and underwear clung to him like Saran wrap. He resolved to take a shower and put on some clean clothes soon.

Lightning jagged over the river. The roar of thunder came moments later, its full-throated bellow accelerating his strides. He dared not sprint the ground was too puddled and uneven for that – but he was moving briskly, having no desire to be struck with a lightning bolt.

FAMED DEBUNKER LAID LOW BY DIVINE JUDGMENT.

He chugged harder, the swirling thunderheads reminding him of a sci-fi movie. Soon an alien mother ship would descend and begin blowing up buildings.

But the only building in view was the Shelby house. The bottom story was lit up, though with the monsoon blowing, its glow was somehow muted, the downstairs windows a burnished red rather than the incandescent oranges and yellows he'd spied the night before from the kayak.

Nearing the house, he glanced askance at the river, which churned and splashed as though superheated by underwater volcanoes. Lightning flashed over the water, created fantastical shapes that glimmered and swirled before his eyes: misshapen horses that shrieked and faceplanted, their hindquarters giving birth to Sherman tanks and prehistoric sea creatures. For a moment David glimpsed a sinister face reefed by squirming pink tendrils and was reminded of the Cthulhu mythos. Lovecraft, he decided, would have delighted in a night like this.

Thunder crashed in the forest just as David reached the Shelbys' yard; he made the final approach at a dead sprint. He leaped onto the porch, skidded onto the sodden welcome mat, and depressed the doorbell. No answer. While he waited, he glanced down at Mike Jr.'s grotesque chalk art and saw it had bled away in drab, defeated streaks. He rang the bell and again there was no answer.

Lips a grim line, he tested the handle and found it unlocked.

He went in.

And was greeted by the sounds of Jim Morrison singing 'Not to Touch the Earth.' David liked the song, had always found it spooky as hell with its horror movie lyrics and its off-kilter vibe. But here, with the storm buffeting the house and the Shelby children at his place hiding, he found the music infuriating. He resolved to turn it off as soon as he located the stereo.

He passed through the foyer, called out, but the music was too deafening.

"Hello?" he said, louder this time. "David Caine here. I've got your kids." He winced at the shady wording. "You two okay? I heard you were…"

(*Raging*)

"…in a quarrel," he finished.

He glanced right and left, but the dining area and sitting room were both vacant.

"Mrs. Shelby?" he called. "Michael?"

No answer, but then again the bass was so loud he could barely hear his own voice.

He reached the family room and was greeted by a gangbang on the projection TV screen. Nude male figures looked on as a drugged-looking woman was rammed by a muscular man in a black leather mask. The woman's body juddered with the man's thrusts, but her face remained beatific, as though her mind were cavorting through fields of posies and butterflies. The film had the grainy quality of a home movie.

David could hardly hear the shouts of the men on screen, so loud was Jim Morrison's voice.

"Mr. Shelby?" David called. His saliva had dried up.

Movement from his left drew his attention.

Michael Shelby was lying naked on his belly on the sectional couch, his hairy butt cheeks smeared with blood. He was weeping.

Disgusted, David headed toward the kitchen.

He found Honey spread-eagled on the tile. She wore nothing save a pink strap-on dildo the size of a junior league baseball bat. She was writhing on the floor and massaging her breasts. Her eye sockets were purpled and slightly bloodied. Her bottom lip, too, was split in half with rivulets of blood wending their way down her throat. She was wetting her fingers in the blood and working it over her nipples.

David escaped. He still hadn't found the source of the music, but screw it, he couldn't remain in this place any longer. Couldn't fathom the children walking into this. What the hell was wrong with people? How could they—

"*Mr. Caaa-aine,*" a voice called.

Shit, he thought. Honey.

He turned in the foyer and discovered her buxom body emerging from the hallway shadows.

"You wanna play with me until my lover arrives?" Her lips were open in a lustful grin, and as David watched, numbed by a sense of unreality, she took hold of the strap on and waggled it.

It took him a moment to find his voice. "I...I have your kids."

"Keep 'em," she said, letting go of the strap-on and straightening, so that her full breasts poked out at him. She was ten feet away and closing. "Why don't you warm me up, Mr. Caine? Why don't you prime me?"

The song barreled to its conclusion, Jim Morrison shouting ferociously She cupped her left breast, leaned down, and tongued the bloody nipple.

"I'm calling the police," David said.

Honey flicked her bloody tongue at him, very close now. "Tha's okay," she said, and he realized she was quite drunk. "Long as you fuck me first."

Honey groped for his shirt, fingernails gathering the fabric. He jerked away, burst through the doorway into the darkness.

"That's all right, you fucking pansy!" Honey called after him. "You can't bone me as deep as he does!"

David loped down the shoreline path, but his limbs were heavy. Even though the rain had ebbed slightly, its onslaught was colder now. He couldn't decide whether it was the chill or the horror show he'd just witnessed that caused him to shiver.

He saw no way around it. He couldn't very well return the kids to the Shelby house – certainly not tonight – and he had to inform the police.

But providing the details, he thought as he reached the halfway point between the houses, would not only be embarrassing – it might be self-defeating. As vile and negligent as the Shelbys were, would their behavior be provable enough to get the kids removed? And if so, removed to where? The prospect of Mike Jr. and Ivy going to live with 'Granddad' made David want to hit someone.

He made it to his yard. The kitchen light had been extinguished. The entire house was black.

Splendid, he thought, hustling toward the porch. Power outage. On top of everything else. He bet Ivy was scared to death.

David passed through the front door and called out to the kids.

No answer.

He stepped toward the kitchen, keenly aware of both the tomblike silence in the house and the tempest raging outside. His shoes squelched on the wooden floor, the rainwater dripping off his hair. "Ivy?" he called. "Mike Jr.?"

He realized with a surge of self-disgust that he'd modulated his voice as if afraid of disturbing any malevolent presence in the house.

Third night here and you're jumping at shadows. Some professor.

He called out again, louder this time. "Kids? You still here?"

His voice came out at a higher volume this time, but it wasn't stronger. In fact, he thought as he stepped into the shrouded dining room, if he were writing this scene, he'd use the word *quavery* to describe his voice.

Dammit.

Lightning chalked the riverside yard and the roar of thunder followed with barely a pause. The heart of the storm was upon them. He imagined it as a monolithic face floating slowly toward the house and settling there, stalling, the murderous eyes marking the gables and directing its wrath at them. He thought about an extended power outage, a night spent in utter blackness.

A bruising thump sounded from above. David jolted, peered at the ceiling in dread.

Ivy's bloodcurdling scream cleaved the night.

CHAPTER SIXTEEN

David made the foyer in six ungainly strides. His limbs were gelatinous, his heart a racing double-bass drum. There'd only been one scream, Ivy's, but he was certain both children were up there. Where else would Mike Jr. have gone?

David took the stairs two at a time, gripping the banister to make sure he didn't totter backward. He imagined ending the night with a broken neck.

FABLED SKEPTIC DIES—

"*Shut up*," he snarled.

He made the landing, screwed up his eyes to see which doors were open. "Ivy? Mike Jr.? Where—"

A scraping sound from his right.

The long bedroom. The one with four single beds. The one whose temperature had, inexplicably, plummeted when he'd ventured inside.

The place that had scared the living shit out of him.

David moved toward it, saw the door was closed. Had the kids locked themselves in? And if so, why?

He tested the knob. Locked.

"Open up, Mike!" he called.

Thunder rumbled over the property. Had there been a whispered voice beneath it?

David rattled the knob. "Mike, Ivy, open the door!"

Gouts of rain assaulted the window, as though the Rappahannock had reached out a watery hand and slapped the storm-beset panes. David strove to quell the tingling in his spine. "Kids, I know you're in there, so just unlock the damned door."

Nice, he told himself. Shout at them. With their psychotic parents and this cataclysmic storm, they haven't been through enough already.

"Kids?" he started, gentler this time. "I know you're frightened – and I don't blame you – but if you let me in, I'll make sure you're safe."

Ivy's voice sounded from the other side of the door. "How do I know it's you?"

David frowned. "It's me, Ivy. Mr. Caine. Will you open the door for me?"

An endless pause. Then a muted *click*.

David opened the door in time to see Ivy scurrying around one of the single beds. Fleeing from him. Unexpectedly, he found a smile forming. "Hey, you don't have to—" Twin lightning strikes lit up the long bedroom, and his smile vanished. The glimpse he'd had of Ivy looked like a child from ages ago. *Centuries* ago. She'd worn white old-fashioned nightclothes, a cotton dress that covered her limbs to the floor, with ruffles encircling the neck.

Where the hell would she get an outfit like that?

"Ivy?" David called, but the room had sunk into gloom. The rain seethed over the windows. He began to creep the length of the bedroom. "Kids? Where'd you go, Ivy?"

He slid his fingers inside his hip pocket, aware not only of the preternatural silence of the old house, but of the drop in temperature in this hospital ward of a bedroom. It's the rain, he told himself. You got soaked to the bone out there and now your clothes are clinging to you like icy barnacles. No wonder you're cold.

But that isn't it, a voice insisted. *It's cold enough to see your breath in here. That's not the storm, and it sure as hell isn't from soggy clothing.*

The phone stuck in his pocket, the fabric clammy, but with a little more fuss David managed to yank it free, the whole pocket turning inside out, a pair of breath mints clacking to the floor and rolling under the third bed.

A gasp from beneath the hanging coverlets.

David stared at the shadowy pool between the second and third beds. "Ivy? You under there?"

Ivy's voice was faint. "Uh-huh."

Thunder rocked the house.

"It's okay, Ivy," he said, stepping forward. "I'm going to turn the light on now."

"Power's out," she answered, her voice floating up to him as if from a deep well.

"No, my phone light," he said, powering it on and swiping the screen.

He pushed the flashlight button and a spill of incandescence washed the shadows between the beds.

A tiny arm jerked away as if stung by the light. The white pajama arm had been old-fashioned, frilly. The sort of thing worn by a kid during the 1700s. David's heart marauded through his chest.

It was the flashlight, he told himself. It's pale enough to make—

—*a lace cuff?* a dubious voice shot back. *It was an old-fashioned nightdress, David. Not your goddamned flashlight.*

The cold was whispering over his shoulders now, its wintry fingers teasing his flesh. The silvery glow from his phone was wobbly, its edges a blur on the coverlets.

"Please come out," he said, but he scarcely recognized his voice.

You're the adult, he reminded himself.

But I'm afraid, came the answer. *I am afraid.*

"You promise you're Mr. Caine?" the voice from under the bed asked.

Relief trickled through him, but he recognized it as superficial relief, one that didn't touch the core of fear still quivering within. He took a step forward, half bent, but didn't lift the blankets that hung an inch from the floor. "Come out, Ivy."

A pause. Something bumped the coverlet from beneath the bed. Then a tiny hand appeared. Another. Bare, walking-stick arms emerged, bloodred ridges spanning their lengths from wrist to shoulder. The face that swiveled slowly up to leer at him was a crimson horror, the eyes vast and milky white. David dropped his phone and scrambled back, gagging. Facedown, the phone light disappeared. But the shape slithering out from beneath the bed, its skin a variegated network of leathery flesh and deep, valleyed scars, crawled forward, its white pupilless eyes fixed on him. David backpedaled and tried to spur his thoughts into motion, but there was only dumb terror, the mutilated, infernal figure clambering after him, its movements jerky, its milky eyes lambent. Lightning strobed over the room, the hateful shape crawling around the foot of the bed, its fleshless lips drawn back to reveal fire-blackened teeth, scorched and mottled with splotches of yellow. David was dimly aware of his surroundings, the first bed to his right, the door not far, but his legs threatened to betray him. Any moment they'd unhinge and then the leering horror would climb over him, would embrace him with its bacon-stripped arms—

A hand darted from beneath the bed and clamped over his ankle.

David bellowed in terror, pinwheeled his arms, and landed on his back. He heard a familiar metallic jangle, but this barely registered. The hand had come loose from his ankle when he fell, but any moment it would batten onto him again, drag him under the bed, and he fancied he saw the creature's shadow at the foot of the bed, the leering thing almost upon him now, and just as he tensed to scramble for the door, he caught a glimpse of the face under the first bed, the frightened face of a little girl, the coverlet framing her panic-stricken eyes.

Ivy.

"Mr. Caine?" she said, her voice choked with fear.

Without thinking, he pushed toward her, seized her by the shoulders, and dragged her from under the first bed. Her wispy muscles were tight, her skin cold. She trembled, but rather than resisting, she pushed away from the floor, came with him as they made for the open door. He spared one backward glance when they reached the doorway, but it was impossible to tell if the creature was following. The shadows at the end of the first bed were chaotic, jagged shards of pitch-black on a tapestry of gunmetal-gray. David thrust Ivy into the hallway – too roughly, he knew – but his body wasn't his own, his movements that of a robot manipulated by a novice. His hands shook so wildly it was only with difficulty that he grasped the doorknob, drew it shut. It creaked back open. He seized it again and heaved it toward him, the brass knob icy in his grip.

Ivy was saying something, but all David could think about was the creature on the other side of the doorway.

Leave, he thought. Take the kids and race down to the Camry. Then peel ass out of here.

David listened, his ear inches from the door. Thunder rolled over the house, but beneath it, beneath the rattling joists and the shivering of the clapboards, had he heard rustling? Something leathery and near the floor?

"Mr. Caine?"

David jumped, braced his palms on the door. "Jesus," he muttered. "What, Ivy?"

"Mike's in the other bedroom."

He stared down at her. She was clutching some object to her chest – her stuffed animal, he realized – and peering up at him. Lightning flickered over her pale oval of a face.

"What other bedroom?"

She pointed across the hall. "That one, I think."

"You *think*?" he repeated. Far too sternly. God, fear had made of him some ruthless authority figure, a colonial schoolmaster who kept order with his fearsome glare and a stinging rod.

"Did you *see* him go in?" he asked.

"I think so. We ran different ways."

He tore his eyes from the base of the door and looked at her. "What was it?"

Ivy didn't answer.

"What made you run, Ivy?"

Tears began to glisten in her eyes.

David took a shuddering breath, licked his lips. He nodded at the door across the hall, which stood open. "You think Mike's in there?"

A nod from Ivy, almost imperceptible.

He stood debating. He didn't want to leave the door to the long bedroom unattended. What was to prevent the creature from escaping?

There is no creature, his rational side declared. *Stop being a fool and take care of these kids. Can't you see Ivy's scared senseless?*

She and I both, he thought.

Ivy crowded against him. Somehow, the press of her tiny body edified him, bolstered his resolve. With a mammoth effort, he let go of the doorknob, stared down at it for ten seconds. It didn't turn.

He rested a hand on Ivy's shoulder, nestled her into his side, and started the slow walk across the hall. He didn't glance over his shoulder, but he was listening for the deep groan of the door behind him, the insectile *clitter* of fire-roughened skin over oak flooring.

"I'm scared," Ivy said.

"Me too. Shitless."

She pressed against his leg.

They reached the doorway. "Mike? You in here?" Another step, Ivy moving with him. "Mike Jr.?" David whispered.

A sulky voice: "Told you not to call me that."

David stepped deeper into the room and realized the bed had been stripped of blankets. Another step revealed where the covers had gone. A rumpled shape was crammed in the far corner of the room. Except for the twin arches of knee that tented the blanket, he'd have never guessed there was a child under there.

David strode over. "Come on, Mike." He reached for the blankets, started to lift them. "We've gotta go."

"Don't!" Mike Jr. gasped.

David compressed his lips. "We're going into town. Now get up."

The blankets slipped over Mike Jr.'s head, but he snatched them back, covered himself from the neck down. "I had an accident."

David scented the urine. He crouched before the boy. "I've had accidents before."

"Bullshit," Mike Jr. answered, but there'd been a flicker of hope in his eyes.

Lightning flashed through the windows. David flinched.

"I've even gone number two before," David said.

"On accident?"

"Right in my truck," David agreed.

Mike Jr.'s eyes narrowed in the gloom. "You don't have a truck."

"Used to," David said. "A Dodge Ram. Patriot blue. I called it The Patriot."

"The Patriots suck," Mike Jr. said.

David fluttered a hand. "Not the New England— Dammit, we've gotta go." He took hold of the blankets, ripped them away despite Mike Jr.'s protest. "Now come on," he said, hauling the boy to his feet.

David glanced sideways to make sure Ivy was still there. She was, but she was ramrod-straight, motionless.

"Ivy?" he asked.

Slowly, she raised an arm, leveled a forefinger through the doorway.

The door to the long bedroom hung open.

CHAPTER SEVENTEEN

"Oh God," David whispered.

"I don't see nothin'," Mike Jr. said, his voice plaintive.

David didn't either. The view was a straight shot all the way to the opposite wall of the long bedroom, and absent of a few shadows, there was nothing to evoke terror.

Except the open door.

Ivy seemed to read his thoughts. "The storm?" she asked.

He nodded irresolutely. "It could've blown the door open."

"You shut it?" Mike Jr. asked.

"Let's go," David said. Ivy came willingly, but he had to drag Mike Jr. He looked down, saw the boy had drawn up the blankets around his waist and was trailing them like a bulky white umbilicus. "Come on," David said. "Let go of the covers."

Mike Jr. sounded on the verge of tears. "You'll see how I pissed myself."

"Oh, for goodness—" David reached down, seized the blankets, and jerked them out of the boy's hands.

"Hey!" Mike Jr. said.

David hauled the kids toward the doorway. "Keep your voice down."

"How come?" Mike Jr. asked.

"Close your trap, Mike," Ivy said.

"Listen to your sister," David said.

They emerged from the bedroom and neared the stairs, David's eyes never leaving the doorway of the long bedroom. Nothing crawling toward them. Shadows, yes. Flickers of lightning. But no leering creatures.

He turned the corner and started down the stairs, unaware of how roughly he was dragging the kids until Mike Jr. said, "You're gonna make me fall."

"Walk faster then."

Somehow they reached the bottom of the staircase, and despite the way the wind rattled the house, David ripped open the front door, towed the children onto the porch.

"You're gonna drive in this?" Mike Jr. asked as they hustled down the steps. Rain pelted them when they reached the yard, the wind powerful enough to swerve them off course.

"It's fuckin' crazy out here!" Mike Jr. yelled.

"I can see that," David said, but he could scarcely hear his voice above the maelstrom.

"We're gonna get 'lectrocuted," Mike Jr. said.

"We're not gonna—" Lightning whipcracked the forest, the thunder instantaneous. "*Fuck*," David gasped.

They dashed forward. Almost to the car. Ivy clung to his hip like a parasite. They reached the Camry, the rain blinding them, and when David stopped at the driver's door, Mike Jr. went stumbling past and landed on his hands and knees. David hardly noticed.

The door was locked. Rain pummeled them.

He thrust a hand into his hip pocket. Empty. He patted his other hip pocket, the lower pockets of his cargo shorts. Nothing.

David froze. He remembered falling in the long bedroom. The way he'd sprawled on the floor.

The jangling sound.

Son of a bitch, he thought. I dropped the keys.

"Mr. Caine?" Ivy asked.

He wasn't going back upstairs for the keys. Not for anything. He glanced toward the woods, beyond which was the Shelby house. He didn't relish the prospect of returning there. Besides, Honey had spoken like someone else was arriving soon, the bacchanal growing a few shades more decadent. He couldn't expose the kids to that.

Mike Jr. was holding his arms out and staring down at his sodden clothes. "You threw me down, you dickhead!"

David barely heard him. He turned and peered through the storm-swept night at Ralph's property. Not only would getting there require a more than two-hundred-yard dash through a dangerous electrical storm, but it appeared to David that Ralph's house was as bereft of power as his was. Granted, there were trees screening Ralph's house from view, but David believed he would still catch glimpses of house lights if they were on.

The entire peninsula was steeped in darkness.

The rain intensified, as cold as sleet and just as biting.

"Why don't you open the car?" Mike Jr. demanded.

"You see any keys?" David snapped.

"Should we go back inside?" Ivy asked. She was shivering against his leg and when he looked down at her, he saw her teeth were chattering. Her tank top and shorts were paltry defenses against the increasingly frigid wind and rain. She was sickly to begin with. He imagined her wasting away of pneumonia.

He reached down, lifted her, and placed her on his hip. She came willingly, burrowed her face into his shoulder.

He started toward the Alexander House.

"You ain't goin' back in there?" Mike Jr. demanded.

David didn't answer, drew nearer the porch.

"You know how stupid that is?" Mike Jr. asked. "Ain't you ever seen a scary movie?"

David grimaced, pushed ahead more rapidly.

"Somethin' spooked you," Mike Jr. persisted. "What'd you see in there anyway?"

"Nothing," David said. He hurried the kids through the den, into the master suite, and closed the door behind them. "I didn't see anything," he said, turning the lock and dragging the heavy birch dresser over to block the door.

CHAPTER EIGHTEEN

They spent the night huddled in the king-sized bed, all three of them dressed in David's clothes. He'd loaned Ivy and Mike Jr. a T-shirt each. David slept in sweatpants.

At a little after eight the next morning, the kids were still asleep.

In a movie, David would have made them both a hot breakfast and maybe mussed Mike Jr.'s hair as they sat eating like a makeshift nuclear family. But the atmosphere of the house was poisoned for him, and he needed to sort things out. He left the doors ajar so the kids would know it was okay to come out of the bedroom when they awoke, made himself some coffee – the power was back on, thank God – and sipped it while he walked the property inspecting the storm damage.

The trees between the river and the house were intact, save a score of downed branches and a couple ill-fated birds' nests. He didn't see any eggs, broken or otherwise, in the nests.

David ended up at the tip of the peninsula, staring out at the island. He'd stood there for perhaps a minute before he realized he was leaning forward, listening for the woman's voice.

Are you losing your mind? his rational side asked.

He sipped his coffee. What he'd seen last night wasn't an illusion. Something…unnatural had crawled toward him in the long bedroom.

The morning haze, the dark waters of the Rappahannock, the coffee mug in his hand, it all faded away, and in its place came that leering abomination, those staring white eyes, that salt-cured body, the dripping, scorched incisors—

"Hi, Mr. Caine," a voice said from his side.

David spasmed, his coffee sloshing, and discovered Ivy peering up at him.

"You've got to warn someone…." He switched the coffee mug to his other hand, snapped the brown droplets off his fingers. Ivy watched him, smiling a little. She wore his Stephen King 'Gunslinger' T-shirt, which said, 'Go then. There are other worlds than these.' The shirt hung all the way to her bare toes.

"You want something to eat?" he asked.

Her face clouded. "I better get home. I don't want them to take my coloring books."

"That's how they punish you?"

Solemn-faced, she nodded.

He extended a hand, which she took without hesitation. "I'll walk with you."

They were halfway to the house when she said, "Mike already left."

"Ah," David said. "Should we get your clothes?"

Her tiny fingers were cold in his grip. "Uh-uh. Mom'll be mad enough we were gone all night."

If she even noticed, David thought.

★   ★   ★

But Honey had noticed, he realized as they walked along the riverside path. Clad in a garish yellow T-shirt that didn't hang nearly as low as Ivy's did, Honey was striding purposefully toward him, her bloodshot eyes grim. "What's wrong with you?" Honey demanded.

Your kids came to me, he started to say, but stopped, not wanting to get Ivy or Mike Jr. in trouble.

Honey grabbed Ivy by the hand and yanked her away from him. The girl didn't fight, but she didn't look happy with the transfer. Her eyes were lowered, her shoulders stooped. Preparing for punishment, he thought. Goddammit, Honey.

"Get home," Honey barked at her daughter. "Your dad's been worried sick."

Sure he has, David thought.

When Ivy had gone, Honey stepped nearer.

"What the hell did you do to them?" Honey demanded.

David stared at her. "Now listen—"

"Mike Jr.'s scared out of his mind, and I wanna know why."

It occurred to him Honey might not even remember the night before, that their surreal encounter might have escaped that spongy tangle of desires that functioned as her brain.

"Your kids were distraught," he said. "Do you even remember the storm?"

Honey folded her arms. "Where'd you put their clothes?"

David flushed. Was this lunatic actually implying…. "They were like drowned rats. They—"

"*Don't you call my kids rats,*" she growled, taking a step toward him. Her bloodshot eyes widened. "Just because Michael and I aren't big-shot writers like you doesn't mean you can mess about with our children. I've a mind to call Sheriff Harkless."

David nodded at Honey's house. "Let's call her now. I'd love to tell her what kind of parents you are."

Like a switch had been flipped, Honey uncrossed her arms, donned a pouty look, and fingered the hem of her T-shirt. "You'd like that, wouldn't you? Like to worm your way into my home." She fondled the shirt, which crept up, revealing a V of turquoise underwear. She stepped closer, her muscular legs flexing. "Michael's still snoozing. Bet you'd like to inspect me a little, wouldn't you, professor?"

She reached out, fingers closing on his crotch.

He shoved her hand away. "What the hell's wrong with you?"

Honey smiled hungrily. "You're gettin' hard, professor. Why not show me how naughty I've been?"

"Do you have the slightest…*conception* of how fucking crazy you are?"

Honey pooched her lips. "*Ooh,* I like it. The buttoned-down professor turns wild man." She twisted the fabric of her T-shirt so that it rode higher, revealing more underwear, which turned out to be sheer, so that her dark thatch of pubic hair showed prominently.

David headed back to the Alexander House. Honey's laughter dogged him for a good twenty paces before it subsided. By the time he'd made it to the house, he'd resolved to call Sheriff Harkless himself. If Honey couldn't be reasoned with, maybe the sheriff would intervene.

What if Honey tells lies about you? a nagging voice wondered.

Then the kids will refute them.

Unless they're too scared of Honey to tell the truth.

The thought stopped him. He'd heard of people being falsely accused of doing things to children. It didn't happen often, but when it did, it was ruinous.

What if Honey made scurrilous accusations?

"Shit," he muttered. He stood on the porch, thinking. If he didn't go to Harkless, what else could he do? He couldn't leave Ivy to languish in that house of horrors. Even Mike Jr., with his filthy mouth and his disturbing chalk art, deserved better parents than Michael and Honey Shelby.

David went in, fixed himself toast with butter. He poured a tall glass of orange juice, downed it in three gulps, and felt better. Yes, he decided. He'd see Sheriff Harkless. He couldn't imagine the children selling him out. Ivy was quality through and through, and despite being a little shit, he suspected Mike Jr. would tell the truth.

Breathing evenly again, David was halfway out the door before he remembered where the car keys were.

Upstairs, on the floor of the long bedroom.

Hell. David stepped inside the foyer, the screen door easing shut behind him. He'd told himself a hundred times to tape the spare Camry key to the back of his license plate, but it remained in his kitchen drawer back home, where he'd deposited it the day he'd bought the car.

He peered up the staircase. There was no other way. Either remain stranded or go up and get the damned keys.

You could get Ralph.

Sure, he thought. That was admirable. Rely on the elderly neighbor for courage. While he was at it, why not enlist Ivy and Mike Jr. to assist him too? Maybe send them upstairs to retrieve the keys while he cowered down here.

"Enough," he muttered.

As David started up the stairs, he recalled last night's disturbing visions.

Yes, visions were exactly what they'd been, he thought, as he advanced through the coolness of the stairwell.

(why is it colder upstairs?)

There'd been a figure in an old-fashioned nightshirt…and the burned, crimson horror with the leering white eyes.

No. One vision at a time, he thought, nearing the second-story landing. The figure in the nightshirt…that could have been a trick of moonlight. The shadows of the wind-worried trees could easily simulate the folds of a gown.

David reached the landing, turned immediately toward the door of the long bedroom. The door was open and the morning sun was slanting through the windows, leaving half the room in shadow, the other swathed in dull umber light. Ignoring the chill atmosphere and the suffocating silence, David inched toward the foot of the first bed. This was where he'd fallen last night. This was where the keys should be.

David reached the foot of the bed.

Stared down at the bare wooden floor.

"This is ridiculous," he said, then regretted it. The aura of this room, though he was loath to admit it, was different than the rest of the house. It was time to employ the pseudo-scientific instruments in the trunk of the Camry, if only to begin the process of proving to himself there was nothing supernatural about the long bedroom. But of course the Camry was locked. And the keys were somewhere in this room.

(unless something took them)

There's nothing up here! he wanted to scream.

He closed his eyes and clenched his fists. He hadn't driven more than eight hundred miles to be thwarted by a few mystifying occurrences. Hadn't he encountered strange phenomena before?

(nothing like this)

He drew in a deep breath, let it out. He moved about the room, glancing between the beds, the tops of the nightstands, but that was foolish of course. Like checking an old coat you hadn't worn in years for a wallet you misplaced an hour ago. He considered kneeling, peering under the beds, for that's where the keys had to be, right? He'd fallen, heard the jangling sound....

Something from across the room drew his attention, a muted twinkle of light.

The car keys lay on the windowsill. At the opposite end of the long bedroom. An area into which he hadn't ventured, last night or any other time.

It was a test, he realized. To reach the keys he'd have to cross the whole room, nearly thirty-five feet of space.

But he was already fifteen feet in. He could make it twenty more.

Knowing he'd lose what frayed nerve he still possessed if he hesitated longer, David strode toward the northern window, his eyes never leaving the keys. He worried that if he looked away, if only for a moment, they'd disappear.

They didn't disappear. David reached the windowsill, snatched the keys from their resting spot, and stuffed them in his hip pocket. He was about to go when he discovered his iPhone lying facedown on the nearest nightstand.

He swallowed, scooped it up.

He'd started back when he noticed something he hadn't before: the four single beds bore the imprints of bodies.

Why this should disconcert him, he couldn't say. After all, he'd only been in this room on two other occasions, one of those during a violent thunderstorm that had played tricks on his perceptions.

What of the other time? the hard, implacable voice asked. *The first time you inspected this room was in full daylight. Why didn't you notice the imprints then?*

Because, he thought with a rush of hope, I was standing in a different part of the room at a different time of day. Light's a funny thing. It can alter the appearance of a place dramatically.

Can it conjure leering, white-eyed monsters?

No, he thought, his mouth going dry. No, not even a change of light could do that.

David hurried from the room.

CHAPTER NINETEEN

He grabbed lunch at a drive-thru in Lancaster. Ten minutes later he was motoring through the countryside with the burger and most of his fries eaten. The Coke was a trifle watery, but it refreshed him. He'd passed over a goodly span of bridge a while back, and he was trending west, in the direction of his house.

But he was on the other side of the Rappahannock now, and the sights were becoming familiar. There was the graveyard he'd once passed in a big white Buick LeSabre. There were the tobacco fields lining a straight shot of country road three miles long.

Ahead was the entrance to Oxrun Park.

David brought the Camry to a halt outside the entrance, where he found a painted brown box atop a splintery wooden post. It resembled a birdhouse, only instead of a hole for birds to climb through, there was a hinged door that read '$5.00.'

David smiled. He'd always liked the honor system and remembered, many years ago, cramming a couple singles and some coins into the box, the three of them – David, Chris, and Anna – having exhausted their cash supply on beer and needing to scrounge the floor for change.

A horn blasted behind him. David glanced in the mirror, discovered a guy in an SUV with a pontoon hitched behind it.

"Take it easy," David muttered. He moved the Camry into gear and pulled forward. After the guy paid and trundled past, David leaned over the steering wheel and saw a slender green sign reading 'Old Bay Road.'

Images flickered through his head:

A woman knifing through the water.

His kayak drifting into the bay.

The woman climbing onto the dock and disappearing up the stairs.

He drove forward, hooked a left turn.

There were only three houses on Old Bay Road. One of the dwellings, situated on a cul-de-sac, was little more than a shack, probably some fisherman's hut without electricity or running water. Another house was larger but not impressive either. If people lived there, they didn't put much stock in upkeep. The front lawn was strewn with junker cars and weeds as tall as David's waist.

It was the house nearest the park he was interested in. Unless he was mistaken, this was the place that connected to the dock he'd spied two nights ago, the one onto which his mischievous sprite had climbed.

It was a modest ranch with yellow aluminum siding. Nestled in the forest, set fifty feet back, the place was the antithesis of the other two houses on Old Bay Road. David parked the Camry along the grassy shoulder and ventured up the drive, which was redolent of honeysuckle, cedar. A hint of lavender.

He noted as he drew nearer how tidy the lawn looked, how many distinguishing features the yard boasted: A hummingbird feeder dangling from a shepherd's hook. Multiple dogwood trees, pink and white and red ones, a few with their flowers still clinging to glory after last night's storm. Vibrantly colored vases, most of them ceramic. Bluebells and irises in bright orange planters bookending the front porch. Terra-cotta pots were positioned strategically about the yard, these housing zinnias and marigolds and a few flowers he didn't recognize. On the right stood a weeping cherry tree larger than any he'd ever seen, which sprouted from its own garden of lush foxtail, blue pansies, and an underlayer of sedum. Beyond that he discovered an unexpected touch: at the bases of two gigantic maple trees crouched a pair of stone gargoyles, each two feet high. Their faces were drawn back in hideous grins, their heather-colored wings eager to hunt.

Smiling, David inspected the layout. Whoever lived here knew her plants and loved them well.

Why do you assume it's a woman? a voice asked. *You love wildlife too.*

But I saw her, David thought. Saw her climb onto the dock in her white two-piece and scurry into the woods.

So go to her door. Demand to know why she tried to strand you.

That made sense, David decided. Yet he hesitated. Despite the stress the woman had caused, he found he wasn't all that angry with her. Mildly annoyed, sure. Who wouldn't be? Yet as far as pranks went, hers had been pretty innocuous.

"I hope you're not here to save my soul," a voice behind him said.

David whirled and beheld an attractive woman grasping a leash. Rather than barking at him, the dog, which was medium-sized, white-haired, and looked almost as old as the woman, simply cocked its head at David as if he were some exotic creature.

The woman and the dog remained at the end of the drive, obviously having returned from a walk. She carried a knotted blue bag of the dog's waste. A responsible pet owner, he thought. Even out here in the sticks where no one was likely to step in one of the dog's surprises.

"What breed is he?" David asked, going toward them.

"The kind that doesn't like aggressive men."

The woman had long hair, parted in the middle and flowing over her shoulders like black silk. She wore a sleeveless white exercise shirt, black leggings that stopped just below her knees. She was curvy and very fit, her calves sculpted, her arms dark and toned. But it was her face he couldn't get over. There was something familiar about her. She wasn't smiling — was maybe close to scowling — but in the shape of her mouth he sensed someone who liked to smile, who frequently laughed. Her cheekbones were prominent, rounded, her lashes long. Her eyes were an atypically deep green, like the forest surrounding her property; her lips had a natural coral tint.

David realized he'd been staring.

He gestured toward the Camry. "I was out for a drive and…."

She lowered her face, waiting.

He opened his mouth, shut it. Chuckled and sighed. He put his hands on his hips and looked at her. "Did you push my kayak into the water?"

"The park closes at nine. You were there at midnight."

He ventured a grin. "Is it your job to enforce the curfew?"

"I live next door," she answered. "What goes on there affects me."

"You act like I was setting fire to the place."

"I don't hear you explaining yourself."

David realized the dog was glancing from face to face, taking in the exchange.

"I don't need to explain myself," David said.

The woman's expression was inscrutable. She glanced at the dog, murmured, "Come on, Sebastian," and when the old dog had finally made it to his feet, the woman started past David and said, "Get off my property."

He ran a hand through his hair. "Ah, come on."

She kept walking.

"Hey," he said, "I'm sorry for trespassing."

She stopped but did not turn. "Now or the other night?"

"I don't...." He hung his head. "Both, I guess. Can we just start over?"

She did turn then. Watched him expressionlessly.

"I botched it," he said. "I shouldn't have surprised you like this."

"You didn't surprise me."

"Well, that's good." He smiled at her, but she didn't smile back. Not giving an inch. "What about starting over?"

She eyed him a moment, then seemed to come to a decision.

"There's no such thing as starting over," she said. And with Sebastian in tow, she walked away.

CHAPTER TWENTY

He drove the back roads a long while, his thoughts consumed by Anna. Anna with her sense of humor and her smoking habit and her un-self-aware beauty. Everyone had recognized her magnificence but her. And in the end, she had felt low enough to—

"Stop it," he muttered, his voice hoarse. Goddammit, he could scarcely breathe, thinking about her.

So stop thinking about her. You can't take it back.

His mood dismal, he drove the final fifty yards to the Alexander House and parked under a towering oak. Midafternoon, another night looming, and a day he'd hoped to spend on his book squandered.

So do something, David. That's what work is for. To distract you from your disastrous personal life.

One corner of his mouth upturned in a grin, David reached down and pushed the trunk button. He went to the trunk and stared down with vague distaste at his ghost-hunting equipment. It was all nonsense, but his editor had impressed upon him the need to give the possibility of the paranormal fair shrift, and the only way to do that was to employ the tools of the true believers.

He chose the rechargeable infrared light. If he plugged it in now, it'd have plenty of juice by nightfall. Next, he selected the thermal camera. He'd need to charge it too. Moving cautiously, he carried everything to the house. The thermal camera, a nifty device that captured high-def video, had cost him more than four grand, and that was half a decade ago. If he broke it, he'd have to pay handsomely for a replacement. He found an outlet in the hallway and set both the infrared light and the thermal camera on to charge.

Returning to his trunk, he scanned his other equipment and eventually settled on the grid scope. Though it was as bogus as the other items he'd brought along, he enjoyed situating it on its tripod and watching the green laser patterns form on walls. One could adjust the type and intensity of the pattern; supposedly, the grid scope was helpful in picking up supernatural movement.

Horseshit.

He lugged the grid scope and tripod into the master suite and put the scope on its charger. Then, feeling good for the first time that day, he undressed and took a shower. The water seethed over him, washing away the oil from his pores and the fear-sweat of the night before. It hadn't occurred to him until now that he'd been avoiding the house. There was no denying he'd seen something last night, but now, standing in the brightly lit bathroom in the middle of the day, the vision seemed gauzy, easier to dismiss.

David finished, toweled off, dressed, and headed to the screened-in porch, where *The Last Haunting* awaited him. After a moment's deliberation, he went to the kitchen and brewed some coffee. It was a quarter of three, and ordinarily he wouldn't have brewed a pot so late, but he'd hardly slept at all last night, and he needed to be sharp.

Steaming blue coffee mug in hand, he returned to the screened-in porch and resumed his position. A post-storm breeze wafted pleasantly over him, the sun glare on the water mild. He bypassed Hartenstein's sleazy introduction and found the first excerpt from John Weir's journal. That was one of the most profound travesties of Hartenstein's smear job, David reflected: the glaring omission of several sections of Weir's journal. It was apparent to him that Hartenstein had selected only the most suggestive chapters to further his narrative: namely, that one of the most famous skeptics in history had succumbed to the spirits he'd set out to disprove.

David took a swig of steaming coffee, began to read. Within moments, the venomous bile of Hartenstein's writing faded, and the warm, engaging tone of John Weir took its place:

Although I've made a career of "raising the blinds" on disreputable hoaxsters, I do admit to being impressed by the sense of antiquity and history imparted by the Alexander House. My first night in the home was uneventful, and though this confession reveals a whimsical streak in my nature, I must here record some small disappointment at this lack of activity.

One of the unjust assumptions frequently written about me, oft-repeated by both the mavens of the supernatural and those offended by my disbelief, is that I approach my work with a scowl and a heartless compulsion to steal joy from others. These individuals view me as a callous destroyer of hope. This assumption wounds me. As I've written elsewhere, I am deeply sympathetic to the needs of the grief-stricken. Haven't I, as a man of advancing years, experienced loss and been bitten by the pitiless sword of despair? Many are the days that I long for the soft comfort of my deceased mother's hand, the edifying advice of my hard-working father, the delicious cooking of my long-departed grandma, or the cheering word from my doggedly optimistic grandfather. Even more frequent are the nights when I imagine my wife's lovely face on the pillow next to mine; I reach for her, but of course she is no longer there. What I wouldn't give to cure the influenza that took her a decade ago! What I wouldn't give to remove the abnormality that caused our marriage to remain childless.

Of course I know suffering. Of course I wish I could go back and remove those elements that brought pain and heartbreak to my life and the lives of those I so dearly loved and love still.

But I cannot. Nor can I in good conscience succor my emotional wounds with fairy tales.

But I digress.

Most dwellings are as ephemeral as their inhabitants. Most homes are as characterless as a harvested cornfield, with its mud and discarded stalks.

But not the Alexander House. Though not as capacious as most purported haunted structures, this dwelling purveys the notion that much has happened here, that its beams and floorboards have witnessed much and are determined to forestall the property's defamation.

Ah, listen to me. Already imbuing the home with animate characteristics!

Indeed one can imagine these walls as sentient beings. Is it such a great leap then to associate the house with its original owner, the notorious Judson Alexander, brother of Senator Theodore Alexander, member of the first United States Congress?

Undeniably insane, Judson was the bane of his father, a wealthy landowner and a businessman of much esteem. Ever power-hungry, the elder Alexander spent much of his life grooming his younger son for a life in politics and taking extravagant measures to contain his elder son's increasingly volatile and disturbing behavior.

David sipped his coffee and settled into his chair. He'd read John Weir's published works many times, but reading this excerpt from Hartenstein's book caused him to rue the elusiveness of the original diary from which it had been culled. For many years the diary had remained with a law firm in Williamsburg, but attempts by David and other Weir enthusiasts – not to mention generations of ghost hunters – to purchase the diary had been spurned without ceremony. Then, inexplicably, the diary had sold to an unnamed individual, and at that point vanished. Why someone would dole out an exorbitant sum and then hoard the diary was beyond comprehension. Yet that was precisely what seemed to have happened.

Shaking his head, David read on.

As is commonly known, Judson Alexander was never a governor of anything, including and especially the State of Virginia, whose first two governors – Patrick Henry and Thomas Jefferson – are among the most respected leaders in our nation's history.

By contrast, Judson Alexander is only remembered for the horrors he perpetrated, acts so reprehensible that they would have ended Theodore Alexander's political career had they come to light during his lifetime.

Here I must make another confession. Though the roof and timbers that comprise the Alexander House are as blameless as any other inanimate object, I find myself remembering the atrocities that occurred here whenever I walk the central hallway or tarry in the gloomy dining room.

Most of all, I find myself recoiling from the western bedroom.

David paused, the mug an inch from his lips. The long bedroom, he thought.

He brought the mug to his lips, tilted it, and grimaced at the acidic taste of the coffee. With an odd mingling of eagerness and dread, he continued the passage:

Though accounts suggest that Judson Alexander perpetrated unspeakable acts throughout the home, the peninsula, even in the neighboring communities, it is in the western bedroom that his malevolent energy seems to have reached its apex.

Look at me! As I pen this, my heart races and my brow grows slick with perspiration. Such is the effect these tales have on my fancy. You see? I am not the hard-hearted cynic my detractors would make of me. I too have imagination.

And never has my imagination been so stirred by a house.

Yet before I chronicle Judson Alexander's repellent exploits, I must provide a backdrop for those horrors.

I admit here to being captivated by advances in the field of psychology. The work of Sigmund Freud is even now irradiating the human condition in a manner that demystifies our behavior and corroborates my long-held suspicion that saints and monsters are molded rather than born. It has taken us until now, the final century of the second millennium, to recognize the wrongheadedness of the Greeks, whose fatalism and obstinate adherence to superstition waged war on logic.

Alas, I've run off the rails! Please forgive an old man his occasional diatribe.

I believe there are traceable factors that contribute to human behavior. Irrational and pernicious prejudices are not embedded in our natures; a newborn does not enter the world, for instance, hating another infant for the color of his skin. Rather, that hatred is cultivated in the child by hateful parents or unfortunate circumstances. I am not exonerating the racist, mind you – merely chronicling his conditioning.

Judson Alexander, on the other hand, was a different beast entirely.

Yes, I called him a beast. It is a word I don't use lightly.

Little is known of Judson's early life precisely because his father, Zacharias, possessed so much wealth and influence. Nearly all records of Judson's childhood, if they ever existed, were suppressed through threats, intimidation, and, I fear, murder.

In this regard, I do suppose whatever impurities dwelt within Judson were nurtured by his father, a single-minded tyrant who ruined anyone who opposed his schemes. In the years subsequent to Zacharias Alexander's death, myriad accounts were published of his ruthlessness in business dealings.

Yet these accounts paled in comparison to his manner of dealing with what he, in letters to his Senator son years later, called 'the Judson problem.'

Despite his icy core, there did reside in Zacharias a tenderness for his two sons. Granted, the lion's share of that paternal warmth was reserved for Theodore, his youngest. Yet he did love Judson, or at least care enough about him to go to Byzantine lengths to ensure his protection.

This, however, is where I find myself unable to levy any further sympathy toward the Alexander patriarch. Indeed, Zacharias's sins are, in their own way, as execrable as his eldest son's.

The first anecdote one is able to find of Judson Alexander stems from his sixth year and involves one of his father's slaves, an unfortunate individual whose identity time has erased.

The unnamed slave was one of a party charged with clearing a field for tobacco planting. Through merciless business practices and an insatiable desire for power, Zacharias had amassed a small army of workers, indentured and otherwise, to help him extend the borders of his empire, and he never scrupled about driving these workers beyond the boundaries of humane treatment.

On the date in question, Judson had requested to ride along with one of his father's most trusted supervisors, a Mr. Jennings, from whose letter (published posthumously) this account is taken.

Mr. Jennings and the young Judson had been lounging in the shade of a nearby tree when the accident happened. The party of ten workers had been engaged in exhuming a sizable boulder from the untilled field when the slave had become trapped under the rock, his right arm pinned beneath the crushing weight. Much discomfited, the workers had clamored for Mr. Jennings to come to the slave's aid.

Jennings rushed to the sun-scorched field, discovered the nature of the accident, and through much toil and effort, he and his men were able to lever the boulder high enough to drag the slave from under it.

The damage, however, had been done. The slave's arm had been crushed beyond repair and he had entered a state of shock. Ever mindful of his employer's pitiless disposition, Jennings then made a fateful decision. He demanded that the other workers return to their task of clearing the rocky field, left young Judson to attend the unconscious slave, and thundered off on his horse to fetch a doctor.

What happened next was not witnessed firsthand, but it can be surmised.

When he arrived with the local doctor, Mr. Jennings noticed something was amiss straightaway. None of the workers was engaged in the field as he had instructed. While the majority of the workers were ambling about in a state of what Mr. Jennings described as 'drunken shock,' two of the slaves were attempting to wrangle a third slave, who was raving at young Judson.

As he strode nearer, Jennings noted that the injured slave's body was motionless. Just as motionless was young Judson Alexander, who gazed expressionlessly down at the slave as if the man were a rock or a stump.

The injured man was dead. While he was unconscious, his nose and mouth had been stuffed with dirt.

The culprit could only have been young Judson. Although the child was only six, Mr. Jennings alluded in his letter to previous infractions authored by the boy. Destruction of cherished family heirlooms. Insolence toward adults and violence toward other children. The torture and slaying of small animals.

Yes, though I'm loath to say it, Judson Alexander makes me believe in innate evil.

Mr. Jennings, upon informing Zacharias of Judson's unspeakable act, was *threatened with termination. In his letter, Mr. Jennings insinuated that the termination might not be limited to his employment.*

The slave who dared berate Judson was summarily scourged, and all present that day were instructed to keep the murder a secret, a secret that was apparently honored until Mr. Jennings's niece garnered a handsome sum to have her uncle's letters published.

As will be demonstrated, this was only the beginning of Judson Alexander's infamous career of depravity.

David closed the book with a pop, rose, and stretched. The sleeplessness was catching up with him, the caffeine insufficient fuel to keep him awake.

He pondered heading up the lane to Ralph's, but as he strode back to the master suite, an object on the right edge of his bed, barely visible in the swaddled blankets, made up his mind for him: Minty, Ivy's stuffed animal.

David realized what was bothering him.

The kids. Were they okay?

Of course they're okay, his rational side declared. *They've spent their whole lives in that house of horrors; why would they be in trouble now?*

Because they stayed the night with me? Because Honey and Michael might not take kindly to an outsider knowing their business?

David went to the landline phone and, after speaking with an operator, finally got in touch with Sheriff Harkless.

CHAPTER TWENTY-ONE

Harkless suggested they meet at The Crawdad, a site that appealed to David on a number of levels. For one, he was eager to discover in person the place Ralph had described; for another, he was hungry, had no appetite for the items in his refrigerator, and had even less desire for fast food. If he could score a Tombstone pizza or a similar delicacy at The Crawdad, he'd be content.

David arrived before Harkless and introduced himself to an attractive young black woman at the front counter.

"Alicia Templeton," she said, offering her hand and showing him teeth that were straight and white. He put her at twenty-two, perhaps a college student working a summer job.

"The Alexander House, huh?" she responded when he told her where he was staying. "You're either brave or stupid."

He maintained his smile, but only with an effort. "A place that old, there're bound to be some creaky stairs."

She straightened one of the displays. "Means you don't *want* to see anything. I get it."

"Now wait—"

"Hey, it's okay," she said. "You don't need to act tough in front of me. My dad's the caretaker, and he doesn't like it one bit."

"I forgot there was a caretaker."

She gave him a look. "Who do you think mows the lawn? The Bell Witch?"

And standing there at the register, the memory nailed him flush in the face: Anna mentioning the Bell Witch one winter's night, David reacting scornfully because anything supernatural reminded him of his mom and her insistence on unseen forces intervening in their lives.

But what if it's real? Anna had asked.

Glaring, David had answered, *What if I get scratched by a werewolf tonight and start howling at the moon?*

That, Anna said, an eyebrow arched, *would never happen because it would require you to change.*

It shouldn't have rankled him, but it did. Looking back, he realized that his occasional spats with Anna about the supernatural – she was a fanatic about the stuff – was where the notion of becoming a debunker was born. He'd detested religion and the occult since childhood; Anna's enthusiasm for ghosts and goblins merely gave purpose to his contempt.

"You still alive?" he heard Alicia Templeton ask.

He jolted, remembering himself. He tried a laugh, but it sounded forced. "You into that stuff? The occult?"

She bent, retrieved a handful of BiC lighters, and began refilling a display. "I've eaten it up since I was a kid."

"You wouldn't have come across any of my books, have you? David Caine?"

"You told me your name already. And no, I haven't read your work."

His cheeks burned. He glanced about the store. "You guys have Dots?"

She cocked an eyebrow. "The candy?"

"It's my weakness."

"I can order you some."

"Don't bother. You've got enough here to tide me over."

He watched her movements as she refilled the lighter display. She mixed up the colors but had a pattern. Red, blue, green, yellow; red, blue, green, yellow.

The bell over the door rang. He turned and beheld a plump black woman, likely in her late forties, coming through the door. Her hair was drawn back in a bun, little makeup with the exception of indigo eye shadow. She wore a light brown police shirt, dark brown slacks, and a silver badge.

"Don't look at me like that, Mr. Caine," the woman said. "You already knew I was a woman. Finding out I'm also black can't be that much of a shock."

He sensed Alicia grinning in his periphery. "I don't get surprised often," he said.

Harkless moved past him. "'Nother way of saying you didn't think I'd be black. A clerk at a humble gas and grocery, sure. But not the sheriff of a big ol' county."

"Hold on," Alicia said. "I'm one semester away from my Master's."

"I barely managed my Bachelor's," Sheriff Harkless answered. "I was boy-crazy back then."

Alicia gave David a glance. "Well, I'm not boy-crazy."

"Thank heavens for that," Harkless said, taking a seat at one of three circular tables in the far corner of the small store. "Your dad would never forgive me if he found out I'd let you run off with some young stud."

Alicia uttered a breathless laugh. "Like you have any say."

"It's my job, dear." Harkless looked at David. "You need a formal invitation?"

David went over and took the chair opposite Sheriff Harkless.

"Nice of you to come on such short notice, Sheriff. I don't—"

"Dispense with the pleasantries, Mr. Caine."

"David, please."

"Um-hm. We'll see. What's your relationship to Mrs. Mayr and Mr. Gardiner?"

"What's that got to do with the children?"

"Funny thing," she said. "Ever since I was a kid, I've enjoyed puzzles. And I despise it when someone tries to do them for me."

"Chris was my best friend at William & Mary. Katherine is his wife."

Sheriff Harkless nodded. "What's with the different name thing?"

"Is the idea of a woman keeping her own name shocking to you?"

He thought he heard Alicia snicker from the counter.

"Well, listen to you," Harkless said and smiled. "Why're you here?"

"To make you aware of an abusive situation."

She shook her head, still smiling. "This *county*, Mr. Caine. What are you doing here in Lancaster County?"

"Oh, that." He told her the story of how he came to be staying at the Alexander House.

When he finished, she raised her eyebrows. "Well?" she asked.

"Well, what?"

"Have you seen anything?"

He glanced at Alicia, who'd come around the counter, ostensibly to restock the Big League Chew bubble gum, but more likely to better hear their conversation.

"Nothing," he said. When Sheriff Harkless only stared at him, he added, "Not a single solitary thing."

"What about a woman's house on Old Bay Road?"

It hit him like a slug to the gut. "She called the cops on me?"

"She called *me*, Mr. Caine. Were you not in her driveway, uninvited?"

"She pushed my kayak into the water, she almost stranded—"

"In the park after curfew," Sheriff Harkless said, nodding. "Your list of offenses is pretty extensive for only having been here a few days."

"Sheriff Harkless—"

"Georgia, please."

"Okay…well, I feel like you've got me wrong."

The pleasant smile hardly wavered. "How have I got you wrong, Mr. Caine?"

"First off, I wasn't doing any harm."

"In the woman's driveway or at Oxrun Park?"

"The woman's – I mean, neither. I wanted to ask her about my kayak."

"You were confronting her."

"I wasn't *confronting* her, I was—"

"Demanding answers?" Alicia called.

"No," he said, glancing over at her. He looked at Harkless. "I was curious."

"She *is* a beautiful woman."

He scowled. "That's not why I went over there."

"No?"

"Of course not."

"So if she were, say, toothless and plagued with acne you'd still have trespassed."

He made a face. "I didn't.… Is it trespassing if you're in someone's driveway?"

Using a forefinger, Sheriff Harkless drew a line parallel to the table edge, said, "The road is here," and connected it to the table edge with an invisible perpendicular line. "The house is here." She indicated the area between the two lines. "Everything between is private property. Including the driveway."

He sat back in the barely padded chair. "Fine. Technically, I trespassed, but I wouldn't in a million years.…"

"Make a woman feel unsafe?"

"Hell no."

Harkless leaned over. "Mind if I tell you what I think, Mr. Caine?"

"That this table's private property and I'm trespassing again?"

"I think you're used to getting by on your looks and reputation."

He spread his hands. "Where's this coming from?"

"Experience. And I Googled you."

"Why would—"

"Big-shot literature professor, darling of the scholarly journal scene...."

"You can't base your opinion—"

"...never married...whoppin' book deals...several movie options...."

"Those are bad things?"

"They're fantastic things," she said. "For you."

"What are you implying?"

"Come on, you're a clever guy."

"I can't believe how ungenerous you're being."

She sat up straighter. "Is it generous to grin that shit-eatin' grin of yours and charm a lady out of her pants and move on as soon as you've had your fill?"

His voice went thin. "You don't know me."

"Tell me I'm wrong."

When he didn't answer, she said, "I know your type. Ain't that many of you, thank goodness, but when one comes around, the hackles on the back of my neck stand up."

He felt as though someone had strung him up by the wrists and beaten him like a rug. "Can I lodge my complaint now?"

She nodded curtly, produced a small flip notebook. "Children's names?"

"Ivy and Mike Shelby Jr."

She scribbled that down, added, "Parents are Michael Shelby and Honey Shelby."

"That's her real name?"

"Been Honey as long as I can remember," Alicia said.

David glanced at her. She was on her knees before a display of Altoids. The sandy rattle of the mints in the tins reminded him of rat claws scratching the floor. Alicia's shirt had ridden up, revealing a toned lower back.

When he turned, he discovered the sheriff staring at him dourly.

David sank deeper into his chair.

Harkless said, "What's the nature of the abuse?"

He hadn't rehearsed what to say. He'd pictured giving his statement in a sterile gray room at the police station, not the back corner of The Crawdad with a beautiful young woman listening in.

He glanced at Alicia. "Should she be…you know…."

Harkless's look was level. "Restocking the Altoids?"

"No, not— This is personal stuff. I feel weird saying it in front of someone so…."

"Gorgeous?"

"Young."

Alicia grunted, kept arranging the displays.

Harkless said, "She's perfectly capable of enduring whatever you share with me. She's gonna witness your statement."

Aw, God, he thought. He blew out a weary breath. "Okay. Let's start with the porn."

"Always good to start with porn," Harkless agreed.

"The first time I was there, there was hardcore pornography on the big screen. Honey was drunk and cussing up a storm and little Ivy was sitting in the corner, about four feet from the sex show, working in her coloring books. She looked like she hadn't eaten in days."

"You spend much time with kids, Mr. Caine?"

"If I did, I sure as hell wouldn't let them stay in the room while I watched porn." He winced, agitated a hand. "Not that I watch porn."

He glanced at Alicia, who appeared to be holding back laughter.

"Denies watching porn," Harkless said, scribbling in her notebook.

David ignored that. "I forgot one detail."

"Yes?"

"Michael – Michael Sr. – looked like he'd been beaten up."

"And how would you describe his attitude about this?"

"About being beaten up?"

Harkless waited.

David shrugged a shoulder. "He seemed okay."

"Would you say," Harkless asked, "that Mr. Shelby was a willing participant in whatever activities he and Mrs. Shelby were engaging in?"

"I guess."

Harkless's pen continued to scratch.

"Last night there was a storm."

"Real whopper," Harkless agreed. "Power was out for half the county."

"Had to take my bath in the dark," Alicia said.

Heat burned David's face as images of Alicia soaping herself in the dark flickered through his head. He stared resolutely back at Sheriff Harkless, whose gaze never wavered.

When it became apparent David wasn't going to speak, she smiled, said, "Go on, Mr. Caine. You were talking about the storm...."

"Somehow the kids got into my house. I did my best to take care of them. Gave them food...a drink besides Kool-Aid."

"That was good of you," Harkless said.

David scoured her face for traces of irony. Finding none, he said, "I ran to their parents' house to make sure they were home. I didn't want to drag the kids through that storm only to have to turn around."

"Were they home?"

David made a scoffing sound. "In body. Michael was prostrate on the couch, weeping. He'd been—" David cleared his throat, "—sodomized."

Sheriff Harkless's eyebrows went up. "There was another man in the house?"

"No, it was...Honey. She was on the kitchen floor, sort of... caressing herself."

"Masturbating?"

David glanced at Alicia. The young woman was straightening a display of chip bags and obviously hanging on every word.

He lowered his voice. "She was fondling her breasts."

"I'm not understanding the sodomy thing."

Ah, man. "Honey had on – was wearing – a, um—" he gestured, "—strap-on thingie."

"Dildo," Harkless supplied.

"Yeah."

"Could you describe the dildo?"

"Come on."

"Black, white, spiked like a medieval mace, what?"

"Pink," David said. "Pink and gigantic."

Harkless nodded staidly. "And you think she used this object to penetrate her husband?"

"Well, what else?"

Harkless stopped writing. "What else what?"

"What else could've made him bleed like that?"

"Mr. Shelby was bleeding? Where?"

David couldn't help writhing a little. "His anus."

Across the room, Alicia made a pained face.

"Look," David said and leaned toward the sheriff. "The kids stayed with me all night. Did their parents even call you, wondering where they were?"

"Maybe they didn't know they were missing."

"*Exactly.*" He pounded the table with a fist. When Sheriff Harkless stared at him, he mumbled, "Sorry."

"So, a kid sneaks out—"

"Two kids," he corrected, "both under the age of ten."

"Two kids sneak out, their parents don't know, and they end up sleeping at a neighbor's—" She paused. "You put them in the guest rooms?"

An image of the long bedroom strobed in his head. "They stayed in my bed. On either side of me."

"Why'd you do that, Mr. Caine?"

David studied Harkless's face, but if there was any accusation there it was well hidden. "The storm was really severe."

"Felt like an apocalypse," Alicia agreed.

"The kids were scared," David continued. "So was I, I guess."

"You were trying to keep them safe," Harkless said.

David nodded.

Harkless appraised him a moment longer, then pocketed her notebook and pen. "Mr. Caine, I can't pretend to like you, but you do seem to care about the children."

"Gee, thanks."

"That's why I'm gonna tell you the situation."

"This about their grandpa?"

Harkless grunted. "And the foster family who tried to get custody of Mike and Ivy a year and a half ago."

David noticed that Alicia had given up the pretense of restocking the shelves and was now watching them, arms folded, shapely hip leaning against a Coke refrigerator.

He said, "There are tons of parents looking to adopt."

"Babies, Mr. Caine. They want babies." Harkless sighed, sat back. "There was hope for the Shelby kids a few years ago, but now I'm afraid their situation is harder to sort out."

"But the abuse—"

"What abuse?" Harkless interrupted. "Did you witness Honey hitting one of them?"

"Well, no, but—"

"Maybe they *are* malnourished, but not enough for it to be provable. Lots of kids are scrawny, Mr. Caine. At least Ivy and Mike Jr. are eating *something*."

"What about the drinking? The porn?"

Harkless nodded. "They could get in trouble for that, but I doubt it'd be enough for CPS to remove them from their home."

"It's not a home."

Harkless nodded. "Agreed, Mr. Caine. By your standards and mine, it isn't. But you gotta remember the severity of what you're demanding. Taking two kids away from their parents, their other family members—"

"Grandpa Pedophile?"

"Hold on," Harkless said, eyes flashing. "Don't you think I'd like to get that grandfather of theirs into a cell and whup his sorry ass? Hell, for that matter, don't you think I'd like to do the same for Michael and Honey?"

"Mr. Caine," Alicia said, coming over, "Georgia's done more to try to help those kids than you'll ever know. She'd like to adopt them herself, give them a proper home. Truth is, it's a dreadful situation created by dreadful people."

David glanced at Harkless and was stunned to see tears threatening in her eyes. She blinked them away and said, "I'll have a coffee to go, Alicia, if you'd be so kind."

"Sure, Georgia."

Harkless pushed herself up from the table – it took an effort – and moved after Alicia, who took a detour toward the coffee station and poured the sheriff a cup. Harkless reached into her pocket. "How much is the tax?"

"Put your money away."

Harkless scowled. "Dammit, I asked you how much."

Quietly, Alicia rang her up. "A dollar and five cents."

Harkless fished a dollar from a rumpled brown billfold, found a nickel in her hip pocket. "Thanks for the coffee."

Without another word, Harkless went out.

"She'll be heading to the Shelbys' now," Alicia said, watching after her. "And tomorrow, the mayor will be in her office bawling her out."

At David's questioning look, Alicia explained, "Honey's father. He's the Mayor of Lancaster."

CHAPTER TWENTY-TWO

David bought more groceries than he needed before saying goodbye to Alicia and returning to the Alexander House. He cooked a pepperoni Tombstone pizza and ate the whole thing. No sign of Ivy or Mike Jr., no trace of Ralph or Chris or Katherine.

He sat down to write on the screened-in porch, hammered out two thousand words, and judged them decent. At dusk he cracked open a beer and checked out the dock, but when he realized he could see hints of the Shelby house from the end of the dock, he returned to the backyard and gazed out sullenly over the water.

Night fell, and David had never felt so alone. Maybe it was having the kids here last night and then not having them. Maybe this was how parents felt when their kids grew up and left them.

"Come on," he said, annoyed with the maudlin run of his thoughts. Being companionless, he'd decided long ago, was preferable to the entanglements of child-rearing and the vagaries of marriage. Just look at the Shelbys. Or his own family, for Christ's sakes. What an ungodly train wreck that had turned out to be.

David's shoulder muscles began to tingle.

He turned and gazed up at the windows. Like the front, the rear had seven dormers. They stared down at him like the eyes of some hostile alien presence, long dormant but slowly awakening.

The ghost-hunting equipment would be fully charged by now.

"Let's get this over with," he muttered, and began his uneasy slog to the house.

★   ★   ★

The grid scope could be adjusted to produce different laser patterns. David judged the fine, uniform spray of green dots to be the most logical setting, but since he'd never actually witnessed anything paranormal with the grid scope and figured he never would, he favored the 'Night Sky' configuration, which simulated a tapestry of stars.

David tested the grid scope on the dining room wall, found it in working order, then cycled through the other gadgets he'd brought in. Everything functioned perfectly. Not that it mattered.

Feeling utterly foolish, the way he invariably felt when puttering around with this equipment, David stashed it in his athletic bag, laid the tripod over his shoulder, and toted it all upstairs. On the way, he flipped on the hall light. It was ten p.m., the glow over the Rappahannock having disappeared as though sucked into a vortex. The familiar chill of the second floor seeped through him, but he stepped through the landing and did his best to ignore the temperature change.

At the threshold of the long bedroom, he paused. The buttery yellow illumination from the hallway seemed to die six inches after entering the long bedroom.

But this was the logical room to make his tests. The only room, really. He could set up the thermal camera somewhere else, but he owed it to himself and his book to be academically honest.

Yes, he realized as he steadied his breathing. This moment would be a crucial one in his book. He could call the chapter 'The Ballad of the Long Bedroom' or 'Better Housekeeping with Judson Alexander.' He smiled but found it difficult to maintain.

"Here we go," he said.

He stepped into the long bedroom and flipped on the light. A single lamp on the nearest nightstand flared to life but left most of the space in shadow. He waded into the room but stopped near the southern window. He rested the athletic bag and tripod on the floor, spread the legs of the tripod, bent, and retrieved the thermal camera. Directly opposite him, at the far end of the bedroom, loomed the northern window, on whose sill he'd discovered his keys this morning.

Had that really been this morning? The day had stretched to ludicrous proportions, and it wasn't even half past ten yet.

Shaking his head ruefully, David screwed the thermal camera onto the tripod mount and opened the camera window. He fussed with the viewer for a few seconds in an attempt to encompass as much of the room as possible, then went over and selected the grid scope.

Knowing what was coming made his heart beat faster, so before he could lose his nerve, he switched off the lamp. There was still the meager glow from the hallway light, but that didn't help much. The long bedroom seemed to swallow illumination like a black hole. His movements unsteady, he returned to the camera and tripod, which he'd positioned near the fireplace, and situated the grid scope on the mantle. He thumbed on the button, experienced a childish thrill of excitement. Multitudinous green lights of varied size and brilliance shone on the walls, the nightstands, the beds.

He went out and doused the hallway light.

There was a small writing desk beneath the southern window. David removed the chair, swung it around, and after a quick debate, he shuffled toward the tripod, arranged the chair beside it, and sat.

After a few moments' silence, however, he grew anxious. True, part of the room was spangled with green lights, but to his right there were roiling motes of Stygian gloom.

The silence deepened.

Now what? Ordinarily, he'd get on his iPhone to surf the internet, but out here in the boonies he couldn't get a signal, not even on the extended network. Still, he brought out his phone, used his thumbprint to activate it, and opened a voice memo.

He cleared his throat, quoted Hawthorne: "'What other dungeon is so dark as one's heart! What jailer so inexorable as one's self!'"

He pushed pause, opted to delete that one. Too bleak.

Poe, then. "'The boundaries which divide Life and Death are at best shadowy and vague. Who shall say where the one ends, and where the other begins?'"

Uh-uh, he thought. Even worse.

He deleted it, started another. In his best southern twang, he began to croon George Strait's 'All My Exes Live in Texas.'

A rustling sound from above.

David's arms went slack, his legs nerveless stalks.

Footsteps sounded directly overhead. Moving toward....

With a fathomless dread, he turned in his chair. Glanced at the trap door in the ceiling. Holy God, he thought. He'd never investigated the third story.

He wanted to rise from the chair, to tiptoe out of the room before the presence revealed itself, but his body wouldn't cooperate. He'd lost the ability to move. Or think, for that matter. Only rudimentary sensory input remained. The sound of the grandfather clock ticking downstairs. The whisper of frigid air on his arms. The vulgar green stars dotting the walls.

David watched in sick fascination as the green lights rippled, as if they reflected on water rather than solid walls. His breathing came in rapid sips, his heart a thundering herd running roughshod through his chest. He stared at the single beds, gape-mouthed. The green lights there were…undulating. As though bodies lay there. Bodies in pain. Bodies being tortured.

The trapdoor in the ceiling flew open and the ladder crashed down beside him.

David screamed, tumbled off his chair.

A footstep sounded from the third floor. Another. A shiny black work boot appeared on the top ladder rung, the wood groaning. Another black boot appeared on the second rung, the figure's pants, dark cloth breeches, now visible.

David moaned and crawled toward the door, conscious of nothing save the figure descending the ladder. David reached the threshold of the long bedroom as the figure's broad waist revealed itself, then the stomach, sturdy and thickly muscled. His whole body tremoring, David clawed his way into the hall, around the corner, his numb legs barely able to navigate the stairs. He heard heavy footfalls from the long bedroom, the creaking of rungs. When the boots reached the floorboards, David was on the third stair. He clambered down the steps, nearly plunged headlong into the closed front door. Then he was fumbling with the locks, certain he hadn't locked the door himself. From above he heard a figure step through the threshold of the long bedroom. David tore the door open, dove toward the porch. He bolted down the lane and didn't look back until the Alexander House was completely out of sight.

PART THREE
CHANGELING

CHAPTER TWENTY-THREE

David had damn near passed Ralph's house before he spotted it in his periphery. Unthinkingly, he veered that way, on some level worried he'd throw a fright into the older man by showing up unannounced at 11:00 at night. But this concern was buried under a slagheap of terror. Whatever David had seen stalking down that ladder had frightened him as badly as had the leering thing of the night before. And that was saying something.

He hustled through the gloomy dooryard and pounded on Ralph's door. When no answer came, he stepped off the porch and peered through the front windows. No sound from within, no light at all.

Was the man asleep?

Such a possibility wasn't farfetched, but in his gut David doubted it. The night they'd drunk beer and gobbled burgers, Ralph had been going strong well into the darkness and had shown no signs of sleepiness. That could have been exuberance over having a visitor in his home for the first time in a blue moon, but David didn't think so. Ralph was a night owl. He'd stake his reputation on it.

The thought made him stop and stare into the massed trees that enclosed Ralph's property.

His reputation. What would happen to David's reputation should this incident become public? Aside from little Ivy, he was the only person who'd witnessed anomalous happenings in the long bedroom.

David frowned. *Had* Ivy seen anything? It dawned on him they hadn't even discussed the matter. He'd been so freaked out by the abomination crawling toward him that he hadn't applied his usual logic....

He couldn't finish the thought. The phrase *usual logic* was farcical in this situation. There was nothing remotely usual or logical about what was happening in the Alexander House.

But how to admit that without becoming a laughing stock?

For one thing, his writing career was predicated on *not* seeing things, on *not* hearing things go bump in the night. How clownish would he seem to his editor, his agent – hell, his *readers* – when he claimed to have been terrorized by not one, but two supernatural entities?

Don't forget the Siren.

Well, shit, he thought. How could he forget the Siren?

David ambled about the yard with no particular goal in mind. It occurred to him how very few his options were. He liked Ralph, but he didn't know the man *that* well. He couldn't exactly rummage around for a spare key and let himself in. If Ralph owned a gun, David might get shot.

But the lack of a car – he'd again left the goddamned keys in the house – and the lack of civilization, compounded by the late hour, meant he was effectively screwed. He couldn't go to the Shelbys'. Hell, Honey might try to hump him on sight. Or hurt him. If Harkless had visited the Shelbys, there could be no doubt who'd sent her. If the Shelbys distrusted David before, they would despise him now.

With a quickening of hope, he remembered The Crawdad. Granted, it was seven miles away, but it was a safe haven, and he suspected Alicia Templeton would help him.

But how exactly?

"Shit," David muttered as reality set in. For one, it was already 11:00, and if The Crawdad weren't closed, it would certainly close by midnight. David was in good shape for a man in his mid-forties, but there was no way he could make seven miles through hilly, tortuous terrain in a single hour. And that was assuming The Crawdad stayed open until midnight, a dubious proposition at best. No, Alicia had most likely closed a while ago.

Which left him alone.

The nearest civilization was fifteen miles away. Running at a decent pace, David figured he could make it in two hours, more likely two and a half. Which would put him there at 1:30 a.m. What would be open then? Not the mom-and-pop motels, surely. And he didn't even have money in his pockets!

He glanced down and received another nasty surprise. He'd worn his sandals, and they sure as hell weren't built for running long distances. Short of finding a hollowed-out oak tree and curling up inside it for the night, what the hell *could* he do?

David reached into his pocket, checked for the iPhone he knew wasn't there, knew was lying on the floor of the long bedroom, where he'd dropped it in mortal terror. He was in serious trouble, and far beyond the immediate trouble of having no place to sleep.

Katherine Mayr had brought him here to prove to him the existence of the supernatural, and in persuading the foremost skeptic in America that ghosts inhabited the Alexander House, the place would become a bona fide tourist attraction. Folks would come from around the world to see the house that defeated him.

But what *did* he believe? Now that he'd seen…inexplicable things… just what did he believe?

That, he realized, was the burning question. Aside from having nowhere to sleep tonight, aside from the worldwide humiliation of being thwarted by the unseen, aside from his careers being derailed – both his writing career and his job at the university, which would surely be forfeit the moment they caught wind of his crackpot conversion – aside from all that…what did this mean for him? For his view of the universe? His thoughts on the afterlife? His belief in the nature of—

His thoughts broke off. There'd been movement from the side of the house, a few feet from the woods. David peered into the tenebrous shadows, a surge of fear-sweat peppering his skin.

The figure was broad-shouldered, it wore work boots, it—

"That you, David?"

Ralph Hooper. David exhaled, the energy sluicing out of him.

Ralph's voice was shaky. "I got a…I got a gun."

"Do you really?" David asked.

Like a delayed mirror image, David saw the older man's shoulders slump. "I've got one, but it's in the house."

"Why didn't you bring it out with you?"

"I wasn't *in* the house." Ralph gestured behind him. "I was fishing."

"Any luck?"

"I damn near shat my pants a second ago. Do we have to stand out here making small talk?"

They entered the house via the screened-in porch, and Ralph fetched them beers. David cracked his open gratefully, took his accustomed chair. Funny, he thought, but neither of them suggested turning on a light. Sure, the illumination might have been comforting, but in another way, it would have felt like revealing their whereabouts to whatever dwelled in the Alexander House.

They sipped their beers in near silence, the only sound the gentle burble of the Rappahannock.

The constancy of the river soothed David's overtaxed nerves. He needed to regroup, to relax, and as long as no more spectral visitors assaulted him tonight, he thought he might make it to dawn with his sanity intact.

Ralph was the first to speak. "I take it this isn't a random moonlight visit."

David sipped his beer. "Not much moonlight tonight."

Ralph was silent awhile. Finally, he shifted in his chair. "Come on, man. We both know something over there spooked you."

David stared down at his sweating Budweiser can. Sighed. "It did."

And he told Ralph both stories, the huge figure tonight and the leering thing of the night before. David could tell by the man's bated silence that he was hanging on every word, but dreading each word and wishing he weren't hearing what he was hearing.

It emboldened David, Ralph's fear. Ralph didn't want these things to be true any more than David did. Less, if possible. Ralph had to live here, after all. In a month David would be gone, and Ralph would have to live with images of the leering thing, with the incident of the ladder chunking down from the ceiling and the black work boots inexorably descending.

"...and then I rapped on your door," David finished. "So what do you think?"

Ralph peered out over the river. "I think that's the creepiest fucking thing I've ever heard."

"The leering thing or the—"

"Does it *matter*?" Ralph snapped.

David gave a shrug. "Guess not."

"Question is," Ralph said, "what are you going to do about it?"

"Meaning what?"

"Meaning," Ralph said, "your stuff is still in there. I assume you're not gonna walk back to Indiana."

"I'll return to the house in the morning."

"Just walk right in."

David glared at him. "Of course. What else?"

"You ever seen a horror movie? You're like those morons who keep going back into the haunted house even though the walls are bleeding and little Asian children are jumping out from under the beds."

David made a face.

"You telling me I'm wrong?" Ralph demanded.

David couldn't meet the older man's eyes. "Those are movies."

"Did you listen to the shit you just told me? You have any idea how dreadful it is?"

"Why you think I'm over here?"

"So you admit to seeing those things, but you're going back over there anyway. How'd you get to be a professor with shit for brains?"

"Daytime is better."

"*Ohhh*," Ralph said, chin upraised, "daytime is *better*. And what about when dusk creeps in tomorrow? You gonna bunk with me again?"

"I hadn't gotten that far."

"David, listen to me." A pause. "Are you listening?"

David returned the man's frank stare.

"There's something wrong with that house. People who go there are in grave danger. Including you." Ralph sipped his beer. "Maybe especially you."

"What's that supposed to mean?"

"Maybe the house wants to flex its muscles for you."

David grinned. "Huh?"

"You heard me. Stop being an asshole."

"I'm not—"

"It's showing off for you, okay? It wants to prove how strong it is. How real it is. Whatever lives there—"

"Nothing lives there."

"Yeah? 'And then the creature opened its dripping mouth, its fleshless jaws pale in the moonlight'—"

"Okay."

"Your words, David. Your words."

"Take it easy." David glanced uneasily through the screen at the murky shadows of the trees.

"You can't reason away the unreasonable."

"I'm not ready to embrace the irrational."

"Of course you're not. You've gotta be a stubborn dipshit and have more proof shoved in your face." A mirthless chuckle. "Maybe get a couple of your friends killed." Ralph leveled a finger at him. "I'm not going over there with you, by the way, so I'll save you the trouble of asking."

"Thanks."

"You're welcome."

David set his beer aside with a clank. "There's got to be an explanation."

"All ears."

"Maybe I ate something…."

"Sure," Ralph agreed. "Food poisoning.

"Projected images…."

"Right. A prank. Or a twisted new reality show." Ralph flourished a theatrical hand. "'Join us next Saturday, when we subject a renowned skeptic to the ultimate paranormal hoax!'"

But David scarcely heard this last. One word Ralph had said had stuck in his mind, and the more he pondered it, the more distinct it became.

"Prank," he murmured.

Ralph cocked an eyebrow at him. "You being that dull-witted movie guy again?"

"Hold on—"

"You're gonna convince yourself it was all a big put-on, and you'll end up just like John Weir."

"You know about Weir?"

"I know all of it, David."

"Then you've heard of Judson Alexander."

Ralph sipped his beer.

"Chris – my friend Chris Gardiner," David explained, "he used to play pranks on people. He was mainly the straight man, the guy who laughed at my jokes. But on occasion he could really startle you with something unexpected."

"Like a crawling, burned-up creature."

"Ease up for a second," David said. "Let me think."

Ralph grunted but didn't otherwise interrupt.

"Ever since he contacted me," David resumed, "Chris acted like he was against all supernatural stuff, that his wife was the fanatic. Chris has been the good cop. The one aligning himself with my beliefs. But the other day, I realized he was − *is* − angry with me. He blames me for something that happened a long time ago."

"What happened?"

"Doesn't matter. What matters is that Chris has a motive to hurt me. To mess with my head. His allegiance would be to his wife, not to me." David mulled it over, nodded. "It makes sense."

"It's like magic," Ralph said. "Just like that you've got it all explained."

"It's easier to swallow than—"

"Than the possibility you don't know everything?"

David picked up his beer can.

They sat in silence for a couple minutes before Ralph said, "I'll let you sleep on my couch on one condition."

David glanced at him. "I'm not giving you a foot rub."

"Dumbass."

"What's the condition?"

"If anything comes for you, you stay the hell out of my bedroom."

CHAPTER TWENTY-FOUR

David slept poorly. After a breakfast of bacon and toast, Ralph shooed him out the door and climbed into his faded red pickup. He claimed he needed groceries, but David suspected Ralph was yearning for a few hours away from the peninsula.

David couldn't blame him.

Still, he watched Ralph pull out of the driveway and felt a good deal better. He tromped down the lane, up the porch steps, and into the dining room of the Alexander House. There, he selected a black wrought-iron poker from the hearth and went immediately up the stairs. If he delayed, he might lose his nerve. Even as he advanced up the final few steps, there was a sizeable region in his brain that threatened to revolt, to steal his resolve and send him clambering down the stairs and out of the house, and at that point there'd be no returning.

He made it to the second-story landing and into the long bedroom.

The equipment was as he'd left it. Only the grid scope was still running, its green stars considerably weakened by the morning sun. The thermal camera, he realized, had run out of battery.

His iPhone lay dead where he'd fumbled it.

The dropdown ladder from the third story, however, was folded into the ceiling, as if it had never crashed down. David stared up at it, unable to decide if this were a positive development or a negative one.

If only he had proof....

"Holy crap," he said. With a rush of excitement, he bent and scooped up the iPhone. In another few seconds, he'd unscrewed the thermal camera from the tripod and was hurrying from the room. He told himself his haste was due to what he might discover on the iPhone and the camera, but he knew it was just as surely because of his strangling fear of the long bedroom.

By the time he'd scuttled around the first floor gathering the chargers, his enthusiasm had been replaced with dread, not only of what he might find on the devices, but of what might still be in the house.

He'd made it to the front door when his shoulders hardened and, as though he were the protagonist in a film, he saw himself, really saw himself standing before the screen door.

An armload of tech equipment: camera, iPhone, charger cords dangling to his knees. Clothes the same ones he'd worn yesterday and smelling like it. His hair mussed and oily from his night's adventure. Hell, he hadn't even brushed his teeth. He loathed morning mouth, couldn't live with himself until he'd banished that dank, yeasty taste.

And where exactly was he going?

More importantly, what did he believe?

Ralph claimed he was like a dumb movie character returning repeatedly to the place that would spell his doom. Last night, he'd have agreed with Ralph.

But wasn't believing in ghosts a greater leap than believing in a hoax?

Yes, he decided. It sure as hell was.

There was a rustic carved teak bench on one side of the hallway, and it was on this bench he placed the camera and iPhone while he plugged in the chargers. He set the devices to charge and strode to the bathroom. He took a hot shower and brushed his teeth simultaneously.

Better. He toweled steam off the mirror and studied his reflection. Slight discoloration under the eyes, but absent of that, no ill effects. His shoulders looked broad, his chest full. He hadn't skipped his workouts, and it showed.

Contrast that with Chris, he thought, moving through the den and into the master suite, where he selected a clean T-shirt, clean underwear, and semi-clean cargo shorts. Chris looked to be doing fine financially, but what was abundantly clear was that Chris wasn't an especially happy human being. More importantly, Chris's venom during their last conversation revealed a black vein of resentment David had never sensed before.

But what if it had been there all along? And now, nurtured by time and memory, it had taken hold in Chris and metastasized like a tumor, allowing Chris to go along with, or even orchestrate, an elaborate hoax with his wife.

David sat on the bed and imagined Katherine laying out her plot to her husband:

...and the Alexander House is the perfect cash cow.

But dear, Chris would say, *there's a reason why it's been uninhabited all these years.*

Because people are imbeciles! she'd answer. *The fact that no one has lived in it since that Raftery family died makes it* ideal. *All we need is your old friend to proclaim it haunted.*

Chris, shaking his head: *David would never believe in spirits.*

Katherine, shiny-eyed: *He will if we* make *him believe. Listen, we'll scare him so badly he'll end up in an asylum. All we need is for him to allow for the* possibility *of the paranormal. We get that in print and we're both rich!*

David nodded. It might not have gone exactly like that, but the essence of it felt true. And which possibility was more difficult to believe?

The world was fraught with ghosts.

Or…

…Chris hated David and was conspiring with his wife to make a fool of him.

David drummed his fingers on his knees. Only one way to be sure….

The camera and the iPhone, he decided, wouldn't be fully juiced by now, but they'd both spent adequate time on their chargers to power on. He went to the hallway, sat on the bench, and thumbed on the camera. He powered on the iPhone too, remembering as he did that he hadn't checked his email since leaving The Crawdad the night before. He found himself itching to drive into better reception territory so he could see if his agent or publisher had contacted him. Checking his email was something of a compulsion.

He flipped out the window of the thermal camera and pushed play.

There'd be nothing for the first couple minutes, he knew, so he fast-forwarded a bit before resuming real time.

Then, just as he remembered, the shadows on the walls began to worry the green lights of the grid scope. The beds themselves began to ripple.

David realized he was holding his breath.

A moment later, from the left corner of the screen he glimpsed a pale flash – the ladder crashing down. The camera, dammit, didn't have audio, but he'd be able to listen to the voice memo on the iPhone for that.

David watched the small screen, his windpipe constricting. If he didn't see anything, that meant…what? That he was cracking up?

Boots appeared on the ladder steps. Every fiber of David's being cried out to leave the Alexander House, but he was staying, dammit, staying and watching this recording. He wasn't running anymore.

The figure came into view.

The man was gigantic. He wore what looked like dark breeches of some sort and a white shirt David associated with – hell, he might as well admit it – Puritans. The hulking figure strode fully into view, paused, and for one horrible instant David was certain the man would swivel his head and grin at the camera.

But he didn't. Only passed by. David stared at the screen, waited for the man to return. When nothing else happened for more than a minute, David fast-forwarded, squinted down at the camera to detect any movement.

Nothing.

He hadn't been able to distinguish any of the man's features, so there could be no way of knowing whether it was Chris or

(*Judson Alexander*)

someone else. He reached the end of the recording and went back to the moment when the figure had stopped before the camera; this time David paused it. For some reason, while the man's hands were ghostly white, the face remained in shadow. It didn't look like Chris's profile, but then again, it didn't look like *anyone*. Just a vague intimation of a large nose, a protuberant brow, a cruel jaw.

David set the camera aside and powered up the iPhone. He found the voice memo, pushed play, and listened to the pertinent section of audio twice, thinking he might hear whispering voices or maybe a snatch of conversation in which the hoaxsters revealed their identities.

But there was nothing. Only the sounds of the crashing ladder, the clumping footsteps, and David's terrified retreat from the room.

David pocketed the iPhone. The atmosphere in the house remained a bit too tense for him to relax, but he did know of a place where he could work on his book: Oxrun Park.

He'd gathered what he needed and was heading to the Camry when he stopped beside the car, the flesh of his arms spreading in goosebumps.

David turned and gazed up at the third-story dormer.

No face stared back at him.

"Was it you, Chris, or did you hire an actor?" David asked.

When no one answered, David climbed inside the Camry, started the engine, and rolled down the lane.

CHAPTER TWENTY-FIVE

Oxrun Park appeared empty. David grabbed his gear from the passenger's seat and made his way to the small shelter that overlooked the beach.

He discovered a socket in a wooden shelter support and plugged in his computer, but an errant glimpse at the island across the bay resuscitated a memory from his senior year in college.

The memory of Anna and their last night together.

They'd made love on the beach, as they'd done many times. Anna had asked him if he'd spend the night with her in the island woods, but the impracticality of it had made David laugh. They had no sleeping bag, no pillows. No blanket, for that matter, their lovemaking a thing of moonlight and wet sand. Besides, he'd told her as they'd swum back to the shore of Oxrun Park, he had tests for which to study. It was Dead Week, and final exams were looming. While Anna wouldn't be graduating anytime soon – she was a year younger, and her attendance at lectures was sporadic – David planned on finishing with honors and moving on with his life.

Truth be told, he was equally anxious to move on from Anna. Not because he was tired of her, but precisely because he wasn't. Through the first three years of his matriculation at William & Mary, he'd never had trouble ending relationships. After a particularly clingy girlfriend during his junior year in high school, he'd made it a habit to tell girls, up front and with brutal clarity, that he wasn't looking for anything long-term, that he believed in living in the moment and not darkening his interactions with false promises.

Of course, this didn't prevent some women from erupting on him. Claims that he'd misled them, willfully hurt them, or even, in one young woman's case, "shattered my soul" still abounded. But his conscience remained clear.

Until Anna.

He'd given her the same warnings he gave every woman he dated:

I will never lie to you.

I will never mistreat you.

I will never marry you.

They were reclining in the shallow water that night, David shirtless, Anna in a lime-colored string bikini that covered very little.

She'd said, "This is the end."

He'd turned to her, eyebrows raised.

"Of our time together," she explained. "I feel it."

"That's what you want?" David asked.

She stared at the brilliant moonlit water, her eyes filling. "You just answered my question."

David, chafing: "I told you this was temporary."

"Ten months, Davey. Nearly a year."

He hung his head. It had endured twice as long as any relationship he'd ever had.

"Saying words that end up being true," she murmured, "is not the same as being honest."

That stopped him. "Anna—"

"Don't worry," she said, not looking at him, "I'm not going to stalk you. I'll let you go."

He reached out, put his hand over hers.

"That's for you," she said.

"Anna—"

"You want to walk away but you don't want to feel bad about it. You'd kiss me right now, hold me, even make love to me, but it would be for you to feel better. You'd be giving me a going-away present, something to remember you by."

He withdrew his hand. "That's a vicious thing to say."

"I won't get mad now, Davey, or at least I won't show it. But you talking about what's vicious is hilariously ironic."

"Just like the others," David muttered.

"Of all the words you've spoken, those might be the cruelest," she said, and he knew she was right. She wasn't like the others, was the opposite of the others, which was why this was so difficult.

"You had a tough childhood," she said.

"Come on. Not that psychoanalytic bullshit."

"At the very least you owe me the chance to speak."

He didn't answer, but he shook his head in disgust.

"A bad childhood can't be a neutral, Davey. It can be a negative or a positive, but it can't be a neutral."

"How exactly can a troubled childhood be a positive?"

"Motivation," she answered. "Someone with a bad childhood knows better than anyone else how painful it is, how little security a person feels."

He suspected where she was going and did all he could to unhear her words, but she was pressing on, and the noose around his throat was tightening and tightening. God, he could scarcely breathe.

"It did something to you," she said. "How could it not? Whatever happens to us when we're young – good or bad – it affects us."

"Could you be any more ambiguous?"

"I'm not as articulate as you. You'll always be the one who charms people, while I'm just...awkward. Goofy. Guys think I'm pretty, but they don't take me seriously. Just a poor girl from a blue collar family trying to punch above her weight." She turned to him. "Did I get that metaphor right?"

He was horrified to find he had an overwhelming urge to hug her and pepper her face with kisses. God help him, he not only loved Anna, he honest-to-goodness *liked* her too. Jesus, how could he not?

"Here's the point," she went on. "I know you make it a habit to have a short memory with relationships, and I don't hold much hope that it'll make a difference for any of the women who'll come after me."

"Can we just go back to the car?"

"Soon. Soon it will all be over. You feel it and I feel it, and you're set on doing this the way you've laid out in your head."

He laced his hands around his knees. "You make me sound so unfeeling."

"I care about you, Davey. I'd tell you again how much I love you, but you'd only accuse me of guilting you for breaking up with me."

"Damn it, Anna—"

"I'm not telling you anything you don't know."

He glared a question at her.

He saw no accusation in her face. Just a sad species of fascination. "It's like...emotional Darwinism. You got hurt as a kid, so you changed emotionally. You created this...I don't know. Filter isn't the perfect word, but it's close."

"I don't have a filter," he said. "I'm just honest."

"You call it honesty, Davey, but it's sifted and processed through this complex system of justifications, and it allows you to move from person to person like an emotional hurricane, leaving them devastated in your wake."

"You're making me into something inhuman."

Her gaze was steady. "That won't work either, Davey. We both know I'm not the one ending it. It's you. It's your decision."

"Goddammit," he muttered, and started to get up, but she threw a hand out, grasped him by the shoulder.

There were tears in her eyes, tears he knew were hot and burning even if they weren't his. The kind of tears he'd cried as a young child, back when his mom had taken him to church and prayed with him at night and he'd lain in bed alone and railed at God for allowing everything to fall apart, his family, his mother, everything. *Pray* was what his mom always said when things were terrible, *pray* was what she said when she should have been doing something to help. Praying was all she did when he was a little kid and his dad kept entering his bed at night and if she'd *done something* instead of praying, David might not have endured hell at those rough hands, that drunk, whiskery face, that fiendish voice.

David realized he was grinding his teeth, yearning to strangle that monstrous son of a bitch who dared call himself a father.

But Anna was going on. "You're leaving me," she said. "We both know it. So please give me this one thing. Please allow me the chance to say what I need to."

Thoughts of his parents abated, yet his body remained rigid. He couldn't look at Anna. "Trying to make me feel bad."

"You already feel bad. I'm just making you aware of that feeling."

"So manipulative...."

"I can't manipulate anybody," she said, and to David she'd never looked so vulnerable. "Least of all you. You're choosing for this to happen, Davey. That's what I need you to know. You're *choosing* to put an end to this. We get along so well, we hardly ever fight."

"Anna...."

"This makes me sound pathetic, but it's over anyway, so I might as well say it."

He was horrified to find tears threatening in his eyes. "I can't—"

"The future you won't allow is a good one. Maybe even a beautiful one. You know I'd be loving. I'd support you, make you laugh, tell you off when you act like a jerk...."

"This isn't doing any good," he said. He could smell her breath, the gum she chewed and the beer she'd drunk reminding him of some fruity mango drink, and the aroma conjured up a vision of Anna at some all-inclusive resort, a bikini top like she wore now but at sunset, with some kind of swim wrap tied at her hip. She'd wear shades, she'd be smiling at him, and as she strode toward him on the beach he realized there was someone else holding his hand. He looked down and there was a kid, *their* kid, and the three of them would come together, Anna and David and their daughter, and it was too much, too perfect, and he did rise from the shore then and stumble into the water.

Anna rose behind him. "You're choosing this."

He was walking away.

"Remember," she said, not moving after him, but her voice dogging him. "You're choosing to end us. Even though it's wonderful...the best thing in my life...."

The tears were flowing down his cheeks, hot and bitter. He kept moving.

"...you'll always know how much I loved you," she called. "How much more we would have shared...."

He could barely see, his eyes were so blurry, but he made it all the way to the Buick, where Chris sat on the hood. He'd evidently been watching the whole exchange.

"Start the car," David said.

The beer bottle dangling between his knees, Chris said, "So that's it, huh?"

"Start the goddamned car!" David shouted, climbing into the back seat. Let Anna sit in the front, he thought. She and Chris could sit there and hate him together.

"I'm getting Anna," was all Chris said, and after a time, David didn't know how long, the car doors opened and closed and the engine started and the Buick began to jostle and sway. David didn't open his eyes, merely reclined his head on the seatback and waited for it to be over. He tried to doze off but couldn't. The drive stretched on forever. When they finally did stop and a door opened, David squinted and saw Anna climbing out. Neither she nor Chris said a word. She began the short walk to her apartment building, where she lived by herself. She worked a full-time job at a pizza place to pay for rent and school and food, and she snuck David and Chris free pizza when her boss wasn't paying attention. She often scrawled David little notes and left them on his car window, telling him she had to go home to take care of her dad, who had stage three cancer, or that she missed David and hoped she could see him later.

Anna, who had no money sense and routinely gave ten-dollar bills to the homeless people they encountered in Richmond, was almost to the door of her apartment building. Anna, who always drove to her little brother's baseball games and her kid sister's softball games, was reaching for the door handle. Anna opened the door, and he thought he'd see her big brown eyes, the eyes that looked at him in a way none had.

But Anna went through the door and disappeared. He couldn't imagine her taking her own life, but that's what she did. And the worst part, the part he could never get over, aside from the loss of that rare, amazing person….

The part he couldn't get over was that when Chris called to tell him she was dead, David wasn't surprised.

CHAPTER TWENTY-SIX

David's head was in his hands, the bench at which he sat hard and unforgiving.

Anna had seen through him. It was difficult to swallow, but there it was. That night on the shore she'd disassembled his finely constructed emotional apparatus in just a few sentences, and though she'd revealed him for the selfish bastard he was, she somehow loved him anyway.

Yet despite that goodness, that capacity for forgiveness, he'd still abandoned her and gone about leading the life she'd exposed as fraudulent.

What did it matter that his last book had flickered at the bottom of *The New York Times* Non-Fiction Bestseller List? What did it matter that his colleagues respected him? In the end, what did he have? What had he done? Taught a few undergrads about the symbolism in *Moby Dick*? Crushed the hopes of those who wanted to believe in the afterlife?

A splashing sound, something hitting the water maybe a hundred feet from where David sat. He tensed, on some level grateful to be dragged from his reverie. David rose, left the shelter, and padded through the deep powdery sand. He waded into the shoal and surveyed the riverbank. When the water reached the tops of his shins, he discovered a figure free-styling away from a dock.

The woman who'd called the cops on him, of course; it was her dog sitting on the dock gazing at her. Feeling vaguely creepy, he watched her swim a gradual loop. As she returned to the dock, her dog – Sebastian, he remembered – stood up, tongue pumping, and did a little dance. She smiled, reached up, and scratched the old dog behind the ears.

She turned in the water and looked at David. "How long have you been spying on me?"

He nodded toward the shelter. "I was over there writing. When I heard a splash, I came to check it out."

"And stayed."

He shrugged. "Well...not that long."

She resumed scratching Sebastian's head and David felt more than ever like a voyeur.

He asked, "Why did you call Harkless on me?"

"A woman lives alone, she has to be vigilant."

"I seem dangerous to you?"

"Hard to tell," she answered. "Some of the worst fiends in history have been outwardly charming."

Sebastian was on his side, panting in ecstasy, as the woman scratched his belly.

"You think I'm charming?"

She gave him a flat look. "Want me to call the sheriff again?"

"Whatever happened to trusting people?"

"Life teaches you how foolhardy that is."

He shook his head, stared out at the island. He thought briefly of the vision he'd glimpsed that first night, the woman in the mist.

"Did I hurt your feelings?" she asked.

He shook himself back to attention. "I haven't been sleeping much."

She watched him.

"I've hardly been sleeping at all," he admitted.

"Stalking must be hard work."

"*Hey.*"

"I'm joking," she said and went back to scratching her dog. She was smiling a little, and though he could only see her in profile, the smile lit up her face, dimples showing at her cheeks and her features coming alive. He wanted to tell her how nice her smile was, what a difference it made, but figured that sounded both stalkery and insulting.

What he did say was, "I'm sorry for startling you."

"Today or the other night?"

"Well...."

"You didn't startle me."

"Oh."

"Jessica," she said.

He opened his mouth to tell her his name, but she said, "I know who you are."

"Did Harkless tell you?"

Rather than answering, she murmured something to Sebastian, gave the dog a final emphatic scratch, and backstroked into the bay.

"Can I talk to you?" he called, cringing at the loudness of his voice. She stopped, frowned. "Huh?"

"I was wondering if we could talk some more." He gestured toward shore. "It can be at the park, if that makes you feel safer."

She treaded water for a few moments, maybe thinking it over, maybe considering calling the cops. Finally, she said, "You know how to swim?"

★   ★   ★

It only took him a couple minutes to return to the shelter, gather his things, and stow them in his car. He shed his shirt and emptied his pockets.

He returned and waded in to his hips, and though the river was frigid on his genitals, the water felt exhilarating. It occurred to him with a sense of mild wonder that he hadn't swum since arriving.

He didn't dive in, instead pushed forward and leaned into the deeper water. He let his head go under, and after the quick snap of surprise wore off, the familiar thrill of sliding through the water gripped him. God, he'd needed this. Despite the drag of his cargo shorts – they probably weighed twenty pounds when wet – he scythed through the water, pausing now and then to stand upright and satisfy his curiosity about the river's depth.

It was fifty yards from the shore to the island, and at the halfway mark, he found he could no longer touch bottom. He bobbed, took a deep breath, sank for maybe eighteen inches before his toes scraped sand. He surfaced, resumed his stroke until he was forty feet from the island. At that point, he merely stood up, the water just above his navel, and strode into shallower water.

Jessica was already reclining on the shore. Fast swimmer, he thought. The last woman he'd seen so at home in the water was Anna, who Chris had often joked was part mermaid.

In fact....

The way Jessica leaned on her elbows, her butt and legs in the inch-deep water, reminded him forcibly of Anna.

He hadn't noticed it during that first encounter, but now that the sun shone fully on Jessica's face, he saw how much she resembled Anna. Yes, there were differences – Jessica's lips were fuller, her muscles slightly more toned. And of course Jessica was older now than Anna had been. The last time he'd seen Anna she'd been twenty-one. He put Jessica in her late thirties, despite her nearly flawless looks.

Here beside her the water was only shin-deep. There were miniscule fish darting about, worrying the hairs of his ankles and tickling his feet.

"Do you have to stand over me?" she asked. "I feel like I'm being reprimanded."

"Sorry." He took a few steps away, studied the island's tree line. It was as pathless and dense as he remembered it.

"You've been here before?" she asked.

"What, the island?"

"You really do need more sleep."

He snorted laughter, knew how dorky he sounded, but the time he might have made a favorable impression had long passed.

"Sit if you want," she said.

He glanced at the minnows darting to and fro. "Don't those things bother you?"

"Worried they're gonna nibble your balls?"

He chuckled, eased down alongside her, and eyed the minnows warily. "You've really changed your tune," he said. "One minute you're calling the cops on me, the next you're inviting me to lounge with you in Minnowland."

She smiled and looked away. "You're too dull-witted to be a serial killer."

He winced. "*Man.*"

"Any reason you're not sleeping?"

"I'm an insomniac," he said. "Melatonin usually works, but lately, not so much."

"I don't sleep well at all," she said.

"Have a hard time shutting off your mind?"

Rather than answering, she swiveled her head in his direction, but stopped short of looking at him, instead fixing on something beyond him.

He turned and saw the Alexander House in the distance.

He shivered. Hoped she didn't notice.

"What do you think of Georgia?" she asked.

"She enjoyed messing with me."

"Maybe you're just insecure."

He laced his hands over his knees. "Did you really feel threatened by me?"

"You're not a small guy," she said. "I'm all alone."

"You seem comfortable now."

She nodded to her left. "There are other houses on the bay. Probably eight roads like mine. I'd wager someone is watching us now."

He followed her gaze, spotted other docks. Above the docks, there were houses, mostly set back from the water and built into the hillside. "They'd have to use binoculars."

"It's safe during the day. At night, not so much. Besides," she said, peering at him, "if you touch me, I'll make you regret it."

He glanced at her fingernails, which appeared healthy and sharp.

A bark carried to them from across the water. They looked at Sebastian. "He gets impatient when I'm over here," Jessica said.

"Don't dogs swim?"

"Not one as old as mine." With barely a pause, she said, "You're in danger."

He glanced at her.

"I mean it," she said. "Your skepticism is going to get you killed."

Oh boy, he thought. One of those.

He couldn't suppress a grin. "You a psychic?"

"Artist," she said. "And graphic designer."

"But you're in touch with spirits...."

"I better get back to Sebastian."

"Hold on," he said, putting out a hand, but stopping when he realized how inappropriate it would be to touch her, even on the forearm. "Sorry. But in my line of work, I run into this all the time. People warning me off places, telling me the undead are going to claim my soul."

"That's not what I said."

"I know. But—"

"You said you weren't sleeping."

"That hardly proves the existence of ghosts."

"David?"

"What?"

"I didn't say anything about ghosts."

He opened his mouth to argue, then realized she was right.

Chastened, he asked, "Then what are you warning me about?"

"You're as sarcastic in person as you are in your books," she said.

He searched her face, but her expression betrayed nothing.

"Which ones did you read?"

"Read or skim?"

He whistled softly. "Ouch."

"You're talented."

"Thanks," he said and meant it. He paused. "But you still skim—"

"I can tell when you're being honest and when you're doing something for effect."

He frowned, splashed the water near his crotch to scare off the minnows. "That's not flattering."

"You need flattery?"

"Uh...."

"Or are you just used to it?"

He laughed, directed a glance at the cloudless sky. The sunlight felt good on his face.

"What's your new book about?" she asked.

"The Alexander House," he answered. He watched her toes twiddle in the water, the minnows darting away. "You know something about that?"

"I might," she said. "Want to make me a co-researcher?"

"Another perspective never hurts."

She stood up, and he got an eyeful of her sand-covered behind. It was a lovely behind.

"Down, tiger," she said.

David cringed. "You know, I'm really not that lecherous. You were right in front of me...."

"I'll help you with the book," she said, "on one condition."

"Only one?"

"I mean it," she said, looking down at him. "If you don't agree, I'm not wasting my time."

"I'm at your mercy," he said, getting to his feet and dusting off the sand. "What's the condition?"

"Take the house seriously."

He saw how earnest her eyes were. Thought of the ladder crashing down, the figure clumping down the steps. The leering thing.

"I'll take it seriously," he said.

"Good," she said. "Race you to the park."

CHAPTER TWENTY-SEVEN

Jessica beat him by twenty yards.

When he discovered how effortlessly she'd smoked him, he eased his pace to catch his breath and restore a trace of his dignity. When she climbed out, he assumed she'd turn around and favor him with a wry grin. Instead, she wrung out her long black hair, flicked it a couple times, and made for the shelter. Somehow, this was worse than being teased.

He caught up to her outside the shelter and asked, "What about Sebastian?"

"Drive me home, and I'll go down to get him."

He started the car, and rolled down the windows. On the way up the park lane, she asked, "You have any dry clothes?"

"They're back at the house."

"Tough luck," she said. "You're not borrowing any of mine."

He leaned toward the open window, let the breeze dry his hair. "I wouldn't look good in your clothes anyway."

"You're right," she agreed. "You'd be a hideous woman."

David smiled.

Soon, they pulled into her drive, and she said, "Take your things to the pergola out back. I'll get Sebastian."

He did as she instructed, and though the pergola was set a goodly ways from the house, when he opened his Mac, a Wi-Fi password prompt appeared. While he waited for Jessica, he gazed at the purple clematis flowers threading their way over the aged cedar rafters.

Soon, Jessica appeared at the forest's edge. She was carrying Sebastian, and though he wasn't a tiny dog, she didn't appear to be laboring at all.

On the way past him, she said, "Gotta get the boy some water. Password's *Mordor*."

He typed it into his phone, and within seconds saw he had three voicemails. One was an automated message from an online pharmaceutical company. The second message was from his editor, who hinted that this could be his biggest book yet and to take his time with it. Which meant his editor was in a hurry to see it. David listened to the rest of the message impatiently, went on to the third, which was from his agent, who informed him that three foreign rights deals for his latest book were pending: Spain, France, and Japan.

Jessica emerged from the house with a glass of ice water in each hand. She'd changed into a black tank top and beige shorts. No shoes or makeup.

She was gorgeous.

"Tell me about the book," she said.

He raised his eyebrows. "I don't usually talk about my work. It's bad luck to talk about a book while you're writing it."

"Luck? That doesn't sound very scientific."

"I'll talk," he said too quickly. She caught it, and he blushed a little. "To tell you the truth, it'd be nice to share what's been happening."

"You haven't made any friends here?"

"One," he said. "A neighbor. But he's too frightened of the house to be of use."

She placed her water on a wrought-iron stand. "You seem a little skittish yourself."

He gulped his ice water, fought off a fierce brain freeze. "I'm not sure where to start."

"You're a writer, David. Start at the beginning."

He did, beginning with the phone call from Chris and ending this morning when he'd watched the video and listened to the recording. Jessica was a good listener and only asked a few questions. Unexpectedly, he found a burden lifting. He'd been oppressed by his experiences in the house. He detected no mockery in her but maybe she was simply a good actress. She might very well believe him a lunatic but was simply keeping it to herself.

Her most dramatic reaction occurred with his revelation about the video. "And you have this with you?" she said. "The footage?"

"Yeah, it's...." He gestured toward the athletic bag.

"Can I watch it?" she asked, smiling a little.

They viewed it together, and though David's spine still tingled at the sound of the footsteps, when the figure appeared this time, it wasn't quite so unsettling.

"You think that was your friend?" she asked when the figure had passed.

"Maybe," he said. "Who else?"

"Someone they hired?"

"It'd take a pretty brave actor," he said, "to stake out the third floor of a haunted house."

"I saw him the other night."

David's legs went numb. "What do you mean you saw him the other night?"

"The night of the storm," she explained. "The weather was haywire until, what, three in the morning?"

"About that," he said, remembering how Mike Jr. had kicked in his sleep.

"Sebastian hates storms," she said. "Storms and fireworks. He shivers all through a storm, so I don't sleep much either."

"He sleeps in your bed?"

"Best bed partner I've ever had," she said. "No snoring, no hogging the blankets. Anyway, he kept me up most of the night, and by the time the downpour ended, I was just…awake. You ever get to that point? Where you know you're not going to sleep, so you get up and do something?"

He nodded.

"The storm had blown over, so I decided to assess the damage. You know, see if my dock was still there…."

She frowned, her voice lowering. "There wasn't much damage, just downed branches and a lot of leaves. But I wondered if the island had been affected. I swam out there—"

"In the middle of the night?"

"Why not?"

"Gutsy."

She smiled. "It's just an island, Davey."

A chill whispered over him at the name.

She didn't appear to notice. "I was walking the shore of the island when I turned toward the Alexander House."

"I wish I'd been awake."

"The storm was over, but there was lightning in the distance. Enough to see by." Her voice went quieter. "There was a figure in your yard. It was looking at the house."

David's mouth was dry. "In the backyard?"

She shook her head. "He was on the right side of the house…to the east. It looked like he was staring at the room over there."

The master suite, David thought. Where he and the kids had been. Jesus.

David cleared his throat. "Did you, um, get a look at—"

"It's a goodly distance," she said. "But it looked like he was wearing a light-colored shirt and dark pants."

David stared at her. She'd seen the footage, of course, but her green eyes betrayed no sign of duplicity.

"You think I'm making this up?" she asked.

"I can't think of any reason why."

"Well," she said, "if I liked you, I might participate in the ghost story to get closer to you."

"*If* you liked me?"

"Merely a hypothetical." Her eyes shone with mirth.

David said, "Seeing someone in the yard – even if it was the man in the video – doesn't mean it was a ghost. In fact, it lends credence to the notion someone is having me on."

"Your friend Chris…is he a tall guy?"

"Not exceptionally."

"That's why I think it's an actor."

He nodded. "The more I think about it, the harder it is to believe that Chris would sit up there in that attic waiting for a chance to scare me. Whoever was up there, he couldn't have known when I was going to enter the long bedroom. It has to be sweltering up there."

"He could have brought a cooler, ice packs to keep himself from overheating."

"Chris was never what you'd call rugged."

"So what's your next move?"

He looked at her, the glass halfway to his lips.

"With the house," she explained. "What other gadgets can you use?"

"Not many. There are a couple other things, but they're just…silly. I only use them to placate the ghost nuts."

"Are you sleeping in the house again tonight?"

"Where else would I stay?"

"One of the motels in town."

"Oh."

She sat forward. "You didn't think I was going to invite you here, did you?"

"Not necessarily."

Her mouth opened in an incredulous smile. "You did!"

"Hey, let's just—"

"You were hoping to parlay this into sex."

"Wait a minute—"

"Don't deny it," she said. "I see the way you look at me."

He tried to swallow, couldn't. "I'll admit I find you attractive."

"Is that so?" She sat up primly.

"But we just met."

"Exactly."

"I have too much respect for you...."

She gave him a flat look.

He flailed a hand. "For women in general...."

She cocked an eyebrow.

"Have mercy," he said. "I swear you and Harkless are in on this together."

Her laughter was lighter this time.

It relaxed him. A little.

He glanced at her. "I would like to take you to dinner though."

"I don't know if we're there yet."

"Six o'clock?"

"Consider it a probationary date. But how do we prove you're being hoaxed?"

"Catch the guy who's playing Judson?"

"The guy you *hope* is playing Judson."

"Man, why did you have to say that?"

★   ★   ★

He peeled off his still-damp shorts in the tiny downstairs bathroom of the Alexander House and told himself not to get too excited. It was just a date, after all. He'd gone on hundreds of them.

Not with someone as interesting as Jessica.

He twisted on the shower. While the water heated up, he brushed his teeth, guzzled a cup of water. It was well water, dank and slightly eggy, but it didn't bother him. He'd never been the sort to require purified water that had been collected from some glacial mountain pass.

He climbed into the shower, let the steamy water spray over him. Damn, it felt nice. He turned up the heat a speck, closed his eyes.

He'd washed his hair this morning, but because of his impending date with Jessica he decided to do it again and eliminate any river residue. He didn't think he smelled like fish, but images of the turd-colored minnows darting around his legs kept recurring, and he wanted to be sure he didn't stink. He worked the shampoo in, exulting in the seething assault of the showerhead.

Hands closed over his shoulders.

David gasped, thrust out against whatever was in the shower stall with him, but the shampoo suds streamed over his eyes, stinging them. The skin against his fingers was pliant and warm, and for a crazy moment he thought, *Jessica?*

The hands slithered over his chest, and he heard laughter. He blinked the suds away, grimaced as the burning in his eyes intensified. He placed a hand on the invader's chest – his fingertips encountering full breasts – and raised his face to the showerhead. The spray washed over him, needling his eyelids and ameliorating some of the sting. When he turned his head and dragged a hand over his smarting eyes, he finally realized who'd invaded his house.

Honey, horribly and gloriously naked, her hands cupping her ample breasts, her tongue licking across her upper lip.

"What…the *fuck*…is wrong with you?" he demanded.

"Not a thing, darlin'," she said. She fondled her nipples, which were taut nubs. "Not a thing."

David reached for the shower door.

But Honey was there, her fleshy hip bumping his hand away. He caught a glimpse of her sodden light brown bush.

"Here," she said, fingers closing over his penis, "let Honey take care of you."

He smacked her hand away, hissed as her thumbnail scratched his glans. "What the hell?"

"We're both adults, David," she said, closing in. Her breath was heavy with alcohol, her fingers insistent on his chest. "Don't pretend you don't wanna be inside me."

He stepped to his right, but not only was the coffin-like space too tight for him to slip past, the low-hanging showerhead slashed his temple. He brought his fingers to the wound, was amazed to discover blood there.

"Let me help with that," Honey said, and took his bloody forefinger into her mouth. He jerked away, but her hands swarmed over him, one rubbing his testicles, the other grinding the crack of his ass.

"*Hey*," he growled, "get your goddamned—" He slapped her hands away. He endeavored to squeeze by on her left, but she pressed her body against his, laughing huskily. Her fingers slithered over his genitals.

"Let's slip this beast inside," she breathed into his ear.

David seized her by the arms, swung her to the back of the shower stall.

Upon impact with the hard plastic wall, Honey's eyes widened. "Oh, *baby*, I *love* it rough!"

She reached for him, but he was pushing away, his heel kicking open the frosted-glass door. She lunged for him, but he was out, and before she could grab him again, he shouldered through the bathroom door, hurried through the den, made it to the master suite just as he heard the slap of footsteps behind him. He looked up as Honey, soaking wet and somehow terrifying in her birthday suit, stumbled into the den, spotted him, and began an ungainly dash in his direction.

"Oh don't you—" she started, but he slammed the door on her, slid shut the lock. She actually thumped against the door, shouting something unintelligible, and began hammering on the wood. David backpedaled, looked around to find something, anything, to improve his predicament.

A landline phone on the nightstand. Thank God.

He only hesitated for a moment before calling the sheriff's office. Georgia Harkless might enjoy busting his balls about this, but he thought she'd believe him. If their conversation last night had been any indication, she wasn't a fan of Honey Shelby either.

"You open the door right now, you goddamned queerboy!" Honey shouted.

The phone rang twice before a woman picked up. Harkless wasn't in, but they could radio her and have her come out. "Please do that," David said. "It's urgent."

"There's a deputy closer," the woman said. "Want me to send him?"

He considered. "Better make it Sheriff Harkless."

He rang off.

Honey pounded on the door. "What's the *matter*, Caine? You not man enough for me?"

"Go back to your husband," David shouted. Thought about the Shelby children. "Better yet, go jump in the river."

The door trembled under Honey's blows. "*Open the door, you fuck!*"

David bit down on his response. The door continued to rattle in the jamb for a good thirty seconds. Then, with a series of muttered expletives, Honey's footfalls squelched away. He stared at the closed door, thinking, Did she walk over here naked, or are her clothes somewhere in my house?

He listened intently, hoped Honey wouldn't attack the door again. He wondered if this was how Shelley Duvall felt in *The Shining*.

But instead of renewing her assault, Honey went out the front door. At least that's how it sounded. He wouldn't put it past her to feign an exit and jump him the moment he opened the bedroom door.

He remained there, listening, for a long time.

★   ★   ★

Twenty minutes later there was a knock from the front porch.

David put his hands on the bedroom door, leaned closer, and listened.

"Mr. Caine?" a woman's voice called.

Sheriff Harkless.

"Thank God," he muttered.

He went to the front door and let Harkless in.

She entered the foyer. "I was told this was urgent." She studied him. "Your hair is wet, and you're shirtless. You trying to seduce me?"

He'd been putting his T-shirt on, but now he stopped and stared at her.

She looked at him, deadpan. "I'm messing with you."

"Honey tried to force herself on me," he said.

"You mean she waited this long?"

"She got in the *shower* with me."

That got Harkless's attention. "You invite her in?"

"No, I didn't invite her. I was washing my hair when she started... groping me, I guess."

"She was naked too, I'm assuming."

"Very naked. Can we go to the porch? I feel like a prisoner in here."

She followed him out. "You're worried she's gonna make an accusation."

"It occurred to me, yes." He plopped down in one of the white metal chairs. "You should've seen her. I wouldn't put anything past that maniac."

"Me either."

David looked at the sheriff. "You think I'm in trouble?"

"Hell, I've thought that since you arrived."

At his aggrieved expression, she smiled. "I believe you, Mr. Caine. But Honey is as unpredictable as a top. Once she starts twirling, there's absolutely no telling which way she'll go."

He hung his head. "Damn."

Harkless's voice was not unsympathetic. "You called me. That was smart. Now the best thing to do is take your mind off it."

"How?"

She shrugged. "Take in a movie. There's one about a deranged neighbor playing at the Lancaster drive-in."

He stared at her.

She was chuckling, a hand on her belly. "Oh, come on. That was a little funny."

He shook his head, was about to comment, when he jolted. "Wait. I've got a date."

She leveled a finger at him. "You better not be sniffin' around Alicia Templeton. I swear I'll take that typewriter of yours and cram it—"

"It's not Alicia," he said, "and I write on a Mac."

"*Better* not be Alicia. Girl's half your age."

"I'm well-preserved, though."

"So help me God," Harkless said and raised an open palm.

David raised his hands in truce. "Kidding! Take it easy."

Harkless settled in her chair. "So who's the lucky woman?"

"Jessica," he said, watching Harkless's face.

"Your stalking paid off."

"I wasn't stalking!"

Harkless gave him a look. "Be nice to her. She's a friend too."

"Is there anyone around here who isn't your friend?"

She stared at him, raised her eyebrows.

"Thanks a lot," he said.

"You walked right into it."

CHAPTER TWENTY-EIGHT

David's date with Jessica went better than he could have imagined. Only afterward did the night go to hell.

She sold him on a Chinese restaurant, which turned out to be not bad. It wasn't, they both agreed, as delicious as Peter Chang's, a place they'd both frequented in Williamsburg, but it was better than your average buffet and a damned sight better than the food David had been eating since he'd arrived.

Afterward, they went for a walk in downtown Lancaster. Not much to see, but there were a few art shops and a bookstore that carried some of David's books. He signed them for the owner, wondered if Jessica was impressed, and decided if she was, she was gifted at concealing it. Leaving the shop, he recognized the beginnings of a crush. Not love – he found the concept too perplexing – but infatuation for sure. Too bad he had to leave in July.

They were walking side by side, the evening sun making the quaint cobbled street glimmer like midafternoon, when Jessica said, "Can I ask you something without your thinking it's an invitation to sex?"

"Wow."

"What I'm wondering is…will you take me to the house?"

A chill whispered over his neck. He glanced at a storefront that featured bridal wear and prom outfits. "Why would I have assumed that was an invitation to sex?"

"You're a guy," she said.

He looked at her. "Now there's a helpful statement."

She shrugged, unabashed. "I've met quite a few Neanderthals."

"As long as we're being honest, I better tell you something."

And he told her the story of Honey, which led to his other experiences with the Shelbys. Jessica gasped when he told her about the mistreatment of the children and occasionally burst out in stunned laughter. Especially the part about Honey trapping him in his bedroom.

"She really called you that? 'Queerboy'? I haven't heard that word since junior high."

"Honey is a bundle of prejudices."

"Was that all of it?"

"Isn't that enough?"

"And you've been here how long?"

His mouth wrinkled in distaste. "Less than a week."

She shook her head wonderingly. "Ghosts, stalking, sexual assault in the shower—"

"Enough."

They took a right down a street devoid of storefronts, the kind of street you'd be scared by in a bigger city. In Lancaster, however, he doubted they were in much danger of being mugged.

"Why did you tell me about Honey?" she asked. When he began to scowl, she put her hands up. "Don't get me wrong – it's interesting, if a little sad. I can't believe they can't get those kids out of that house...."

"It's tragic," he agreed. "Mike Jr.'s a pain in the ass, but Ivy is a sweet girl. They deserve better."

Jessica's eyes remained downcast.

Into the silence he said, "I guess I told you about it because if Honey shows up naked, you won't think I've got a thing for her."

"She really that rapacious?"

"I've met aggressive women before, but she's on another level. Those hands of hers were everywhere. I felt like I was fending off that Indian goddess, the one with all the hands?"

"Durga."

"That's the one."

"You know, if I were Hindu, I wouldn't want you sexualizing one of my deities."

"Are you Hindu?"

She gave him a look. "Do you care?"

They turned right again, on a residential street this time, trending in the direction of where they'd parked.

"Believe what you want to believe," he said.

"And you'll keep on doubting."

"Hey...."

"It's your god, isn't it? Doubt?"

"Come on."

She halted in front of him. "Isn't it?"

He had to stop to keep from running into her. The old-growth trees lining the road and the height of the historical homes cast her face in a softer light, and though she was youthful to begin with, in this muted apricot glow she looked young enough to pass for one of his undergrads.

No, a voice in his head amended, *not one of your students. Another young woman…Anna….*

"What?" she asked.

You remind me of someone, he almost said. Instead, he took her hand, got them moving again.

"I haven't held hands with anyone in years," she said.

"We could stop."

"I'd prefer that."

At his shocked expression, she nudged him with her shoulder. "Kidding! Sheesh, David. Are you always this serious?"

Only when I think of Anna, he thought.

★   ★   ★

Because of the packed forest choking the countryside, David and Jessica didn't see the flashing lights until they had nearly reached the Alexander House, and then they only noticed the lights because of the way they reflected on the Rappahannock and the trees across the river.

"That doesn't look good," Jessica said.

David leaned closer to the windshield. He could see plainly that the flashing lights weren't on his property. Given the direction from which they were emanating, they could only be coming from the Shelbys'.

His first thought: *Dammit, Honey, what did you do now?*

His second: *The kids.*

This thought galvanized him, compelled him to stop the Camry too abruptly, to shove the gearshift into park and fling off his seat belt.

To her credit, Jessica didn't question him as he took off toward the path that connected the properties. Judging from the sounds of her footfalls, she was jogging a little ways behind him. Soon the property opened up, and it was worse than he thought: five police cars, two others he figured were unmarked cruisers. There was a fire truck, an ambulance, and no sign at all of any Shelbys.

Did you kill him, Honey? Did you kill your husband?

David pushed the thought away, spotted Georgia Harkless on the front porch addressing a loose semicircle of cops on the grass. Several of the cops stood taller than Harkless even though she was perched on the porch.

When she saw David and Jessica, she held up a forefinger but didn't pause her monologue: "…and I'll need you to grab as many volunteers as you can. That'll start at dawn tomorrow. Balagtas, Prettyman, you take two men each into the woods to the north and south of the lane." The sheriff turned to a stone-faced man with shoulders like an offensive lineman. "Sergeant Speaker, no reason for an Amber Alert yet, but if you hear of any suspicious activity, please declare one immediately. No need to confer about it."

Oh God, David thought. Which kid is it?

Sergeant Speaker nodded, told his officers to get moving, and soon three state police cars were rumbling into the forest. Shortly after that, several more officers fanned out into the yard and entered the adjacent forest, their flashlights spearing the dense underbrush.

Which one? David wondered as he approached Harkless, who'd taken out a walkie-talkie and had her head cocked, listening to the scratchy voices coming through.

When he reached the porch, Harkless twisted off the walkie-talkie and said without looking at him, "Can you account for your whereabouts over the past twenty-four hours?"

"He's been with me since noon," Jessica said.

"I didn't ask you, Jessie. Plus, I happen to know you weren't with Mr. Caine between five thirty and six because *I* was with him."

Jessie? David thought and gave her a look, which she shook off with visible annoyance.

"Who's missing?" David asked, but before Harkless could speak, he got his answer.

Mike Jr. was watching him through the glass panel beside the main door.

Oh man, David thought. Poor Ivy.

His throat constricted. "How long has she been gone?"

"Can't answer that until you take me through your day."

He rested his hands on his hips. "You really think I abducted her?"

"Work backward," she said. "You've been out with Ms. Green since, what, six thirty?"

It occurred to him he hadn't even known her last name was Green.

"David picked me up at six forty-three," Jessica said. "He was late."

He glanced at her.

She shrugged. "You were."

"That's because I was mauled in the shower," he said and looked at Harkless. "Which you'll no doubt remember. That takes us back to, what, five o'clock?"

"He was with me before that," Jessica said. "I went for a swim off my dock at around noon, and that's about when we started talking."

Harkless shifted her gaze to David. "Before that?"

"I was at Ralph Hooper's last night from eleven p.m. until well into the morning."

"Mr. Hooper was with you?"

He considered making a smartass remark but decided now was not the time. "Yes, he was there too."

"'Well into the morning,' she repeated. "What does that mean?"

"Ten? Ten thirty?"

"Which is it?"

He thought about it, ran a hand through his hair. "Ten, I guess."

"No one with you between ten and noon?" she said.

David stiffened. "That's not a long time."

Harkless didn't respond.

Faint static crackled from the sheriff's walkie-talkie. She dialed the volume higher, listened. Sergeant Speaker was barking at one of his underlings, but the words were lost in a sea of white noise. How anyone communicated that way, David had no idea.

Harkless dialed the volume down and stepped off the porch. Standing at ground level before David and Jessica, she seemed less like a vengeful executioner and more like a human being.

"Near as we can tell, Ivy went missing some time in the night. Or this morning, before her folks finally hauled their sorry asses out of bed."

"When was the last time she was seen?" Jessica asked.

"That's foggy," Harkless said. "Mike Jr. claims she wasn't in her bed when he got done playing videogames around midnight, but Honey says she tucked Ivy in at nine o'clock after reading her some bedtime stories."

"Bullshit," David muttered.

"Most likely," Harkless agreed. "Only thing Honey reads is the label on her vodka bottle."

David made a fist, tapped it against his thigh.

"Can we help, Georgia?" Jessica asked. "You need people to search?"

"We're gonna try tonight," Harkless said. "But finding her is gonna be a hell of a thing, even if she is in these woods."

Something dawned in Jessica's face. "You don't think she's in the woods."

Harkless glanced down at her walkie-talkie. "Kid goes missing near the river, it's usually one thing. We're treating it like she got lost, but… the divers are coming at dawn."

David's stomach clenched. He hadn't considered the possibility she'd drowned, but now that the thought had been planted, all sorts of grisly images assailed him: Ivy, having filled up her coloring books, wades into the water. The girl splashing around. Ivy wandering a little too far and realizing the water is deeper than she thought. Over her head. Floundering….

"My God," David said, moving away from them. Hot tears stung his eyes; an invisible blowtorch burned the tender lining of his throat.

"David," Harkless said.

He drew in a shuddering breath, tried to keep his eyes off the Rappahannock, which now resembled a lurking sea monster, eager to drag helpless victims down.

"You wanna do something for me?" Harkless asked.

"Anything," he breathed.

Harkless said something to Jessica, and a few seconds later, Harkless was opening the door and ushering Mike Jr. outside. The boy looked like he'd lost weight, which was extraordinary given his already gaunt state. It was dim on the porch, but David could see well enough the purple half-moons under Mike Jr.'s eyes, the pitiful way his lips trembled. Gone was the defiant miscreant from their early interactions, in its place a fallen thing, the husk of a child whose essential self had been torn out violently by the roots.

"…my fault," Mike Jr. was saying. "Ivy bein' gone is my fault."

Harkless started to speak, but it was Jessica who squatted before the boy.

"Can you show me your videogames?"

Mike Jr. sniffed. "You any good?"

"Probably not," Jessica conceded.

"Ivy sucks. We always fail co-op missions because of her."

A sharp pain stabbed David's heart.

"I'll just watch you play," Jessica said. "How would that be?"

"Dad says watching someone play videogames is the most boring thing in the world."

David decided that, for once, he agreed with Michael Shelby.

"I can learn by watching you," Jessica said.

"It don't work like that," Mike Jr. said, "but you can watch if you want."

"Are your parents in the family room?" Harkless asked the boy.

"Mom's shitfaced," he said. "I don't know where Dad is."

"Jessica?" Harkless said. "Can you…."

Jessica nodded, and they started through the doorway, her hand on Mike Jr.'s shoulder. "What game are you playing now?"

"The new *Grand Theft Auto*," Mike Jr. said.

David and Sheriff Harkless exchanged a look.

"That's lovely," David said.

Harkless watched sourly after Jessica and the boy. She ran her tongue around the inside of her cheek. Glanced at David. "You ready to aid me in an official police investigation?"

★   ★   ★

Honey was on the couch, an almost-empty glass wedged in the crotch of her sundress, which had ridden way up her thighs, the half-empty bottle positioned between her bare feet. She was staring at the blank TV screen.

"Where's your husband, Mrs. Shelby?" Harkless asked.

Instead of answering, Honey raised the glass, drained it, set to munching on a hunk of ice.

Harkless crossed to the couch, jerked the glass from Honey's hand, and chucked it at the wall. It shattered, the glass shards pelting the side of the projection TV. Honey looked after the glass sluggishly, no emotion registering on her face. Harkless bent, retrieved the vodka bottle – 'Grey Goose,' the label read – and without hesitation dumped its entire contents over Honey's head.

Honey's arms shot out in surprise, her mouth open. David couldn't see her eyes because the vodka had matted her hair down over them.

"Mr. Caine," Harkless said, "I've got a toolbox in the trunk of my cruiser. Please fetch it for me."

David started out of the room, but paused. "Which car is yours?"

Harkless looked at him sweetly. "The one that says 'Sheriff' on the door."

David went out. The toolbox was where Harkless said it would be, and within a minute he was returning, the heavy tan box banging against the side of his leg.

He was just in time to see Harkless leading Michael Shelby down the hallway, his left earlobe pinched between her thumb and forefinger.

"What are you *doing*?" Shelby asked, reaching the family room. "Why are— Honey, you're soaking wet."

Honey uttered something obscene-sounding.

Shelby started to speak, but Harkless squeezed his ear harder, eliciting a high-pitched moan. Harkless whipped him toward the couch, where he jounced down beside his wife.

Shelby rubbed his ear with one hand, touched the sectional cushion with the other. "Why, the couch is drenched!"

Staring down at the Shelbys, Harkless said, "Open the toolbox, Mr. Caine."

David bent and unfolded the clasps. He raised the lid, revealing a tray of wrenches and screwdrivers, but Harkless said, "The main compartment. Under the trays."

David lifted the trays. In the main compartment of the toolbox he found an embarrassment of heavy tools: a rubber mallet, an enormous adjustable wrench that showed some rust on the handle, a sturdy black hammer, bungee cords, and several other implements. David was reminded of Mary Poppins's bottomless suitcase.

"Hand me those bungee cords, Mr. Caine." He started to comply, but she amended, "The red ones, not the green."

He dropped the green bungee cords, which were shorter, and selected four red ones, each of which was as thick as his middle finger and as long as his forearm.

Wordlessly, Harkless set to wrapping up Honey Shelby in a pair of bungees, one for her arms and torso, the other around her knees. Honey was too stunned to react while Harkless was binding her upper body, but when the sheriff started in on her legs, Honey began to kick. Without hesitation, Harkless smacked Honey an open-handed blow on the cheek. Honey's mouth fell open, but she didn't kick at Harkless again.

When the sheriff was done winding the red bungee around Honey's considerable legs, she said, "Mr. Caine?"

David jarred to attention, set to confining Michael Shelby in the remaining bungee cords. He thought Shelby would fight, but the man remained docile throughout, maybe figuring if Honey was cowed by the sheriff, he stood no chance.

When David finished, he stood beside the sheriff.

"First thing we need to get straight," Harkless said, "is you two are pieces of shit."

"I want a lawyer," Shelby said.

"Shut the fuck up," Harkless said.

Shelby shut the fuck up.

Harkless turned to Honey. "You got somethin' to say, Little Miss Shower Rapist?"

David didn't think it was possible, but Honey's jaw drooped even lower.

Shelby frowned at his wife. "What's she talking about?"

"Piss off," Honey told him.

"You're probably wondering why I didn't just cuff you," Harkless began.

Honey and Michael looked at each other.

"It's because," the sheriff explained, "I only use those in case of an arrest. And you two aren't officially under arrest."

Slurring a little, Shelby said, "Our daughter has been kidnapped. How *dare* you imply we're in trouble."

"Oh, you're in trouble all right," Harkless said. "This is one of the worst cases of negligence I've ever seen. How old's your daughter?"

A beat. Then Honey muttered, "Almost five. Her birthday's in December."

The corners of Harkless's mouth turned down. "This is June, you dipshit."

Shelby said, "What's her age—"

"Four years old," Harkless said, "and you didn't even know she was gone this morning."

"Kids like to roam," Shelby said.

"Near one of the biggest damned rivers in the state."

Honey looked at Harkless. "You don't think she's...."

"Drowned? I hope to hell not, but let's talk some more about you two assholes. What were you doin' when you were supposed to be making your kids breakfast?"

Shelby muttered something unintelligible.

"Sleeping it off, I reckon." Harkless glanced at David. "How many times you witnessed the Shelbys inebriated in front of their kids?"

"Every time I've been here," David answered, "day or night."

Honey fixed him with a baleful look. "You don't know what you're messin' with."

"What about lunch?" Harkless asked. "Your daughter was gone all morning, but you just figured she was sleeping in? Didn't need any breakfast? Not even a goddamned glass of milk?"

David glanced at Harkless and realized the sheriff's eyes were moist.

Shelby said, "We have Lunchables, goldfish crackers. Ivy knows where that stuff is."

Harkless slapped him.

So loud was the crack of her palm on his cheek and so violent the blow that for a moment, no one in the room reacted.

It was Harkless who spoke first. "Normal people – responsible people – they realize their four-year-old is missing, they give it maybe an hour. Two, tops. But probably not that long if they live by a river."

Shelby watched the sheriff in horrified fascination. Honey's expression was unreadable.

Harkless went on. "They're frantic. They look everywhere. They call me by noon. One o'clock at the very latest."

Shelby scowled, looked like he was going to argue, but Harkless didn't give him a chance. She seized him by the face and squeezed so that his lips bunched together like a kid pretending to be a chubby baby.

"You didn't call my office until *nine* tonight. That's eight hours you wasted guzzling vodka and grabbing people's peckers."

Shelby tried to pull his face away, but Harkless's fingers tightened.

She jerked his face, hard, her voice becoming a harsh rasp. "And even when you called, you were hesitant, like you weren't sure there was anything wrong. Like you don't even have a parental instinct."

"You ain't a mother," Honey murmured.

Quicker than David would have thought possible, Harkless backhanded Honey, the taller woman's face whipping sideways and a stream of drool spattering on the leather sofa. Harkless gripped her by the chin, and got nose-to-nose. "You're done, Honey. You hear me? You had your chance to be a mother, and you squandered it."

Shelby was staring at Harkless, aghast. "You can't assault my wife. I'll have our attorney on you so fast—"

"David," Harkless said.

David moved forward, grasped a handful of Shelby's hair, and said, "Not another word."

Whatever Shelby saw in David's face, he evidently believed the threat. Shelby lowered his eyes.

Still gripping Honey's chin, Harkless said, "I'm sending Mike Jr. to a safe place tonight." When Honey started to speak, Harkless overrode her. "You're not gonna know where it is, so don't even ask. And if you look like you're gonna do something stupid, I'll bungee your ass again and throw you in the river."

"You can't take our kids away," Honey said, her voice garbled by drink.

"You already lost one of them," Harkless said. "I'm just taking the other to make sure you don't misplace him too."

Honey didn't answer, only gazed at Harkless with measureless hate.

Shelby looked like a man mired in a nightmare. "What are we supposed to do?"

Straightening, Harkless said, "I'm gonna take your car keys to make sure you don't try to run."

"I'm telling my father-in-law," Shelby said.

Harkless ignored him. "You two lumps of shit are gonna get up and start looking for your daughter."

Shelby shook his head. "We've been looking, we haven't found any—"

"Look again," Harkless said. "If my people are gonna risk their necks stumbling around these woods at night, you're sure as hell gonna join them. You're the shitheads who caused this mess."

Honey's voice was surprisingly level. "It ain't our fault Ivy got herself lost."

Harkless made a move for Honey, but David said, "You have any clue what your daughter wants?"

Honey glowered at him. "What are you talkin' about?"

"That night she and Mike Jr. stayed with me," David continued, "all she wanted was somebody to show they cared. Someone to make her a sandwich. To look at her when she was talking."

Honey's eyes were widening.

"During the storm, you didn't even know she was gone. What if she hadn't come to my house that night? She would've been in bed hiding under the covers, scared to death of the thunder."

Honey's mouth twitched.

"All she wanted was a mom," David said. He nodded at Shelby. "A dad. But you were too busy doing everything *but* caring for her. When all Ivy needed was a little attention. A little love."

Then, horribly, Honey's self-control crumbled, and she was sobbing, the sounds like a dying animal, the sight of her snot-streaked face too much to bear.

David looked at Harkless, who was staring at Honey without an iota of pity.

"You wanna stay with these sad sacks while I get Mike Jr. out of here?" Harkless asked.

"Happy to," David said.

"Gimme a five-minute start," Harkless said. "And don't take off the bungees until they've given you their keys."

Harkless started out, but David asked, "What then? How can I help?"

"I'd tell you to get some sleep, but I know you won't be able to. You want, you and Jessica can look for Ivy. To my knowledge, nobody's searched your side of the peninsula yet."

"Done," David said.

Harkless looked at him a moment. Then she went around to the staircase and called up to Jessica and Mike Jr.

When David returned to the family room, Shelby was sobbing along with his wife.

CHAPTER TWENTY-NINE

Ten minutes later, David was walking the river path with Jessica. When Shelby had finally told David where their car keys were, David pocketed them, loosed the Shelbys of their fetters, and gotten the hell out of there.

Jessica's voice was hushed. "Where do you think Ivy is?"

David shook his head, not wanting to give voice to his worst suspicion.

"Mike Jr.'s not so bad once you get to know him," Jessica said.

"He's a pain in the ass."

Jessica smiled quickly at him. "He sort of is, isn't he?"

David almost smiled too. Then his good humor faded when he heard the distant sounds of voices in the woods, the nighttime search party calling out to Ivy on the off-chance she'd gotten lost in the forest. He had no idea how he knew it, but David was certain Ivy was not in these woods. Tomorrow, a larger search party would be formed, but he suspected it would be fruitless.

He thought of Ivy's willowy body clinging to his side. Thought of her carrying around a stuffed animal for comfort.

"I'm sorry, David."

He looked at Jessica. Her eyes were large and liquid in the moonglow.

"You care about her," she said.

He nodded but didn't speak. What was there to say?

"There's a flashlight in my trunk," he said as they drew nearer his property. "I think there's another under the sink."

They'd passed the dock and rounded the edge of the woods when Jessica stopped short, her body rigid. David followed her shocked gaze to the house, and at first could only frown. Other than the way the siding glowed a spectral white in the moonlight, the Alexander House looked the way it always did.

Then he realized what was wrong.

The front door stood wide open.

"David?" she said. "You think?"

"I don't know," he said, but he was already hurrying toward the house.

★   ★   ★

"Ivy?" he called in the entryway. He rushed into the kitchen, the dining room, flipping on lights as he went.

"Ivy?" Jessica called. She'd headed the other direction, toward the den and master suite. David moved to the hallway and the screened-in porch, hoping against hope he'd discover the girl huddled in a corner, frightened but safe.

The porch was empty.

He met Jessica in the hallway. "Nothing in this part of the house," she said. "I checked under your bed, the closets...."

David nodded absently and started up the stairs. Jessica followed but didn't speak. Without thinking he went immediately to the long bedroom, switched on the nearest lamp, and proceeded to fire up the other two lamps, which still didn't lend adequate light to the murky space. He lowered on his knees and began drawing up the bedclothes to make sure Ivy wasn't hiding there. Peripherally, he could see Jessica doing the same.

Into the silence, she said, "The room is deeper than it looked in the video."

With a start he remembered he'd shown her the thermal camera recording, had made her privy to all he knew about the house.

Forgetting Ivy for a moment, he studied Jessica's face, the nervous way she fiddled with the hem of her black shirt. "You feel it too," he said.

"I always wondered..." she started, but trailed off as if catching herself.

He tried to smile. "What is it?"

Her face clouded. She gripped her elbows. "Let's look in the other rooms."

They did, by mutual consent shunning the third story. After all, he told himself, there was no way Ivy could leap into the air, pull down a heavy ladder, and, once she reached the third-floor dormer, heave the whole apparatus back into position.

That's right, a voice teased. *Only Judson Alexander can do all that.*

He bared his teeth against the taunt, told himself to focus. Even if Ivy wasn't here now, she *might* have been here, and if she had, it was possible she'd left a clue.

In his opinion, there were several reasons why she might have ventured inside his house, the most basic of which being a desire to see him. He'd felt a strong bond with the child the night of the storm, and he believed the regard was mutual. She might have come while he was on his date with Jessica.

The front door wasn't open when you and Jessica arrived here from Lancaster.

That was true, he acknowledged. But the door *had* been open when they'd returned from the Shelbys'.

Jessica had moved into the bedroom across the hall, but David froze on the landing, a horrid thought dawning.

Jessica emerged from the bedroom and saw the look on his face. "What?"

He looked at her. "What if Ivy was in the house when we first got here, but by the time we left the Shelbys' she was gone?"

"Why would she do that?"

David's heart thumped dully in his chest. "I don't think she did anything."

"David," Jessica said, moving closer. "You aren't making sense."

"I think...." He swallowed. "I think someone had her hidden here, then took her while we were at the Shelbys'."

★　　★　　★

Flashlight beams dueling, they crisscrossed the broad stretch of vacant land between the Alexander property and Ralph Hooper's. Whenever they neared the shore, David's muscles tightened, an atavistic fear of discovering Ivy's body floating facedown in a rock pool overmastering him. But each time they ventured near the shore, the only objects their flashlights revealed were wet rocks, a scum of brown bubbles reefed by vegetation, and a dead fish, its putrid body alabaster.

When they'd made it halfway across the lot without spotting any sign of Ivy, Jessica said, "What makes you think she was taken? Isn't it just as possible she was hiding in your house and made a break for it when we went over to her house?"

David thought of the way the screen door had hung open, like a whiff of violence on the air.

"For that matter," Jessica pressed on, "why are you so sure it *was* Ivy? Georgia's people were already combing the area when we were at the Shelbys'. Maybe one of them checked your place."

"And left the door wide open?"

"It's an emotional time. People don't behave rationally."

"I don't know," he said. "Maybe I just want Ivy to be alive so badly I'm telling myself she was the one who left the door open." He looked at her, could barely discern the delicate outline of her face in the moonlight. "If it was Ivy, that would mean she was alive not twenty minutes ago."

Near the edge of the lane, they turned southward, the tall wild grass enameling their shins with dew.

"You think she's running away?" Jessica asked.

"Wouldn't you?"

Jessica didn't answer. David's body jolted as he stepped into a depression. A bolt of pain shot through his knee.

"Careful," he said, shining the light into the hole, which was disguised by skeins of violet thistles and goldenrod.

David rubbed his knee, tested it.

"That you, Caine?" a man's voice called.

"Ralph?" he asked.

Jessica's beam picked him out. Ralph Hooper stood about twenty feet before the tree line that enclosed his property. He carried no flashlight, but he was clutching a shotgun.

"Why do you have that?" David asked.

Ralph brought up a hand, visored his eyes. "Miss, do you mind...."

"Sorry," she said, lowering the flashlight beam.

"Why are the cops out here?" Ralph asked them.

Coming nearer, David told him of Ivy's disappearance.

Ralph nodded. "Thought it might be an escaped criminal or something. They used to...." He looked away.

"Used to what?" David asked.

"Never mind," Ralph said. "There's no sign of her?"

"Nothing definitive," Jessica said. "You haven't seen anything, have you?"

Ralph shook his head. "You guys wanna come in?"

"Can we search your woods?" David asked.

Something hooded came over Ralph's face. "Ransack my house if you want."

David grimaced. "I'm not accusing you."

"Well, that's how you act," Ralph snapped. "A kid goes missing and all of a sudden I'm John Wayne Gacy. You forget who took you in last night?"

David shone the light over Ralph's shoulder. "She might be hiding in your grove."

"Uh-huh."

"It's been a traumatic night," Jessica explained. "The Shelbys... they're—"

"Trash," Ralph said. "You don't have to tell me. I heard a gunshot over there a few months ago."

David took a step toward him. "Do you know the little girl?"

"Sure I know her. Comes by for popsicles now and then. Her and that foul-mouthed urchin."

"The sheriff took Mike Jr. somewhere safe," Jessica said.

Ralph nodded. "It'll get him the hell out of that house."

They'd neared the edge of the thicket when David stopped, put a hand on Ralph's arm. "I've had enough mystery, Ralph. What did you mean a little while ago?" When Ralph only looked at him blankly, David said, "About escaped criminals."

Ralph reached into his pocket and produced a crinkled pouch of Red Man. "It's a complicated business."

"Ralph's talking about Judson Alexander," Jessica said.

David turned. Jessica's gaze was steady.

"The Alexander House is my hobby," she explained. "You might call it an obsession."

"We spent the day talking about it. I showed you the video...." He shook his head. "Why didn't you say anything?"

"I didn't want you to think I was using you to get information."

"Were you?"

She folded her arms. "Is that what you believe?" When he didn't answer, she said, "Apparently you do. Maybe it's best that you drive me home now."

David watched her. "Why did you act like you didn't know anything?"

"I didn't know," she said. "Not most of it, at least. The stuff involving you. How *would* I know about it?"

Ralph seemed about to say something, but Jessica stilled him with a sharp glance. David looked from one to the other. "Wait a minute. You two know each other?"

Jessica stared back at him defiantly.

Ralph was scratching the back of his neck. "I can see you two need time to sort things out. I'll just head back—"

"You're staying," David said. He looked at Jessica. "And I'm not taking you anywhere. We're gonna go to Ralph's and you're gonna tell me what the hell is going on."

Jessica and Ralph exchanged a look. Ralph ventured a sheepish grin. "The Red Sox *are* on tonight."

★   ★   ★

Ralph had the game on, but he turned it down almost to inaudibility when they took their seats on the screened-in porch. David snagged a wooden chair from the kitchen so Ralph and Jessica could have the gliding rockers, and though the chair wasn't as comfortable, it did allow him to face the pair. It also spared him a view of the river, which loomed more and more ominous with each passing minute.

"Talk," David said. He nodded at Jessica. "You first."

She sat back in the rocker. "What would you like to know, Davey?"

"Why are you obsessed with the Alexander House?"

Though the lamp in Ralph's kitchen tossed light onto the screened-in porch, Jessica's features were difficult to make out. Her eyes were riveted on him, but they resembled the eyes of an antique doll, glassy and emotionless.

"I think you know," she said.

He felt a heat building at the base of his neck because, God help him, he *did* suspect why she was so obsessed with the place. But to give voice to the suspicion was unthinkable.

David tapped his fingers on his knees. "Are you familiar with Chris and Katherine?"

Jessica was smiling now.

"You in on it with them?" David demanded.

"Easy, David," Ralph murmured.

But David scarcely heard him. "*Tell me.*"

Jessica didn't speak, but her smile broadened.

"You...you knew Anna." The words cost him an effort.

At utterance of the name, something triumphant shone in Jessica's face.

His hands curled into fists. "You've been playing me."

Her maddening smile never wavered. "I've been nothing but genuine."

"It's true, David," Ralph said.

"Shut up," David snapped. He turned to Jessica. "How did you know her?"

Jessica didn't answer.

David pushed to his feet, the wooden chair nearly overturning. "How did you know her?"

"David," Ralph said gently.

"How?" he demanded.

Jessica gazed up at him. "Sit and I'll tell you."

David glanced from face to face, dragged a wrist over his mouth, and sat. "Goddamn you two," he muttered.

Jessica glanced down at her folded hands. "Anna was my sister."

CHAPTER THIRTY

Into the thunderstruck silence, Ralph said, "I think I'll just—"

"You're not going anywhere," David said. To Jessica: "So this is about revenge. You've been working with Chris and Katherine to… undo me? To discredit me?"

She tilted her head. "You're rather full of yourself, you know that, Davey?"

"I can't believe you'd deny it."

"She's telling the truth," Ralph said.

David glowered at him. "You're as treacherous as she is."

"More self-importance," she said.

He scooted his chair forward so their knees touched; Jessica didn't pull away. "The other night, you sicced the sheriff on me even though I'd done nothing wrong."

"You do have a habit of showing up unannounced," Ralph put in.

David ignored that, glared at Jessica. "Then, all of a sudden, we're buddies. You're nice to me, eager to help with my…." He gestured inarticulately.

"Situation," she said.

"…and then you go on a *date* with me? Visit all those art shops and the bookstore, and…." His mouth opened wider. "How much of what I told you did you already know?"

"I don't know Chris and Katherine," she said. When he made a scoffing sound, she said, "Or I barely know them. Chris was at Anna's funeral."

David flashed a grin. "Did you two date?"

"Don't be petty, Davey. It's unbecoming."

David's grin curdled. He glanced at Ralph, who was watching him with good humor. "What?" David demanded.

"She's right," Ralph said. "It is unbecoming."

"As for Katherine," she said, "I've only met her in passing."

"Why should I believe you?"

"I don't give a damn what you believe."

He grunted. "You always able to do that? Flip your emotions on and off?"

"Maybe you should ask yourself what you're so angry about."

"Are you serious? The two of you have been deliberately withholding information from me."

"We've spent a day and an evening together. I've hardly had time to withhold much of anything."

"You had plenty of chances."

"Did it ever occur to you that it's painful for her to talk about?" Ralph asked.

"But it's—"

"And you were the one who came to *me*," she reminded him. "It's not like I lured you over there."

An image flickered across his mind, barely glimpsed but in some way momentous. He faltered, grasping for it, but when Ralph spoke again, it flittered away.

"To my way of thinking, Miss Green is showing a lot of kindness, given the way you treated her sister."

David's arm muscles hardened. "I moved away after college. Quit acting like I murdered someone."

"It's that easy," she said, and he was alarmed to hear the emotion in her voice. "It's that easy to talk about Anna."

It's the opposite of easy, he thought. It's eating me alive.

He said, "I better get you home."

"I can take her," Ralph said.

Jessica nodded. "It's fine, Ralph. I have a few more things I need to say to him."

"We're done," David said, rising.

Ralph got up too, said to Jessica, "If you don't want to go with him—"

"Thanks, Ralph," she answered. "This is how it has to be."

Ralph eyed her bleakly but didn't otherwise protest. David went out, had moved through the side yard and was almost to the lane when he heard her voice call, "You're omitting some things."

He angled toward the Alexander House.

"I could tell earlier," Jessica said, hustling up beside him. "You're not being forthright."

He shone his flashlight into the woods. "I've got to hand it to you. You were a damned good actress. Extracting information, pretending you knew nothing about the house…. You should have been a spy. You could have bedded foreign dignitaries, learned state secrets."

"Tell me what else you saw."

"I told you everything."

She aimed her flashlight beam at his face. He shielded himself with an upflung arm. "Don't do that."

"You're a crummy liar," she said.

They soon reached the Camry, and without further discussion, he drove her down the lane, past Ralph's, onto Governor's Road, neither of them speaking. They made the highway, cruised past The Crawdad, which was dark.

"How much are Chris and Katherine paying you?" he asked as they buzzed over the bridge, the bugs catching the headlights and splattering over the windshield.

"Have you seen Anna's ghost?" she asked.

David nearly swerved off the road.

"She moves on the water," Jessica explained. "She prefers a veil of mist, but sometimes she walks on land."

Stop talking, David wanted to say, but he was afraid his voice would betray his disquiet. The woman on the water…that first night…had she looked like Anna?

My God, he thought. She had.

They'd turned onto Old Bay Road and were nearing Jessica's house when she said, "You've treated me almost as coldly as you did my sister."

David's throat was dry. "Your name's Green…why was hers Spalding?"

"Different fathers. She was my half sister, but her father left when she was so young. They never went through the legal adoption process, but she considered my dad her real one. Is that really the only question you want to ask me?"

He pulled into the drive, coasted to a stop. Cut the engine and heard Sebastian's eager bark within the yellow ranch. She reached for the door.

David looked around. "Why here?"

Her fingers on the handle, Jessica glanced at him.

"Why this house?" he asked. "Why this area? Anna and I only came here a few times. Sure, it was special to us…the island, the park…."

Her expression had changed.

"What?" he asked.

She shook her head wonderingly. "You didn't even look into what happened to her, did you? That's how self-centered you are."

"You don't know me."

"I knew you even before you devastated Anna."

He gritted his teeth. "I didn't— For Christ's sakes, I was twenty-two!"

"We all knew," she said. "My dad, my brother, everyone. We knew from the way Anna talked about you. It was only a matter of time before you screwed her over."

"Stop."

"It was just a game to you, but to my sister, you were the whole world."

"Get out."

"You were everything, and you ripped it all away from her and you didn't even have the guts to do it with any grace."

"Get out of the car!"

"You want to know why I live here?"

David's face twisted. "I don't care, I want you—"

"Anne killed herself in the Alexander House."

David's body turned to stone. He stared at Jessica.

"You didn't even know," she said. She shook her head. "My God, you didn't even know."

He could scarcely breathe.

"And you know what else?" she said.

He opened his mouth to answer, but her fist shot toward him, caught him in the jaw. The blow rocked his head back. His vision swirled.

"That's for my sister," she said.

Jessica got out, slammed her door, and disappeared inside the house.

PART FOUR
THE SIREN

CHAPTER THIRTY-ONE

David barely registered the drive back to the Alexander House. He couldn't believe how blind he'd been, how oblivious. As a professor and author, he relied on research, on facts. Now, in what he suspected was the most vital case in his career, he'd been willfully ignorant, a sleepwalker instead of a scholar.

In the driveway of the Alexander House, he shut off the engine and gazed through the windshield at the dormer of the long bedroom. What if, he asked himself, Jessica *wasn't* in league with Chris and Katherine?

Another question, unavoidable now: did he really want to spend another night here?

Hell yes, he thought, climbing out. He closed the Camry door and listened, but if Harkless's officers were still combing the woods, they'd moved on to other parts. The only sounds he heard now were the chirring of the crickets and the subtle lapping of the Rappahannock.

No, he was certain the search had been called off for the night. A thick mist had settled over the peninsula, and they'd never find anything until it lifted in the morning.

He started for the house. Maybe Jessica didn't know about Chris and Katherine's plot to make him look like a fool, but could there be any doubt she wanted revenge on him for what she believed he'd done to Anna?

What you did *to Anna.*

He entered the house and pulled the door shut behind him. The question was, how did all this relate to Ivy? Had she learned something about the Alexander House and paid for it?

That was preposterous. She was a little kid. What could she have possibly discovered?

It was much likelier she'd gotten sick of her parents' behavior and decided to run away. His only hope was that she'd headed inland.

He shivered, not wanting to consider the possibility of drowning. On his list of fears, drowning was foremost. Many were the nights he'd been plagued by nightmares of his car plowing through a bridge guardrail, of the frigid waters closing over his hood, his windshield, the sky replaced by darkness, the door refusing to budge while the water swallowed his legs and torso—

He reached for the light switch but paused, thinking.

No. No more flooding the house with illumination. No more trembling at shadows and listening for raps on the walls. There was too much evidence of a hoax and too little proof of the supernatural.

David went to the Camry, lugged in the athletic bag full of his research. If he wanted to awaken before dawn to join the search for Ivy, he'd need a few hours of sleep to recharge. Maybe after a couple minutes of reading, he'd be able to nod off.

Grateful to have a sense of purpose, David slid into bed, arranged the covers over his chest, and opened the book. Skipping through Hartenstein's smarmy interlude, David began on a Weir section:

I confess to not recording my thoughts for nearly a week. The reason for my silence is ignominious, but were I to withhold it from my own journal, I should be guilty of the selfsame hypocrisy I have many times leveled against my critics. I refuse to relate only what supports my beliefs and to omit those facts that do not. The true scholar must not quail at the confounding; he must confront all information with equal disinterest.

Therefore, I confess to experiencing a pair of terrible frights, one this morning, the other nearly a week past. These events have disoriented me and for the first time made me feel my age. I do not possess the stamina or, though I'm galled to admit it, the same mettle I did as a younger man. Oh, to be thirty again! Thirty and married and possessed of the brashness that allowed me to blaze a career in the field of letters and the revelation of truth!

But that youthful crusader is gone, and in his place sits a feeble, skittish old man, bereft of fire or steel. In years past I possessed the fortitude to dismiss the occasional nervousness and remain fixed on my purpose.

Yet now....

Look at me! Look at my hand, shaking like an April leaf.

It's that damnable Judson Alexander.

Although Alexander died early in the nineteenth century, I can still imagine him peering out of his third-story lair, absorbed in his infernal vigil.

I might as well confess it now, dear journal. This was the first inexplicable event: six days ago I saw Judson Alexander watching me from the uppermost dormer.

Had I not beheld the bald, mountainous figure with my own eyes, I would have laughed at such an assertion. Men dead for over a century do not suddenly appear alive and whole. Nor do they gaze bloodlessly down at houseguests who blink and rub their eyes to expunge the sight.

I have ruminated on the problem since then, and have yet to reach a satisfactory explanation.

I had taken breakfast in the kitchen, bathed, and completed my morning constitutional. It was perhaps half past nine when I strode down the steps with the intention of walking the countryside to clear my head. I had nearly reached the lane when, unaccountably, I was overcome with the sensation of being watched. I surveyed the forest, yet I knew that was not the direction from which the interloper watched me. I swiveled my head to take in the western view, but the Rappahannock remained as blameless as always. When I continued my revolution, I noticed nothing. The Alexander House was as I had left it: silent, inanimate.

Only when my eyes crawled up its pallid surface did I discover the enormous figure watching me.

It could only have been Judson Alexander. Or some unaccountable approximation of him. I admit now that my reading and my overstimulated senses might have conspired to conjure the apparition, but there could be no doubt that a man powerfully resembling Judson Alexander gazed down at me from the third-story dormer. No pictures of Judson were taken after his twenty-third year – the year of his exile – yet there exist numerous drawings of the man as he'd been in his later years. And as he'd been depicted in these sketches, the man in the window was gigantic, Judson's size imbuing him with an appalling vigor, an impression of inexhaustible virility. As I watched, the bald figure grinned at me and beckoned me toward the house.

I allowed superstition to overmaster logic. I fled. True, I made a poor job of it with my temperamental knee and my old birch cane, but still I fled from the house gripped by the certainty that Judson — the 'Governor,' as he is still ghoulishly referred to in these parts — was charging toward me, his vast muscles writhing like vipers.

Panting and perspiring, I reached the end of the lane before I chanced a look behind me. Nothing had pursued me, of course, yet I could not shake the feeling that I had narrowly averted calamity. Indeed, I was sure that if I'd remained near the Alexander House one minute longer, Judson would have claimed me as he claimed so many other victims.

I must here confess the true state of my physical infirmity. In public I essay the role of the venerable yet well-preserved scholar. Many are the days when someone comments on my upright posture, my youthful physique.

But alas, it is all artifice.

My stomach, I fear, has grown too large for my belt, and only with an effort can I keep it drawn in while in the presence of others. My chest and arms are gradually withering, and I rely more and more on the birch cane that has been in my family for four generations, an aid I once used as an affectation but must now rely upon as did my forefathers before me.

Here, I think, lies the root of my alarm. The figure in the window may merely be a fleeting, illusory representation of my own lost virility. For isn't it his potency for which Judson was renowned? That and his madness?

I admit here how captivated I am by Judson's exploits. When I last wrote in you, my faithful journal, I related the tale of young Judson and the doomed slave, and although any wrongdoing on the part of the six-year-old was left unspoken at the time of the incident, Judson's later behavior sheds an unflinching light on the truth: that Judson was the individual who asphyxiated the fallen slave with soil.

During Judson's twelfth year another incident occurred, this one also unwitnessed yet no less dreadful.

Because Judson and Theodore's mother died attempting to bring a third son into the world (the child too died in childbirth), their father, the ignoble Zacharias (who was now in his late thirties), took as his wife a girl not yet seventeen. This young woman, whose name was Angelica, soon bore Zacharias a child, a healthy baby named Sarah.

As one would expect from a tobacco baron of Zacharias's stature, little Sarah was given every advantage: nannies, wet nurses, and frequent visitations by local doctors. Angelica doted on her daughter, as did young Theodore, who took an especial shine to the infant. Even Zacharias, in his own saturnine way, evinced an unaccustomed affection for the child, and in this manner, the family's felicity swelled to a level previously unknown.

Then Baby Sarah died.

The suddenness of her passing devastated not only her mother, but the entire estate. Though the succession hadn't been made public, many in the community had considered it likely that Sarah might one day help shepherd the family's agricultural empire. It was widely known that Zacharias was grooming his youngest son for a career in politics, and Judson's strangeness made him a poor fit for the mantle of family leadership.

Perhaps Judson surmised in Sarah a rival, for he never displayed affection for his sister, and when she was discovered blue-faced and lifeless in her crib, Judson was the only family member who evinced no sign of grief.

No one can know what precisely happened in that upstairs nursery of the Alexander plantation. All that is known are the following facts:

On the night of Sarah's death, the nanny assigned to the infant's care between the hours of ten p.m. and five a.m. received an urgent letter informing her of a family emergency two counties away. The nanny rushed to the hostelry, where the night watchman volunteered to convey her, via a coach, to her parents' homestead. As it was already three a.m., the nanny was loath to awaken her employers, and because young Sarah was sleeping soundly, the nanny believed the child would continue to rest peacefully until the wet nurse appeared for the predawn feeding.

When the nanny arrived at her parents' homestead some hours later, her mother and father were dumbfounded by their daughter's state of agitation. The letter the nanny received was proven to be a forgery, as neither her mother nor her father admitted to having authored it.

These facts are public record. And though the following information might be apocryphal, the evidence suggests it contains at least traces of veracity, despite its macabre nature.

A governess, fired abruptly after the infant's death and afterward unwilling to speak to anyone about the incident, accused Judson of killing young Sarah. The governess produced sketches Judson had made of the most unspeakable atrocities. "Drawings that would make Hieronymus Bosch shriek in fright," the governess declared. When Zacharias, red-faced, condemned the implied connection between Judson and the recently deceased Sarah, the governess then produced a sample of Judson's handwriting, which matched in every detail the counterfeit letter given to the nanny.

The governess was dismissed and lived out the rest of her days a skittish pauper, constantly afraid of Judson hunting her down and exacting revenge.

But the evidence doesn't cease there. Another servant, who died under mysterious circumstances less than a month later, revealed to a local reporter (who later redacted the story and himself disappeared) that she had seen young Judson stealing up to the nursery via the back hallway at around four a.m. The servant had marked the time because of the disquiet she had experienced at the twelve-year-old's furtiveness, but had refrained from pursuing Judson because she assumed the nanny was still watching over Sarah.

This brings me to the reason I am so frightened today.

Yes, dear journal, as I sit here by the riverside in the calm light of midmorning, I confess that I am overcome with dread at the prospect of reentering the Alexander House.

It was just after six a.m. when I was awakened by a noise so clear yet so illogical that I was at first convinced I still dreamt. But as I opened my eyes and patted my face to reassure myself I was truly conscious, I understood that what I was hearing was no fancy, that it was in fact emanating from the second story of the Alexander House.

It was the shrieking of a child.

And not just any child, an infant. The baby, by my reckoning, must be no older than six months, for its squalls were too incoherent for a toddler, yet too powerful to be produced by a newborn. I lay in bed, wide-eyed, unwilling to credit what I was hearing. But hearing it I was, and eventually (I'll not admit how long it took me to peel back the sweaty bedclothes and set foot on solid ground) I tottered my way to the stairs. Even as I began the climb, I cursed myself for neglecting my birch cane, not only because it steadied me, but because some childish region in my brain had long ago imbued the cane with talismanic powers. It had been passed down by better men than me, men whose belief in God had fortified them against whatever evil dwelt in the earthly realm. That I was not also a believer was immaterial. Because their belief was so unwavering, their faith represented something unbreakable, and that stalwart faith, I suspected, had somehow communicated itself to the cane, the secret weapon I kept as a boon companion.

But now I moved without it. The journey up the staircase was the longest thirty seconds of my life. For as I climbed each successive step, so too did the urgency in the child's voice grow. When I reached the second-story landing, the brays of the infant were well-nigh deafening. That there could be no child in the house at this or any hour did not occur to me then. So compelled was I to bring solace to that squalling newborn that I eschewed logic for passion. I was reaching *for the doorknob of the western bedroom (a door I could not remember closing!) when I heard the quality of the child's screams change.*

Note that I didn't say the screams ceased; I said they changed. Oh, how I wish they'd ceased instead! Dear God, were that the case I might even now be sitting in the Alexander House working on my book rather than trembling out here in the shade of an elm tree, my body shivering with a terror-spawned ague despite the torrid heat of the day.

When my fingers closed on the doorknob, the child's cries grew muffled, not as though the child's agitation had been mollified, but rather because someone or something had covered the child's mouth.

I, too, covered my mouth, and though I know I should have entered the accursed bedroom, I was too horrorstruck to do aught but hold my breath and hope the child would be permitted to breathe freely again.

At length, the screams grew choked, ragged.

Within moments, they stopped.

I stood there quaking, unable to either enter the bedroom or escape down the staircase.

Then…though I wish I could forget the entire affair…then, with God as my witness, the doorknob began to turn. Whoever had smothered the child was coming now for me.

This was sufficient to throw me into a paroxysm of terror. I thundered down the stairs, and since that moment, nearly three hours past, I have not reentered the Alexander House. Only because I had left my notebook and pencil on the porch the day before have I been able to record here the phantasmagorical happenings within the house looming behind me.

I know it is a risk to give voice to these musings, for if something happens to me, this journal will prove my undoing. Yet the Catholics, despite the flawed basis of their dogma, do understand the cathartic quality of confession. Sharing these thoughts with you, dear journal, has provided a measure of solace. I shall continue to inscribe my experiences no matter how irrational they might sound, and in so doing I will palliate my nerves sufficiently to disprove the legends surrounding this property and its erstwhile owner, Judson Alexander.

I will reenter the house soon, but before I do, I will admit to one alteration in my beliefs. Prior to studying the account of Judson Alexander, I believed in the corruptive influence of money and the impure taint of power. Now, I must confess a newfound belief in evil. Not, as some would have it, as a floating chimera or a creature with horns and a pitchfork, but rather as an innate hunger for inflicting suffering.

Judson Alexander, I believe, was a manifestation of darkest evil.

Was, I say, such a manifestation. Not is.

It will take more than a figure in a window and the cry of a child to persuade me otherwise.

David closed the book, extricated his legs from the covers, and sat on the edge of the bed.

It was time to implement a more proactive approach.

Yes, he thought, pushing to his feet. Chris Gardiner and Katherine Mayr, he was sure, were conspiring against him. Chris's attitude the other day all but confirmed it. Jessica and Ralph knew far more than they'd let on, and though he didn't regard them with the same contempt he felt for Chris and his wife, he understood the folly of trusting them.

Time to formulate a plan.

Step One: Get a couple hours of sleep and rejoin the search for Ivy.

Step Two: Confront Chris and Katherine, at their Williamsburg home if necessary.

Step Three?

Step Three, he decided, was the simplest of all: Write the damned book. He needed to be more disciplined, more confident in his own abilities. Okay, so he'd underestimated the effect the Alexander House and its macabre history would have on him. He'd underestimate it no longer. He'd take measures to guard against the onset of panic. He'd make sure Chris and Katherine couldn't make sport of him again.

Good, he thought. Good. He opened the door of the master suite, went to the hallway to make sure the front and back doors were locked. Then he returned to the downstairs bathroom, shook out a quartet of Melatonin tablets – too many, he knew, but he was desperate – and downed them with a cup of water.

He returned to bed, set his phone alarm, picked up *The Last Haunting*, and continued reading for the next forty minutes. Only when he reached the Hartenstein chapters did his eyes begin to grow heavy. At around one in the morning he fell into a dreamless sleep.

Only in the deepest level of his subconscious was he aware of someone watching him through his bedroom window, or the way the figure floated twenty inches off the ground.

CHAPTER THIRTY-TWO

David jumped awake and knew immediately something was wrong. For one thing, the light in the bedroom was too bright; for another, he felt too good, too strong, to have slept only the four hours or so on which he'd planned. He fumbled for the iPhone, thumbed on the power, but the screen remained black. He leaned over, checked to make sure the charging cord was plugged into the wall, and of course it wasn't. Dammit! And now…

…now the search party would be deep into the woods.

Cursing, he flung the covers aside and hustled into the bathroom. He wanted a shower, but feeling oily and unkempt was better than failing Ivy.

He splashed water on his face and realized that's exactly how he felt – like he'd failed the girl. When or how he'd begun to feel responsible for her he didn't know, but the fact was, he believed her wellbeing was dependent on him.

He rushed into the kitchen, saw it was 8:25 – dammit – and grabbed a granola bar. He wolfed it in four bites, forced it down with a glass of water, and moved to the master suite to get dressed.

In another minute he was out of the house and hurrying through the yard, but even before he neared the Shelby property, he knew something was amiss. For one, there were no voices in the woods, no signs of a search party. For another – and he was inexpressibly glad of this – there were no boats in the river, no indications that the water was being dragged.

Yet rather than relaxing him, this struck a deeper chord of unrest in his heart. What if they'd found the body? He was reminded of an axiom his father once uttered when David was a child: an ambulance with its siren blaring was a hopeful sign; it meant its occupant was still alive.

A silent ambulance meant death.

My God, David thought. Was the silence that lay over the peninsula the equivalent of a quiet ambulance?

Jogging on legs he couldn't feel, David made it to the Shelby house and was met with a sight he didn't know how to interpret. There were only a trio of cars in the driveway, and only one belonged to a policeman.

Police*woman*, David amended, drawing nearer. It was Harkless's cruiser. The other cars were a cobalt blue Subaru Forester and a white Cadillac Escalade.

David heard voices before he rang the doorbell.

The hand that opened the door belonged to Mike Jr.

David gaped down at him, was about to ask the boy what was going on, but before he could, Sheriff Harkless stepped into view and waved him inside. Mike Jr. looked like he'd donated too much blood, frail and ashen-skinned.

"You okay?" David asked and put a hand on the child's shoulder, but when he did, Mike Jr. tensed, shot a look toward Harkless.

David let him go and moved toward Harkless, whom he now saw was in the sitting room talking to a young woman with a hank of long brown hair gathered in a ponytail, khaki pants, and a teal blouse.

The other occupant could only be Honey's father, the Mayor of Lancaster.

The moment he saw David, his expression changed. The mayor's grin, if it could be called that, looked more like a rictus of pain. His eyes gleamed.

"Ah," the mayor said, "if it isn't the king of the sleepovers!"

Harkless sighed, said, "David Caine, meet Jim Warner."

They didn't shake hands. With an effort, David broke the stare-down with the mayor and asked Harkless, "Any news?"

"You haven't heard?"

He swallowed, terrified of asking. If something had happened to Ivy....

Maybe Harkless read this in his face because she nodded down the hallway. "Go see for yourself."

As David moved toward the family room, he could hear Honey Shelby singing a soft, surprisingly melodic lullaby, saw Michael Shelby on the sofa reaching out to stroke someone's hair.

Ivy's, he saw. The child was lying in her mother's arms, seemingly safe, her eyes closed but her breathing steady.

David looked from mother to child. "Is she…?"

"Healthy?" Honey asked. "She's cozy and warm, not that it's any of your business."

David took a step forward.

"You touch her," Shelby said, "and we tell Harkless what happened the night you kept our kids at your house."

David stared at him blankly. The words refused to register. *Kept our kids*, he thought. *Kept our kids....*

"David?" Harkless called.

David turned and saw her waiting halfway down the hallway. She waved him over.

He looked at Ivy, saw her eyes were open.

He smiled. "It's good to see you safe. I was—"

"Please leave," Ivy said.

David stared at the girl. Her eyes were utterly bereft of warmth.

"Don't come near me," Ivy said, her expression fierce.

David's lips worked, but he couldn't speak.

"You heard her," Honey said, smiling a little. "Get your ass out."

Numbly, he left the room and joined Harkless. His mouth had filled with a noxious taste. "Sheriff, there's something wrong."

"Agreed," she said. "This all stinks, but I need time to think about it."

For the first time he realized how shaken Harkless was. He'd never seen her look like that, and in a way, this was as disturbing as the change in Ivy.

He knew he should be celebrating. The girl was safe. A few minutes ago he'd been sick with worry. Now she was in her mother's arms.

"You with me?" Harkless asked.

"Sorry," he said. "I don't get it. Where was she last night?"

"Your cellar."

"*What?*"

"She told us..." Harkless's lips thinned, "...some story this morning about her folks quarreling and not wanting to be in the house. Claims she hid in your cellar most of the day and all last night."

"That's not possible," he said, but even as he spoke the words he knew it *was* possible.

"Ivy claims she went in your house when you and Jessica were here last night. Says she was hungry and went in there to raid your refrigerator. She needed a snack."

"That's crazy."

"She heard voices approaching and had to get out in a hurry. That's why she left the front door hanging open."

And as insane as it sounded, it jibed with what had happened. The question was, why had she hidden in the cellar in the first place?

"Hey, David?" Harkless said, lowering her voice. "There're some things you need to know. Mr. Fancy Pants over there—" a nod at Honey's father, "—he and his daughter seem to have concocted a really… damning story about you. I know it's not true, but you need to know."

David's heartbeat was a hollow thump. When he glanced at the mayor, he realized the man was grinning at him the way a nasty child grins at an insect he's trapped.

"There's something else," Harkless said. "Something about Jessica."

Before David could respond, the mayor was striding over to him. David moved forward, preferring to meet him head-on.

Though older, the man was rangy and appeared to be in good physical shape. David put him in his late sixties, with a broad, tanned face and gleaming white teeth. He resembled a television evangelist, David decided, including the hypocrisy.

"You make it a habit," the mayor drawled, "to upset families every time you write one of your screeds?"

The last word scarcely registered. "What do you mean, 'upset families'?"

"Why, this one," the mayor answered, his long arms out to encompass the Shelby home. "My Honey and her family were perfectly content before you started smuggling our children into your bed."

David glanced at Harkless, who was watching the mayor sourly.

David said, "They were with me because your daughter and son-in-law are substance abusers. Why don't you ask Honey—"

"Defamation of character," the mayor cut in, "is a grave matter. These allegations are unfounded and sickening. What evidence do you have?"

David noticed the woman, who was evidently from Child Protective Services, looking on with interest.

Harkless stepped closer. "Both times I've stopped by – including the night of Ivy's disappearance – Mr. and Mrs. Shelby were under the influence of alcohol, at the very least."

"In their own home," the mayor said.

The woman from CPS said, "A parent needs to be a good role model no matter where she is." Her voice was quiet and controlled, but David sensed a strength there and experienced a moment's hope that this might turn out sanely.

Then the mayor spoke again and his hope vanished.

"My lawyers are preparing charges, Tina," he said to the CPS woman. "The sheriff acted unconscionably last night when she wrested Mike Jr. from the house when he needed his parents most." The sharkish smile. "And that's not even mentioning the unlawful confinement or the police brutality. *Bungee cords*, Georgia?"

"It's Sheriff Harkless," she said in a low voice, "and I'm not one of your appointees." She tapped the star on her chest. "I was elected, and I'll be re-elected next cycle."

"I doubt that," he said. "Not when the facts of this sordid affair are made public."

"You have no proof of any unlawful confinement," David said.

The mayor smiled. "Just as you have no proof of any wrongdoing on my daughter's part. It's hearsay, Mr. Caine. Unsubstantiated and uncorroborated by anyone save Sheriff Harkless."

David gritted his teeth.

"And that's not even getting into the…*disturbing* details Ivy has shared with us since returning," the mayor said. "If I were you, I'd consider legal representation, Mr. Caine."

"What are you—"

"Don't tell him anything, David," Harkless said, taking his arm and leading him past the mayor.

"She's right, Mr. Caine," the mayor said as David passed. For a moment they were close enough for David to smell the mayor's breath, and though the dominant scent was spearmint, beneath that he detected an undercurrent of halitosis, rank and unkillable. "Our granddaughter has provided ample ammunition for your prosecution."

David stopped, shrugged Harkless off. "What the hell are you implying?"

The mayor looked at him in mock surprise, more like a televangelist than ever. "All sorts of interesting facts have come to light this morning. How you sowed unrest in this home. How your overtures toward my daughter have caused a rift between her and her husband."

"Your daughter is a sex-crazed psycho—"

"David," Harkless said.

"—who broke into my house and tried to force herself on me."

Harkless took him by the biceps. "*David.*"

"She's a pitiful excuse for a human being, much less a fit mother."

"You pathetic, conniving little *shit*," the mayor growled.

"Let's go," Harkless said, dragging David away.

"Go to hell," David snapped, "you fucking child molester."

The mayor froze, the televangelist gone, in its place something scarlet and slithery, an ancient reptile with a thirst for blood. "How...*dare* you say such a thing? Do you have any idea who I am?"

"We know," the woman from CPS said. "Unfortunately."

"You're out of a job," the mayor said, poking a forefinger at her. "By the end of the day, mark my words." He turned to David. "And you...I will *scourge* you."

"That sounded like a physical threat," Harkless said. "I need to take you in?"

"You won't take me anywhere, Georgia. Your career is over."

Harkless's expression didn't change. "You're only one vote, Jim."

The mayor turned to David and jabbed the air with a forefinger. "You'll pay dearly. You put my granddaughter in peril. You nearly had my grandson handed over to *strangers*. I promise you, Mr. Caine. There'll be an accounting for what you've done."

David started to answer, but Harkless jerked his arm so hard he nearly stumbled. She was short, but she was a good deal stronger than she looked. They went out to the lawn, the CPS woman following Harkless and looking glum.

"We're screwed," the CPS woman muttered.

"Nobody's screwed, Tina," Harkless said. "Least of all you."

"Would one of you...." David started, dragged a hand through his hair. "Just what the hell happened with Ivy?"

Harkless shrugged. "She evidently let herself into her house this morning some time between three and five a.m., so that by the time we arrived to start our search, her folks were awake and in full attack mode."

"What could they possibly say?"

"That Ivy wants her family like it used to be," Harkless said, looking like she'd smelled something awful.

"This came from Honey and Michael?" David asked.

"It came from Ivy," Tina said. "That's why it's so troubling. I've been out here half a dozen times over the last year and a half, and it's like pulling teeth getting that girl to say anything. But…it's like she aged ten years overnight."

David looked at Harkless, who nodded grimly. "She said *you* were the problem, David."

"*What?*"

"Claimed you brought all the sorrow – she used that word – to the peninsula. Said once you left, it would all be better."

David searched Harkless's face. "You heard her say this."

Harkless dropped her gaze. It was answer enough.

Tina sighed, started back to her car. "I gotta get some work done. This is a nightmare."

She started her car, reversed around the mayor's Escalade, and trundled into the forest.

David watched after her. "I'm sorry, Sheriff, but this doesn't make a damned bit of sense."

"You're right. It doesn't."

"Why is Mike Jr. here? I thought he was—"

"Ivy changed everything," Harkless said. "The stuff she told us this morning, plus the entrance of Mr. Smug Politician in there, it put us in a bad position."

"What did Ivy say?"

"That her mom and dad drank sometimes but they were good people. That they were only squabbling because you were flirting with her mom."

"How the hell could she say that? Aside from all of it being untrue, she's *four*, for Christ's sakes. How would she even know what flirting is?"

"Tina said it right," Harkless said. "It's like Ivy aged ten years in one night."

The rage was bleeding out of him, in its place a desolation that was far worse. He shook his head. "I can't accept this. The kid I know, she'd never say those things."

Harkless regarded the sky, which showed some incipient sun. "One thing I've learned in this job…people can surprise you. Sometimes in good ways, more often in bad."

"But Ivy…."

"I know, David. I know."

Head down, he took a few steps toward the path, but Harkless called out to him. "About Jessica."

He turned, regarded her wearily.

"You got her wrong," Harkless said. "She was here this morning. For the search. Said you'd told her off last night."

"If she would've been honest from the start, we never would have—"

"You wanna find enemies, you're looking in the wrong place. Jessica's good people. Remember, you sought her out, not the other way around."

With that, Harkless moved toward her cruiser. David headed toward the path, thinking not of Jessica, but of what Harkless said about looking in the wrong place for enemies. He was nearing the Alexander House when the thought clarified:

Chris and Katherine.

He took a shower, ate breakfast, and within fifteen minutes was on the road to Williamsburg.

CHAPTER THIRTY-THREE

In a little over an hour, he found himself in an upscale neighborhood. Not gated, but otherwise everything he'd expect from a couple with money to spare and no children to spend it on.

David parked, rang the bell, and waited. He was opening his mouth to lay into his so-called friend when a woman he'd never seen before answered.

"Hello," she said, her face and voice pleasant. She was sixtyish, with curly peroxided hair and a lot of eye shadow.

David put on what he hoped was a disarming smile. "I'm an old friend of Chris's. We went to school together. I was hoping I could talk to him."

Evidently deciding David wasn't a threat, she smiled an apology. "They're in the Colonial District having brunch." She gestured over her shoulder. "You're welcome to wait. They should be back within an hour or two."

He started down the steps. "That's okay. I'll surprise them there." He paused. "You are…?"

A smile. "I clean for them once a week."

"Ah," he said, and thanked her for her time.

Ten minutes brought him to colonial Williamsburg. While at William & Mary, he, Anna, and Chris had spent a great many evenings here eating in the restaurants, strolling down the brick streets, and buying books from Barnes & Noble. Unless Chris had changed completely, David had a good idea where he'd be.

David passed under a poplar tree and stepped onto the porch of the Dog Street Pub, a place they'd once frequented when they had the money. From the looks of Chris's waistline, his old friend was eating plenty these days.

David was greeted by a skinny guy in his mid-twenties. "Dining alone?" the guy asked.

"Meeting friends," David said and moved past.

Chris and Katherine were about halfway in at a window table.

David was fifteen feet away when Chris saw him, paled, and looked around as if searching for a place to flee. David snagged a chair from a vacant table and sat down between Chris and his wife.

Katherine smiled. "David! So happy to see you."

He ignored her, said to Chris, "How did you do it?"

Chris opened his mouth, shut it.

"Do what, David?" Katherine asked, unruffled. The woman had the poise of a veteran news anchor.

"I can't imagine you'd have the guts to pull it off," David said, his eyes never leaving Chris's reddening face. "So you must've hired people."

Katherine's voice was rapturous. "Sounds to me like Mr. Caine has experienced the wonders of the Alexander House."

"If you mean I've seen weird things," David said, "you're right. But that doesn't mean I believe in ghosts."

"The spirits need no validation from you, David."

"You need to leave," Chris said.

David turned back to his friend, whose short-sleeved polo was pitting out badly. "I'm sorry about Anna," David said. "But you're a bastard for being complicit in this."

"Tell us what you saw," Katherine said, leaning forward with her chin on her fists.

David glanced at her. "How does it feel to have a husband who's in love with a memory?"

The occasional Katherine – the freezing one – surfaced. "You have absolutely no business talking about that."

David took in her hissing sibilants, her fierce gaze. "You hate me because I immortalized your husband's lovesickness."

"He is *not*—"

"It's an exorcism," David said to her. "You knew Anna died in that house, and you hate her for it. Now if you can make money from it, exploit Anna and the rest of the house's history, you can cheapen her memory."

"She's *dead* because of you," Chris said, pounding the table. The silverware jumped, and Katherine jerked backward, her shoulder brushing a curtain.

David scooted his chair nearer to Chris, so close their legs were touching. David grasped him by the shoulders. Chris tried to pull away, but David pinned him effortlessly in place.

"I'm going to say this one time, old friend, and you better listen. Not a day has gone by in the last twenty-two years that I haven't regretted leaving the way I did. If I'd known what would happen—"

"You *did* know!" Chris shouted, causing several people to turn. "You knew, and you did it anyway!"

David took a steadying breath. "Maybe I suspected what Anna would do. That hurts worse than anything." When Chris started to speak, David cut him off. "I deserve that pain. I deserve the knowledge that a…wonderful person would still be alive if not for me. You don't think I know that? You don't think I've begged for the chance to take it all back?"

Katherine's voice was haughty. "You don't believe in the supernatural."

He ignored her, gave Chris's shoulders a squeeze. "I've made mistakes, I've been a bad person at times. But I'm not the monster you're making me out to be. And I sure as hell don't deserve the shit you've been pulling."

Chris's eyes twitched to something on David's right. David looked up and saw the greeter standing there, the young guy's face tight. "Do I need to call security?"

"Do what you want," David said. He nodded at Chris, gave his shoulders a final squeeze, and got to his feet.

Reminded of David's size, the greeter took a step back.

David said to Chris, "You need to stop living in the past." He glanced down at Katherine. "And I'll tell you something, because I know you've been wondering."

She showed her teeth. "This ought to be funny."

"Anna Spalding was a hundred times the woman you'll ever be. I don't blame Chris for being obsessed with her. Or for ignoring you."

He left Katherine openmouthed behind him.

★   ★   ★

He took a detour through a fast-food drive-thru and made it to Jessica's house by one o'clock. He was sure she was gone, but he rolled up the drive anyway and got out expecting to hear Sebastian woofing at him from inside the yellow ranch.

He did hear Sebastian barking, but the dog's voice, which sounded more like a wheezy cough, seemed to originate from the backyard. David moved through the side yard and discovered Jessica inspecting a canvas on an easel, a paintbrush in her hand and the midday sunlight revealing hints of scarlet in her hair he'd never noticed before. She wore a droopy gray University of Virginia tank top with a black sports bra showing at the sides and a snug pair of black capri pants.

Sebastian ceased barking when he saw David.

"Can I talk to you without getting shot?" David asked.

She didn't look up from the canvas. "I have the sheriff on speed dial."

He went over, scratched Sebastian's head.

"You were awfully cold last night," she said.

"You punched me in the face."

"You deserve worse."

Sebastian allowed David to scratch him, but the dog kept his eyes on Jessica, as if awaiting instruction.

She studied her painting, which David could not see from where he stood. "Was that how you treated my sister?"

David lowered his eyes, the ache in him instantaneous. "I...I shouldn't have—"

"Why don't you tell me why you're here?" she said, and now she made no pretense about being absorbed in her painting. She was watching him with a rawness that was so like her sister's that David could scarcely meet her gaze.

He said, "I'm sorry for everything."

She glowered at him. Sebastian nudged his hand to recommence the petting.

"I'm sorry for lumping you in with Chris and Katherine," he said.

Jessica's eyes narrowed. "You still believe it's a hoax?"

"Has to be," he said. "I confronted them today and they acted guilty as hell."

"Katherine is intolerable," Jessica said, returning to her painting. "Chris is...."

"Ineffectual?"

"He's that," she agreed, "but there's more to it. He's desperate.

Cowardly. That's a dangerous combination."

David took a step closer. "How'd you meet them?"

"I remembered Chris from my sister's funeral. I met Katherine recently. They wanted me in on the ghost tour. Figured I'd provide a juicy backstory. They came by one afternoon and—damn." She made a face, went over to the little café table, retrieved a plain white sheet of paper, and began to dab at the canvas. "Got distracted," she murmured. "They even offered me a fee – a pittance – to exploit my sister."

"You tell them to get lost?"

"With a couple profanities," she agreed. "Chris looked like a puffer fish. I thought he'd explode with embarrassment. But Katherine, it was almost as if she enjoyed it. I must remind her of my sister." Jessica paused, squinting. Then she reached out, gently pressed a corner of the white paper to the canvas.

"Hey, Jessica?"

"Mm."

"I'm a horrible person."

She became motionless before the canvas. "I'm listening."

"It doesn't matter that I justify my behavior according to some code. Not if the rest of the world lives by a different...better set of rules."

"People prey on each other every day. Cheat on each other. Abuse one another. Why do you think I got divorced?"

That stopped him. "I didn't know you were married."

"You didn't show any interest in my past. We were too busy talking about you."

He groaned softly. "You're right. I'm a selfish bastard."

"Maybe you are," she said, returning to her canvas, "but at least you're aware of it. That's a start."

"You don't give in much, do you?"

"Never," she said, smiling.

He scratched behind Sebastian's ears. One of the dog's hind legs began to hammer the patio. "I suppose it's too late to start over. You knowing what a bad person I am."

"Maybe that was the problem."

"Huh?"

"Not knowing the truth about each other. I knew who you were right away. The ghouls – Chris and Katherine?"

He nodded.

"They mentioned bringing you here. That was their big play. They'd use you to drum up publicity for the house. Then they'd start the tours and include all the salacious details about my sister."

"Did they talk about trying to scare me? Hiring actors to play the ghosts?"

Jessica gave him a long, calculating look. "Come here."

David stepped over to stand beside her.

And felt his legs liquefy.

The canvas depicted the ghostly woman he'd seen his first night at the house. The scene was bathed in deep blue night; the moon cast a snowy luminescence over the river and the figure floating above it. Her bare toes not quite skimming the water's surface, the woman's creamy white dress seemed to undulate before David's eyes. The arms were spread in supplication. There could be no doubt the face was Anna's.

"How many times have you seen her?" Jessica asked.

David found his voice. "Once."

"She'll come again."

"I take it you've seen…."

"Anna," she finished.

David swallowed.

"I bought this house five years ago," she said, "and I've seen her at least once a month since then."

"My God."

"Ready to believe?"

He stared into the depthless eyes, the incalculable pain and yearning captured in Jessica's brushstrokes. "I guess I have to."

"That's not good enough."

He couldn't behold the painting any longer. He turned away, gazed sightlessly toward the forest.

"I can't…." he began.

"Look at me, David."

Grudgingly, he did.

"If you don't have the strength to admit what's right in front of you, the rest is pointless. We can't go on unless you can be honest with yourself."

He sighed. "Okay."

"No," she said. She nested the brush in the slim trench beneath the canvas, wiped a hand on her hip. He saw a tiny comma of magenta paint smeared on her black capri pants.

She moved closer. Because she was barefoot, she wasn't as tall as he remembered, but despite this, she'd never appeared more powerful. She gripped his hands. "You have to say the words."

No point in pretending he didn't understand. "I saw the woman in this painting the first night I was here."

She gave his hands a tug. "That's not enough. You have to admit you believe."

He took a breath, let it out. "I believe."

Her eyes roved over his face for several seconds. She smiled, her dimples reappearing. "I'm gonna show you something that'll scare the hell out of you."

★   ★   ★

Orderly and smelling of bay leaves, the interior of Jessica's house was predominantly gray and ivory, with hints of yellow and an occasional splash of blue. The living room received a healthy dose of daylight from a large picture window. There were a couch and a loveseat, both yellow, which popped on the gray background. The gray walls weren't dreary, but instead sophisticated, like something from a magazine.

"What do you call this style," he asked, "shabby chic?"

She chuckled. "Mid-Century Modern. Come on."

He followed her down a hallway to the last door on the right. Jessica's bedroom.

Like the living room, this one featured a broad picture window overlooking the backyard. The bed was made, the comforter gray and yellow and ivory. He remarked that she favored those colors.

She lowered her nose. "It's not yellow; it's chartreuse. And yes, I find those colors attractive."

He looked around. "You do all your painting outside?"

"When the weather's nice. The other bedrooms...one is my art room, the other's my library."

A flurry of movement and a loud thump drew his attention.

"Sebastian," she explained, going over to the dog. "He still thinks he can jump up onto the bed." She hoisted Sebastian onto the comforter, where he immediately turned to David, apparently wanting him to be impressed that he had achieved such a height, even if it had been accomplished with help.

David glanced at Jessica, realized she was looking at him closely. "I say something wrong?"

She folded her arms. "I'm just trying to decide how I feel about you being in my bedroom."

He didn't trust himself to answer.

"Am I betraying Anna?" she asked. "Or would she understand?"

David waited.

Apparently deciding something, Jessica went to her nightstand and opened a drawer. For a crazy instant he was afraid she was going to pull out a gun and shoot him, but then he saw the faded green book, and his alarm melted into bemusement.

"No one knows I have this," she said, "and if you tell anybody…or try to steal it…."

David came closer. "Why would I— Hold on, that isn't—"

"John Weir's diary," she said.

CHAPTER THIRTY-FOUR

"*You're* the one who purchased it?"

"The owner was sympathetic to my plight." She pulled the diary away. "Don't look at me like that. I didn't sleep with him or anything."

"You wouldn't have to," he said. "Just being you is persuasion enough."

She made a scoffing sound. "I'm not some temptress, Davey."

"Can I see it?"

She started to hand it over but hesitated. "Your eyes are shining like Gollum's."

"Can you blame me? That diary is the holy grail of ghost hunters and skeptics the world over."

She patted the comforter beside her. He sat and she handed him the diary.

It was lighter than he expected and well-preserved. Roughly the dimensions of a mass-market paperback, he estimated it to be a hundred and fifty pages, though they were unnumbered. He noted without surprise that the last twenty pages or so were blank. Weir had not, however, ceased writing in mid-sentence or left some jagged scrawl at the end as if he'd been dragged away screaming to some hellish fate.

"Incredible," he murmured.

"Do me a favor?" she said, watching him closely.

He riffled through the pages, spellbound. "What?"

"Look at a passage for me."

"I'd like to read the whole damned thing." Though it pained him, he allowed her to take it back.

"You will," she said, "as long as you're good."

She flipped through the diary and paused halfway through. She ran a forefinger over a page, turned it over, scoured the text again. Then she gave him the diary, and with a finger still on the page, said, "Here."

David read....

When Lula returned to her family's farm, jubilation ensued. The only daughter in a family of boys, Lula's parents showered her with affection and gifts. Her brothers, who had previously displayed only the nominal warmth accorded by boys to their sisters, became more protective and even ceased teasing the child. For a time, all was felicitous in the Anderson homestead. Their only daughter and sister had returned. Life was good.

At some point, however, the dynamic at the Anderson farm altered. Despite her young age – Lula was seven at the time of her disappearance – she soon exerted a more than natural influence over her family's daily life. If she wanted her father to take her into Lancaster, he abandoned his current project and obliged her. If Lula demanded a certain dish be prepared for dinner, her mother acquiesced, no matter how inconvenient the request was. Her brothers, likewise, lived in superstitious fear of incurring their baby sister's ire. So intent on doing her bidding were the boys that they took to vying with one another to win Lula's favor.

Soon came the day Lula instructed her brothers to harm a schoolyard rival who had once mocked Lula's hair.

David paused, glanced at Jessica. "Lula was abducted and came back changed."

When Jessica didn't answer, he said, "You think this relates to Ivy."

"Identical scenarios."

"Ivy wasn't abducted."

She gave him a look.

"Well, she wasn't," he persisted. "According to Honey's dad—"

"He's rotten and you know it. Why would you take his word for it?"

"But Ivy said—"

"All we know is she disappeared and showed up again. There are a hundred possibilities."

He glanced at the book. "Jessica…."

"Sheriff Harkless told me about the accusations," she said.

Hell, he thought. He'd somehow managed to not think about the heinous things the mayor had said.

Jessica turned on the bed, folded a leg so she could face him. "Do you believe Ivy – the real Ivy – would say those things about you?"

When he didn't answer, she reached down, flipped the page, tapped a paragraph. "It says here that Lula Anderson was a sweet, unassuming little girl before she was taken. But afterward she was like a…a vengeful goddess. She made people do bad things." Jessica paused. "She had her brothers kill someone."

David stared at her, appalled. "The bully on the playground?"

Jessica shook her head. "Lula's teacher."

His flesh gathering into tight nodes, he turned back to the book.

But Jessica lifted it out of his hands, placed it on the nightstand. "I'll let you read it on a couple conditions."

"You put conditions on everything?"

She took a steadying breath, brought her other foot onto the bed to sit cross-legged. "Our beliefs are so different, it's like we exist in alternate realities."

"I'm coming around," he said, smiling wanly.

"Not fast enough," she said. "What I need from you is open-mindedness. Actual, authentic open-mindedness, not that condescending humoring attitude you usually have."

He drew back. "*Damn.*"

"The time for politeness is over, David. Something terrible is happening, and I need you to face it."

"I'm doing my best."

She seized his hand. "You've got to do better. Frankly, your best has sucked. I need you to consider the possibility that you've been wrong about everything."

He liked the feel of her hand in his. The sensation wasn't erotic. Not exactly. But it was edifying.

"Pay attention," she said, giving his hand a squeeze.

He met her gaze.

"The painting you saw out there," she said, nodding toward the backyard. "The ghost it depicts is real. You saw her with your own eyes. If you can't accept that, we can't accomplish anything."

He chewed the inside of his mouth, sighed. "I can't see any way around it. It had to be real."

She began to shake her head, but he cut her off. "I'm agreeing with you, okay? It's just difficult for someone as hardheaded as me to accept."

"But you do accept it."

He mulled it over. "I do."

She scrutinized him for a full ten seconds; then, evidently convinced by what she saw, she exhaled and withdrew her hand. He tried not to show his disappointment.

"Judson Alexander," she said, "was a monster."

"He was a violent criminal."

"You don't understand," she said. "If all you've read of him comes from *The Last Haunting*, you don't understand."

"Cramming dirt into an unconscious slave's throat?" he said. "Murdering his own baby sister?"

"Unspeakable atrocities," Jessica agreed.

"Then what—"

"The understanding I'm alluding to," she broke in, "is of the *scope* of what he did. The *longevity* of his reign." She leaned forward. "Do you realize that Judson didn't die until he was in his sixties? Have you ever considered how isolated the peninsula is?"

He grunted ruefully. "I consider it every day. I don't even get a cell signal out there."

"Judson's reign lasted more than four decades, David. His father, that wretch Zacharias, purchased the house, the peninsula, and most of the surrounding land in order to quarantine his son. The problem was, Judson wouldn't stay put. When he'd get…I don't know, hungry? He'd ride his black mare into Lancaster and people would scatter. No one ever got close enough to measure him, but some estimated he was well over six and a half feet tall, and likely closer to six eight. He was bald on top, but he had these thick black eyebrows that never whitened, even as the years progressed. The eyes themselves were coal-black."

Jessica resituated herself on the bed, drew up her knees and cupped them with her palms. "Judson would lumber down the chief thoroughfare and denigrate anyone who deigned to look at him. He'd sneer and call women raunchy names, use racial epithets, embarrass men in front of their wives and children. On one occasion a local barrister by the name of Lockett stood up to Judson. It cost him his life. The story goes that Judson insulted Lockett's wife, Lockett demanded an apology, and Judson beat him to death in the street. Some called for Judson to stand trial, but ultimately nothing came of it.

"He picked up the nickname 'Governor.' He had no job, no real position, but because of his family's importance and because people were terrified of him, he was utterly untouchable. Though he was undoubtedly insane, he was also of above average intelligence. He was well-read, eloquent even. He'd hold court in the Lancaster pubs, often treating the patrons to drinks. In the next breath, he'd humiliate or physically abuse one of them. The town lived in fear."

Jessica's phone rang. A landline.

"I'll let the machine get it," she said. "Anyway, the disappearances started some time later, after Judson had lived on the peninsula for a year or two. The victims were families who lived near his territory, but he was never investigated. At least not seriously. And here's one of the most important parts: when it was an adult who went missing, he or she was never seen again." She leaned forward. "But when it was a child, the disappearance was almost always short-term. The boys and girls came back, but they came back changed."

"Oh man."

"Oh man is right. The children, even the ones who'd been kindhearted before, became cruel. Ruthless. Sadistic, in some cases. Again, no one confronted Judson about it. The authorities, such as they were, had seen what happened to those who messed with the Alexander family, and they weren't about to put themselves in Zacharias's crosshairs."

"Or Judson's."

"Exactly. By the time Judson had resided on the peninsula for five or six years, everyone was cowering in terror, but no one was willing to do anything about it. A few families moved, but you know what a difficulty that is. Even now, it's hard to uproot a family. Think about how harrowing it must have been back then."

David scowled. "Still hard to believe no one stood up to him."

"A few did." She tapped the diary. "Weir gives a few accounts of citizens trying to take back their self-respect. In one case, a new constable tried to haul Judson in for questioning, but his horse was later found roaming free across a tobacco field."

"No one found the constable?"

She shook her head. "Some months later, a group of five stout men journeyed to the peninsula. It appears that Judson hunted them one by one and left their eviscerated bodies for the animals. Then someone got a ghastly idea. It was two-fold, a means of containing Judson."

"Appeasing him."

"People can be cowards," she said. "Especially when they're protecting their families."

"What was the solution?"

"The first part was building a house for one of Zacharias's most trusted employees. You remember Mr. Jennings?"

"The supervisor."

She nodded. "He was advancing in years by that time, but Zacharias trusted him, and more importantly, Zacharias knew he wouldn't harm Judson."

"Did Judson kill Jennings?"

Her face went grim. "No, but he raped Jennings's granddaughter."

"Christ."

"Jennings did nothing. Likely pretended it was consensual. Pretty soon, the girl, who couldn't have been more than fourteen, was Judson's personal plaything. Whenever he got the urge, he'd go over and…."

"Oh, man. Don't tell me…the Shelby house?"

"On that plot of land," Jessica agreed. "When Honey inherited the lot, she and her husband – on Daddy's coin, I'm sure – built a nice new home. They're situated where Jennings and his family lived. If you could call what they did living."

David blew out a disgusted breath. "That's how they dealt with Judson?"

"That was half of it. The other half was sending unsuspecting travelers down Governor's Road."

"Offering them up."

"Exactly. Whenever folks would pass through town, they were sent on a detour."

David stared at her. "The whole town was in on this."

"The whole *area*."

He started to shake his head, but she broke in, "It didn't have to be everyone. I imagine most of Lancaster kept silent. That's what people typically do, isn't it? When an injustice is happening?"

"This was more than an injustice."

Jessica nodded. "It worked, though. For a time."

"What does that mean?"

"It means—" She broke off as her landline rang again. "I better see who it is."

David watched her leave the room. He was reading a passage near the end of the diary when Jessica reentered, smiling.

"What?" he asked.

"Alicia Templeton," she said. "You must've made an impression on her."

At his quizzical look, she sat and explained, "She ordered you a bulk package of Dots and is planning to drop it off at your house."

He laughed, but Jessica's eyes had narrowed to slits. "What?" he asked.

"You're not planning on reciprocating, are you?"

"You mean, buy her some Junior Mints?"

She whacked him on the shoulder.

"Hey!" he said.

"I know what an operator you are."

"I'm not— Listen, Harkless said it herself, Alicia's half my age."

"And smart and funny and ravishing."

"You lobbying for her?"

"I'm trying to protect her."

He drew away slightly. "How do you know each other, anyway?"

Jessica sobered. "After I moved here, I started investigating what happened to Anna. I talked to Alicia's dad, since he was the only one who'd gone in or out of the house for ages." She shrugged. "Alicia and I became friends."

"Co-conspirators."

"You never answered my question."

He put his hands up. "I don't have designs on Alicia, okay? She seems terrific, but…the age difference. And I suspect if I did ask her out, her dad might shoot me."

"Or Harkless would."

David glanced out the window at the easel. "Can I see more of your work?"

Jessica bit her bottom lip. "Sure. If you don't mind nightmares."

★ ★ ★

He came through the door that Jessica had opened and stopped, awestruck. The bedroom was larger than he'd anticipated, roughly eighteen by eighteen. There were various works-in-progress leaning on easels, a desktop Mac, and a desk strewn with sketchpads and pencils.

The walls were crammed with paintings of Anna.

Only most of them weren't Anna as he'd known her, the smartass-yet-sincere young woman who'd beguiled him as a younger man and whose memory haunted him still. No, most of the paintings – some oil, some acrylic – featured a phantasmal version of Anna, sometimes achingly beautiful, at others bestial and terrifying. In the latter category her eyes were pupilless whites. The teeth were elongated: hooklike canines, jagged molars, the incisors sharpened to feral points.

In the bestial depictions, the Anna-thing was leering maniacally.

It knocked his wind out. "Shit," he whispered.

Jessica was watching him closely. "Any of these look familiar?"

Rather than answering – he didn't trust himself to – he paced over to one of the less disturbing portraits, but the closer he drew to this one, the more he regretted choosing it. Though the Anna in this oil painting was the young woman he'd known back in college, the sight of her unnerved him more than the ferocious images did. She was sitting at the base of a tree, gazing up at the artist from over her left shoulder. Her bare arm and shoulder were dappled with pools of sunlight, the rest of her shadowed by the tree. She wore a mauve baseball cap backward, her tank top the same color; her khaki shorts revealed glorious, coltish legs; she'd applied lampblack under her eyes in thick stripes. Her big brown eyes watched him with profoundest melancholy.

"It's from one of my softball games," Jessica said from beside him. "Our school colors were burgundy and gold, like Gryffindor." A small laugh. "Anna used to put that black grease under her eyes to support us."

David couldn't have looked away from the painted Anna had he wanted to. Held by that gaze, he said in a soft voice, "I never deserved her."

Jessica said nothing.

"I'm so sorry," he said. He realized with some amazement he was on the verge of tears. "She didn't.... I never should have left. You must hate me."

"Hearing you beat yourself up helps."

He frowned at her, but she shook her head, said, "I mean it. Words are just words, but...sometimes they're better than nothing."

"Wish I could give you more than that." He looked at the painting. "I wish I could give you your sister back."

"David?"

He looked down at her. She moved to stand in front of him, took his hands in hers. She leaned up on tiptoes, kissed him on the side of the mouth. Drawing away, she said, "There's something you can do."

He waited.

"Help me solve the mystery."

"We know why she took her own life."

Jessica lowered her chin. "I don't believe my sister committed suicide. I think she was murdered."

CHAPTER THIRTY-FIVE

They spent the day together, focusing on Weir's diary, his disappearance, and what bearing it might have on the events of the past week. They talked little of Anna. Jessica claimed she'd discuss her theory about her sister's death when David showed more willingness to believe.

After a lousy supper at a Mexican restaurant, they rode to the Alexander House in uneasy silence. The day had been sunny until midafternoon, but now early evening clouds had appeared, throwing the road and the surrounding woods into a basalt-colored gloom.

"You know," David said as they motored down Governor's Road, "you can't just say you believe Anna was...."

"Murdered."

"You can't announce something like that and just clam up." He turned onto the peninsula lane.

"It's hard enough to talk about, but knowing how you are about the supernatural...."

"How am I gonna grow more enlightened if you don't help me?"

The look she shot him made his balls shrink. "Don't tease me, David. Not about this."

Chastened, he returned his gaze to the rutted lane. They'd just passed Ralph's property when Jessica sat up and leaned toward the windshield. "That's Alicia's car."

David saw a white Nissan Sentra parked outside the Alexander House. "She said she was bringing me Dots, right?"

"Five hours ago," Jessica said. "Why's her car still here?"

David had no answer for that.

They pulled up next to the Sentra. Jessica climbed out and peered inside. "Keys are in the ignition."

"Maybe she locked them in by accident."

Jessica tested the door. It opened.

Seeing the look on Jessica's face, he said, "Hey, there's nothing to worry about. She probably...."

"Probably what?"

He realized he had no answer. He went up the walk and was starting to use the key when, on a whim, he tried the front knob. The door opened freely.

Jessica's voice was tight. "Did you lock it?"

"Maybe I forgot."

"*Did* you forget?"

He thought about it. "No. Not since Honey barged into my shower."

They stared into the sludgy foyer.

"Alicia would have a key, right?" he asked. "From her dad?"

"Why would he loan her the key?"

"Hell, I don't know."

He went in, called Alicia's name, but got no reply. Jessica went immediately up the stairs. To escape from the mental chill the long bedroom brought on, David checked the master suite, the den and bathroom. Empty. As were the dining room, screened-in porch, and kitchen. He returned to the entryway and nearly plowed into Jessica.

"Jesus," she said, a hand on her chest. "You scared me."

His heart was whamming too. "I should've gone up there with you."

"You're right," she said. "You should have."

"Sorry."

"You think she's somewhere outside?" she asked.

"It's possible. We can— Hold on."

"What?"

Wordlessly, he went out the front door, down the porch steps, around the front of the house to the western side. To the basement door.

Which stood ajar.

Jessica's voice was thin. "Why would she go down there?"

David shook his head faintly, stepped down the grassy incline to the door. It wasn't wide open, but the gap was large enough to accommodate Alicia. He forced it open another few inches and squeezed through.

Jessica entered behind him, asked, "Flashlight?"

He reached into his cargo shorts, took out his iPhone, and activated the flashlight. She did the same with her phone. He scanned the walls, strafed the junk heaps with silvery light. Nothing different than it had been the first time he'd been down here. He was about to say so when Jessica said, "Look, David. The floor."

He followed her gaze. Saw tiny footprints – Ivy, from last night, presumably – and beside those....

"Please tell me those are yours," Jessica said.

He shook his head, moved forward and placed his shoe in one of the prints. The print on the dank cellar floor dwarfed David's shoe easily.

"I wear thirteens," he said. "Fourteens when I want to wiggle my toes." He regarded the gigantic prints, of which there were several.

A furtive scuttling sound from the rear of the cellar. David gasped, swung his iPhone in that direction but could make out nothing save old chairs and deflated rafts.

"What if something happened to Alicia?" Jessica asked.

David opened his mouth to answer, but the sight of the footprints stopped him. The tiny ones and the giant ones. He kept looking from one to the other, some thought, inchoate yet urgent, slowly crystallizing.

Then he had it.

"Come on," he said.

He went out, mounted the steps, and hastened through the front door. He didn't give himself time to think, simply clattered up the stairs. He passed into the long bedroom and barely spared the four single beds a glance. Instead, he crossed to the trapdoor, reached up, and tugged on the rope. Some primitive region in his brain recoiled at the thought of ascending the ladder, but before he could lose his nerve, he gripped the handrail and climbed the ladder.

He realized Alicia had been here.

A canary-yellow box nested on the windowsill. Dots candy, the box open, with a blood smear on the flaps.

There were other objects up here. A globe, a throne-like chair. Stacks of books and a rope dangling from a rafter.

Jessica was calling his name from below, but David didn't answer, couldn't answer. He could only pivot slowly toward the corner of the unfinished dormer, where he spotted an antique birch cane, upside down and resting on its curved handle.

On the floor a few feet away, eyes and mouth sewn shut with black thread, was Alicia Templeton's severed head.

CHAPTER THIRTY-SIX

Their flight to Ralph's house was a dimly glimpsed nightmare. David had a foggy memory of encountering Jessica in the long bedroom, of convincing her they had to get out of the house, of her repeated questions and furrowed brow. He experienced a curious lack of sensory input as they moved down the lane. Jessica's voice came through, but it was wrapped in cotton. There was no birdsong or river noise. He couldn't smell, couldn't taste, couldn't even feel his feet. It was as though his body, besieged as it was by the horror of what he'd seen, had staged a strategic withdrawal, his essential self now holed up within some deep and protected enclave.

Ralph, thank God, was pulling in just as they staggered into his drive, and seeing his cheerful expression morph into one of confusion helped rouse David from his stupor. Jessica did the talking, but then again, Jessica didn't know what was in the third story of the Alexander House, and David wasn't yet able to articulate it. It wasn't until David called Harkless on Ralph's landline and explained the abomination he'd encountered that Jessica and Ralph learned why he was so whey-faced.

Harkless, a deputy, and two state cops showed up within ten minutes. The coroner arrived shortly after, and more official-looking men and women trickled in as evening encroached. To David's dismay, he and Jessica were brought back to the Alexander House, but were at least spared reentering. Maybe they wanted to see David's reaction as he was grilled about his activities that day. Maybe Harkless and the lead detective simply didn't feel like tramping up and down the lane each time they had a question.

The detective, whose hair was graying and receding, wore a half smile most of the time, but after the first twenty seconds of their interaction, David realized the smile conveyed nothing but suspicion.

Q: What was your relationship with the deceased?

A: I met her once at The Crawdad.

Q: Were you attracted to her?

A: Anyone would have been. She was gorgeous.

Q: Were you jealous of her boyfriend?

A: I didn't know she had a boyfriend. But if I'd have known, I'd have envied him. Even if she was too young for me.

Q: Did that make you mad? That she was too young for you?

A: It made me feel old.

Q: She rejected your overtures.

A: There *were* no overtures. Sheriff Harkless was there most of the time.

Q: What'd you talk about before Harkless showed up?

A: Tombstone pizzas? Her father being caretaker of the Alexander House.

Q: Ah, yes. The Alexander House. Why'd she show up here?

A: Didn't the message she sent Jessica explain that?

Q: About the candy.

A: Right.

Q: I'm sorry, Mr. Caine, but why the hell would a luscious, nubile girl like Alicia drive all the way out here to bring you a box of candy?

A: I don't like the way you said that.

Q: Hurt your pride, Mr. Caine?

A: It isn't that. You're talking about her looks.

Q: You found her sexy, didn't you?

A: Maybe you're projecting.

It went downhill from there. Harkless stepped in when it became apparent that David and the detective, whose name turned out to be Baldwin, despised each other.

Harkless accompanied David to the southern shore, where they stood facing the Rappahannock. In the dying light, the water carried an unnatural purple hue.

"I know you had nothing to do with this," Harkless said in a toneless voice.

David realized she'd been crying.

"Good to hear," he said.

"But it doesn't look promising. First, Ivy goes missing and turns out to have been hiding in your house..."

"When I wasn't there."

"...then Alicia is found dead in your house."

David stared at her. "It's not my house. I'm only here a month."

"Don't make any travel plans."

"I'm a suspect?"

She waved him off, sighed. "How am I gonna tell her dad?"

He looked at her. She was short to begin with, but tonight she looked even smaller than normal.

"When does the notification usually happen?"

She grunted. "An hour ago."

He regarded his sandals. He didn't want to ask it, but he had to know. "You find her body yet?"

"Hell, you're gonna bring that up now?"

"Sorry."

"No trace of it."

They turned at the sound of raised voices.

To the east of the house, where the lawn began to merge with the weed-strewn vacant lot, Ralph Hooper was shouting at Baldwin, the detective. Jessica stood between the two men, uttering calming words to Ralph, but whatever they were, they weren't working.

Harkless and David hurried over and heard Baldwin saying, "… reaction is interesting, Hooper. I only asked you—"

"—if I found the dead woman pretty," Ralph interrupted. "Uh-huh, I know what you said, and I know what you mean. Am I some kind of depraved, dirty old man is what you're really asking."

"Not at all," Baldwin said in that same maddeningly reasonable tone. "But I do find your anger interesting."

"Of course you do," Ralph barked. "You find the fact that I live alone interesting. The fact that I don't have an alibi interesting." His voice rose to a shout. "You're just interested as shit, aren't you?"

Baldwin saw Harkless and David approaching and grinned his cheerless grin. "Come on over, Sheriff. We're almost to the part where Mr. Hooper here lawyers up. That about right, Hooper?"

"You can fuck right off," Ralph growled.

"Go home, Ralph," Harkless said.

Baldwin gaped at her. "I don't think I heard you right."

"He's not gonna run, and you know it," Harkless said. She glanced at Ralph. "Are you?"

Ralph blinked at Harkless, ran a shaking hand through his white hair. "Search my house if you need to. I've got nothing to hide."

"We'll let you know," Harkless said.

Baldwin folded his arms. "Why are you protecting him, Sheriff? And why wasn't I notified when the Shelby girl went missing?"

"Another detective was closer," she said. "Guess I didn't realize how brokenhearted you'd be about the snub."

They continued bickering as Jessica led Ralph away, David following. He heard Baldwin ask, "Where are they going?", but Harkless told him to chill out, and the rest was lost as another vehicle rumbled up the lane. A red GMC Jimmy, old but well maintained.

Oh hell, David thought when he saw the driver. Alicia's dad.

By tacit agreement, the trio walked faster. David had no desire to witness Mr. Templeton's reaction to his daughter's murder.

They reached Ralph's yard and without discussing it, they ambled around the thicket so they'd be screened from the Alexander House. Once there, however, something occurred to David.

"I can't stay in that house tonight," he said.

"Georgia says forty-eight hours minimum," Jessica agreed.

David rasped a hand over his stubbly jaw. "All my stuff's there. I don't even have a toothbrush."

"I got a couple extra," Ralph said.

David glanced at him.

"They're still in the package," Ralph added, looking a little insulted.

★   ★   ★

They dropped Jessica off, and when they returned to the highway, David remembered to check his iPhone. His email was choked with messages – nothing urgent – and there were seven missed calls, three of which were from Chris and Katherine.

To hell with 'em, he decided.

It was nearly 11:00. The Alexander House, they saw before they turned into Ralph's drive, was lit up, the driveway resembling a used car lot during an end-of-summer sale.

"They're combing every inch of it," Ralph said, his truck idling in the lane.

"What time are we going over there?"

Ralph turned in his seat to face David. "Come again?"

"They'll be there until well past midnight," David said. "Maybe later." He nodded. "We'll get some sleep and head over there at four, before first light."

Ralph had drained of color. "Are you out of your goddamned mind? Of all the places on earth I least want to be, the Alexander House is number one by a sizeable margin."

"We need to set up my equipment."

Ralph squinted at him. "What equipment?"

"My ghost-hunting stuff."

"I thought you believed all that was bunk."

"Part of me still does."

"But...."

"But there comes a point when disbelief turns into stupidity."

"I'd say we got there quite a while ago."

For the first time since the gruesome discovery, David smiled.

★   ★   ★

David was consigned to the couch and dubious about his sleep prospects. Ralph emerged from the bathroom with a pair of white pills and a Dixie cup of water.

"Ambien," Ralph explained.

David hesitated. "I hear this stuff makes people hallucinate. I don't want to wake up sewing your mouth shut."

Ralph winced. "Jesus. Has anyone ever told you that you have a sick sense of humor?"

"Every day," David said and knocked back the pills.

They didn't give him hallucinations, but he did have a bad dream. In it, he was making love to Jessica, which should have been delightful, but before they reached climax, Jessica's face became Anna's. When he discovered this and attempted to apologize for the way he'd treated her, he found there wasn't a body beneath him. He was addressing Anna's severed head.

He woke with a start, saw it was only 1:00 a.m., and though he tried to fall asleep again, he gave up around 3:30 and went out to the dock. From there, he could see the Alexander House, which was dark and apparently abandoned. He gave it another fifteen minutes, at which point his resolve crumbled and he went into Ralph's bedroom.

Ralph had his back to David, and David experienced a momentary fear that Ralph, too, had been decapitated. Then he heard a sharp intake of breath. Ralph jerked his head around, and stared at David in the semidark.

"What the *hell* is wrong with you?" Ralph snapped.

"It's time."

"I never said I'd go over there."

"Then I'll go alone."

"You do that." Ralph resumed his sleeping position.

"Wouldn't you like to know whether it's something supernatural over there or just a run-of-the-mill psycho?"

Ralph remained facing away from him.

"If I go and something happens to me, that detective will be over here pounding on your door."

The white head on the pillow lifted fractionally.

"Plus, if I'm at the Alexander House, you'll be here. Alone."

"So?" Ralph asked, still not turning.

"That's why you had me stay, isn't it? You wanted the company, living so close to the murder site?"

Ralph threw off the covers and sat up. "Darn it. What makes you so ruthless?"

"I'm just trying to solve the murder."

"You're trying to get rich," Ralph said, swinging his legs over the edge of the bed, his white hair poking up at crazy diagonals. "You're no better than that buddy of yours."

"Chris isn't my friend," David said. "Not anymore." He took a knee before Ralph, the older man gazing down at him in surprise. "Don't worry, I'm not going to propose."

"Let me sleep."

"Sorry. I need your help."

"For *what*? We set up that equipment and don't find anything, we're no better off and they know we trespassed on a crime scene."

"They won't know we were there."

"They always know! You've seen those shows. I'll leave a fingerprint or a lock of hair or maybe I'll piss myself. Hell, I do that every time I sneeze."

"I need someone with me."

"What the hell for?"

David opened his mouth, but no believable lie presented itself. He sighed, regarded the hard wooden floorboards. "The truth is, I'm scared."

"You're right to be," Ralph answered. "But at least you get to leave soon. I'm stuck here. I'd sell this place, but the thought of relocating makes my head throb."

"Isn't that a reason to get to the bottom of the mystery?"

"You mean risk our lives."

"If there are two of us…"

"…then two of us could die. That sounds fantastic."

"Just go with me," David persisted. "We'll only be there long enough to set up the thermal camera and the grid scope."

"The what?"

"Five minutes. Ten tops."

"That's what Alicia said."

David grabbed Ralph's pajama-clad knee, which was bony and trembling. "Isn't that reason to do this? For her?"

Ralph knocked his hand away. "You're a manipulative prick."

David sighed. "You believe certain things your whole life. Those beliefs, they dig grooves in your brain, like a record player, and the needle doesn't leave the grooves. For many years you don't see anything – even in sites that are supposedly haunted – to knock the needle out of place."

Ralph was watching him, interested.

"Then you start to see things to disabuse you of your beliefs." David laughed humorlessly. "The two sides – believers and non-believers – they're so contemptuous of each other. The non-believers, they look at the believers with scorn, like they're beneath contempt. Not only do they buy into fairy tales, we argue, but they do it knowing how illogical they are."

Ralph's mouth twisted. "Tell Alicia your logic."

David nodded. "Alicia's at the heart of this. I keep thinking about who could've done that to her, and I can't sort it out. No one had a motive."

Ralph didn't answer.

"There're the Shelbys, but I can't see either of them doing it. Michael is too…inoffensive. Honey would be strong enough, but why the hell would she hurt someone?"

"Jealousy? Alicia must've liked you to drive all the way out here."

"I just don't see it. Whoever did this is either unhinged or so full of rage that…but that doesn't work either. There was hardly any blood up there. This thing, it was done with the precision of a surgeon. The stitches in her mouth and—"

"Do we have to talk about that?"

"How do you hide all that blood? How do you—"

"Enough."

"Then you've got the outlier possibilities. Someone following her here, an angry ex-boyfriend. He kills her and frames me. Or you."

"*Hey.*"

"You've got Chris and Katherine. They want this place turned into an attraction. A gruesome murder falls right in line with that, but I can't believe they'd do such a thing."

Ralph rubbed the back of his neck. "The part I get stuck on is us stealing over there in the middle of the night and trespassing on a crime scene."

"I'm not too keen on it either."

"Then why—"

"You want me to say it, I'll say it. I'm crossing over into belief."

Ralph grunted. "Took you long enough."

"I'm not saying I believe in everything. I'm not wearing a tinfoil hat and fiddling with Ouija boards. I'm just allowing that there might be more going on here."

Ralph cocked an eyebrow. "That's mighty big of you."

"Something unnatural is happening over there, and I want proof." He gave Ralph's knee a squeeze. "Please help me."

Ralph gazed back at him for several seconds. Then he sighed. "Well, fuck."

He rose, groaning with the effort, and shuffled out of the bedroom.

A few minutes later he was dressed and walking with David toward the truck. "I'm sure as hell gonna have a way out of there if something goes wrong," he explained as he climbed behind the wheel.

They crunched down the lane without headlights. There were clouds, but what moon and stars bled through provided enough illumination to make the two hundred yards without rolling off the lane.

In the driveway, the truck idling, Ralph said, "Maybe I should wait here. That way we can leave as soon as you set up."

David just looked at him.

"Dammit," Ralph muttered and cut the engine.

They got out and peered at the third-floor dormer. The house looked more imposing than ever.

"They're just gonna take your equipment down once they find it," Ralph said. "Then you're gonna be in bigger trouble than you already are."

"We're coming back at dawn to collect it. They'll never know we were here."

Ralph didn't respond. David moved toward the house, reached the police tape strung around the porch pillars, ducked under it, and drew out his key. He unlocked the door, wrapped the knob with the belly of his shirt, and opened it. Inside, he glanced back to see if Ralph had followed

He had. The older man looked miserable, but at least he'd come.

Cool air rolled down the stairs.

Beside him, his eyes raised, Ralph asked, "You running the AC up there?"

David shook his head. "All on the same unit."

"I rescind my offer."

David reached out and put a hand on Ralph's shoulder. "I need you."

"I'm dead weight," Ralph murmured.

"Hey," David said. "I'm as scared as you are."

Ralph licked his lips but didn't speak.

David moved down the hall to the charging area, disconnected the thermal camera and grid scope and brought them back to the base of the stairs, where he found Ralph still gazing upward in dread.

"It's time," David said.

"Aw, man."

"In and out."

"Can't I wait down here?"

"Alone?"

Ralph's shoulders sagged. "Shit."

They crept up the stairs, David in the lead. Halfway up, he froze, listening. "Did you hear that?"

Ralph's voice was cracked. "Don't make it worse."

David cocked his head, listening. "It came from downstairs. My bedroom."

As if in answer, something above them creaked.

Ralph stared at the open doorway of the long bedroom. "That didn't come from downstairs."

David swallowed. "Come on."

"Let's leave," Ralph croaked.

David reached the top step. "We'll be fast."

The look of abject fear on Ralph's face brought on a pang of guilt. He hadn't taken Jessica along because, yes, Jessica meant more to him.

You're a rotten bastard, a voice in his head declared.

I'm trying to solve Alicia's murder!

And dragging a terrified septuagenarian with you.

He had no answer to that.

But Ralph was making his way up the steps, his face so plagued with terror that he looked like an engraving from some nineteenth-century ghost story: 'The old man climbs to his doom.'

David reached out, helped Ralph up the last step. He expected Ralph to smack his hand away, but he didn't seem to register David's touch. He was gazing at the doorway with wide-eyed dread.

"The tripod's already set up," David explained in a whisper. "I'll just mount the camera, position the grid scope, push record, and then we're out of here."

Ralph showed no sign of having understood.

Selfish, the voice said.

Too late now, he thought. He crossed the threshold and the cold washed over him, a punishing February cold, the kind that bypasses the skin and goes straight for the bones.

Ralph made an inarticulate sound. David paused a few feet from the tripod and looked back at his friend, who in turn was peering at the nearest single bed. David glanced that way, saw the indentation of where a body had lain, told himself the shape wasn't different than the last time he'd been here.

The floorboards creaked as Ralph tottered deeper into the room.

The clouds outside shifted, the room brightening, but rather than buoying David's spirits, the change dampened them. Much better to sneak in here than to make their presence known. Better not to rouse whatever dwelled here.

Judson.

David moved to the tripod with barely controlled panic and made to screw the thermal camera onto the mount, but his fingers trembled so violently he needed several attempts before the camera revolved smoothly on the threaded screw.

The light from the windows was absolutely pouring in now, casting the beds and the rest of the room into stark relief. David attempted to keep his eyes on the camera, but his peripheral vision betrayed him. He kept stealing sidelong looks at the pools of darkness between the beds, the spawning ground of the leering thing.

"David?" Ralph asked, causing him to jump and damn near upset the tripod.

"What?" he demanded.

"I forgot the gun."

"Never mind that."

Ralph's voice was querulous. "There's something else. I can't keep it to myself any longer."

"Not now."

"It has to be now," Ralph said. "I've seen him. He came to me the night I moved into my house."

David's guts did a somersault. "What are you talking about?"

"He made me promise…"

"Ralph."

"…made me promise to send him people every now and then."

The words scarcely registered. The air in the long bedroom was kissed with frost.

"I went by The Crawdad," Ralph said, his voice a brittle whisper. "Alicia mentioned you, and I suggested she bring you the candy."

Something rustled above them.

He glanced at Ralph, but Ralph's gaze was riveted on the trapdoor.

The groan of a floorboard. The unmistakable sound of a footstep.

"Oh my God," Ralph moaned. "I wasn't supposed to tell."

The trapdoor swung open and the ladder crashed down. David threw out his arms, upsetting the tripod, and sprawled sideways against a bed. The carved mahogany footboard thumped his rib cage, and as he lay on his side he saw a figure descending the ladder. Work boots. Jeans. Not the same as the figure of the other night, but the minutiae didn't matter, what mattered was the shotgun leveled at him, the crazed rolling eyes. David scrabbled back, cast a glance at Ralph, who looked waxen, corpselike, ravaged by terror.

"On your feet, you sick fuck!" the wielder of the shotgun bellowed.

David realized with a sense of unreality that this wasn't Judson Alexander, wasn't Chris Gardiner or some actor he'd hired to play Judson.

It was Alicia Templeton's father.

Templeton looked to be in his mid-fifties, his hair prematurely white, his face deranged, the eyes darting from David to Ralph and back again. To David the twin bores of the shotgun seemed as large as bathtub drains.

"They say killers revisit the scene of the crime," Templeton muttered. "That what you two doing? Coming back to relive my baby's murder?"

David remained paralyzed. Any response he auditioned in his brain was certain to bring about their doom. There was no give in Templeton's face, no leeway for bargaining.

This was the end.

Templeton nodded. "On your feet."

David somehow managed to stand.

Templeton motioned with the barrel of the shotgun. "Over there. Next to Ralph." A hunger permeated Templeton's features. "That's right. Two sick, twisted fucks huddled together. You two mess with my baby before you killed her? You sons of bitches touch my little girl?" His voice became a raw plea. "How could you do that? All the people in the world, you had to prey on my Alicia. She's all I had! You understand, goddamn you? She was all I…."

Templeton's expression changed. He was staring, David realized, out the southern window, and when David turned he beheld a sight that knocked his breath out, erased thought, the man holding him at gunpoint momentarily forgotten.

The woman floating outside the window could only be Anna Spalding.

The flowing white dress undulated as she hung in the air, staring in at them with unblinking white eyes. Unable to stare at the apparition for long, David shifted his gaze to Ralph, who had his back to the window. The older man's eyes rolled to the extreme corners of his vision. Then Ralph performed a slow, tottering pivot, and when he faced the figure in the window, he said in a breathless voice, "Oh my."

Ralph crumpled to the floor.

Heart thundering, David looked up at the figure, realized it was watching him.

"Make it go away," Templeton urged.

David couldn't answer, could only gaze at the apparition. He watched in terrified fascination as a pale, pellucid hand reached out and brushed the windowpane with long black nails. They grazed the pane slowly, leaving razor-thin gouges in the glass.

"*My...Jesus,*" Templeton said.

David managed to say, in a low, thick voice, "I didn't kill your daughter. I came here to find who did."

Anna hovered outside the window.

Something nudged his forearm. Templeton was kneeling beside him, reaching for Ralph. "Got to get him out of here," Templeton murmured. "He's still breathing."

David nodded. Bent to help.

Ralph's body was motionless as David grasped him under the armpits. Templeton took Ralph by the ankles, and they carried the older man toward the door. David started down the stairs, backpedaling, and beyond Templeton's shoulder he saw the window of the landing, waited for the floating wraith to appear there, the pupilless white eyes to batten on his.

He looked away before it could appear.

Soon they reached Ralph's idling truck. "You get the door," David said.

Templeton did, and with some trouble they muscled Ralph into the truck. David hustled around, got in.

David had just reached for the gearshift when Templeton seized his arm. "*Listen.*"

David heard it immediately, couldn't believe he hadn't noticed it before.

The song. A woman's mournful voice. As he and Templeton sat forward, something caught David's eye. He glanced and saw, from the western side of the house, something white materializing near the roof.

"Drive," Templeton said.

David jerked the truck into reverse, swung the back end around, and gunned it down the lane.

Neither he nor Templeton spared the wraith a backward glance.

PART FIVE
THE SPECTER

CHAPTER THIRTY-SEVEN

Ironically, without Templeton's account of the incident, Sheriff Harkless might have murdered David.

At just after six a.m., outside Ralph's room in the intensive care ward, David faced the sheriff with Templeton at their sides like a referee preparing to step in should the conflict escalate.

Harkless was ranting, "…and ignored the fact that my people will need to get back in there. I oughta arrest your dumb ass on the spot."

"I was just getting my things," he said. "I left my computer and my—"

"Don't lie to me!" Harkless shouted, drawing the attention of a passing nurse. Harkless glared at her. "And you can fuck right off."

The nurse scurried away.

Templeton said, "Hey, Sheriff…."

She shot him a look. "The only reason I'm not on you too is what happened to Alicia." She blinked, softened her tone. "I'm so sorry, Charles."

Templeton turned away.

Harkless's eyes narrowed as they latched onto David. "And you—" she jabbed him in the chest, "—do you have any idea how thoughtless it was of you to barge back in there the same night…." Harkless glanced at Templeton, lowered her voice. "And dragging Ralph up there with you? What the hell were you *thinking*?"

"I was—"

"—being a dumbass," Harkless finished. "Uh-huh. I see that. And that poor old man suffered a heart attack because of you."

"Doc said he'd be okay in a couple days," Templeton ventured.

"Sure," Harkless answered. "No harm done, huh?"

Harkless's eyes shifted to something behind David. He turned and discovered Jessica, attired in baggy gray sweatpants and a green-and-gold William & Mary T-shirt. Her hair was tied up in the kind of topknot he associated with undergrads burning the midnight oil during finals week. He recognized the familiar clenching of his guts at the sight of her and realized why.

She looked eerily like Anna.

Like the apparition in the window.

David fled from the thought.

"How is he?" Jessica asked.

"Not great," Harkless said. "But alive is better than dead, right?"

Jessica blew out a relieved breath.

Templeton frowned at Jessica. "How did you—"

"I called her," Harkless explained. She nodded at David. "For reasons I can't fathom, Jessica seems to have feelings for this dipshit."

David winced.

"I still don't know how you went from wanting to shoot this guy to helping him carry Ralph down the stairs," Harkless said to Templeton.

Templeton gave David a rueful look. "I'm not sure either. It's all so crazy."

"Crazy," David said, "is becoming the normal state of things."

Harkless squinted at him. "Do me a favor and shut up."

Jessica glanced at David, wide-eyed. He shrugged.

"You were saying?" Harkless prompted Templeton.

Templeton shook his head wearily. "I was going to shoot Mr. Caine. I really was."

"I wouldn't have blamed you," Harkless said.

Templeton sighed. "It was the Siren."

Harkless lowered her chin, her eyes widening. "Siren? As in Odysseus and an island covered with bones?"

Jessica watched Harkless fixedly. "You've heard the legend."

Harkless agitated a hand at her. "Course I've heard the legend.

I've also heard of the Loch Ness Monster and the Easter Bunny, but that doesn't mean I believe in 'em."

David glanced from one face to another. "Why haven't I—"

"A couple reasons," Harkless said. "For one, we've got a nice ghoulish legend already. Why waste time on a variation of an arcane Greek story when there's Judson Alexander to keep us entertained?"

Cool air misted over his skin. "What are you talking about?"

"Our nation is young," Harkless said, "but this country is old. Do you even know where the river got its name?"

"The Rappahannock tribe," David said with some heat. "They met Captain John Smith in 1607."

"The Rappahannocks were around a hell of a lot longer than that," Harkless said. "And when the white men came, the natives warned them to stay off the island."

David glanced at Jessica. "The island across from your house?"

"You're pretty damned slow for a professor," Harkless said.

"Men are curious creatures," Jessica said. "The Siren uses that to lure them to the island."

"Not that they need much luring," Harkless put in.

"And they're never seen again?" David said, unable to suppress a smirk.

"The story," Jessica said, "is that a Native American woman… someone hundreds of years before John Smith…this woman's husband strayed. He left her with several mouths to feed and no way of taking care of them."

David asked, "Did the other men…?"

"No. But the chieftain, who was smitten with the woman, he forbade the other members of the tribe to help her unless she'd accept him as her new master." Jessica paused. "She took her children to the island, where they lived until the winter."

"And then?" David asked.

"They starved," Harkless said.

David glanced at the sheriff, whose sour expression was leavened with what might have been pity.

"Since then," Jessica resumed, "she's haunted the island, drawing wayward men to a clearing, where she seduces them and dines on their flesh." She peered at Templeton. "You saw her?"

Templeton nodded.

"I did too," David said.

They all looked at him.

He shrugged helplessly. "No point in pretending I didn't. The problem is…"

…*the Siren looked like Anna,* he thought but didn't say. Jessica was watching him closely, but he couldn't meet her gaze.

"Well, shit," Harkless said. "No wonder poor Ralph's heart gave out. That'd put a scare into anybody."

There was a dour silence. Into it, Templeton said, "You have any idea who did this to my girl?"

"I don't," Harkless said. "Not yet. But I'll find him. Alicia was the best person I knew."

"*Is* the best person," Templeton corrected, his voice hoarse. "*Is* the best person. She's not gone. Not forever. She still lives in here." He tapped his chest. He nodded heavenward. "And up there."

No one contradicted him.

★   ★   ★

Jessica suggested David come to her house to get some sleep. It wasn't until he was driving Ralph's truck back to Ralph's house, with Jessica following, that he realized how displaced he was. He couldn't enter the Alexander House. Harkless had nearly suffered an aneurism when he'd asked her if he could go inside to gather some of his things. He had no clean clothes, no toothbrush, no anything save some books and his iPhone.

After dropping off Ralph's truck, he walked down to the Alexander House with Jessica idling in the lane behind him. It was nine a.m. and already sunny, but the sight of the many dormers and the glare of the eastern sunlight on the side of the house lent the structure a cruel, pitiless aura. David was reminded of Judson Alexander striding through Lancaster and hurling insults at everyone he met. They said that married couples began to look alike after living together for a long time.

Why not a house and its owner?

Tall, pale, ruthless, the Alexander House stood ready to unleash destruction.

David finally reached his Camry, opened the door, but hesitated, a forearm on the roof, his eyes fixed on the third-floor dormer.

The others could say all they wanted about Native American women and wayward husbands, but David knew what he had seen – twice – and he knew whom the Siren resembled. David got in, his eyes on the dormer.

He thought, Maybe the Siren looks different to everyone.

But that wasn't right either. Jessica's paintings verified the kinship between Anna and the Siren, and he was certain that if Templeton or Ralph were asked to compare the wraith with the paintings Jessica had crafted, they'd come to the same conclusion.

Something tapped on the driver's side window.

David cried out, a hand clutching his chest. He peered up at Jessica, who watched him amusedly.

He opened his door. "You have any idea how much you scared me?"

She smiled an apology. "I thought you were in a trance."

He laughed softly, rubbed an eye with the heel of his hand. "God, am I tired."

She reached down and touched his cheek. "Come on. You can have my bed for the day."

He looked at her.

"My *bed*," she clarified. "Not me."

His cheeks burned.

★　　★　　★

He was dubious about his ability to sleep, but within minutes of drawing Jessica's covers over his shoulders, he was out. Once, he opened his eyes and glimpsed Jessica crossing toward the master bathroom. She was lathered with sweat, clad only in a sports bra and spandex shorts. Dimly, he heard the sound of the shower and soon felt the subtle kiss of warm mist on his skin. He was tempted to turn and peer through the doorway, which was partially open, but decided if she wanted him to see her nude, she'd make it clear in her own time.

He drifted back to sleep.

When he awoke and checked his iPhone he was flabbergasted to discover it was late afternoon. He pushed back the covers, shambled into the bathroom, and voided his bladder. He yearned for a shower, but even more pressingly, he needed to brush his teeth. On the nightstand he discovered a menagerie of toiletries. A travel-sized tube of toothpaste, a similarly small bottle of mouthwash. Next to that a toothbrush, a razor, and a can of shaving cream.

"Incredible," he murmured.

He brushed his teeth, showered, shaved, and got his clothes on. When he came out, he was promptly beset by Sebastian, who whimpered and heaved himself against David's shins. David bent, scratched the dog's back. Sebastian flopped over and offered up his belly. David obliged him by scratching him until his legs began to kick.

"He's been whining to get into the bedroom all day," Jessica explained.

"I didn't hear him," David said, getting to his feet. Going over to where she sat on the couch, he recognized the book in her hands as one of his: *Road to Damnation: The Legend of Moody Lane*.

"Are you skimming?" he asked, sitting beside her.

"It's fine so far."

He grimaced. "*Fine?*"

"I'm thirty pages in."

He shook his head. "Fine."

"I never pegged you as a sensitive artist."

He stretched. "Thanks for letting me sleep. The thing is…I want to find Alicia's killer."

"As it happens," she said, placing the book on the ivory coffee table, "I've got our night plotted out."

"Does it involve you showering with the door open?"

She blushed. "I thought you were asleep."

"I was."

"Wait, you didn't see…."

"No, but I wish I had."

She smiled, swatted his shoulder with a backhand. "Pig."

"What's the plan?" he asked her.

"I'm taking Charlie Templeton dinner," she said, "and you're going to stay with Ralph."

"Oh." He lowered his eyes. He'd forgotten about Ralph.

For the first time since they'd seen the apparition floating in the window of the long bedroom, David remembered what Ralph had said: *He made me promise to send him people every now and then.*

Was it possible? David wondered. Could Ralph have really had something to do with Alicia's murder?

Jessica was going on. "That should take us till well after sundown. Then we cross the river."

He raised his eyebrows.

"In kayaks," she explained. "I want to know what's happening in the Shelby house. Somehow, I think that's the key."

"What makes you—"

"Remember Jennings?"

"The guy who offered up his granddaughter for Judson's gratification."

"The Shelby property has been linked to Judson from the beginning. And now there's this weirdness with Ivy…." She shook her head. "Don't you think there's a correlation?"

David considered. "There could be. But I'm not keen on getting caught again."

"Caught doing what? Kayaking? The river is state property. We're perfectly within our rights."

"Am I a bad person for being interested in you?"

She grew very still. He felt the blood rise to his cheeks, wondered if he'd overstepped a boundary, and if he had, how egregiously. It wouldn't have surprised him if she'd thrown him out. Or condemned him for what happened to Anna.

Instead, she said in a subdued voice, "Not half as bad as me."

Before he could answer, she pushed to her feet, said, "Come on. Charlie needs to eat, and Ralph needs watching over."

"Wait."

"David, I can't think about this right now."

"It's not about us."

She looked at him.

"It's about the Alexander House," he said.

Her face darkened. "What about it?"

"Maybe we should burn it down."

Unexpectedly, she favored him with a wry smile.

"What?" he demanded.

"Weir was the only one to dig up all the history, and almost no one has seen his diary. I suppose it's part of why he was killed. You know, revealing all Judson's secrets."

"Would you just—"

"The townspeople – the ones with consciences, anyway – they eventually rose up. After four decades of permitting Judson to degrade or butcher anyone he desired, a group of maybe thirty citizens formed a lynch mob. They journeyed to the peninsula and split into two groups. One branched off toward the Jennings house, the other went to Judson's. They burned the Jennings place. By that time there were several…I don't know, concubines? They were corrupted by Judson and savagely loyal to him. There was gunfire from both directions. The people living in the Jennings house barricaded themselves in."

"The villagers burned it?"

"It went up like a bonfire. It's said that the spirits of Judson's concubines still reside in the long bedroom, where he often bedded them, one after the other."

My God, David thought. The leering thing.

He shook his head, the stomach acid rising in his throat. "But why would they fight for him?"

"Why does anyone support a tyrant?" Jessica asked. "They're brainwashed. Or fearful of their master. It comes to the same thing."

David tried to stifle the chill her words brought on but made a poor job of it. "So they burned down the Jennings house, and everyone inside it died."

"Or was shot trying to escape."

"These were Lancaster's decent people?"

"I didn't say 'decent,'" she corrected. "I said they had consciences."

He grunted.

She went on. "I'm not saying they were justified, but we're talking more than forty years of horror, David. Dozens of people slaughtered or…warped by Judson. Maybe hundreds. No one knows for sure. The town kept his secrets."

"Why'd they do it then? Why when he was in his sixties?"

"Even though he was older, he wasn't really aging. He'd gone bald, but that had happened long before. I think the reason they finally went out there was that Judson seemed to be growing stronger. Feeding on his own Luciferian acts."

David studied her face. "You don't believe that."

"I do. There are too many bizarre facets of the case for me to get hung up on a man growing more virile as he aged."

He decided to let it go. "The other group," he prompted. "The one that went to Judson's...."

She took a deep drag of air. "They found Judson watching them from the third story. You know the highest dormer?"

David nodded.

"He didn't offer any resistance. He didn't have to. No matter what the mob did, they couldn't burn the house. Couldn't even get inside."

"That's crazy."

"No crazier than the rest of the story. The house...it's like a citadel. Judson's bastion. The torches they lobbed at the windows deflected off. When they attempted to set it aflame, the fire refused to spread. Like it had the ability to choke out the flames, deprive them of oxygen."

"Jessica."

"You want to read the diary? This all comes from Weir."

David looked away. "Maybe Weir was going senile. And those passages could be forged."

"You know it wasn't forged. You've seen the handwriting."

"Houses don't just become fireproof, Jessica. If they wanted in, they could get in."

"They did," she agreed. "Eventually. But it was well into the next day that the house's defenses started to break down. Maybe because Judson allowed them to."

"Come on...."

"They crept inside, their weapons ready. The house was like ice. Several members of the party refused to go up the stairs, but a few brave people did. They found Judson dangling from the third-floor rafter. He'd hanged himself."

David stared at her. Outside the window, a night bird unleashed a plangent cry.

"Providing all this is true," David said slowly, "why would Judson commit suicide? You've made him out to be some kind of colonial-era supervillain. If he had nothing to fear...."

"I think he understood he couldn't hold out forever. And maybe he believed he'd done enough to prepare for death."

David raised his eyebrows. "Prepare for death?"

"Survival is the most basic human urge. Judson had all that time out there by himself. He was a voracious reader. He was particularly interested in the occult. Who knows what secrets he discovered?"

David had nothing to say to that. He was relieved when Jessica said, "You need to check on Ralph."

Five minutes later he was in his Camry motoring toward the hospital. More than once he glanced over his shoulder to make sure there was no one in the backseat.

★ ★ ★

When David was allowed in to see Ralph, the man's appearance shocked him. David knew a heart attack could be fatal, so he figured Ralph would show some strain from last night's incident, but the figure awaiting him on the bed looked like something featured in a wake. Ralph's cheekbones protruded from a tarp of papery skin. Yesterday Ralph could've passed for a man in his early sixties. Tonight he looked like a resident in a full-service nursing home, the kind who didn't recognize his own children.

Of course, Ralph *had* no children, and it was this thought that brought on tears. They caught David off guard. He'd liked Ralph, yet he hadn't realized until now just how much. Despite Ralph's terrible revelation – *he made me promise to send him people every now and then* – and David's anger at him, a part of David couldn't help feeling sorry for the old man. Ralph was utterly alone in the world, his only possessions a house, a beat-up truck, and a few fishing poles. Oh, and a radio for Red Sox games.

The thought filled David with a horrible desolation.

Was this, he wondered, where he was heading? He had friends, sure, but they were his age or older, which meant they'd either die off before him or be in the same physical state when he got old. He had no kids, and as an only child, there were no nieces or nephews.

He was completely alone.

It was a grim thought.

The nurse informed David his time was up. He took a seat in the waiting room, glanced about furtively, and when he was satisfied no one was watching, withdrew John Weir's diary from the pocket of his cargo shorts.

He drew in a deep breath, riffled through the diary, and selected a passage twenty pages from the end:

Tonight I took a walk through Lancaster's business district, and as I strode down those cobbled streets, I fancied I heard Judson Alexander's laughter drifting out of a local pub. Although I didn't peek inside, I felt Judson's presence, despite his death many years ago.

And in the cool October breeze, I began to contemplate my own beliefs. Before the dire events of the past month, I believed spirits and demons were matters of jest and inimical to science. Yet how could a man who has witnessed what I have witnessed doubt that the Alexander House is plagued by something unnatural?

The lights overhead gave a brief flicker. A nurse down the hallway muttered something, but David couldn't make out what. He continued reading.

Nevertheless, I now believe that Judson Alexander's reach is not bound by the house in which he wrought such hellish deeds, nor even to the peninsula, which served as his chief hunting grounds for so many years.

From one of the intensive care rooms, a monitor began to beep. The lights flickered again, and David looked around uneasily. Dangerous thing, a power outage in a hospital. His thoughts went briefly to Ralph, wired as he was to all those machines. He hoped the interruption in electricity wouldn't affect his convalescence.

He returned to the passage.

Lancaster bears the taint of Judson Alexander. Not just the man himself, a powerful enough force, but the stain of complicity perpetrated by the area's populace.

Evil can only triumph when good people allow it to.

The wickedness began when Judson was enabled by his father, but it was nurtured by people like Jennings and Jennings's son, who made concubines of their female family members.

As I sit here in dread of another night in the Alexander House – a dwelling I am increasingly certain does play host to Judson's spirit – my thoughts continually drift toward those poor young women, the Jennings girls, who during their exploitation ranged from thirty years all the way down to ten. Judson did not discriminate on the basis of age, nor did he scruple to maltreat his concubines in the meanest possible ways.

And after all that mistreatment, after living lives of fear and torment, the Jennings women were dealt the final insult, suffering a fate so savage and unfeeling at the hands of the villagers who journeyed to the peninsula, that I question who was the real villain, or whether there was any goodness at all in Lancaster back then.

"Did you go in there?" a voice snapped.

David stared dumbly up at a guy in green scrubs, an orderly perhaps, with a shaggy mane of black hair and a sallow, unshaven face.

The orderly bustled by, pointed at Ralph's door. "The guy in 209? You went in there, right? His monitors are off line."

David shook his head as he got shakily to his feet. He started after the orderly, almost forgot Weir's diary on the padded bench, went back for it and crammed it into his pocket. By the time he reached Ralph's room, the orderly was opening the door.

The lights went out.

The door half-open, the orderly glanced up at the lights. "What the hell? The generator's supposed to kick on automatically." He bounced on his heels. "Come on, come on...."

But David barely heard. His attention had been transfixed by what he glimpsed within the half-open door. Though it was dark, there was enough moonlight spilling through the window to cast Ralph's room into greater relief than the hallway in which David and the orderly stood. And within Ralph's room David beheld something so stunning he lost the ability to speak.

A gigantic figure in a white shirt and dark breeches stood between Ralph's bed and the window. Ralph's feet were dangling high above the floor, the figure clutching him by the throat. David saw with a pang of helplessness that Ralph's eyes were open. Without thinking, David pushed forward, knocked the orderly out of the way.

"Hey, what the hell—" the orderly began, but then he saw what was happening by the hospital bed and whispered, "Holy God."

The shadowy figure shot David a look. For a moment, the figure's eyes seemed to bore into David. Then the giant turned, smashed Ralph into the wall, the older man's head punching through the sheetrock. David moved on nerveless legs toward Ralph, whom he was sure was dead of a shattered skull. Then the giant pivoted and heaved Ralph's boneless body toward the wall opposite. Aghast, David watched the body crash against it, and in the next moment, the giant stalked toward David. Behind him the orderly was squealing, but David scarcely heard. The smell of the giant flooded his nostrils, the odor of an untended dog kennel, rank with violence and watery spoor.

The lights flickered on and off, and David glimpsed the man – it could only be Judson Alexander – in clarion detail: boulder-like head perched atop broad, muscular shoulders; thick black eyebrows arched in sadistic glee; balding pate rimmed by greasy black hair that hung in lank strings down his bull neck; a simple white shirt discolored with crimson stains; legs that stretched the dark breeches to bursting.

Judson reached for him.

Breath clotted in his throat, David raised an arm to ward him off. The lights overhead strobed, and he felt the brush of Judson's fingertips on his cheek.

The lights clicked on, and David was staring into empty space.

The orderly's voice was hushed. "Is he gone?"

David, still frozen in that warding-off stance, swiveled his head toward the orderly, who'd taken refuge behind a chair.

"You saw him?" David asked.

"You nuts? Of *course* I saw him. He killed that old man."

Trembling, David crossed to where the old man's body lay spread-eagled on the floor.

CHAPTER THIRTY-EIGHT

At least, David thought, as he followed Jessica back to her house around midnight, there'd been a witness. In movies and novels beyond counting, the hero would be charged with a crime he didn't commit.

The orderly saved him.

Harkless, thank goodness, arrived at the Lancaster hospital before Detective Baldwin did. In a vacant custodian's closet a few doors from Ralph's room, the two of them stood nose-to-nose in the tight space, the aromas of cleaning products nearly overpowering:

Harkless: You realize how goddamned crazy that sounds?

David: Don't you think I know that?

Harkless: A week ago the biggest problem I had was speeders on Highway 21. And Honey Shelby.

David: You hear from her? Or the mayor?

Harkless: Who the hell are you to ask that? That's police business.

David: There's something else.

Harkless: I don't wanna hear it.

David: It's Ralph. Something he said in the Alexander House.

Harkless: Is this about the floating harpy?

David: He said he encouraged Alicia to come.

(A pause.)

Harkless: What?

David: He told me he made a bargain with…it had to be Judson.

Harkless: Dammit, David….

David: Said he agreed to lead people to the Alexander House now and then. Almost like…like an offering.

Harkless: That doesn't help a damn bit.

David: That's all he told me.

Harkless: What I need is something without rattling chains and psychotic Puritans.

David: Remember when you made fun of me for being a non-believer?

Harkless: I didn't mean for you to swing so far the other way. Next thing you know, you'll be reading palms and conducting séances.

David (frowning): I do have one more thing.

Harkless: Don't tell me it's another body.

David (pulls out Weir's diary): Jessica let me borrow this.

Harkless (eyeing the little green book): I already have a Bible.

David: It's Weir's. There's so much in here about Judson—

Harkless: Would you come off that? Hell, I don't know why I'm standing here in a closet. That Baldwin is probably out there right now making everything worse.

David: I better get going.

Harkless: Oh yeah? Who you gonna get killed now?

David: Hey—

Harkless: I'm serious. Alicia gets butchered going to see you, Ralph gets his head smashed in—

David: I had nothing to do with those!

Harkless: —and now you're gonna go to Jessica's and put her in harm's way.

David: That's not fair.

Harkless: Fair? Tell that to Charlie Templeton. Tell that to his daughter.

Soon after, Jessica arrived and saved him from Harkless.

Now, as he followed Jessica's car toward Old Bay Road, he thought of what Ralph had said. David hadn't realized it at the time, but looking back, it couldn't have been plainer: Ralph was racked with guilt. He'd sent Alicia to the Alexander House knowing something insidious might be awaiting her there.

Ralph had sent her to her death.

When they reached Jessica's drive, she parked in the garage, waved him into the empty garage stall, and pushed the clicker to lower the garage door. He noticed several signs on the wall: 'QUIDDITCH PLAYER PARKING ONLY: VIOLATORS WILL BE CURSED'; movie posters for *Jaws* and *Star Wars* on wooden placards; a Poe quote in white cursive script on a rectangle of bronze: 'All that we see is but a dream within a dream.'

"You okay?" Jessica asked as he neared.

"No," he answered. She led him to the living room. Sebastian went straight for Jessica; she picked him up and let him lick her cheek. Something about the way she stood there in the center of the room made David pause. Something familiar....

She noticed his scrutiny. "What is it?"

He blinked, the moment passing. "Just a bad night, is all."

"You want something to drink?"

"Water," he said. "I can get it."

They went to the kitchen, where she retrieved a pair of glasses. She filled them from the filtered refrigerator spout and handed him his glass. "I'm sorry about Ralph."

He sipped his water. "Me too."

"Do they know who...?"

He shook his head. "Harkless asked me who else I was going to get killed."

"She's in a bad mood."

"I don't blame her. Since I've come, there've been two deaths, an abduction."

"Ivy was just hiding."

"She's changed," he said. "I could tell, just looking at her. I feel responsible."

"Did you kidnap her?"

He made a face. "Come on."

"Did you kill Ralph? Or Alicia for that matter?"

"You know I didn't."

She placed her glass on the counter. "Could it be you've got an overly guilty conscience over what happened with my sister?"

His mouth went dry. "Do you think I should?"

"It's not for me to say."

"Can't you just tell me how you feel?"

She watched him for a long time. She took a long draw of air and let it out. "I hated you. Anna was everything to me. No mother around, Dad with health problems, Anna was the one who did the heavy lifting. Not just the flashy stuff, the showing up for softball games and helping me get ready for a dance, but the subtler things, the things no one notices until there's no one there to do them. She cooked for us most of the time. She cleaned, did our laundry. Or she demanded that we do it. But she taught us how." Jessica smeared away a tear. "She taught me everything. Except how to cope with losing her."

Sebastian was rubbing himself against David's calves, but David scarcely noticed. It was just Jessica's voice and the indelible images of Anna. Of Anna making dinner for her siblings. Of her reprimanding them for not putting their dirty clothes in the hamper.

"One time when I was eleven," Jessica went on, "I hit a home run in softball." She grinned crookedly. "My only home run. It was early in the game, but I hit it out, actually hit it over the fence. I was so surprised, I must've forgotten to touch home plate. The other coach, some twat who was probably a frustrated ex-athlete, he appealed the play, and I get called out. I was crushed. What should have been my happiest moment as a player turned into my worst moment. My friends were all there, what family I had…it was humiliating. Like I was too dumb to step on home plate."

She smiled and the tears leaked out of her eyes. "Anna had just gotten her license, and she had plans with her friends. But instead of going with them, she drove me around for what must have been an hour while I cried and screamed and cussed out the coach and the umpire."

David smiled, picturing it.

"She got me fast food and drove toward home, but I knew my brother and my dad would want to talk about the game. I told her to drop me off and let me walk so I wouldn't have to face them. She told me not to be stupid, but instead of taking me home, she drove to a country road, pulled over, and listened to me. I was mad about what had happened, but I was aware enough to know Anna was putting off going out with her friends. So I kept talking. Pretty soon we were both talking. At one point her friends called, and Anna said she couldn't go with them. We ended up going home and watching a movie together in the basement. *Say Anything* with John Cusack."

"Great film."

"You see?" she said. "That was Anna. She was willing to do the unglamorous stuff. I think that's real love. Real love isn't just playing the part when others are around. Real love is doing the stuff that never gets noticed, the stuff that's purely for the other person. True love is willing to do what's tedious when the other person needs it."

And ten feet away from Jessica with the overhead fluorescents accentuating her perfect cheekbones and the exotic contour of her nose,

David found himself wanting to go to her. But he couldn't. He could only watch the tears crawl slowly down her cheeks.

She wiped her eyes. "I hated you. When I found out how you'd treated my big sister, I wanted to find you and claw your eyes out."

David said nothing, merely took it. God knew he deserved it.

"Then I got depressed. I was down for a long time. I was a sophomore in high school when Anna…." She reached out, ripped a sheet of paper towel off the roll, dabbed her face with it. "I got into drugs. Nothing heavy, but that was out of character for me. I wasn't an angel, but I wasn't some huge partier, so for me it was pretty brazen behavior. College was a good distraction. I missed Anna, but my classes and my friends helped me climb out of the hole I was in. Since then…there's been a void. It's like this empty, aching place that nothing can fill."

He swallowed. "I won't tell you what you already know, that I was an idiot and a selfish son of a bitch. I guess I still am."

Jessica lowered her eyes. "If I thought that, you wouldn't be standing in my kitchen."

"I'm sorry, Jessica. I know that's not enough. It will never be enough. But I'm sorry. I wish I could take it back."

"You're right. You can't. The only thing we can do for my sister is figure out who killed her."

He hesitated. "Why are you so sure she was murdered?"

"If you were going to commit suicide, would you do it in a haunted house?"

He frowned.

She nodded. "You've been to a ton of supposedly haunted places, David. I bet you've experienced all sorts of emotions. But at any time, did you feel suicidal?"

"I never went through what Anna did."

"You're right," she said and flashed a bitter smile. "You didn't. But I don't believe Anna would have killed herself at the Alexander House. She went there searching for something. In that final month, she'd become obsessed with the legend. I think she got too close to the answer, and someone killed her because of it."

An image of Ralph Hooper dangling two feet off the ground raced through his mind's eye. The gigantic figure smashing Ralph's head into the wall.

He said, "You think it was Judson?"

She shook her head. "I believe it was Honey's dad. I think the Mayor of Lancaster murdered my sister."

★　　★　　★

The moon was preternaturally bright. Jessica stored her kayaks in a shed near the shoreline, and when she and David nudged them into the water, their yellow hard-plastic shells shone like polished silver. He held her kayak steady as she climbed inside. Then he did his best to step into his and scull it away from the dock. He managed to avoid tipping, and soon they were skimming through the sable water of the bay.

"You could've borrowed a life jacket," she said. "It's a long way across the river." She wore jean shorts and a black bikini top, a combination David found pretty damned distracting. She had her hair tied in a bun with what looked like a pair of blue darning needles that formed an X.

Jessica must've noticed him looking, because she said, "They're called Oriental hairpins."

"They look sharp."

"Should we get the life jacket?"

"I can swim," he said.

"I've seen you swim," she answered, rowing on the starboard side.

"Not all of us are part dolphin."

The moonlight gleamed on her smiling teeth.

They rowed for a while, the crosscurrent rendering their progress gradual. David worked up a fine layer of sweat, but Jessica continued to manipulate the oar with apparent ease. Many times he allowed the nose of his kayak to drift too far toward the broad expanse of the Rappahannock. Once he overcorrected too severely, and before he could check his progress, he was rotating counterclockwise, the kayak spun around by the flow of the river.

To her credit, Jessica kept her wisecracks to herself. When they reached the bend, Jessica led the way, veering left, straight into the heart of the current. She'd chosen to navigate the center of the river, David knew, because the shoreline was littered with deadfalls and lurking stumps. Who knew what manner of hazards lay beneath the river's surface? In addition to trees, rocks, and manmade objects, there could be snapping turtles, snakes, oversized catfish with gaping, misshapen mouths. David shivered.

He realized he'd been purposely avoiding a glance at the Alexander House, but now he looked that way and noticed how the shadows encased it. It was half past midnight, he estimated.

He expected Jessica to head toward the weathered dock, but she surprised him by bypassing the Alexander property altogether and rowing farther upstream.

"Where are we going?" he asked in a carrying whisper.

"Honey's," she said.

He gestured toward the dock. "If we anchor here, we can—"

"There's someone at the Alexander House."

He stopped rowing, the current hauling him instantly backward. He rowed vigorously to catch up. "What are you—"

"The forest," she explained. "Look to the left of the lane."

He did and at first saw nothing. Then, leaning forward and squinting, he spotted the glint of a car roof nestled in the woods.

"Charlie Templeton," she explained. "Waiting for his daughter's killer."

David switched his oar from starboard to port, splashing his bare chest in the process. "Poor guy."

Jessica's triceps stood out momentarily as she corrected her course. "That 'poor guy' is gonna kill an innocent person if he's not careful. He almost did last night."

They labored against the current.

David looked at the moonlight scintillating on the water. "Won't they see us out here? We're not exactly camouflaged."

"Charlie's watching the house, not the river."

David considered this quite an assumption but didn't say so.

"What are we expecting to see at the Shelbys'?" he asked.

"Something depraved, I'm sure."

They'd reached the midway point of the Shelby house. "I can tell you what's happening there," David said. "Honey's watching a porno…four guys violating a horse or something. She and her husband are shitfaced, and the kids are off on their own. Ivy's probably asleep, and Mike Jr.'s playing some game unfit for a teenager, much less a child."

"Look," she said.

He did and was surprised to see Michael and Honey on different floors. Michael stood framed in the downstairs picture window, a drink in hand, gazing out at the water. If he hadn't spotted them already, he would soon.

Upstairs, Honey paced back and forth in what had to be the master suite. All the lights were on, Honey bedecked in a white negligee, her full breasts mostly unshielded by the drooping material.

Something in the front yard drew his attention.

"Ivy," Jessica said.

David noticed with misgiving that Ivy wore a formal white dress, like the flower girl in a wedding. Her hair was curled in tight ringlets, her ears and throat glimmering with earrings and a string of pearls.

There was no sign of Mike Jr.

"What's she doing?" Jessica asked, though it wasn't really a question. They could see well enough what was happening.

Like her parents, Ivy was waiting.

David and Jessica oared against the stream, the sweat flowing freely now. The current wasn't brisk, but it was constant, and in order not to get swept backward, they had to toil to maintain a view of the Shelby property.

Two minutes passed, and there was no change in the Shelbys' behavior. Somewhere upstream, a dog began to emit a high-pitched bark. A primitive fear tickled at the nape of David's neck. His back muscles burned from the unceasing effort. His arms had begun to go numb. Upstream, the dog yipped louder.

"I don't think I can keep this up," Jessica said.

Thank God, he thought. He detested the prospect of admitting his fatigue to Jessica, particularly after she'd made that crack about his swimming.

Out of breath, he nodded toward the Shelby property, where the yard was swallowed up by woods. "Let's land there."

A hundred feet beyond the house, Jessica veered toward the grassy shore, and David followed. While her kayak seemed to cut smoothly through the moist bank sand, David's thunked against land and threw him forward as though he'd rear-ended someone with his car. When he joined Jessica in dragging their kayaks ashore, he noticed she was stifling a grin.

Wordlessly, he followed her through the weedy area between the shore and the forest. She'd worn rubberized water shoes, and it occurred to him she might have done this before, used the river to spy on someone.

What if she'd done so to him?

David faltered, Jessica pulling away a little. A nasty thought had bloomed in his mind, and despite its outlandishness, it refused to be displaced.

What if Jessica had been toying with him all along?

Though she seemed not to despise him for his role in her sister's suicide, murder, whatever it had been, what if it was all a plot to strike back at him?

Do you realize how insane you sound?

But it was *all* insane. The notion of a Native American woman haunting an island or David's long-dead girlfriend turned floating spirit or some despicable colonist transformed into a revenant capable of lifting an old man off his hospital bed and dashing his brains out against the wall. Crazy, every last bit of it.

So is it really so crazy to believe Jessica is playing you? After all, who painted those portraits?

He watched her stealing through the weeds, twenty feet ahead of him now.

You believed the Siren looked like Anna, but doesn't Anna look like her sister?

Yes and no, he decided. Different fathers and all that.

But what if….

"*David,*" she said in a harsh whisper. "*Get moving.*"

What are you going to show me? he wondered. What new and horrible trick awaits us? Do you know what's coming, Jessica? Are you part of all this?

He got moving, but his feet felt leaden, his sweat a patina of chilled slime. He noted without surprise the white Escalade in the driveway. So the mayor was here too. The prospect of encountering the cretin turned David's stomach.

Ahead, Jessica was a subtly bobbing shape, a gleam of shoulder flesh, a hint of black bikini top.

Could this woman really be perpetrating some kind of vengeful hoax?

Don't you see? a voice suddenly bellowed. Your skepticism is your curse! Even when the evidence points toward the supernatural, you still cling to cynicism, and this time the results will be disastrous. At best you're going to lose your chance with a fantastic woman. At worst....

Jessica halted on the edge of the forest, cast a glance back at him. David hurried along, disgusted with himself but unable to fully shake the suspicion. It came down to this: you either believed in people or you didn't.

"What's wrong?" she asked as he drew even with her.

He hunkered beside her, took a moment to memorize her features. From this perspective, with the moonlight resplendent on her face, he couldn't imagine her deceiving him.

David stared at her. Jessica stared back at him.

He leaned toward her, tilted his head.

"Not now," she said, turning toward the Shelby house.

"Ouch," he whispered, but they were both smiling.

David strained to see into the night. Beyond the Shelby house, just visible where the yard ended and the path to the Alexander House began, he spotted Ivy in her formal white dress. What she was doing there he had no idea, but he was certain that, were he to sneak around to the waterside of the Shelby house, he'd find Michael and Honey still engaged in their vigil. The question was, what the hell were they waiting for?

David decided he no longer wanted to know. The temperature had dipped several degrees. A chill wind kicked up and bit at his bare torso; there were goosebumps on Jessica's arms. Nearby, a grackle let loose with a metallic shriek and winged away into the darkness.

"David," she said.

A figure was striding up the path toward Ivy. Tall, burly, appareled in the same colonial garb David had glimpsed in the hospital, the figure moved with a grace that belied its ursine frame. At some point, Jessica had taken David's hand, and he was glad of it, for the figure kept blurring, one moment substantial, the next like a poorly developed photograph. Had Ivy not remained unchanging in the foreground, David would have chalked it up to a trick of the moonlight. But the girl, grown very still, remained constant, as did the Shelby house and the path and the forest. Only the figure wavered, clarified, as it moved inexorably closer.

As David watched, appalled, Ivy reached up, took the figure by the hand, and led it toward her house.

CHAPTER THIRTY-NINE

"We've got to go in," David said.

He expected – maybe even hoped – for Jessica to disagree, but she only nodded. At least he wasn't the only one terrified of what they'd just glimpsed. At least he wasn't the only one convinced they'd just seen a ghost.

"Mike Jr. has to be there," she said, giving voice to one of his primary concerns. When David had last seen the boy, Mike Jr. had seemed beaten-down, his fieriness become a bewildered resignation.

They had to get him out of the house.

As for Ivy....

"Maybe we should get Harkless," Jessica said.

"We should have," he agreed. "But we can't now. Whatever it is...I think it's going to happen now."

He rose, a shiver coursing from his shoulders all the way to his thighs.

Jessica joined him and twined her fingers with his. He was glad of it. Though her hand was cool to the touch, it was the bracing sensation he needed.

They reached the front porch and found the wooden door ajar, as if in invitation. David exchanged a glance with Jessica and found himself wishing he'd kissed her.

No matter. The moment was gone.

He started through the door, and she put a hand on his arm, whispered, "I'll find Mike Jr."

He nodded. "I'll get Ivy."

"What then? Even if we get them out, where do we meet up?"

"The kayaks," he said. "There's room enough for them."

"What if Ivy doesn't want to go?" she asked.

"I take her by force."

"That's kidnapping."

"Once you get Mike Jr., don't wait for me. Just get out of there."

"That's the worst plan I've ever heard."

"You're beginning to sound like Harkless," he said and slipped through the door.

★   ★   ★

He led the way up the stairs. As they ascended, two sounds masked their footfalls. One was the unmistakable clamor generated by Mike Jr.'s Xbox. Whatever game the boy was playing, it involved a great deal of shooting. The machine gun fire was punctuated only by cries of pain and frequent shouted profanities.

The other sound chilled David's blood.

Moans of carnal pleasure. Echoing through the door to Honey's room.

He reached the landing and crept forward so Jessica could pass. She padded down the hallway toward Mike Jr.'s room. Once Jessica reached the boy, he'd either go willingly with her, or he'd sound the alarm. David's time was short.

He glanced behind him expecting to find Michael Shelby or the mayor at the base of the staircase, but for now the space remained empty. David stepped forward, the master suite evidently situated in the center of the home. Strange, he thought, though not as strange as the noises echoing through the door. Moaning. Grunting.

His stomach churning, David grasped the knob, twisted it, and opened the master suite door.

The lights had been doused, so only the ghostly moon illumined the master suite. He inched forward until he beheld the scene, Honey spread-eagled on the bed, her hands grasping the brass rails behind her, her mouth half opened in ecstasy.

To David's left, the mayor – for God's sake, Honey's *father* – stood naked and tan and wrinkled, masturbating furiously, eyes fixed on his daughter, who was being defiled by a giant, one whose massive frame blurred and clarified, one moment as insubstantial as smoke, the next as clearly delineated as Honey.

"He's here!" a reedy voice shrieked. "The intruder!"

David spun, and with an unbelieving gasp realized it was Ivy, her accusatory stare and tiny forefinger betraying him; he raised his hands in a stupid placating gesture and saw her little face spread in a look of ancient cunning, her eyes battened onto something over his shoulder. David turned in time to see the giant shoving off the bed, away from Honey's glistening sex. Before Judson blurred, David saw the mad gleam in his eyes, the bushy black eyebrows. The sadist's leer.

He retreated, but far too late. Judson's great arms thrust out at him, and David was driven backward, his feet not touching the floor. He sprawled in the doorway and his head cracked painfully on the hardwood floor. Between him and the ghost he saw Ivy's matching leer; the girl grinned at David with vicious glee.

He was scrabbling onto the landing when he bumped against someone's shins. He looked up expecting to find Jessica, but instead stared into the muzzle of a black handgun.

"Man, this is gonna feel good," Michael Shelby said.

★ ★ ★

David prepared for the impact. Shelby had trained the gun on his face, and there wasn't the slightest hope of escaping. I don't want to die, he thought, and even as the thought flitted through his head like the pitiful joke it was, something crashed against Shelby, throwing the man sideways. David scrambled to his feet and found Mike Jr. a few feet away, but the boy's eyes were fixed on the struggling pair on the floor: Michael Shelby, whose gun had tumbled down the hall, and Jessica, who'd tackled Shelby and saved David's life.

Shelby slapped at Jessica's face, the sound a dull crack. Jessica was shoved sideways, stunned by the blow. Shelby was pushing Jessica away, clearly intent on retrieving his gun, but then David surged forward, descended on Shelby, and hammered the man in the nose. Shelby yelped, blood splurting out of his nostrils. David raised his fist to smash Shelby again, but cool air whispered over his bare back, and he knew Judson was coming. Unthinkingly, he shoved away from Shelby, got Jessica around the waist, and staggered toward the staircase.

"Mike Jr.," David snapped. "Come on!"

But Mike Jr. only stared mutely toward the master suite, where Ivy was glowering at David with measureless loathing.

David took a step toward the girl, but before he entered the master suite the monstrous figure blurred toward him. The great arms snatched at David, and involuntarily he jerked away.

He turned and was heartened to note that Jessica had hefted Mike Jr. onto her shoulder and was hauling him toward the stairs. David followed, seeing from his left Michael Shelby crawling toward the gun. Jessica clattered down the steps with David on her heels. They swept across the foyer and Jessica had just burst through the door when a gunshot erupted behind them. David reached the doorway, leaped through to the accompaniment of another gunshot. He tensed for the impact but there was only the night air, the sight of Jessica carrying Mike Jr. on her shoulder and dashing toward the Alexander House. Beyond Jessica and Mike Jr. another figure was hurrying along the path toward them.

Charlie Templeton. The man was clutching a shotgun.

"Who the hell are— *Jessica?*" Templeton said.

"Help us," Jessica called.

Templeton spotted David, raised the shotgun, and for a terrible moment David glimpsed the scene from Templeton's perspective: a woman and child being pursued by a shirtless madman. Templeton would shoot him, believing he was saving Jessica and Mike Jr., but from behind them another shot sounded, and David didn't have to look to know that Michael Shelby hadn't given up.

"Holy shit," Templeton muttered. He stepped sideways, aimed his shotgun toward the Shelby house, and unleashed with both barrels.

The noise was shocking, even out here in the open. David listened but heard no cry of pain. He wondered if Templeton had only fired to warn Shelby off the hunt. Or maybe Templeton was a poor shot.

"Come on," Templeton was saying to Jessica. "My car's over here."

David had no idea if Shelby were still giving chase, and even if he wasn't, there was the very real prospect of Shelby or his father-in-law heading them off at the end of the lane.

"Give him to me," David said when he pulled even with Jessica. She allowed David to lift Mike Jr. off her shoulder, and though she didn't speak, her grateful look at David spoke volumes. He knew he should thank her for saving his ass, but that could come later.

First, they had to get the hell off the peninsula.

Templeton ran well for a man in his late fifties. Jessica streaked along beside him. David fell behind, but not by much. Carrying Mike Jr. was like toting a sack of mulch, the boy's legs bouncing against David's chest.

Ahead, Templeton ducked into the woods, and a moment later the interior light of Templeton's SUV lit up the trees. David followed, a stitch piercing his side, and was relieved to see Jessica tearing open the back door and awaiting David's arrival.

He knifed between the trees. Jessica stepped aside to let him pass, and without pause he fed Mike Jr. into the backseat of the SUV. David winced at the way Mike Jr. slouched sideways in the seat, but there was no time to diagnose the kid now.

Jessica hurried around to the passenger's seat. David scooted in beside Mike Jr. and yanked the door shut. "Drive."

Templeton reversed the Jimmy, moving too briskly given the closeness of the forest and the gravity of their plight. David cast a glance behind them, sure they'd slam into a tree. Then the SUV burst out of the forest and skidded on the lane.

"You think you can beat the Shelbys to the main road?" Jessica asked.

Templeton glanced at her but didn't answer.

"We need to get to Harkless," David said.

"Assuming she's not in on it," Templeton answered.

David stared at Templeton in the overhead mirror, appalled.

Jessica was watching Templeton, wide-eyed. "There's no way Georgia's in league with them. Why would you say such a thing?"

Templeton regarded her dourly. "Would you have suspected Ralph Hooper?"

Jessica seemed to deflate.

Shit, David thought.

They rocketed past Ralph's, swerved onto Governor's Road. Templeton was driving like a movie stuntman, and while David worried they'd overturn on a curve and die in a fiery crash, he said nothing, understanding as well as Templeton did that if the Shelbys headed them off, they'd be just as screwed.

"How is he?" Jessica asked, peering over her shoulder at Mike Jr.

David glanced at the boy's wan face and thought, *Blighted*. He's been blighted by whatever's happening in that house, ruined by his parents and his grandpa and that fucking….

Ghost, his mind finished.

He couldn't believe it. The specter was real.

He was thinking this when they rumbled around a bend and discovered the white Escalade parked diagonally across the road. Templeton stomped on the brakes, the Jimmy skidding sideways. Templeton fought the skid, cut the wheel, but they'd swung too far. They came to a stop facing the other direction. The car stalled, a persistent ding and a flashing yellow light announcing engine trouble. A shadow appeared from their right and they heard a loud clack against the passenger's window.

Michael Shelby grinned through the window at them.

He had the gun trained on Jessica's face.

★   ★   ★

"Drive," Jessica said in a low voice.

"You nuts?" Templeton asked. "Hell no, I'm not driving. He'll put a hole in your head."

"Drive, dammit," Jessica said. "If they catch us, we're done anyway."

"Charlie's right," David said, taking in Shelby's demented grin. "He'll kill you for sure. Our only chance is to take the gun away from him."

"Daddy likes movies where they kill for fun," Mike Jr. said.

They all turned and stared at the boy.

His expression never changed, his eyes sleepy. "I seen Daddy kill one a few months back. A man they found in Richmond, was supposed to fuck Mommy. The guy started causing trouble, givin' Daddy shit. Daddy told him he wanted to go outside and talk things over. Shot him in the back of the head, right there on the lawn."

God, David thought. He remembered what Ralph had said about the Shelbys: *I heard a gunshot over there a few months ago.*

Shelby tapped the muzzle against Jessica's window, causing them all to jolt. Templeton sighed, reached for the keys, but Jessica gripped his forearm. "Drive away, Charlie. Now, while you still—"

The passenger window imploded. Glass sprayed over Jessica, and then Shelby, having smashed the window with the butt of the gun, jammed the muzzle against Jessica's temple. "Get out of the car," he said, eyes aglitter. "Right fucking now."

This time Jessica listened. In the moment before Shelby's gun receded from the car, David considered lunging for his wrist.

But the risk was too great, his feelings for Jessica too strong. He realized, as Shelby seized her arm and wrenched her away from the SUV, he cared more about her than any woman since Anna. And he was about to lose her....

David was out of the SUV and circling its back end. "I'll go with you," he said.

Shelby whirled, trained the gun on David's chest. "Stay back!"

David showed Shelby his palms. "Just let her go. This is my fault anyway."

Shelby, his eyes showing too much white, swung Jessica around, cinched a forearm under her chin, and ground the muzzle into her hair. "None of you are getting out. Don't you see that?" Shelby glanced at Templeton, who was still behind the wheel of the SUV. "Get the hell out of the car!"

David took a step toward Shelby. "Take it easy. Your son's in the backseat."

"You don't think I know that?" Shelby snapped, spittle flying from his mouth. For a hideous moment he was sure Shelby would blow Jessica's head off. David held his breath.

"It's okay," Templeton said, stepping out of the Jimmy. In the moments before he edged around the front of the SUV, David half hoped the man had brought his shotgun out with him, perhaps concealing it behind his back.

Templeton stopped before the headlights and raised his arms.

No gun.

"Maybe I should do it now," Shelby said, the demented grin widening. He nodded at Templeton. "Maybe I should do you first."

The barrel had begun to swivel toward Templeton when something drew everyone's attention.

Two cars were winding up the lane.

Jessica's face went slack, but Shelby merely looked interested. That seemed like a bad sign, David decided. If the newcomers were part of the Shelbys' twisted cabal, the situation would go from terrible to hellish.

If, on the other hand....

The first car nosed around a curve; the sign on the door read 'SHERIFF.' David's heart jackhammered.

Thank God. Harkless.

David frowned. The second vehicle was Chris and Katherine's Mercedes.

Harkless and a deputy eased to a halt several feet from the Escalade. The deputy was a broad-shouldered man about David's height, with a bushy red mustache and thick red hair combed over like a seventies-era sports broadcaster.

"Stand where I can see you!" Shelby yelled.

But the deputy crowded against the forest to Shelby's left, Harkless fanning out the opposite way on Shelby's extreme right.

Shelby resembled a trapped animal, his eyes darting both ways, the muzzle of the gun pressed far too forcefully against Jessica's temple.

Evidently Harkless saw the expression of pain on Jessica's face. "Lighten up, Michael," Harkless said. "We're just going to talk." A nod. "Isn't that right, Deputy Vallee?"

The red-haired deputy nodded.

"Drop your guns!" Shelby commanded. "You know I'll shoot her."

Vallee's hand, like Harkless's, was resting on the handle of his gun.

"You need to breathe, Michael," Harkless said. "This doesn't have to end badly." She shot a look at the deputy. "Be careful, Andrew."

David's muscles still thrummed, but the presence of Harkless and her deputy had restored his hope. He glanced at the deputy in time to see a small, sleek object poke out of the forest. The deputy's eyes widened.

Harkless's eyes shifted that way. "Don't—" she started to say and then the side of the deputy's head exploded.

David stared in horror as what was left of the deputy sank to its knees and pitched forward, blood gushing from the head wound. A second later, the mayor, shirtless and grinning, emerged from the dense trees and trained his handgun on Harkless.

It wasn't until Katherine spoke that David realized she and Chris had gotten out of their Mercedes.

"Now that this nonsense is over," she said, "we can go home."

"You mean Williamsburg?" Harkless asked in a dull voice.

"I mean home," Katherine said and flashed her remorseless smile. "I mean the Alexander House."

CHAPTER FORTY

Katherine drove the Mercedes with Chris holding a gun on Jessica and Mike Jr. The rest of them – David, Harkless, and Templeton – were packed into the back seat of the Escalade with the mayor at the wheel and Michael Shelby in the passenger's seat, his gun pointed lazily at David's midsection. Templeton said nothing on the short ride to the Alexander House. Harkless looked stunned. David couldn't blame her. The deputy had probably been her friend as well as her colleague, and seeing him murdered like that....

He whispered out of the side of his mouth, "Does anyone know you're here?"

Without looking at him, she said, "Uh-uh. Mr. Gardiner told us they wanted into the house to retrieve a couple important papers." A hollow laugh. "I brought Andrew with me just in case anything was out of joint."

Poor Andrew, he thought, but the image of the deputy lying in a pool of his own blood and brains vanished swiftly.

They were approaching the Alexander House.

Chris and Katherine were in the lead, so it was by the Mercedes' high beams that David first spied Honey and Ivy emerging from the river path. Honey wore her ivory negligee, Ivy clad in her formal gown. But what bothered him was the impish smile on Ivy's face, the girl behaving as though this were all some amusing game.

The Escalade halted beside the Mercedes, and when both vehicles' headlights were extinguished, the only thing he could see clearly was the Alexander House, the blazing starlight lending it a spectral glow, the shadowed dormers like gaping black eye sockets.

The mayor climbed out. Shelby never lowered his gun, so there was no question of escape. The side door opened, and the mayor said, "Get your asses out."

Harkless went first, and as David followed he saw the mayor had backed away, his gun at the ready. Templeton joined David and Harkless, and within seconds the whole procession, including Jessica and Mike Jr., were herded toward the front porch.

"Where the hell you going?" the mayor snapped.

Mike Jr. turned and stared up at his grandfather.

"He's ruined," Honey said with a look of disdain. "Let him go."

The mayor looked at his daughter incredulously. "Are you out of your fucking mind?" He stormed over, grasped the boy by the shoulder, and yanked him away from Jessica. "He's my *grandson*. He'll come around."

"Don't want any of this," Mike Jr. muttered.

The mayor gave him a rough shake. "You will respect your grandfather, goddammit. Now shut your mouth unless you want to end up like that deputy."

With a pang of disgust, David realized the boy had witnessed the deputy's execution.

David's head swam as he trooped up the steps. So much bloodshed, so much depravity. What else awaited them in the Alexander House? How could the Shelby kids ever recover, provided they lived through the night?

He'd barely registered the absence of the police tape when Honey stepped forward and opened the front door.

"Thank you, darling," the mayor said, grinning his saurian grin. The bastard was every crooked politician David had ever met. The sight of his hand on Mike Jr.'s shoulder made David's stomach do a slow, sick roll.

Shelby moved ahead, backpedaling into the house, his gun shifting from Harkless to David. The mayor kept the handgun poised on them.

Chris watched impassively from the right side of the porch. "Go on," he said.

Jessica was just ahead of David in the procession. She stopped and regarded Chris silently.

"Don't look at me," he said.

Jessica didn't look away, didn't move. "You know something about my sister," she said.

"Don't *look* at me," Chris said, raising the gun.

Something jabbed David in the side. He turned and saw the mayor glowering at him, the white teeth aglow in the moonlight. "Tell your bitch to move," the mayor snarled.

Jessica finally got moving. She, David, Harkless, and Templeton crowded together in the foyer.

"Where to now?" Harkless said. David glanced at her, was heartened to note that she looked more animated now, more herself.

"You know where," someone said from above.

They looked that way and saw Katherine beaming down at them.

"Shit," Harkless said. But she started up the stairs anyway with Templeton in tow. Jessica came next.

David stared over his shoulder at Chris. He remembered the first time they'd met their freshman year in the dorm, David scared but not wanting to show it, Chris petrified but much worse at hiding it. The two of them thrust together because everyone else seemed to know each other. David and Chris soon realized that they both loved movies, both enjoyed the same kinds of music. Not a natural pairing, but one that deepened quickly, the two of them ordering pizza together and devouring two large pepperoni-and-sausages by themselves. Watching movies and staying up until four a.m. playing videogames. Turning twenty-one a few years later, both of them preferred bars rather than fraternity keggers. And somewhere along the line, there'd been Anna. Anna, who had first strengthened their bond and ultimately destroyed it.

No, David, a voice reminded. *You destroyed it.*

"Hey, Chris…." David began.

"Don't," Chris said.

David studied his old friend's face for a brief time, hoping he'd find a trace of warmth. But there was none. Only a callousness so complete that no reconciliation was possible.

David climbed the steps to the long bedroom.

★   ★   ★

They were herded to the landing and made to wait while the rest of the party entered the long bedroom. When David and the others were ushered in, David was chilled to discover the way the kids had been arranged.

Ivy lay on the bed closest to the door. Mike Jr. on the one next to her. The next two beds were untenanted, but the deep impressions made from long-ago bodies remained clearly stamped on the sheets.

Honey moved about the room lighting candles, and despite the fact that there were soon more than a dozen shimmering from the room's various surfaces, they provided little light and even less heat, the deep chill causing David to shiver.

"Close the door," the mayor instructed his son-in-law.

Shelby did as he was told, and soon the three gunmen – Shelby, Chris, and the mayor – formed a triangle around the four prisoners.

"On the floor," Chris said.

Templeton was the first to comply. Jessica followed. Harkless looked like she'd swallowed a bug, but she sat down anyway. David hunkered down last.

Honey and Katherine stood beneath the trapdoor like sisters, the former busty and half-naked, the other icily elegant.

A silence fell.

Harkless sat cross-legged. "I got a question," she said.

"No one wants to hear it," Shelby answered.

"How do we get started?" she said, ignoring him. "Do y'all mutter some incantations? Sacrifice a llama?" She looked from face to face, but their captors remained expressionless. "That is what we're doing here, right? Summoning the spirits?"

The mayor showed white teeth. "We merely need wait."

David studied the older man, the tanned chest tufted with white hair, the muscles not large but chiseled for a guy his age. Yet there was something indecent about the mayor's shirtlessness; maybe, David mused, it was because of the scene in Honey's bedroom, the sick son of a bitch pleasuring himself while his daughter was defiled by a ghost.

By Judson.

Whether it was real or his imagination, the thought of Judson brought with it an awareness of the room's increasing frigidity. A terrible energy charged the air. The others felt it too, apparently, for Shelby's expression had shifted from hostile to awestruck. To David, he looked very much like the Nazis in the climactic sequence of *Raiders of the Lost Ark*, gape-mouthed and enchanted.

Until the swirling spirits transformed into avenging angels and reduced them to overheated soup and exploding heads.

"He's coming," Katherine whispered.

Harkless looked around. "I don't feel a thing."

But David did. His skin was tingling and his scrotum was drawing taut. He glanced at Jessica, but she showed no signs of being disturbed. Instead she stared fixedly at Chris Gardiner.

"What?" David asked her.

"I just realized," she said.

He watched her. "Jessica?"

She said to Chris, who stood with his gun hanging at his side, "You did it."

Chris didn't answer, didn't look at her, but to David it appeared that Chris was attempting to *not* look at her, was studiously avoiding eye contact.

"The most obvious suspect," she murmured, "but I'd convinced myself it wasn't true."

Katherine was frowning at her husband. "What's she talking about?"

"My sister," Jessica said. "You murdered her."

Katherine looked like she'd been slapped. She said to Chris, "Tell her you had nothing to do with it. Tell her to shut her filthy mouth."

Chris's lips were closed so tightly they'd all but disappeared. The gun, David noticed, was tapping against his thigh.

The room grew colder, as if the walls were leeching the heat from the air.

"Tell me how it happened," Jessica said.

Katherine strode over and spoke through clenched teeth. "Shut *up*. Shut up and don't speak to my husband again."

"*Uhhhhh,*" a voice moaned. It was Mike Jr., who writhed on the bed as if in pain.

"What's wrong with him?" David asked.

The moaning crescendoed; Mike Jr.'s head began to thrash.

"Make it stop," Jessica said.

"You better tell me what the hell's happening," Harkless said to Mayor Warner, but the mayor merely twitched the gun in her direction.

"He's communicating with my grandson," the mayor said.

Harkless's eyebrows went up. "He?"

Mike Jr.'s chest rose, an anguished keening issuing from his mouth.

"Dammit," David said, pushing to his feet. "Do something for him."

"We are," the mayor said, the gun coming to rest on David's face. "Now sit down before I use this."

Mike Jr. thrashed his head from side to side, his teeth bared, a choked gurgle sounding in his throat.

"You'll kill him!" David shouted. He glanced wildly about the room until his eyes came to rest on Michael Shelby. "He's your son, for Christ's sakes. Help him!"

Eyes on Shelby, the mayor nodded. "Deal with Mr. Caine."

Michael Shelby stared blankly at his father-in-law a moment, then looked at David. A diseased smile spread on his face. Shelby raised the gun.

"Not here," the mayor said, nodding toward the southern window. "Do it over there."

"You're going to kill him?" Katherine asked.

Honey gave her an incredulous look. "What'd you think we were here to do? Have an ice cream social?"

Shelby strode toward David, gun extended. "On your feet. I've been yearning to do this since the day we met."

But Katherine was casting pleading looks about the room. She went to her husband. "It was supposed to be about convincing him."

Chris barely glanced at his wife. "After he disappears, this place will supply you with all the vacations you want, all the plastic surgeries."

David expected Katherine to be affronted, but she barely seemed to hear her husband. She took a step toward Shelby. "You can't—"

Chris seized her by the arm and yanked her toward him.

"By the window," Shelby told David.

David took a step in that direction.

Jessica rose. "Can I tell him something?"

"*Sit,*" the mayor ordered.

But Shelby was grinning coldly. "Sure. Tell him something."

Jessica moved close to David, stared up at him. He felt the eyes of everyone in the room on them, but it was Jessica from whom he couldn't look away.

She whispered, "Save Ivy and Mike Jr."

"Well, ain't that sweet," Honey said.

Shelby's grin had evaporated. "My kids don't need saving. They're part of something momentous."

Jessica looked up and said, "The trapdoor is moving."

As they turned that way, Jessica reached back, something in her hand now. Shelby was just glancing in her direction when she jabbed the Oriental hair needle. The tapered point punctured Shelby's left eye and sank in. The gun exploded, and Jessica cried out, twisted, and Michael Shelby dropped to his knees, runnels of blood slopping down his cheek.

David reached for Jessica, distinguished a dark patch on her side, but he also spotted the gun beside Shelby's motionless body. He knew this was their only chance. He lunged for the gun, cried out when another shot exploded and pain lanced his left forearm. Instinctively, he jerked the arm back, covered the bloody wound, and the mayor, who must've been the one who'd shot him, kicked out at him and sent him sprawling on his side. Without pause, the mayor swept his foot at the gun and sent it skittering under Ivy's bed.

Harkless clambered toward the bed to retrieve the gun, but Chris hurried over, shoved his gun against the side of her head. Harkless froze, a frustrated grimace contorting her face.

"Katherine, dear," the mayor said. "Would you kindly retrieve my dead, shiftless son-in-law's pistol for me?"

Katherine glanced dumbly at the mayor. Honey looked at her twitching husband like he was an unexciting zoo exhibit. Templeton watched Harkless and Chris, looking like he might make a move to intervene. The Shelby children lay on their backs, immobile, barely even breathing.

"Katherine?" the mayor repeated, an edge to his voice.

Her trance broke, and Katherine scurried to the bed, beneath which the gun had disappeared. She lowered to her knees, reached toward the gap between the blankets and the hardwood floor.

Honey's face tightened. "Wait—"

But she didn't have time to say more.

Something had seized Katherine's forearms. David watched, horrified, as the leering thing slithered out from beneath the bed, the scorched, bloody fingers already piercing Katherine's flesh. She tried to pull away, her mouth open in a soundless scream, but the leering thing held on, the mottled fingernails digging troughs in her flesh. She drew back from the creature, but its pupilless eyes opened wider. Its denuded jaws spread in ghastly hunger. Katherine finally found her voice, but it was silenced as the leering thing's razor-like teeth sank into her throat, and her blood sprayed out either side of the creature's face. Katherine's eyes rolled as the leering thing shook her in its champing teeth and blurred her head like a Rottweiler's chew toy.

Chris watched his wife die, his expression unchanging.

Something beyond the leering thing drew David's attention: Charlie Templeton had lunged toward the bed and was scooping up Ivy Shelby.

The mayor bellowed, "Put her down! Put her down, damn you!" But the mayor didn't fire his weapon, nor did Chris. Yet.

Templeton spun with Ivy toward the closed door, and David had time to think *Don't turn your back* before the mayor did shoot, and a gout of blood splashed from Templeton's back and spattered the wall.

Templeton gasped but didn't stop. He only reached awkwardly for the doorknob. He got through. The mayor followed. David heard a door slam, a lock click, someone hammering on wood. Templeton, David realized, had locked himself and Ivy inside the bedroom across the hall.

How long until the mayor starts shooting through the door? David wondered.

Chris and Harkless were staring one another down, the sheriff's expression grim in the semidarkness of the long bedroom.

"Oh, fuck this," Harkless said and rose.

"You stupid—" Chris started, and then Harkless was surging forward.

Chris would have killed her, David was absolutely certain of it, had Harkless not been so fast. Chris's gun went off, but the shot was wild. The sheriff hit Chris in the midsection like a linebacker taking down a quarterback. Chris jackknifed, stumbled back, pawed at Harkless, but she kept driving him backward until their feet tangled and they went sprawling into the alcove of the northern dormer. There was a thud – Chris's head on the floor – and then Harkless was rising and aiming a brutal kick at Chris's face.

As Harkless reached down and took possession of Chris's gun, David became aware of his own wound. His forearm throbbed, the momentary numbness giving way to pain. Ahead of him the leering thing had Katherine's corpse pinioned to the floor, was feeding on her larynx, the blood frothing over its red-black face, the gobbets of meat and tissue splattering on the down-hanging ivory coverlets.

David crawled toward Jessica, saw her eyes were squeezed tight in pain.

"Can you hear me?" he whispered.

Her eyes still closed, Jessica nodded.

"Can I—" he said, reaching for her side, but he froze, his stomach lurching.

The leering thing had left off Katherine's corpse, was staring at him.

No, he amended. Not at *him*. At the blood on his forearm.

The creature sprung. David shot an arm up, his good arm, but the creature battened onto it, snarling and tearing. With a cry, David twisted, and the leering thing, which weighed little despite its ferocity, went tumbling into the blackened fireplace. On impulse David seized a poker from the implement holder. The leering thing darted at him again, and he just had time to bring the poker up, interpose it between himself and those lethal teeth. The black iron tip of the poker sank into the throat of the creature and pierced through the back of its neck. But it kept coming, champing and growling. The thing's claws had sunk into his shoulders; it hauled itself nearer, the poker sliding through its throat. But how, David wondered crazily, did you slay a ghost, if that's what this was?

The creature jolted, and David jerked his head around to find Harkless bearing down on the leering thing, her gun extended. Harkless fired again, and the leering thing howled.

David shoved the leering thing away, staggered to his feet, and grasped its ravaged body by the hips. Thoughts swirled in his head as he lifted the abhorrent creature: this was once a woman, likely a very young woman, who'd been victimized by Judson Alexander; but the shrieking, charred thing in his grip no longer understood anything save hunger…and serving its master. Although the poker had impaled the creature's throat and Harkless had shot it twice, the creature still twisted and fought with indefatigable energy. Even now, as David strode toward the window, the creature was reaching back for him, clawing at his arms, yearning for his blood. David pivoted and hurled the creature through the window. When he turned, he saw Harkless lifting Mike Jr. from the bed.

He cast a glance toward Jessica, who lay on her side, moving very little.

A gunshot from the hallway. David glanced at Harkless.

"Shooting through the door," Harkless said in a hushed voice. "Charlie won't be able to keep the mayor out for long."

David glanced at Mike Jr. "Should we…."

Harkless took a steadying breath. "Keep the kid safe."

David nodded, took Mike Jr. by the hand, and moved against the wall where he could observe Harkless.

Harkless stepped into the doorway, gun extended.

"Mayor Warner!" she shouted.

David watched Harkless's fierce eyes widen. "Well, shit," she said. And then she was firing, her body braced low and the gun raised. David heard the mayor cry out, a clattering thud, then Harkless lowered the gun, looking nothing but overtired.

David said to Mike Jr. "Wait here." He came around the corner and peered over Harkless's shoulder at the sagging corpse of Mayor Warner. Harkless's aim had been true. There were three ragged blooms pumping cherry-red blood from the vicinity of the mayor's heart. The bare-chested man looked more obscene than ever lying there in a heap, his eyes staring sightlessly at the ceiling. The mingled odors of gunsmoke and fresh excrement filled the landing.

"One less pedophile," Harkless said. She stepped across the hall. "Open up, Charlie. We got him."

No answer.

Harkless glanced at David, frowning, and reached for the knob, which hung loose and dented in its splintered housing. She nudged the door, which swung inward.

Revealing what lay just inside the bedroom. Charlie Templeton was sprawled on his chest with little Ivy sitting astride his back. The child's fingernails were digging at a wound in his back, more than eight inches in diameter. The raw crater was ruby-colored and glistening with blood and vertebrae. David could only make out the edges of the wound because Ivy's face was buried in its center. He became aware of the slurping sounds as Ivy feasted on Templeton's viscera.

"Oh my holy God," Harkless said.

Ivy paused, her shoulder blades like tiny harrows inside the formal gown. Then she looked up from the gory hole from which she'd been feeding and grinned at them.

CHAPTER FORTY-ONE

"No," Harkless whimpered. "Please, no."

Ivy's grin widened, her anemic little face rimed with blood and bits of cartilage. The front of her white dress was stained a deep burgundy, the blood having soaked through the silken material to her skin.

"What did you do, child?" Harkless said, a question David judged unnecessary. *What the hell does it look like?* he wanted to ask. *She's feasting on the man who tried to save her.*

"Where's my sister?" a voice asked. He turned and saw Mike Jr. staring past him toward Ivy and Templeton, and before David could move to block Mike Jr.'s view, the boy's face crumpled, and he began shaking his head.

"Sheriff," David said, "please get Mike Jr. out of here."

Harkless seemed transfixed by the sight of Ivy's blood-smeared face, but murmured, "Okay."

Harkless turned away from the nightmarish tableau and took Mike Jr. by the hand. Mike Jr. allowed himself to be led down the stairs, but he kept casting glances back at David. "Aren't you coming?" the boy asked.

"I've got to get someone," David said.

"But you'll come?" Mike Jr. said.

Soft laughter from across the hallway.

Ivy, David thought. Jesus.

"I'll put the boy in one of the cars and come back up," Harkless said. She and Mike Jr. were nearing the bottom of the stairs.

"Drive to town," David said. "Get him somewhere safe."

"Bullshit," she said.

"We'll be right behind you."

Harkless didn't answer, but she did lead Mike Jr. across the foyer and out the door.

As soon as they were gone, David turned toward Ivy, whose laughter was deepening, the voice as unnatural as the cannibalism.

"Shut up," David said.

Ivy's laugh grew louder, deeper.

"You're not Ivy," he said.

"The hell she ain't," came a voice from behind him.

He whirled and stared into the muzzle of a gun. Michael Shelby's, he realized. The gun that had gone spinning under one of the beds.

With the gun extended, Honey smiled a slow, languid smile. "Forgot all about me, didn't you?"

★   ★   ★

After bending to scoop up her dead father's gun, Honey led David back into the long bedroom. While it was the last place he wanted to be, he was grateful to be shot of the sight of Ivy ripping and tearing at Templeton's back.

A current of rage sizzled through him. Templeton had saved Ivy's life, or had tried to. He'd taken a bullet for the girl, and though he might have died from the gunshot, he deserved better than to have his body defiled by a possessed child.

And Ivy *was* possessed. There was no other explanation. Whatever had happened the night she'd gone missing, all the goodness in her had been extracted and had been replaced by malice, by sadism, by an irrational allegiance to a being so fearsome not even death could vanquish him.

Chris had roused and was leaning groggily against the farthest bed. David barely spared Katherine's body a glance, though he wondered what had become of the leering thing. Was it still alive, or were its powers limited to the house? And if it did still lurk outside, would it attack Harkless and Mike Jr.?

Ignoring Honey and Chris, David hurried over to where Jessica lay on her side, the puddle of blood beneath her having doubled in size. He knelt, got a hand under her head, and rolled her toward him. He placed a hand on her wound, applied pressure, and gritted his teeth.

Goddammit, he thought. Goddamn these fiends and their loyalty to a monster.

Honey said, "Don't get all huffy. There're other women."

David's arms trembled. "You...vile excuse—"

"Save it," Honey said lightly. "You wouldn't have been man enough for me anyway." A lascivious smile. "There's only one who is."

"She's right, you know," Chris said.

"You bastard," David said. "This is your fault."

Chris stepped around the edge of the bed. "At least you're giving me credit for something. The whole time we've known each other, all you've done is marginalize me."

"You're a coward."

Chris's eyes flashed dangerously. "I killed her."

It knocked David's breath out.

Chris grinned nastily. "That's right. I drove Anna here because she asked me to. She *was* suicidal – you're not off the hook for that – and she had a bucket list. One item was spending the night in the Alexander House."

David listened, and though he was intensely interested, he was even more desperate to get Jessica to a hospital. Had Harkless listened to him and taken Mike Jr. to safety, or was she even now sneaking up the stairs in an attempt to ambush Honey and Chris?

And what about Ivy? he wondered.

God. David couldn't think about her. A vision of the girl licking the ragged fringe of Templeton's wound arose, and he had to fight off a wave of nausea.

"Give me that gun," Chris said to Honey.

She handed Chris her father's gun and smiled at David. "Aren't you gonna ask your buddy how he killed your old girlfriend?"

"I don't care," David said, but God help him, he did.

"You'll enjoy the story," Chris said. "You always did enjoy humiliating me."

"That's not true."

"*It is!*" Chris shouted and suddenly lashed out with the gun. It caught David on the side of the face and knocked him backward. Jessica's head, released from David's support, thudded smartly on the floor. David pushed up on his elbows and started to move toward Jessica, but Chris was there, the muzzle three inches from David's nose.

Chris's face was a rictus of loathing. "You're a narcissist, Davey. You expect everyone to serve you, and when you're done with them, you cast them aside."

David didn't bother arguing. The staring black eye of the gun made it impossible to think, much less speak.

"You were all she talked about," Chris said, smiling bitterly. "That night we broke in here, we ended up in this room. She said without you there was no point in living, that she'd never love anyone as much as she loved you." Chris's face twisted. "When I was *right here in front of her*. I wanted to scream, 'I'm here! I love you more than he ever will!' But do you think she listened? You think she gave one shit about me? It was like I wasn't even alive!"

"Let us go," David said.

Honey barked out laughter, but Chris's eyes remained lost, unfocused, his mind firmly on that night twenty-two years ago. "I hugged her. You know, to comfort her. She leaned into me, and I thought she might let me kiss her. I…" Chris licked his lips, "…I put my mouth on hers, but she jerked away, her eyes wide open…Jesus Christ, like she'd been stung or something. She acted like I was some kind of rapist."

Jessica stirred. David watched her face, her eyes rolling under her shut lids.

Chris went on. "I knew then. Even though I loved her – maybe *because* I loved her – I knew I had to end it." He smiled. "She'd already written a suicide note. You believe that? Showed it to me. Carried it around with her. I only had to make it look like she'd done it herself. I told her how sorry I was. She wasn't hard to convince. She always saw me as this…." He bared his teeth. "This harmless troll. She turned her back on me, started to walk out."

"Chris…."

"I tackled her, drove her face first onto the bed." He nodded toward the nearest bed. "I grabbed her around the throat, grabbed her from behind. I just…choked her. When it was done, I couldn't believe it. I thought I'd be crushed, that I'd want to die too. But you know how I felt?"

Chris leaned closer, his grin terrible. "I felt free! I knew no one else would have her. Would ever kiss her…or fuck her."

Jessica sucked in breath, let out a wet, rattling cough.

"She's dying," Honey said in a bland voice.

Chris didn't seem to notice. "There was a rope, thank God, in the cellar. I had to hunt around for one, but there it was, attached to an inner tube. I brought it up here, pulled down the ladder, and tied that ski rope to the third-floor rafter. I lugged her up to the attic, fitted the rope around her throat where I'd throttled her. Then I pushed her body through the opening and heard her neck crack."

He chuckled. "I was sure there'd be an investigation, but the note saved everything. She'd written it, she'd been talking about it to a couple other friends. Everyone was sad, but there was no reason to suspect murder. Do you see the irony, Davey? *You saved me.* By goading her into suicide, you saved my life."

David clenched his fists. "You're going to hell."

Chris's face spread in an amazed grin. "But you don't *believe* in hell. Do you, Davey? You don't believe in anything. Just your books and your sterling goddamn reputation."

"I believe," David said.

Chris's expression darkened. He was about to pull the trigger – David could see it in his eyes – but at that moment the door to the long bedroom slammed shut.

Freezing air scurried up and down David's backbone. Chris was looking about with a look of stupefaction.

But Honey was smiling hungrily and tracing a line with her fingernails over her breastbone. "He's here," she said. "Judson's come."

★   ★   ★

As it had on the night he'd videotaped the long bedroom, the energy began to change, the air to swirl. The atmosphere grew charged even while the temperature plummeted. What was more, David could see shapes on the bed clarifying. He thought of what Jessica had told him about the mob of Lancaster's denizens burning down the Jennings house, and though it turned his stomach, beneath the ozone stench permeating the bedroom, he caught the odor of charred flesh and blackened bones.

A knocking began from the third story. The joists overhead started to groan. The candles guttered. The light slanting through the windows flickered, died, like a jet blasting through moonless night, its engines failing and its doomed shell spiraling toward earth.

Chris murmured, "Can't believe it," and on his face David saw wonder warring with dread.

He's never seen Judson, David thought.

Humanoid figures materialized on the beds. David cast a glance at Katherine's mangled carcass, felt the throb of his own forearm, where the leering thing had battened onto him and begun to chew. He'd barely been able to best one creature; how difficult would it be to battle multiple charred horrors?

Jessica coughed, and he saw a trickle of blood at the corners of her lips. He looked up at Chris. "We have to get out of here."

"I'm not going anywhere," Chris said, but his voice shook.

"He'll kill you," David said.

Chris's face clouded, his eyes darting about the long bedroom as the meager light flickered.

From below, David heard Harkless hammering on the front door.

It won't let her in, he thought, remembering the mob's inability to enter the Alexander House. No matter what she does, we're on our own in here.

"Come to me!" Honey called, and when David glanced that way, he saw she'd turned her back on him, was gazing raptly up at the trapdoor, her arms spread in worshipful anticipation. The negligee had ridden up her thighs; forgotten, her gun drooping toward the western wall.

Now, David thought. It has to be now.

As if in confirmation, Jessica coughed again. A dime-sized splat of blood hit the floor.

He glanced at Honey, at Chris.

He went for Chris.

His old friend had turned toward the nearest bed, and because of this David closed half the distance before Chris noticed him. When Chris did look up, David leaped, and at the last moment, before their bodies collided, David was sure he'd missed his chance, that the gun, which was pointed at David's head, would spit fire and David's face would be turned to pulp.

David slammed into him, the pistol detonating, and they both crashed into the pooled darkness between the last bed and the northern dormer. The noise of the gunshot so close to his head started a horrid ringing in his ears, and somehow, Chris had kept hold of the gun. Chris swung it toward David's face, but David deflected it. He worried Honey would shoot him in the back, but he couldn't prevent that. He had to disarm Chris before Chris killed him.

The gun wavered toward him again, but David reached out and seized Chris's wrist.

David groaned, the wound in his forearm weakening his grip. The pain was a conflagration, and worse, Chris was winning the struggle. The gun trembled higher, higher, angled toward David's head. Desperately, he reared back with his free fist, hammered down at Chris's face. The blow was a solid one, but it awakened a screeching agony where the leering thing had torn into him. At the thought, David became aware of a shape on the bed nearest him, a writhing, twisting, hungry shape that needed only to fully materialize before it could sate its bloodlust.

From above, footsteps sounded. Heavy, clunking footsteps. David's stomach roiled at the thought of the giant descending the stairs.

Chris appeared dazed, yet he was bucking beneath David, fighting to unseat him. David groped for the gun. His fingers closed on it. He was sure he could wrest it from Chris's grip, but Chris's free hand landed on David's bitten wrist, the fingers sliding into the ragged gouges. David gasped, tried to wrench his arm away, but Chris's fingers had cored into the wound and were squirming through tissue. David cried out in pain, concentrated all his force on the gun. He clutched Chris's hand, bashed it on the floor. The gun loosened in Chris's grip but didn't fall. Chris's fingernails harrowed the tendons in David's wrist. Nauseated by the pain, David tried to jerk away, but the pain wrought by Chris's probing fingers incapacitated him. Desperately, he slammed Chris's hand down again, and this time the gun skittered into a corner. David strained forward, but Chris, with two good hands, latched onto him and held him fast. David sprawled on top of him, wriggled to free himself, but Chris wouldn't let go.

"You doomed her," Chris said, his grin triumphant. "You doomed Anna, you doomed yourself. Now you've brought her sister here to be defiled by Judson."

Chris's words scythed through his fear of Judson Alexander and the leering abominations. In its place came a panicked guilt. Was Jessica still alive? He heard Honey back there, importuning her lover to take her, to give her what she needed. But what about Jessica, the woman so loyal to her dead sister that she'd devoted her adulthood to unraveling the mystery of her death?

And now, David realized, though he knew the truth about Anna, Jessica might never hear it.

"That's right," Chris said, misreading David's wide-eyed stare. "Judson might even play with *you* a little."

With what strength he could muster, David yanked his arms down, breaking Chris's hold. Chris twisted onto his side and strained toward the gun, which lay just out of reach.

David took Chris by the throat, began to squeeze. Chris's eyes went wide, and he pushed against David, but David held on, bore all his weight to pin Chris on his back.

"Uh-uh," David said. "I want you to see me killing you. You fucking monster. You couldn't even look at Anna while you strangled her."

The name seemed to ignite a greater panic in Chris. He slapped at David's hands. His tongue lolled out, his eyes rolling white. David no longer felt his fingers, no longer governed his own body. The muscles flexed of their own accord. His teeth ground together in mindless hatred.

A lazy voice drawled, "Let go of him if you don't want to be killed."

David froze. Slowly, he turned and looked at Honey, who'd interrupted her Judson-worship to train the gun on him.

"Did you really think I'd let you strangle him?" she asked. "Hell, he's the only friend I have left." The grin broadened. "At least, the only living one."

David lay atop Chris, indecisive. He knew there was nothing to be done. His fingers slackened. Beneath him, Chris sucked in hoarse, desperate breath. He coughed wetly, his body tremoring. To David's right, the shape in the nearest bed was rippling beneath the covers, a hint of scorched flesh showing at the rim of the blanket. And from above, the sounds of heavy footfalls. Judson was materializing, preparing to unleash his malice on David and his unspeakable lust on Honey.

And Jessica, a hideous voice whispered.

Honey had the gun extended and was peering up in fascination at the trapdoor, and because of this she didn't see the gleaming slender object piston toward her bare right foot. The spike – Jessica's remaining hair needle – punctured the webbing between Honey's toes and hammered all the way to the floor. Honey flung her arms up and howled in agony, and David scrambled off Chris, leaped for

Chris's gun, got hold of it. He swung it around to face Honey, who'd remembered her own weapon, was bringing it down toward Jessica, the one who'd stabbed her.

"You *cunt*," Honey growled, teeth bared.

"Hey, Honey?" David said.

She looked at him and he fired. The slug shattered her sternum, a purplish blossom opening between her breasts. She gaped down at it, staggered. He fired again, this time nailing her in the heart, and she slumped to the floor beside Jessica, who no longer appeared to be moving.

Above their bodies, the trapdoor jolted.

David surged toward Jessica, but something seized him around the legs. David stumbled and pushed against his assailant. It was Chris, weak from the near-strangulation, but intent on fighting him. Chris's eyes were glazed over but he was still climbing up David's body. David cracked an elbow into the side of Chris's head, disentangling him, but when David moved toward Jessica – they had to escape this fucking house! – Chris fell against him again, wrapped his arms around David's midsection. David pumped a knee into Chris's gut, lifted him off his feet. He reached down, seized a handful of Chris's receding hair, drew his head back to expose his face, and slammed the pistol against his cheek. He felt the cheekbone collapse, heard his old friend emit a surprised bleat, and then Chris blundered sideways onto the bed.

Where a charred creature rose up behind him.

David stepped back involuntarily as the gnarled, blackened arms snaked around Chris's chest. Chris's eyes cleared and flooded with terror. The leering thing opened its fanged maw and clamped down on the meat of Chris's shoulder just below the neck. David looked away, but not before he saw another shape dart off the next bed and swarm over Chris's chest, biting and tearing and ribboning his flesh. Chris's wails became a phlegmy gurgle. Sickened, David lurched toward Jessica, his forearm and wrist screaming, his vision gauzy from blood loss.

He bent to scoop her up. A boom sounded above him. Despite the pain in his limbs, David managed to get his arms under Jessica's limp body, push to his feet, and hurry toward the door.

Ahead of him, a creature hurtled off the second bed and hit the floor with a revolting squelch. Another creature slithered off the first bed and began dragging itself on fire-blackened claws to bar his way. Briefly, David considered vaulting them or climbing onto the beds to evade them, but he saw the figure in the doorway then watched in numb terror as it stepped forward, the door shutting behind it of its own accord.

Ivy's blood-rimed cheeks spread in a sly grin.

"Do you believe yet?" she asked.

★   ★   ★

Jessica lay heavy in his arms, her neck pressing his bitten wrist. He couldn't hold her much longer.

"Move," he told Ivy.

The moonlight strobed and danced.

"You can't get past three of us," she said.

David made the mistake of glancing at the creatures, saw one actually lick its chops with a scorched earthworm tongue, both of them crawling inexorably toward where he stood. Across the room, the other two creatures were ripping Chris's body apart, the blood spouting over their faces, soaking the bedsheets.

"Even if you got past us," Ivy said, her tone conversational, "you'd never get out of the house. His power is too great."

A leering thing darted toward his legs. David danced backward, nearly toppled, and heard the creature's teeth click together. It let out a frustrated hiss.

A groaning sound from above.

David had just pivoted toward the trapdoor when it burst open, the hinged bottom section swinging down with a crack as explosive as a pistol report. Jessica stirred in his arms. He spared Jessica a glance, discerned the pinched look on her face, and was overcome with a gust of desolation more powerful than any he'd ever experienced. Never in his life had he so wanted to protect someone; never in his life had he felt so inept.

She wasn't Anna, and there was no way to take back the pain he'd inflicted on Anna. But if he could save Jessica…even if he didn't save himself….

Fingers closed around his ankle. David gasped and jerked away. The leering thing reared up on its knees, chortled deep in its ruined throat. An uncontrollable shudder gripped him, the sensation of the creature's fingers indelible on his calf, like curling strips of burned bacon crackling against his skin.

"Papa's here," Ivy murmured.

David's chest turned to stone. He rotated slowly and beheld the giant work boots, the dark breeches.

From below, David heard thuds, Harkless attempting to gain entry.

But there was no entry into the Alexander House; he knew that now. Whatever power resided here girded the dwelling against invaders. That long-ago mob from Lancaster had tried for hours to break into the Alexander House, had attempted to set fire to it. What chance did Georgia Harkless have if so many had tried and failed?

Judson Alexander clumped methodically down the ladder steps, his movements like, yet unlike, those of a living being. In the shadow of the descending behemoth, David felt insignificant. The light dimmed, flickered, as if absorbed by the massive figure.

David backed away but froze when he brushed a leering thing. It swiped at his calves. There was nowhere to go.

David turned as Judson's white shirt came into view, a pale swath of chest. His broad bull's throat.

Judson stepped down onto the hardwood and stared at David, who stood eight feet away. The thick black eyebrows arched and moved like separate creatures. The black hair hung lank and greasy on Judson's shoulders, the tendons of his neck bristling with unspeakable power. A goatish smell flooded the bedroom.

The light pulsed, faded. David was aware of his heartbeat, deep and thornlike, each beat damaging him, nudging him closer to unconsciousness.

Judson lowered his face, the deranged gaze riveting on Jessica.

His meaning was plain. Judson wanted her.

In confirmation, he extended his great arms, his eyes dancing with childish anticipation.

With Jessica slumped in his arms, David took a step toward the door. The leering things leaped at him.

His instinct was to shield Jessica, but when he did, they fell on his back, biting and scratching. David squealed, the revulsion of having the creatures affixed to his back only equaled by the agony of their wicked claws and their shredding teeth. With no other choice – he'd die if he didn't protect himself – he deposited Jessica on the bed closest to the door, and then he was pawing at the creatures, crying out at the pain in his back. He knocked one off, but as it fell away, he felt a tearing, another leering thing having bitten out a chunk of flesh. He reached back, groped for the other creature. Unable to displace it, he staggered toward the wall and smashed his back into the plaster. Trapped between David's body and the wall, the creature gave off biting, swept its talons toward David's temples. David gasped and wrenched away, sheets of blood pouring down his cheeks.

Dazed, bleeding, he retreated toward the window, but the sight that awaited him on the bed blasted away his pain, erased all other thought.

Judson loomed over Jessica. David expected Judson to reach for her, to defile her the way he had so many others.

Then he saw the tiny figure climbing onto the bed near Jessica's torso.

Ivy braced her hands on Jessica's unmoving shoulders.

In a deep, insectile voice, Judson said, "*Feed, my child. Feed.*"

CHAPTER FORTY-TWO

Her white gown stained a rusty crimson, her hair stringy and caked with blood, Ivy opened her mouth. The leering creatures watched with rapt anticipation. Judson gazed beatifically down at Ivy, whose teeth were inches from Jessica's throat.

David took two strides, threw a shoulder into Ivy's side, and knocked the child off the bed. A part of him recoiled at treating a child so roughly, but Ivy was no longer the child she'd been

Judson roared, and before David could react, immense fingers closed over his neck and propelled him through the air. He hit the northern wall near the floor, the impact with the plaster dulling his senses.

Jessica, he thought. Have to get to Jessica.

He remembered the ravenous look on Ivy's face, the ceremonial attitudes of Judson and the leering creatures. And though he'd always considered anything to do with the occult unadulterated rubbish, he'd studied it extensively and recalled snatches of it now.

Judson derived regenerative power from living victims. So did his roasted sex slaves. Of special interest to Judson was the degradation of children, and the more Ivy fed on human flesh, the further gone she would be.

She's already gone, a voice insisted. *So is Jessica – she's bled to death. Your only hope now is saving yourself.*

David pushed to his feet, swayed a little. Ivy was turning back to her meal.

Had she already bitten into Jessica's flesh?

No time, he thought. There's no time.

He took a step around the edge of the fourth bed and nearly tumbled headlong. The toe of his sandal had landed on something, and stumbling, he realized what it was.

Honey's gun.

Unthinkingly, David picked it up and aimed it at Ivy, whose tiny face was descending, descending. In another moment she'd bite into Jessica's throat. But though that prospect filled David with horror, he couldn't pull the trigger, couldn't murder a child.

He leveled the gun at Judson Alexander and squeezed the trigger.

He expected the slug to travel straight through the giant, but Judson's arms splayed out, the great head thrown back in pain.

Ivy scrambled to her feet and glowered at David. "Don't you hurt him!"

Amazed, David took aim again, thinking that it made a primitive sort of sense: to do damage in the corporeal realm – to bash Ralph Hooper's brains out on a hospital wall, for instance – Judson had to become physical matter. And as a creature of physical matter, Judson was susceptible to pain, to damage, and David squeezed the trigger again, exulted in the gout of brackish gruel that splashed from the side of Judson's neck. The leering things were squalling, their lidless white eyes gaping moons. Ivy looked unhinged, her fists bunched and shaking. Her scream was somehow worse than those of the leering things. She was already vaulting off the bed and scuttling toward him.

Judson did a slow, staggering pivot, and fixed David with a look of outrage.

David strode closer, took aim, squeezed the trigger and blasted away a portion of Judson's face, the right jaw denuded of flesh, the roots of Judson's molars showing like some hideous anatomical diagram.

A shadow rocketed toward him. Ivy, he knew, the child mad with fury and whirring with fingernails and hair. David started to speak but closed his mouth, knowing no words would halt Ivy's onslaught, knowing she would have to be met with force. David sidestepped and brought a forearm down against her shoulder. She deflected off him, twisted in the air, and thudded against the brass feet of the third bed. She raised her head slowly and fixed him with a look so fraught with hatred that he almost forgot about Judson.

The giant drew his gaze. Though bleeding, Judson didn't appear weakened. To the contrary, his damaged face was spread in a goblin's leer, his eyebrows drawn downward in wicked glee.

David aimed, fired at Judson's face.

Empty.

No! David thought. But it was true. He squeezed the trigger again and again, but there was nothing left, nothing to do but throw the gun at the giant's face. It ricocheted off and landed on the floor.

Arms extended, Judson started toward David.

There was no question of evading him. The giant was so broad and his limbs so long, he would snatch David out of the air the moment David attempted to slip past him. Just as troublingly, two of the leering things had arranged themselves before the bedroom door, another trailing Judson like a hungry cur, the fourth perched atop Jessica's legs like a hyena guarding a kill. And more leering things were forming on the beds, more servants of this deathless fiend.

Nowhere to go, he thought. Nothing to do.

From below, like a sick, ghoulish joke, came the sounds of someone battering a window. David heard Harkless's voice, as if rising from an impossibly deep well, and beneath that, he thought he made out the sounds of Mike Jr.'s pleas, the poor kid having lost his parents, his grandpa, and almost certainly his sister on the same night.

But the house wouldn't let them in. *Judson* wouldn't let them in.

Judson's hands shot out, groping for him.

David jerked away, his knees nearly buckling. He retreated though he knew there was nowhere to go. Judson towered over him, grinning.

David's heel bumped something, and he tumbled backward. With a start he realized he'd fallen against the ladder, and though he detested the notion of abandoning Jessica, his feet began to climb, his hands gripping the ladder's sideboards as he rose. He cast a desperate glance at Jessica, saw that, for now at least, the leering thing holding her captive was making no move to feed on her. He couldn't tell whether her chest still rose and fell.

Judson snatched at his foot. David bared his teeth, climbed faster. Then he was standing in the large third-floor dormer, the A-framed space running the length of the house, the packed shadows only mitigated by the northern and southern windows.

David cast about for something with which to defend himself. He spotted the globe, the stacks of books, the throne-like chair. There were candleholders and other useless objects, but there was nothing resembling a weapon up here. True, he hadn't walked the length of the attic yet, but a perfunctory scan told him the remainder of the space was barren.

David shot a glance at the rafters, where the rope dangled.

An image of Anna, pinned on the bed, her face straining from lack of air, flashed through his head. In the end, Anna had learned there was no escaping this place.

And now, he thought, his breath hitching, he was trapped too. He and Jessica were about to die, if she hadn't died already.

David was backing toward the window when a thought occurred to him, one so fundamental that he couldn't believe he hadn't considered it earlier.

His hands knotted into fists.

If Judson Alexander were so invulnerable, why did he need the protection of the house?

Why hadn't he, on the night of his demise, just waded into the throng of villagers and slaughtered them one by one?

The answer was clear: Judson *wasn't* impervious. At least, he hadn't been in life.

And David had wounded him tonight, had done Judson injury even in death.

That meant he could be destroyed.

The giant's footfalls boomed on the laddered steps. David rushed to the window, saw Harkless gazing impotently up at him, Mike Jr. staring likewise by her side. They couldn't help him. Any help had to come from up here.

He cast about desperately, knowing already he wouldn't find anything, knowing he was wasting precious seconds while the giant ascended. His eyes fell on the stacks of books, and though he knew none of these could help him, one small, green volume caught his eye, stirred a memory that refused to be dismissed.

John Weir's diary looked a lot like that little green book. One passage from the diary had seemed unremarkable when he'd first encountered it, but now the passage struck David with titanic force:

It had been passed down by better men than me, men whose belief in God had fortified them against whatever evil dwelt in the earthly realm. That I was not also a believer was immaterial. Because their beliefs were so unwavering, their faith represented something unbreakable, and that stalwart faith, I believed, had somehow communicated itself to the cane, the secret weapon I kept as a boon companion.

The cane, he thought. John Weir, Prince of Skeptics, had believed in the cane's power.

Deep laughter sounded behind him.

Judson was coming.

As Judson's leering face appeared, an obscenely merry expression arching his thick eyebrows and animating his coal-black eyes, David lunged toward the alcove in which the cane reposed, snatched it up, and turned to confront Judson. Framed as he was by the tunneled darkness of the attic, Judson appeared impossibly large, his shoulders great slabs of meat, his midsection bulging with bands of muscle.

David backed toward the northern dormer. For reasons he couldn't articulate he wanted to be closer to the moonlight.

When Judson spoke, the voice was buzzing and unnatural yet surprisingly urbane. "*You carry the walking stick of your fallen hero. What a waste of good birch.*"

David was so taken aback at being addressed by a ghost that he merely stared at Judson a moment. When he found his voice, he said, "Weir was a great man who deserved better."

Judson grasped the chest flaps of his open-throated white shirt, set his legs apart as if delivering a public speech. "'*Deserve' is a meaningless word. A coward's word. Mice like you can utter it all you like, yet its meaning changes not a whit. I declare such blather false hope.*"

A rustling sound came from below, movement in the long bedroom. David imagined Jessica's unconscious body down there with the leering things. Were they even now devouring her? He had to act.

"*Yes, make your move!*" Judson crowed. "*Swing that cane like a brittle old woman. See where your human devices get you!*"

David raised the walking stick, but before he could strike, Judson's limbs blurred in the gloom, a cudgel fist shooting out and catching David flush on the jaw. He was lifted off his feet, the cane skittered away, the back of his head cracking against the windowsill. He lay several feet from the giant, groggy and, despite all he'd seen, astonished by Judson's strength.

The heavy boots clumped nearer. Judson bent at the waist, blotting out most of the light. "*I am eternal, Mr. Caine,*" he said in his buzzing voice. "*I am the god of pain. You have taken my Honey from me, the best of my cherished vassals.*" Judson's grin dissolved. "*I will exult in your wails.*"

Judson reached for him. David barely had time to raise an arm, but Judson was unstoppable. The massive fingers closed around David's shoulder and began to squeeze. Pain like he'd never known flowed through him as the granite-like fingers compressed his flesh, puncturing his skin, splitting his sinew and probing the tender tissue beneath. David was dimly aware of his own shrieks, his head thrown back, his arms palsied and powerless.

"*Ah, a low tolerance for pain,*" Judson remarked. "*We must remedy that, Mr. Caine. We must burn the weakness away!*"

Giant fingers closed on the sides of his head, the thumbs probing under his jaws, like a potter gone mad and punishing his clay. David shrilled out a scream, pawed at Judson's hands, but the giant continued his explorations unperturbed. The merry, buzzing voice came to him as through a cotton blanket. "*You're like a fairy tale wanderer, Mr. Caine. You happened upon a lonely house in the woods, and you ventured inside.*"

Torrents of blood spilled from David's underjaw, a hot drizzling on his neck and chest. Judson had hinted at a protracted suffering, but David knew he couldn't hold out much longer. This torture was too violent, too barbaric to be sustained.

"*We need to check inside your trousers, Mr. Caine.*" A hand went away from David's neck, slithered toward his groin. "*We need to make of you a gelding!*"

Instinctively, David thrust his hands down to cover himself, but Judson's movements were implacable. The fingers closed over David's genitals and began to squeeze.

His consciousness dimmed. He was still screaming, but his cries were no longer his own, were the noises of a dying animal in a steel trap after days of trying to wriggle free.

"*You shall die a failure,*" Judson breathed, his iron grip tightening. "*Unloved, unmourned—*"

Judson let go of him. So overwhelming was David's agony that he scarcely noticed. He slumped to the floor, wondered briefly if he'd already died. He opened his eyes and saw with amazement that Judson was striding past the trapdoor to stand on the other side of it, to gaze upon something that approached from the darkness of the southern dormer, from the direction of the river.

When David beheld what lay beyond Judson, he was certain he'd passed into death. It was surely a vision, David's last few synapses firing illogically.

Anna Spalding hovered in the attic, gazing at Judson Alexander. As they'd been in life, her liquid eyes were large and candid, her mouth relaxed yet somehow steely.

"*What's this?*" Judson asked with an interest David judged too keen.

Anna did not speak. David coughed, his jaws and genitals ablaze with pain. Yet the sight of his former love transfixed him. Grimacing, he pushed to his feet. He retrieved the cane.

Judson addressed Anna. "*Speak, lass. I have seen glimpses of you about, but haven't yet sampled of your comely form.*"

David shuffled over to the throne in which Judson had so many times waited, peering through the dormer windowpanes for fresh victims. David climbed onto the chair and easily reached the rope, which, many years before, had been fashioned into a noose.

"*I said* speak!" Judson thundered. It took all David had not to stare at Anna. Though her form shimmered and pulsed, he felt the undiluted power of her gaze, the innate goodness emanating from her in bright waves.

David stepped down off the chair, noose in hand. He crept toward Judson, hoping the rope would stretch far enough.

It did.

Judson bellowed at Anna, "*Get on your knees, wench. I'll show you how I treat haughty quims such as you.*"

David slipped the noose around Judson's neck.

Judson whirled, eyes blazing, and David swung the cane in a vicious arc. Judson was knocked off balance and stumbled sideways toward the trapdoor opening. Righting himself, Judson reached up, grasped the noose, but David swung again, whipping the cane like a baseball bat, cracking Judson in the jaw, where the flesh had been torn away by the gunshot. Judson roared, windmilled his arms on the edge of the opening, then took an ungainly step toward David.

David plunged the cane into Judson's chest. The impact stood Judson straight up, made him teeter on the edge of the opening. David gritted his teeth, thrust the cane deeper, the brackish blood spewing over David's fingers, and then Judson was shrieking, flailing his arms as he tipped backward, his enormous weight hauling him down like a millstone. Judson plummeted through the opening, the rope jerked taut, and there came a bone-chilling snap. The rope strained, the rafter groaned, but the noose held fast.

David clambered forward to see if Judson were really dead, or if the fiend had found another way to cheat death. The massive form pendulumed slowly, the giant's boots nearly, but not quite, scraping the ladder. Judson's body didn't even twitch.

There came a whispering of air. David peered through the aperture into the long bedroom, saw the giant's long hair rustling, glimpsed the outmoded clothes stirring. The illumination dimmed, went out, and Judson's body flickered with it. The starlight from the windows darkened, went black, and when David could again see, the noose hung empty.

Heart pounding, David peered into the long attic and saw, with an indefinable sense of loss, that Anna's figure, too, had disappeared.

His breath caught.

Jessica, he thought.

David descended the steps, barely noticing the birch cane, which lay on the floor at the base of the ladder. He expected the leering things to dart at him, to finish the attack Judson had begun, but instead was met with a sight so shocking he could only stop and stare fifteen feet from where Jessica lay on the bed.

Six figures stood on either side of the bed, their faces downturned to Jessica's inert form. They were cloaked in white gowns not unlike Ivy's. David judged the young women's ages anywhere between twelve and twenty. These, he understood, were the leering things as they'd been before the fire, perhaps even before Judson had tormented and abused them. They wore expressions of such empathy that David found a thickness forming in his throat.

On the edge of the bed sat Ivy, her dress marred with gore but her face pinched with quiet sobs. He stepped closer, and Ivy looked up at him, the tears streaming down her cheeks. "She's dying, Mr. Caine. We have to save her."

He rushed to Jessica, worked his arms under her neck and legs. Despite his wounds, he managed to lift her, and below he heard the front door slam open, heard Harkless's voice shouting up to him. Ivy's hand was on his lower back as he came around the corner onto the second-story landing. He spotted Harkless, already halfway up the stairs. Mike Jr. peered up at them from below.

"Is she...." Harkless began.

"Start the car," David said, and moved down the steps.

CHAPTER FORTY-THREE

Because activity at the hospital had been light that day, they were given a room next to Jessica's in intensive care.

Harkless sat in a green recliner alongside David's bed, Ivy on a single bed they'd wheeled in, Mike Jr. asleep on a cot, his scrawny limbs buried under a spill of white blankets.

It was 7:14 in the morning.

David hadn't slept since being admitted, and though he and Harkless had fought to see Jessica, thus far the doctors had not relented. Memories of Judson hoisting Ralph into the air kept flitting through David's head, and no matter what he'd glimpsed within the Alexander House, he couldn't permit himself to believe that the terrible specter was truly vanquished.

"Will you check on her?" he asked Harkless in a voice he hoped wouldn't awaken the kids.

"Trying to get me thrown out?" Harkless asked. "Wasn't ten minutes ago I was over there getting the stink eye from her nurse."

David licked his lips, couldn't bring himself to utter Judson's name.

Harkless stared back at him, not unkindly. "It's over, David. All we can do now is pray for her." Her look soured. "Or whatever it is you'd rather do."

David said nothing.

Six feet away, Ivy moaned. Harkless was on her feet instantly. She stroked Ivy's hair, murmured soothing words. Ivy's forehead unfurrowed. She let out a tired sigh.

David turned and discovered that Mike had flopped over onto his stomach. The cot, which was navy blue, was darker around Mike Jr.'s mouth, the boy drooling in his sleep. The position looked incredibly uncomfortable, but with all the wires and tubes connected to David's arms, he couldn't roll the boy over if he wanted to. Mouth open, Mike Jr. snored softly.

"Poor Ivy," Harkless said, moving to stand beside David. "I wonder if they'll do anything about her stomach…or just let her pass what's in there."

David blanched, thinking of what Ivy had done to Templeton when under Judson's spell.

He looked up at Harkless. "What have you told them?"

Harkless pursed her lips. "A load of bullshit. Detective Baldwin insists the investigation is his, but this was my show from beginning to end, and I'm gonna control the narrative."

"Which is?"

"The Shelbys and Chris and Katherine were part of a sinister cult."

At David's look, Harkless's eyes widened. "It's the truth, isn't it? They're the ones who killed Templeton, the ones who shot you and Jessica and tried to kill me and Mike."

David glanced at Ivy. "How do you…?"

"The bite marks on Templeton are gonna be hard to explain, but if I can talk to Ivy…you know, coach her a little…."

Ivy twitched in her sleep.

Harkless said, "She doesn't remember a thing. Not after she went missing."

David sat up. "Nothing?"

"She said she had some nightmares…mentioned a big man taking her by the hand…she described those creatures."

"The leering things."

"Enough." Harkless shivered. "I don't think she'll incriminate herself. After all, she's only four. It's not like they're gonna be predisposed against her." A humorless laugh. "Then again, Baldwin is a complete peckerwood. He'll do anything to cause me trouble."

The door opened and a doctor and nurse entered. The nurse was blond, short, and very young; the doctor appeared to be of Middle Eastern descent. His badge said 'Anayat Wardag.'

"Is she okay?" David asked.

Wardag put a palm up. "I just came on a few minutes ago. Let's check you first. You sustained serious trauma. Your back, your throat, arms, shoulders— What are you doing?"

David was climbing off the bed, but the nurse was there before David could get up, her small but strong hands already pushing him back. "You pull that out," she said, nodding at the needle piercing his wrist, "and you'll spray blood all over."

"You think that bothers me?"

"It should," Dr. Wardag said. "You've lost too much blood already. We don't want to have to transfuse."

David compressed his lips. "I was just grazed."

"That's right," Dr. Wardag agreed. "And bitten. By…what did you say?" He leafed through the pages of a clipboard.

"A cult member," Harkless supplied. "Her name was Honey Shelby."

Wardag eyed the sheriff. "I think Mr. Caine can answer on his own, Sheriff Harkless."

"Honey bit me," David said. "How's Jessica?"

Wardag stored the clipboard against his side. "Miss Green has suffered severe trauma. She will live, but her recovery will be slow."

"She awake?" Harkless asked.

Wardag grunted noncommittally. "She was able to answer some of my questions. Others, she had no answers for."

"You're not a cop," Harkless said. "You have no business conducting an investigation."

Wardag's tone remained patient. "I asked her questions pertinent to her injuries. She was able to tell me she was shot by Michael Shelby." He looked at Harkless. "Mr. Shelby is now deceased?"

"That's none of your business," Harkless snapped. "And yes, he's very deceased."

Wardag appeared to consider. The nurse had gone over to attend to Ivy.

Wardag nodded. "Miss Green is responding well to transfusions. She will have severe scarring on her side. The spleen was perforated but not damaged egregiously by the slug. She shouldn't lose any functionality."

David's muscles unclenched a bit.

"The muscles of *your* forearms," Wardag continued, "were damaged. They'll take time to heal."

"And Ivy?" Harkless asked.

Wardag's face clouded. He flipped the pages on his clipboard. "I understand she's suffering from severe shock."

"Why don't you look at her?" David said with some heat.

Wardag glanced at Harkless. "It's irregular to have so many patients in one room."

"Being attacked by crazed cult members is irregular too," Harkless said. "No way that girl is getting out of my sight again. Hey," she said, stepping closer to Wardag. "That reminds me. When do we get to see Jessica?"

"She's sleeping, Sheriff Harkless."

"That's not what I asked, Dr. Wardag."

The doctor held Harkless's stare a long time. Then he sighed. "She was awake when I first came on. She asked for Mr. Caine and became agitated when I told her to rest. We sedated her."

"Then I won't be hurting anything by looking in on her," Harkless said.

Wardag cocked an eyebrow. Finally, he grinned ruefully and gestured toward the door. "Five minutes."

Harkless winked at David and went out. The doctor and nurse followed.

He'd lain there for a couple minutes when a small voice said, "What's severe shock?"

Mike Jr. was lying on his side on the cot, only his pale face showing between the white blanket and pillowcase.

"It means Ivy's been through something terrible, and it'll take a while for her to feel normal again."

"How long?"

David auditioned several lies but decided Mike had been deceived enough. "There's no way to know."

Mike's bottom lip quivered. "Are they gonna split us up?"

With a pang of self-recrimination, David realized how selfish his thinking had been over the past several hours. While he cared about the kids' wellbeing, his thoughts had chiefly tended toward Jessica.

But studying Mike now...God, the kid had lost everyone but Ivy, and he was terrified of losing her too. In the pale, lost face on the cot, David saw none of the petulance he'd glimpsed that first day on the peninsula. Only a heartbroken, orphaned child who needed comforting.

"Hey," David said and had to clear his throat. "Hey, Mike, why don't you come over here?"

Automatically, Mike climbed off the cot and wandered over to David's bedside. With an effort, David scooted over. "Get in," he said.

Mike frowned. "What about all those wires? I don't want to unplug you."

"I'm not a microwave."

Mike bit his bottom lip. "Will it kill you?"

"You're not going to kill me. Now are you coming up or not? I'm tired."

Wordlessly, Mike crawled onto the bed, his eyes never leaving the wires and tubes connecting David to the monitors and drip bag. Mike lay back, and with some fuss, David lifted the hospital blanket so the kid could slide under.

They were lying there, David half dozing, when Mike asked, "What's in the sack?"

"Huh?"

"That one," Mike said and nodded toward the dangling drip sack.

"Oh, that. It's super-soldier serum. Like they gave Captain America."

Mike looked at him blankly. Then he scowled. "You're full of shit."

David laughed softly. Within a minute or so, Mike fell asleep.

David had begun to drift off when he became aware of someone staring at him. He sucked in breath, turned, and saw Ivy watching him at his bedside.

"I had a nightmare," she said.

Your life has been a nightmare, he thought.

"Wanna join us?" he asked.

She climbed in. She burrowed into his side, bumping one of his arms in the process, and though it revived a throbbing pain, he didn't mind.

"Mr. Caine?" she said.

"Yeah?" he whispered, trying not to wake Mike.

"I'm scared."

David drew her closer, caressed her skinny arm. "The bad man is gone, Ivy. He won't hurt you again."

Ivy was silent so long he thought she'd gone to sleep. Then she whispered, "I'm scared of myself."

He saw her gazing up at him with wide eyes. "I trust you, Ivy. You'd never hurt anyone."

Her face started to crumple. "I think I did."

Her sobs were nearly noiseless, but her body shuddered with them. He clutched her tighter, his throat burning, and when she'd gotten some of it out, he said, "Ivy?"

She looked up at him, her face shiny with tears.

"Can I tell you the truth?"

She nodded.

He took a breath. "Some people should never be parents. Mine were like that." He swallowed. "Yours were too. But that doesn't mean that you and I don't deserve to live, right? We deserve a chance, don't we?"

Her eyes were huge in the near-darkness of the hospital room.

"Don't we?" he asked.

She nodded, her eyes never leaving his.

"You're a great kid, Ivy. You're going to have a happy life. Me, Jessica, Sheriff Harkless…we'll make sure of it."

Her mouth twitched. "You will?"

"None of it is your fault, Ivy. None of it. But it's gonna be better now. I promise."

She watched him for a long time. Then, evidently satisfied by what she saw, she relaxed and placed her head on his chest. He leaned down and kissed the top of her head.

Soon, they joined Mike in sleep.

★　　★　　★

They kept David two days. In that time, both Mike and Ivy returned to their normal personalities, more or less. Harkless and Tina, the CPS woman, decided that Harkless would take temporary charge of the kids, and Mike and Ivy didn't seem to mind. On the day David was discharged, they ate lunch with him – an almost indigestible combination of tepid soup and dust-dry peanut butter-and-jelly sandwiches.

When David was finally allowed to see Jessica, he was awed to discover her sitting up in bed, looking a trifle wan but otherwise beautiful in the early afternoon sunlight. Crossing to her, David realized with a start that she'd been given the same room in which Ralph Hooper had been murdered. He was sure she'd noted the coincidence too but had opted not to mention it.

What she did say was, "Georgia overstated how bad you look."

He grunted laughter. "That was kind of Georgia."

He took her hand. Her fingers accepted his, and he thought, What if….

"Where will you go?" she asked. Her expression remained calm, but there was something raw, something naked in her voice.

"I'll stay in one of the motels, work on my book."

"That's not what I meant."

He lowered his gaze. "I know. But it's a complicated question."

"David?"

He looked up at her.

"The time for messing around is over," she said.

Despite the directness of her gaze, her hand in his was relaxed, her thumb slowly stroking one of his bandages.

He swallowed. "I'd like to stay with you."

Whatever she was looking for, this seemed to satisfy her. "The spare key is taped under the café table by the pergola. Sebastian's food is in the pantry. Georgia will be glad she won't have to feed and walk him any more. With Mike and Ivy, she already has her hands full."

He nodded. "That'll be better than a motel."

Her eyes narrowed. "Pick up after yourself. I don't want my house looking like a frat party when I come home."

AFTER

He drove Jessica home twelve days after she'd been admitted. Her surgery had gone well, and she was expected to make a full recovery. As June wound to a close, David spent time with her when she was awake and worked while she rested. He'd titled his book *The First Haunting: The True Story of the Alexander Specter*, and though reliving the nightmarish events proved emotionally taxing, shaping the story to fit the lies they'd told the authorities proved a stimulating challenge.

"How do we explain Georgia not entering the house when Chris and Honey held you at gunpoint?" Jessica asked.

She was reclined on a cushioned gliding lounger he'd purchased for her. After her surgery, sitting in a traditional chair awakened a glancing throb in her side.

He tapped a pencil on his notebook. "She was protecting Mike Jr. by keeping him away from the gunfire."

"While Ivy remained in harm's way?"

He frowned, then snapped his fingers. "Ivy went with Sheriff Harkless to the car too. She wasn't in the house when Judson made his appearance."

"That could work. But it diverges from the story you told."

He paused. "You sure you want me to finish this project?"

"People need to know how my sister died. For twenty-two years everyone's believed she killed herself."

David gazed down at his notebook.

Jessica swung her legs around and placed her bare feet on the deck. "It isn't just vindictiveness, David. It's…you…John Weir…."

He nodded. In a way, the book was to be David's apology. He'd erected a career on skepticism, and despite the pride-swallowing it entailed, he felt an obligation to admit to the world he'd experienced a conversion to the side of belief. Belief in what, he could work out in time, but at the very least, he had to accept the fact that there were powers he would have never dreamed possible.

His editor and agent were giddy about the project. His agent kept hinting that maybe they should open up the book to other bidders, and while the prospect was tempting, David had come to appreciate loyalty more than ever before. His current publishing house had treated him well and paid him handsomely even before his books started making money. *The First Haunting* would return their investment tenfold.

The only problem was, there was an ending yet to be lived....

He looked at Jessica.

"What?" she asked, smiling a little.

"I'm falling for you."

The smile disappeared.

"Does that bother you?" he asked.

She fidgeted with her beige shorts. She wore them low on her hips, not to be alluring, but so the fabric wouldn't irritate her stitches.

"How do you think John Weir would feel about the project?" she asked.

"Nice subject change. I think he'd be happy the truth was being told."

She looked at him then. "What is the truth?"

"About Weir? I think Judson got him. Or the leering things."

"Isn't that what *The Last Haunting* claimed?"

David reached down, scratched Sebastian's belly. The dog's forepaws extended, like a cartoon sleepwalker. "It isn't what Hartenstein wrote, it's how he wrote it. Like he was delighted by Weir's death."

"Weir deserved better," she said.

"We'll give him better. We'll include parts of the diary that *The Last Haunting* left out. We'll—"

"David?"

"Yes?"

"I'm falling for you too."

At length he said, "Well, that changes things."

The ghost of a smile. "Yeah?"

"I'm going to ask my department head if I can take a semester off."

"Will she go for it?"

"I think so. Either way, I'm staying."

Her smile grew, then faded. "What then?"

He shrugged. "Then we've got decisions to make."

"Sleep in my bed tonight."

It knocked his wind out. "Okay."

"We can't have sex yet," she hurried on. "You know…the stitches."

"Right. The stitches."

"But I'd like you to hold me. Kiss me some."

He smiled. "I kiss you every day."

Her eyes held him. "Not in my bed."

★   ★   ★

They did make love that night. They began almost shyly, but in the end she'd moaned into his ear, licked and bit his lobe, and it had taken all his self-possession not to devolve into animalistic thrusting. Just before David climaxed, Sebastian somehow clambered onto the bed and began sniffing at David's butt crack. He reached back to push the dog away, but Sebastian had begun to lick the backs of his legs, at which point David knew there was no salvaging the moment. Laughing along with Jessica, he rolled off her and vigorously scratched the dog's forehead. Sebastian bounded between them, happy to be included in the festivities.

They fell into a comfortable sleep, but David awoke a few minutes shy of two a.m. and realized what had been nagging at him. He stood in the dark bedroom, naked, his pulse racing, and stared out the picture window into the inky blue night.

He put on his cargo shorts and sandals. Careful not to wake Sebastian, who slept atop the covers at Jessica's feet, David slipped out of the bedroom and moved to the kitchen. He poured himself a glass of tap water, hands trembling. He guzzled it, wiped his mouth, and went out the back door. The moon was overlarge and tinged with scarlet, the stars like avid eyes watching his every move.

Watching to see if he'd lose his nerve.

He wouldn't, though. Couldn't. In spite of how much he felt for Jessica, the truth had been digging at him with greater urgency each day. It had gotten so he could scarcely sleep, no matter what measures he took. He had to do this.

David crossed the backyard and entered the trail to the wooden steps, which he descended purposefully, eyes straight ahead, his will concentrated on the necessity of this, no matter the peril.

He reached the dock and removed his sandals. He spread his arms and brought them together as he leaped. The summer water was a tick warmer than the air. David kicked, cupped his hands, and parted the water before him, the moonlight full on his face. He pushed on, moving deeper into the bay. He knew the Alexander House would appear soon in his periphery, and though it took an effort, he kept his eyes from drifting in that direction. In between strokes he caught glimpses of the dappled water, silver coruscating on black, and when he'd swum for a while, he finally allowed himself to look at what lay straight ahead.

The island.

If it were to happen, he knew, it must be here. The Alexander House, though rife with grisly memories, was now restful. Or at least he believed it to be. He certainly wasn't going to return to test his theory. More than once Jessica had suggested burning the place down, but as the Shelby property had proved, houses could be rebuilt. If evil could survive death, it could survive fire.

Under the water's surface, his fingertips scraped sand. David stood and strode toward the shore.

Funny, he thought, but when he and Anna had been here many years ago, and again when he and Jessica had visited the island this summer, he hadn't noticed a gap in the trees, much less a worn path where they could enter the forest.

But here it lay, as obvious as could be. Knowing he'd lose his nerve if he delayed further, David took the path.

The island trail was smooth and weedless and meandered for perhaps twenty yards before opening to a vast clearing he wouldn't have believed possible, for from the water and the shore, the forest appeared unbroken. Yet now he stood on the verge of a broad stretch of packed dirt as wide as…

…as some ancient temple. Yes, he thought, stepping into the clearing. There was something holy about this place, something awe-inspiring. The soil was packed so firmly that the earth glimmered. He realized as he advanced that the far edge of the clearing rose in a mound, beyond which the ground plummeted for maybe fifty feet before being overtaken once more by forest. Atop the mound lay a sprawling deadfall of alabaster branches, likely washed up by a long-ago flood and bleached pale by the sun when the noonday light blazed straight down.

David performed a slow revolution, surveying the scarlet-tinged leaves of the towering trees, their boughs intertwining like the arms of kindred gods, their trunks so closely massed that they seemed like parts of the same organism.

He cast a glance backward to make sure the trail on which he'd entered was still there. It was, of course, and he smiled at himself for doubting it would be, and when he turned to face the clearing he discovered a figure striding toward him, only twenty feet away.

Anna Spalding.

As she had the night he'd encountered her in the attic of the Alexander House – the night she'd saved his life by distracting Judson – Anna's long dark hair was swept back from her face. Unlike that ghastly night in the Alexander House, however, Anna no longer flickered and blurred before his eyes. Now she wore a simple black dress, her feet bare as always, on her face an expression he couldn't interpret. At one moment he detected a hint of knowing good humor around her mouth, and a dozen happy memories would flood through him; the next moment he'd sense a predator's cunning in her eyes.

But when she drew nearer, these musings vanished and were replaced by the time when he and Anna had spread a blanket on a bridge and watched the sun sink over the Rappahannock…the day the two of them had played tennis, David getting huffy because Anna had whipped him, David eventually apologizing for his immaturity…the weekend they'd spent on Chesapeake Bay, David spending more money than he should have to rent a cabin on the water…making love to Anna, and afterward, the two of them sitting side by side on the deck, cocooned in a blanket, the full moon not as lurid as this but just as dazzling.

Now Anna stood a mere three feet away, and David realized he was weeping. He lowered his head, shook it slowly, and muttered an apology.

Anna didn't stir.

He saw her bare toes, remembered how she'd taken off her flip-flops even in movie theaters and nested her bare feet on the seatback, and the memory warmed him, and he looked into her face and saw she was smiling.

Yet for some reason, this brought fresh tears to his eyes. He saw her through a shimmering curtain, his throat and chest seared by jagged sabers of heat.

"I'm so sorry," he whispered.

Her smile went away, but the expression that replaced it wasn't hostile. He said it again, his voice cracking. Anna watched him.

"Please forgive me," he continued. "I don't deserve it, but please… I'd give anything to take it back."

His chest shuddered. He fought it as long as he could but realized this was elemental, as unconquerable as the tides. Anna merely watched him weep, and after a time, her hand rose, her fingers nearing his face. Her expression was warm, generous. He didn't deserve forgiveness, he knew, but that was Anna. One of the kindest human beings he'd ever met. Not a pushover, not a quiet, saintly figure – when enraged she could cuss and storm violently – but at her core, where it really mattered, her heart was beautiful.

Her fingertips touched his cheek, caressed him, and he dared to meet her gaze. Her smile was subtle, but it was there, and what was more, there was a satisfied placidity in her eyes. Whatever she'd been looking for, she'd evidently seen it.

Anna drew nearer, nearer, only inches from his face. She was shorter than he, but because she stood uphill from him, they regarded each other eye to eye, equals in the scarlet moonlight.

She cupped his cheeks in her hands, leaned closer, and for a moment he believed she would kiss him. Though a part of him would always love her, a wave of guilt rolled through him at the prospect. He'd just made love to Jessica for the first time; how would Jessica feel about David accepting a kiss from her long-dead sister?

Anna seemed to sense David's reticence because her wry smile appeared, that sardonic curving of her lips. Her nose two inches from his, she fixed him with her large, liquid eyes. Her smile faded, in its place a gravity that brought a chill to his spine.

Staring into his eyes, she uttered a single word.

"*Run.*"

Around the clearing, the trees convulsed as if they'd been gripped by a fatal ague. The ground underfoot vibrated, and releasing him, Anna retreated slowly, her expression alarmed. As a terrible, deep-throated hum reached his ears, he realized something was coming, something from the forest ahead, beyond the rising mound of earth, beyond the clearing.

The meaning of Anna's message, as simple as it was, finally took root in him, started his feet to backpedaling, his eyes riveted on the forest, where he heard sticks breaking, the crack of pine boughs. David set off in a nerveless jog, his gaze over his shoulder at the place where the earth rose, that shimmering mound of dirt that reminded him so forcibly of an altar.

He was ten feet from the woods when the Siren exploded over the rise.

The wraithlike figure sent a shockwave over the clearing, soil and pebbles spraying over the earth. The weeds at the forest's edge were flattened by the concussive force. Even the trees leaned away.

The wraith gleamed a dreadful bone-colored white, garbed in flowing garments of the same hue. Even from this distance he could see the straight black hair parted down the middle and radiating out behind her. If not for the hideous expression of loathing stamped on her features, the face would have been lovely.

The mouth yawned open, revealing teeth like glowing scimitars.

Gasping, David plunged into the forest.

He heard her swooping progress in the clearing behind him and a deep, machinelike roar. But this wraith was older than any machinery, older even than the trees. This, he thought with frantic terror, was the Rappahannock woman who'd been banished to this island so many centuries ago, the one who became a Siren, luring untold men to gruesome fates.

David leaped around a curve, his bare feet slapping the trail in mindless terror. The pile of branches he'd glimpsed atop the mound wasn't a deadfall after all, was a pile of human bones accumulated over the many years the Siren had ruled the island. He recalled the ferocity in those white eyes, knew if he didn't escape that his bones would be gnawed clean and heaped upon the mound.

David burst out of the forest and heard the Siren winging after him, her taloned fingers ripping through leaves and branches, her awesome vitality bending the trees and groaning their stout trunks.

He took three leaping strides and dove into the river. His chest scraped the shallows, but he barely noticed it, only kicked as he'd never kicked before, his arms swinging wildly. Even with his ears underwater he heard the deep bullhorn blast of the Siren as she rocketed out of the forest. He didn't need to glance over his shoulder to see the wraithlike figure floating toward him over the water.

David swam for his life. He gulped water, spluttered and gasped. The river grew cooler with the Siren's approach. David was halfway across the bay when he realized the water had turned frigid, the wind bringing gooseflesh despite the vigor of his strokes.

His strength began to flag, his arms like blocks of marble. He kicked against the increasingly freezing water, and when he was fifty feet from the dock, he sensed it, the stare of the Siren on his back. Frost tingled his shoulder blades, the Siren's talons harrowing his flesh. David sucked in breath, plunged beneath the water's surface, breast-stroked with arms he no longer felt. Frantic, David rolled in the water, glanced up and saw the floating Siren, the features turned bestial, the mouth a monstrous leer, the scimitar fangs curved and dripping, the eyes glowing Jack-o-lantern orange, the face a nightmare of lunatic hunger.

At sight of it, David's body went limp. Through the water sounded the dirge he'd heard that first night on the peninsula, the melody no longer sorrowful, but instead gloating, the infernal aria of demons.

The Siren's claws groped for him.

David pushed lower, going deeper despite the water flowing into his throat. In an ecstasy of terror, David heard the sound of something hit the water nearby, but maybe that was imagination. Above him the claws curled, extended, the Siren's face a mask of delight just above the water's surface. Gagging, David slapped at the talons, felt his hand sliced open, the blood awakening an even more perverse glee in the Siren's face. The water went fizzy with his expiring breath, the Siren's claws scrabbling for him, and then his chest spasmed, someone grasping him from behind and hauling him upward.

His face breached the surface, and he vomited water in a sizzling gout. He barely noticed.

He realized it was Jessica grasping him under the arms, Jessica kicking them toward the dock, which was very near. The Siren hovered over the water a few feet away, her face etched with wide-eyed fury. The Siren brayed at them, a soul-freezing combination of misery and desire, the voice otherworldly. David joined with Jessica's efforts to reach the dock; within seconds, they did. Twenty feet away and deprived of her quarry, the Siren bellowed in rage. Jessica scaled the short ladder, helped David do the same, and once they were out of the water, she wrapped an arm around his side in a protective gesture, both of them watching the Siren.

David shivered uncontrollably, his limbs enervated by his flight.

"Come on," Jessica whispered.

David nodded and allowed her to lead him toward the staircase. Together, they climbed the steps, Jessica's arm never leaving his waist. Several times, he glanced back at the Siren, and each time he found her hovering over the water. His great fear was that the face would become Anna's.

But it didn't.

As he and Jessica reached the top of the stairs and completed the short jaunt through the woods to the backyard, he decided that Anna would finally rest.

Hand in hand, David and Jessica made their way through the soothing carpet of grass. The moonlight bathed them in its healing light, their wounds still aching, but the pain no longer impeding their progress.

Sebastian was waiting for them at the back door.

Together, the three of them went inside.

ACKNOWLEDGMENTS

Thank you to Don D'Auria for believing in me; Brian Keene for mentoring and supporting me; Tod, Tim, and Kimberly for being fabulous pre-readers; Joe Lansdale, Tim Waggoner, Paul Tremblay, and Jeff Strand for being so helpful; and Stephen King for inspiring me to read and write. Thank you most of all to my amazing wife and my three extraordinary children for being the best parts of my life.

FLAME TREE PRESS
FICTION WITHOUT FRONTIERS
Award-Winning Authors & Original Voices

Flame Tree Press is the trade fiction imprint of Flame Tree Publishing, focusing on excellent writing in horror and the supernatural, crime and mystery, science fiction and fantasy. Our aim is to explore beyond the boundaries of the everyday, with tales from both award–winners and original voices.

•

Other titles available include:

Thirteen Days by Sunset Beach by Ramsey Campbell
Think Yourself Lucky by Ramsey Campbell
The House by the Cemetery by John Everson
The Toy Thief by D.W. Gillespie
The Sorrows by Jonathan Janz
Kosmos by Adrian Laing
The Sky Woman by J.D. Moyer
Creature by Hunter Shea
The Bad Neighbor by David Tallerman
Ten Thousand Thunders by Brian Trent
Night Shift by Robin Triggs
The Mouth of the Dark by Tim Waggoner

•

Join our mailing list for free short stories, new release details, news about our authors and special promotions:

flametreepress.com